the **KING** has **FALLEN**

The Kingdom of the Krow: Book 1

By Aimee Lynn

For Alan

For being my protector,
even against the worst of myself.

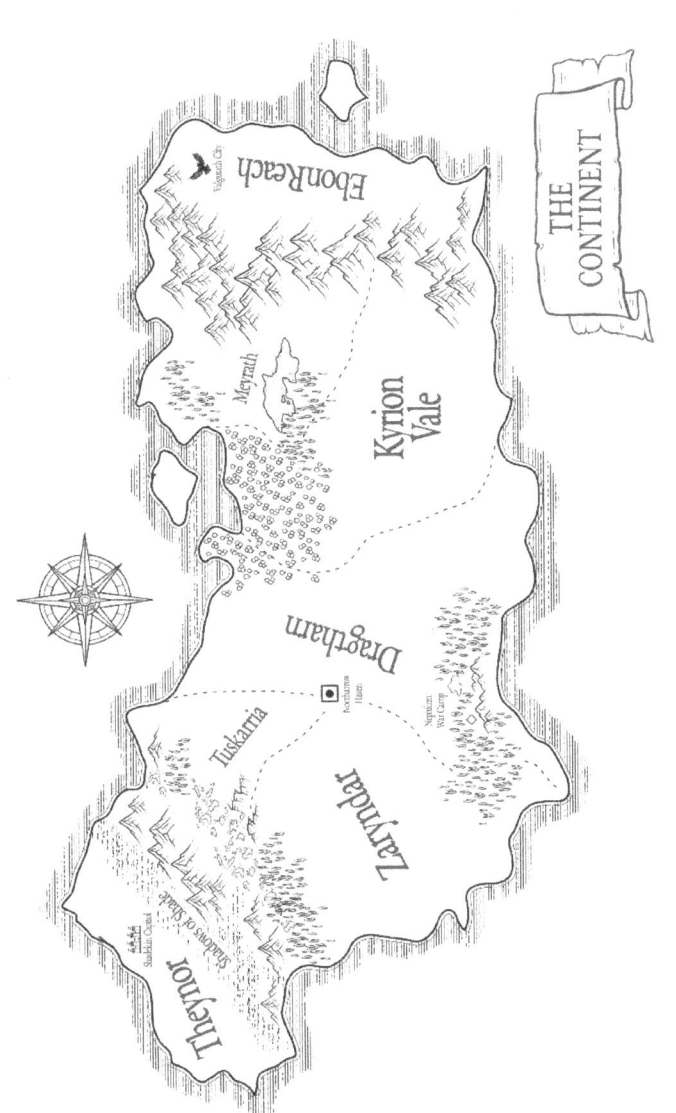

THE CONTINENT

EbonReach

Vagrasil City

Meyrath

Kyrion Vale

Dragtharn

Tuskarna

Averthorne Haven

Nepirian War Camp

Zarivpar

Theynor

Shadows of Silash

Starless Chasm

1. In My Shadow

~ YILAN (Yee-LAHN) ~

If there was one thing that could be said for the Nephilim it was that they cut disgustingly fine masculine figures. Shoulders broader than bhoars, thighs like tree trunks, biceps that could crush weynuts. And if the size of their armor sheaths weren't *optimistic*, cocks that could compete with the trunk of a—

I sank deeper into the shadow between the extravagantly carved armoire and the canvas wall as two royal soldiers marched into the massive King's tent, hurriedly kneeling and clasping fists over their chests and bowing their heads.

"Sire, the General has returned and pleads for an immediate audience."

I inhaled sharply. Melek was here? *Finally!*

At the messenger's words, the King grunted, looking up from where he'd been pinching the ass of a nervous slave. This disgusting pig of a sovereign appeared fit, strong, and relatively young, though I knew the angelic blood running in Nephilim veins kept their bodies from aging normally. Yet, despite his apparent vigor, he spent most of his days sprawled in the furs while his people fought and bled. Today alone I had already been forced to listen to his bestial howls as he inexpertly pumped his seed into one of his human vessels.

Twice.

Please, God, let the General distract the King. I cannot bear another round of hide-the-royal-scepter.

"Send him in," the King muttered as he let go of the slave who scuttled away. In the moments that the guards leaned out of the tent to call the General, the King's heavy brows pinched down over his nose in an expression that, admittedly, set off his rugged features beautifully, and made his golden eyes shine out from the gloom, as if tiny suns existed within the shadows there.

Then the tent flap twitched aside, and suddenly *he* was there.

General Melek Handras.

He must have come straight from the battlefield, half a day's travel away. He was huge—forced to duck his head to enter the tent through the flap they called a door. When he straightened inside I instinctively drew back. The only male bigger was the King himself, and that pig didn't cut nearly as impressive a figure.

The famed General Melek seemed to be carved from rippling steel that had been refined in the fiery furnace of war until every impurity had been burned away.

His hair was short on the sides with strange patterns shaved in, but the warrior's length—a thick chunk of hair that a Neph soldier left uncut from the day of his first kill in battle—flowed from a leather tie at the back of his skull, rippling behind him as he strode into the tent because he had made his first kill decades earlier.

Though he looked much younger thanks to that angelic blood, Melek Handras was at least forty in human years.

As he started towards the King, every male in the tent shrank a bit.

I drank in the sight and my heart beat faster.

I'd been waiting for this man. Targeting him for *weeks*. Wondering if somehow I had missed him in my constant traverse through the shadows of this camp. But no. There would be no mistaking anyone else for this creature. Melek Handras didn't just walk into a space... he *possessed* it.

As Melek debased himself, folded his massive body to take a knee before the King, my mouth went dry. He was stripped to the waist except for the empty weapon straps crossing his massive chest. He had removed his weapons to stand before his ruler and I grieved the loss. I'd longed to see the gleam of his famed twin spears rising behind him. The legends claimed he'd had those lances smithed entirely from metal, each of a single piece, in an effort to stop losing spear heads in the ribs of his enemies.

It was also claimed he notched the handles for every kill, and that his kills were so numerous those nicks offered the traction needed for his grip on such a slick surface.

Melek was the reason I was here. He was quite possibly the most daring and desirable man alive.

Pity I had to kill him.

The King, being the petty, juvenile creature that he was, didn't immediately call the General to his feet. Every face in the room was bowed in obeisance to their idiotic King, so I could indulge myself by leaning slightly closer, drinking in the sight of the soldier who had single-handedly conquered every land between mine and the Eastern coast.

And drink him in, I did. Like a fine wine.

That wide, square jaw that twitched when he clenched his teeth. Full lips that would be stunning when pulled into a smile—provided he hadn't lost teeth. High cheekbones emphasizing those stunning eyes, which were shadowed by brows that were rugged and heavy, but lacking the thickness of mental-density so apparent in the man he served.

"Rise," the King muttered finally, sitting up to swing his legs off the lounge and facing the man who truly led his people.

Did the King know his own imposing form was little more than a statue to his own pride? That *everyone* knew his accomplishments were attained by another man? Or was he *so* stupid that he believed his own bard-songs?

"Speak."

The General's lips tightened and he smacked his glistening, dirty chest with that fist in a warrior's salute that made my eyes roll. If I could, I would have hissed in his ear that his King did not deserve the honor of those who lived to fall.

"There is evidence that the *Fetch* have finally chosen to join us," Melek said without preamble, biting off the word that simultaneously made me smile and my upper lip curl back from my teeth. The *Fetch* we had been named by those who feared us, in an attempt to diminish the shadow we cast over their cowardly hearts. So, *Fetch* we had become. Let any man tremble when they sensed our presence. But Melek didn't tremble. He *seethed.*

"Reports of theft in the battle ranks have tripled, with similar accounts here in camp," he muttered. "Two of our strategists have disappeared without a trace. And a dozen animals have been poisoned—while in guarded pens."

I mentally applauded my brothers. The assassinations were strategic, but the rest merely a way to fuck with the Neph.

The King's upper lip curled back. "Find them."

Every man in the room went still, watching Melek, waiting for him to answer that ridiculous order. I had to bite my lip to stifle a laugh.

Find them, he said. Like we were mushrooms in the dark, just waiting to be plucked.

I eyed Melek, slowly tilting my head to see him more clearly.

How would he deal with his infantile and uninformed King?

"Sire, we watch for them, of course," Melek said carefully. "But... as you know, the Fetch are... difficult to pin down."

I very nearly snorted at the understatement—delivered in a tone as dry as the Raven Desert itself.

"So set traps. We have hunters. Let them hunt."

Every man in the room shifted his weight or eyed his neighbor at the King's thickheaded ignorance.

And they claimed this man carried the blood of the *divine?*

"Again, Sire, we *search* for them, of course. But they are... very skilled. And we cannot risk them informing our enemies of our plans. I ask your permission to call the hounds."

My skin prickled at that. The Nephilim hounds were notorious—creatures of the dark who'd been blood-magiked, a hybrid monstrosity melding wolves and falcons. They were believed to walk in the physical world but see into the next realm, thus no skill of silence or obscurity could deter them. They followed the scent of one's *soul.* Not just to identify the soul's owner, but to devour it. At least, that was what was whispered in the dark among the Nephilim's enemies. Soulless creatures that they were, they yearned for the connection to the divine that a soul offered, and hence were as likely to devour anyone in their path in possession of one as the enemy they'd been set to find.

I'd never seen one and had desperately hoped they were a myth, a rumor started by the Nephilim themselves to create unease in their enemies and discourage thieves.

Nervous, I caught myself shifting my weight uneasily and tugged the hem of my tunic closer to my thigh so it wouldn't find the light.

The King grunted. "The last time we loosed the hounds I lost three girls before they were leashed again."

Melek's full lips pressed thin as he nodded. "It is a risk; however, I believe we were *cocky* in our attempts last time. With the right instructions to the handlers, I believe we could keep our own humans safe." Then Melek lifted his gaze to lock eyes with his King, and once again my breathing shallowed.

The man was *stunning*. Yet, something was wrong.

When a fallen angel mated a human woman, their children were born massive, and regardless of hair or skin color, their eyes were always a deep, pure gold that glowed like sunlight. All the Nephilim had those incredible eyes.

But because the Nephilim were *always* born male, their only recourse for reproduction was to mate another human woman—usually violently. That meant that each subsequent offspring in a line had less and less angelic blood running in his veins.

While their royal lines always possessed eyes of gold, the servants and lowborn of their people—furthest from the fallen angels—had eyes of deep emerald, with every shade between represented in the ranks of their society. Until, many branches down the family tree, the children were merely human with eyes of any normal color and none of the Nephilim's size or power.

I had always been taught that *only* the golden-eyed among the Nephilim were allowed to carry significant rank. Yet, to my shock, Melek's eyes were a startling, bright glow that was more green than gold. By every legend, those eyes should mean he was mostly human and lacking in the supernatural size and strength for which their kind were so feared. Though clearly that was not the case.

I gaped at this warrior of such renown, whose flesh carried the scars of battle on every inch. Even facing the King there was no hint of retreat in his posture.

Fascinating.

My breathing shallowed as the implications of that fact clicked into place: Was it possible this man *had a soul?*

And if so, did he possess a conscience to match?

Adrenaline rocketed through my veins, my breath stopping completely as my mind explored the potential as avidly as any hound of the dark.

And I saw it. All of it. What was needed of me. And how changing the plan could change the world.

There was no time to question. No room for doubt. I sent a silent prayer to the God against whom these creatures had rebelled before letting go of my tunic hem and slowly slipping my hand into the hidden sheath of my favorite blade strapped against my ribs.

The King began to speak at the same moment Melek's eyes cut to the shadow in which I'd secreted myself for the past five hours, his attention caught by the flutter of my hem. The warrior reacted with the speed of a lion, and the precision of a bird of prey.

"THE ENEMY IS HERE! GUARDS TO THE KING!" he roared as he launched himself past the King's lounge... and straight for me.

2. In Your Hands

SOUNDTRACK: Crucify Me by Rosey Reign

~ YILAN ~

With a hiss, I threw myself to the floor as his clawed hand swiped to grasp me, his nail scraping my cheekbone so I flinched as I tucked and rolled, aiming for that thin slice I'd left in the back of the King's tent.

I had a tiny frame compared to these creatures, which helped me hide in their shadows, but even I couldn't fit broadside through the slit I'd used to enter.

The side of the tent caught me like a lover's embrace, the slit widening against my spine, but not tearing, so the surrounding canvas hugged my body.

Still rolling, the dagger's hilt gripped in my fist, I threw the hand wide to swing the blade through the canvas and spit me out on the other side—which would mean running in daylight through an army camp of Nephilim. But I'd take my chances among those ranks over facing the famed General hand-to-hand any day.

Unfortunately, the blade caught his forearm as he grabbed for me a second time.

He roared but, unlike me, didn't flinch.

There was a thunder in my ear, a nervy jolt in my hand as my blade clinked to the dirt, and then the spinning stopped.

I was on the ground, still hugged on one side by the tent, but pinned under the weight of a Nephilim warrior.

The Nephilim warrior.

I couldn't breathe. And not just because he was slowly crushing me.

He muttered one curse, then planted his hand on my throat and used that arm to brace his weight and push himself up, looming over me, golden-green gaze murderous and piercing. Blood spatter from the wound on his arm dripped slowly down his cheek as he bared his very white, very unmarred teeth.

"The King's wish is my honor," he snarled, and his grip tightened on my throat so I could not breathe. "I caught the Fetch, Sire."

As the King grunted in approval and his guards hurried to take positions between us, Melek slid my dagger out from under my shoulder where it had fallen and I'd rolled onto it, then he lifted it, examining the blade that was smeared with *his* blood, and dirt.

I watched, awed, as Melek licked his own blood off the blade with the flat of his long, thick tongue and my belly quivered. Then he cut that stunning, golden-green gaze down to meet my eyes and he smiled maliciously.

My vision was already beginning to tunnel from lack of oxygen when he laid the razor-edge of that dagger against my skin just above where he gripped my neck.

"You have two choices, *Fetch*. I can bleed you dead right now, or you can bow before my King and offer your dubious *honor* to the anointing on him. Tell him every secret you ever stole. Which will it be?"

He arched one brow, his eyes promising violence, no matter what I chose.

I was gripping his wrist in both my hands, though I knew it was pointless. But his sheer strength rendered all my other options moot: A knifehand blow applied to his ribs would only aggravate him. He'd moved so fast, I had no doubt he'd have me bleeding—at the edge of my own blade—before I could reach to grab the dagger strapped at my ankle. And he was just too damn heavy for me to flip him, especially shoved up against the side of the tent as I was.

No. I was utterly at his mercy.

Given that he'd pinned my lower body to the dirt with his hips, and he was braced over me with his back arched and that sizable *manhood* pressed against my flesh... there were ways and means I could have wished he'd taken me instead. But wishes were butterfly farts in the wind. Right now, I needed to *live*.

I opened my mouth, but his grip was so strong, I couldn't speak. And my eyes were beginning to blur.

"It wants to speak," someone said from behind him. Someone with psychic gifts, clearly.

Father's *light*. How had these creatures bested most of the continent?

But Melek's grip eased on my throat, so I wheezed, sucking in a lungful of blessed, pure air, ignoring the stench of sweaty, bloody male, and thanking God for the gift of life.

"Speak up, Fetch," he growled.

I swallowed, wincing at the pain in my throat, praying he hadn't broken anything. "I'll... I'll surrender," I croaked.

His eyes flashed like blades in the sun. Something deep in my belly clenched. His nostrils flared and his eyes narrowed, but before I could say anything more, he drew his knees up, planting his feet under him, and hooked his free hand—dagger still gripped in his fist, though he held it so the blade flattened against his wrist—under my armpit, pulling me up to follow.

I choked as his grip on my throat tightened again, but within moments I stood swaying, able to breathe again, but now surrounded by a handful of these creatures, all staring down at me like hungry wolves on a carcass.

"Bring her to me," the King said, his voice gruff and irritated, as if my appearance was more *annoying* than dangerous.

Ignorant fuck.

Melek dragged me forward, turned me to face him, and planted a hand between my shoulder blades, pushing me to my knees. I did not fight.

I would be a compliant and easy prisoner.

Until I wasn't.

Melek stood behind where I knelt, one boot planted between my knees ready to kick either leg out from under me if I attempted to stand, one hand gripping my shoulder hard enough to bruise, the other holding the knife to my throat.

"Look at me, Fetch," the King growled.

Lifting my chin, I met his eyes as instructed, and had to fight not to smile.

If only he knew how close he'd come to dying by my hand already today. It would wipe that arrogant smirk off his face.

"How many of your... companions are here?"

"None," I said truthfully. "Only me."

The King arched one brow. "You want me to believe your people sent a single female among us without—"

"I am particularly skilled. The others trust me. I've been here since Firstday."

The King scowled. "A liar *and* a thief. There's nothing to be gained by—"

"On Firstday, you poked four of your *bayan* girls—one took it in the ass because she feared your offspring would... how did she put it, *split her from pudang to sternum?*"

The King blinked.

"On Secondday, your apothecary provided services that I'm happy to recount if you wish, but I assume you will not want your men to hear those *very private details*. And this morning—"

"Enough," the King snapped.

I felt Melek go still behind me and had to fight another grin. "I know when I am bested, *Sire*. I have watched you for days. I cannot overwhelm your brute strength. I will serve you to save my skin."

The King glared at me and for a moment I feared I'd gone too far when he leaned in, shoving Melek's blade-hand away, and gripped my throat with his meatfist, leaning into my ear so his hot breath played on my cheek and sent shudders of dread down my spine.

"I don't care what you've seen of me, you putrid little *cunt*. I am the son of a god, and I can do as I wish. I care only what you know of my enemies. Now... I hope that ground isn't too hard. You're going to be on your knees for a very, very long time. And when I get tired of listening to you, you'll stay on your knees, and *I'll* fill your throat. Bestow a gift of the gods' seed for you to swallow, you lucky bitch. Then perhaps *you'll* be the one to take it up the ass, hmmm? That is, if I can bring myself to touch a Fetch..." He inhaled deeply, then wrinkled his hooked nose. "You stink."

I had no doubt it was true. Surveillance was a dirty game— especially in a military camp. Smelling like your surroundings made it far less likely for anyone to notice your presence. And frankly, these males were awful. There was little choice but to let my body reek in order to blend in. But I thought wistfully of a bath every hour.

Still, my stomach churned at very vivid pictures he had painted in my mind. I'd seen him viciously plow several women already. But I didn't flinch.

"I am your servant, of course," I said quietly. Timidly. "And you could take my life at any moment. I cannot deny that. But I should warn you that if you put your cock in my mouth, I will bite it off. And if you rape me, I will scream every word of your conversation with the visitors you had two nights ago. Every. Single. Word."

His eyes narrowed to slits. "You can't scream with my fist around your throat."

"I'm a Fetch. Try me."

Please, God, let him believe the legends. Please, let him believe we speak telepathically. Please can he—

The King snorted air from his nose and leaned back, though he still kept his grip on my throat, his face twisted with hate and disgust.

The feeling is mutual, Sire.

"Start talking," he muttered a moment later, ignoring the looks cutting between the men around us who'd heard the entire exchange.

"Certainly. What would you like me to talk about? The way the light scatters off the hair on your ass while you're pumping? Or—"

"Enough, Fetch!" he bellowed so harshly, spit flicked to my face and I blinked. He leaned back down, leveling a finger at my nose. "One more barb at me and I will drop you where you stand, then desecrate your body until you are nothing but a bloody pulp. You do not open that mouth in my presence unless it is to inform me about my enemies, or receive my *blessing.* Do you understand?"

"Sire, she knows many things, but the Fetch have no scruples. I should have killed her the moment I saw her. Forgive me. Let me do so now, and—"

The King shot Melek a quelling look and that handsome jaw closed so quickly his teeth clicked.

"She is a tool, a gift provided by God to bless me as His son. She will remain until I choose to snap her neck. And since you were the one who caught her, you will be responsible for her. If she gets loose with the things she knows, I will hold you responsible, Melek. You understand?"

Every man in the room witnessing that cocksure threat went utterly still.

Melek was frozen. "But... *Sire,* she's a *Fetch—*"

"Do not toy with me. Our progress has been slowed for weeks. These... *creatures* are holding us at bay. Do not think I haven't noticed."

I gaped at the King.

The legendary fighter and now General in Command for the Fallen King, Melek had single-handedly led the Nephilim's troops from the eastern ranges of the Raven Peaks behind which the Nephilim had always hidden their society, sweeping unexpectedly across the continent, conquering every tribe and people in their path.

Months earlier, they had suddenly taken Meyrath—the human nation in which I gathered most of their female slaves were born—and were already crossing into Kyrion Vale and taking down the Centaurs before the rest of the world even knew they'd left their own lands.

The carnage was swift, and undeniable. And led by the male now bowing before the King.

And Melek *truly* led. Unlike his King, who we now knew remained hidden in his tents many miles from the front, the General didn't shield his own life behind the bodies of his troops.

No, the man roared onto the battlefield, steering his brothers to victory.

And so far, they'd responded with fervor.

But now, *three* of their enemies had allied and joined forces and were holding the line *together.*

Yet, still, Melek and his troops didn't lose ground.

Any other King would have been *ecstatic* to make it this far unhindered. But this man blamed his General for holding fast in a battle against *five times his numbers?*

If only I was free to speak telepathically to Melek. I would have told him to kill this man and take his throne. That the ranks knowingly—and willingly—followed their General, Melek, not this fool.

I could tell him that without lying. And as a fighter myself, I understood why.

Strength followed strength.

Intelligence followed cunning.

And character followed honor.

Melek possessed all three. This pissant King possessed *none.*

But I couldn't tell either of them that. Not yet.

I would be honest with this stupid King about his enemies—in fact, I would *help* Melek defeat those assholes. Far better for the Nephilim to eradicate them for us, than having to fight them ourselves.

But I would not do it for the honor of this cunt. No. I would help Melek because it would give me the chance to sow the seed of dissent among our foes.

There was a reason my people were rumored to hold supernatural gifts that could control the minds of those around us. Because we were manipulative fuckers who understood something the Nephilim never could: Human nature.

The soulless would *never* understand the vulnerabilities—or strengths—of those with an immortal, impressionable soul.

But I did.

And it was the most valuable weapon in my armory.

These men had *no clue* what they were dealing with.

Which was exactly why I would win.

3. F*cking Fetch

~ *MELEK* ~

Gault, the King, was being foolish again. I ground my teeth as he reclined on his furs and instructed the Fetch to begin talking and not to stop until he told her to.

As she gathered herself and eyed him darkly, I knew she would comply. But the truth you heard from a Fetch was rarely the truth you *thought* you heard. I had fought alongside ancients that claimed to have entered the Fetch city, though I was never certain whether they could be trusted either. They said these creatures were wisps on the wind. They danced the shadows and killed like breathing.

If it was true she'd been watching Gault for three days already, then perhaps the ancients hadn't been exaggerating. I couldn't know. I hadn't been in camp. But we'd seen evidence of the Fetch near the battlefield, so I had come to request the hounds knowing Gault wouldn't release them to anyone else—only to find that the signs were here, too.

And now… here we were.

She licked her lips, never taking her eyes off the King, though her expression was empty—no hint of what she felt or thought. And when she spoke, her voice was quiet, *submissive.*

"I will share what I know with the King, of course," she said quietly. "But much of what I know is… sensitive, even here. Your enemies learn of you, you understand? You may not wish me to speak these things with an audience?" She eyed the guards and servants on either side of her, and around the King, then waited.

Cunning bitch.

Gault opened his mouth, his expression dark and suspicious, but his eyes darting side to side, probably because she'd revealed that she already knew *his* secrets. I couldn't let her manipulate him so that she escaped. I cleared my throat.

"It is worth remembering, Sire, that the Fetch are deceivers and thieves. Slippery with both words and body. Do not trust her."

"I don't," Gault said bluntly. "But the point is valid. I also don't trust the dull minds of those who do not carry the blood of the Light Bearer. Clear the tent—you stay, Melek. But everyone else, *out.*"

I gritted my teeth as everyone—including the guards— immediately turned for the door.

"Remain outside and form a perimeter around the *entire* tent," I said quietly, catching the elbow of the Lieutenant as they all hurried for the door. "And send for the tentmaker—she's cut the side in the corner over there. Get someone to repair it today."

The man ducked his head once, then marched for the door, urging the others to hurry. None of them wishing to incite Gault's ire.

I turned back to the Fetch, to find her and Gault staring at each other like two strange cats.

"Sire—"

"You're here, Melek. If you have caution, use it. But I would hear her speak." Then he eyed her again. "Do not tell yourself my threats are empty. The moment I discover you have deceived me, I will open your belly with my teeth and drag you through the tent-city by your intestines—and when you die, I will fuck your remains." Then he smiled and licked his lips, leaning in close to her. "Be careful what comes out of that mouth, you cunning little thing, or I will fill it with *my* truth. And if I must do it to your dead carcass, well… a wet hole is a wet hole."

Despite my disgust, I was impressed that she didn't even blink.

"What do you wish to know first?" she asked as if they were having casual conversation.

Gault smiled and sat back on his lounge, spreading his legs to display the threat of his bulge to her as he reclined. "Tell me… why we have been sitting here for over a week already?" he said with a flap of his hand to indicate the war camp. "What weapons have my enemies developed? What has arrested our progress?"

Her eyes narrowed slightly before she answered. "The enemy of my enemy is my friend," she said quietly. Gault grunted and waited for her to continue. She sighed. "News of your advance reached my people months ago—which means that those pinned between your people and mine heard you were coming weeks before you arrived. They have wisely determined that banding together to defeat you is better than falling alone."

It was exactly what I'd told him a week earlier, the first time we were turned back. We'd seen banners for both the Tuskarrians and the Zaryndar among the fighters. Had he not believed me? Or was he only checking her for honesty?

"Even banded together, they should not hold us so easily," Gault growled with a dark look at me. "How do they manage it."

She raised one brow. "You truly do not know?"

Gault's expression didn't change, but the air suddenly went thin with his disapproval.

She licked her lips and glanced at me before she spoke.

"The terrain at the western end of the continent does not give you the freedom to simply overwhelm them. Even you cannot just sweep through a battle waged among trees, swamps, and ravines. You must be much more strategic in your approach. Add to that… they have Aethereans among them. At least four, that we are aware of."

I cursed. The Aethereans were wraithlike creatures with the ability to soul-bond—create links between themselves and others that would feed strength, energy, and power between parties and enhance any abilities that already existed. Some could communicate telepathically and even heal.

But a bonded Aetherean also took on some of whatever was within those they bonded. Which was why they avoided the Nephilim as if we were poison. Because to them, we were. After all, it was impossible to soulbond to something that lacked a soul. An Aetherean attempting to bond a Nephilim was suicide.

It was no surprise that they would choose to stand against us. But the Aetherean weren't only rare, they were notorious loners, incredibly sensitive to the emotions of others, even those they hadn't bonded. Standing on a battlefield would be torment to them.

To have one join a warring faction against us was stunning. Let alone *four*. That small fact changed the entire landscape of this war, and filled me with trepidation. But also relief. Because it explained how our most recent enemies seemed to coordinate their attacks—and retreats—so perfectly. And how our efforts to take the front so far had been met with such seamless maneuvering that we could never gain traction.

The first time we had advanced, we'd almost been surrounded. They'd kept me sweating ever since.

Shit.

"Is this true?" Gault growled at me.

"It makes sense," I replied reluctantly.

Gault's eyes narrowed as he turned back to the Fetch. "Do *your* people enjoy this... alliance?"

The Fetch shook her head. "We have no need. Our land creates a natural barrier and our reputation discourages confidence. Our neighbors have already learned to respect our boundaries. If *they* win, they'll leave us alone. And if you do... well, we will defeat you without tying ourselves to the soul-suckers," she said viciously.

It was said that while the Aethereans strengthened and enhanced any creature they bonded, *their* strength came from subtly pilfering some of the life-essence of the bonded one.

Did her comment mean that was true? Or was it just a curse on a people that she clearly despised?

I huffed, amused by her arrogance, but Gault's expression went dark with loathing.

Quick as a snake, he stood and took her by the neck, lifting her off her feet and shaking her like a doll. She tried to fight, but his grip was too tight, and just as she had with me, she ended up only gripping his wrist and fighting for air while he held her by the throat and snarled in her face.

"The only reason you still live is because of my *mercy,* bitch. You will not live a moment beyond your usefulness—and your people will not survive beyond my descent. Answer my questions without taunts or barbs, or I will prove to you how powerless you are by turning my men on you to rip your flesh from your bones."

Still gripping his wrist, she nodded. Or tried to. She couldn't breathe and he was holding her entire bodyweight by that one fist clamped at her throat.

Despite my natural aversion to harming females, I couldn't say I regretted his aggression. The Fetch were a massive threat to us—if for nothing else than that they could inform our enemies about us. Having one of them caught *and* informing was a coup.

Mind you, she wouldn't be informing much longer if he didn't let her breathe soon.

"Gault," I said quietly. "She possesses very useful information—insight that could be the key to us finally taking this battle. If you kill her..."

He stared at me for a moment as if he were considering whether or not my words were disrespectful. Then he dropped her without a word, snorting when she landed on the ground with a thump and a wheeze. Then he turned on his heel and went back to his lounge.

I grabbed her upper arm so that she couldn't flee. Her limb was so narrow I circled her bicep completely, my fingers overlapping in the fist. Her lithe stature tempted me to complacency. But I'd heard how easily a Fetch could melt into shadows to escape, even in broad daylight. I didn't know if the rumors were true, but if she'd stayed hidden here for three days, there seemed no point testing them.

"I weary of this," Gault muttered. "Take her. Interrogate her. Whatever you need to do, you have my permission. Get the information from her. Make sure she doesn't escape. Then go win this fucking war so we can return home."

"Yes, Sire, I just—"

"Do not forget that I hold you personally responsible for her, Melek. Do *not* let her escape. Kill her first."

"Yes. Of course. Only—"

"Only *what?*"

I kept my eyes low, gritting my teeth. "Only... I am supposed to return to the front tomorrow. The information she provides may pave the way for our victory. But I cannot be in two places at once."

Gault looked up from where he'd been scratching at a stain on his tunic. His eyes were gleaming, and his half-smile had an edge that made the hair on my neck stand up.

"The *great* warrior and General, Melek Handras, admits there is something he cannot do? How can it be?" he drawled. "The legends are clear, Melek: You regularly achieve the impossible. Or... haven't you heard?"

I didn't back down. These dark moods hit Gault every so often, and the Fetch's taunts had no doubt landed a lot harder than he'd let on. So I swallowed back the curse and shrugged.

"I've told you how dangerous it is to listen to rumor, Gault," I said with a wry smile.

The man snorted and flapped one hand. "Figure it out, Melek. Do what needs to be done."

"I would just like your permission—"

"I said, *figure it out*. And bathe her while you're at it. She reeks. If I'm to question her again or be in her presence, she needs to be clean."

"Yes, Sire," I said through my teeth, bowing to the King, and forcing the Fetch to her knees in front of him, before turning and pulling her out of his presence, my head spinning both with the knowledge she'd provided that needed further exploration, and with the problem of *what the fuck was I supposed to do with her?*

I was about to step out of the tent when I realized that while she was pale, there was new color in the high points of her cheeks, and we were about to cross the tent city.

I couldn't risk losing her. And I didn't want her dead—yet. Which meant I couldn't risk her taunting any of the others who would leap into a rage at the smallest excuse.

I turned back to Gault, and cleared my throat.

"What?"

"You said *anything*… Can I make use of one of your ball gags?"

Gault's head snapped up, his brows high—then he broke into a throaty laugh. "Melek Handras, Purveyor of the Impossible, and Pervert. Please, be my guest."

He nodded towards one of the chests in the corner and I dragged her in that direction, ignoring the look of horror on her face as I used one hand to flip the heavy lid of the chest open and stir the contents within until I found what I was looking for—a ball-gag the size of a small apple on a pair of leather straps.

Her eyes went wide as I turned her around and shoved the ball into her mouth—or tried to. At first she fought me like a horse resisting the bit—teeth clenched and lips pressed tightly down.

"Take it, *Fetch,*" I growled. "It's this, or death. There are no alternatives."

Her brow furrowed, but a moment later she let go of her breath and reluctantly opened her mouth so that the ball slipped in behind her teeth, but over her tongue—keeping her jaw open but her mouth full. Even if she tried to speak, nothing would be discernable.

"Good girl," I purred, just to piss her off as I turned her to tie the leather straps behind her head, tugging them tight.

A low, angry noise started in her throat that reminded me of a cat. But I ignored it. Nodding my thanks to Gault one final time, I pulled her hands behind her back and clamped both of her wrists in one hand, while I took a fistful of her hair and the gag-ties in the other and steered her for the door, snapping at the guards outside that we were coming out.

The guards—both those assigned to the royal tent, and the others that we'd sent to circle the perimeter—snapped to attention as I shoved her through the tent flap and out into the camp and we were bathed in the watery sunlight of the Dragtharn plains. A fist of my men surrounded me the moment we were clear of the King's guards, all of them surprised and curious when they saw my prisoner, but there wasn't time to explain. I marched forward, growling at them to keep eyes out for more intruders, then kept my own gaze peeled for any sign of her comrades that I had no doubt were watching, even if from a distance.

Fucking Fetch.

The sky overhead was mostly gray, matching the rugged boulders and craggy rock formations that pushed out of the dirt here like pimples on the ass of a giant. Formations that became more plentiful, and larger, the closer we got to the hills.

As near as we could measure it, our camp was at the southernmost border where the plains of Dragtharn became rolling forests and met Zaryndar. Our shelters sprawled at the base of a cluster of hills that shielded us from sight on the Zaryndar side.

The battlefront was half a day away and north—beyond Noctharrow Haven, the Dark City. Positioned at the intersection of the borders of three lands and populated mostly by thieves, it was a haven for refugees, merchants and travelers. But few within its fortress walls were willing to put their lives on the line for someone else's nation. Even the Mercenaries went to Noctharrow to rest and relax. Most were more concerned with saving their own skins, and as long as they were offered safe passage, wouldn't fight unless they were being paid coin. So, we'd taken the city almost effortlessly.

And yet, an hour's march beyond that, where Zaryndar shared a border with Tuskarria and the plains turned to low mountains surrounded by swampland, we'd finally been forced to slow our advance.

When they weren't fighting, our soldiers were camped a mile inside the front. But the strategic minds and the King couldn't be within reach of the front in case we were turned back.

So, I placed the war camp here because the gnarled forest, rocky hills, and strange, scarred land allowed us to place watchers on high ground and in trees, and made the position difficult to approach unseen. At least, by creatures who walked with their feet on the ground.

The camp sprawled in a bowl of land that lay at the foot of the largest rock formations in this area. However, the strategic position for scouts and patrols left daily life wallowing in the mud of the hollow.

Hundreds of soldiers tents and campfires lay in an ever-widening spiral around the central, critical structures: The stables that housed our animals—a tent so large it was practically a pavilion and the only place we erected temporary fences—the segmented tents and bivouacs for medical aid, cook tents, blacksmiths, weaponry masters, hounds and handlers, and the countless other resources and people that were needed to keep an army alive and winning. And of course, the Royal marquee just south and west of center, because I'd urged Gault to make use of the rise of the land to position himself in a place even harder to be reached by enemies, and protected on every side by every able-bodied warrior in camp.

Or so I'd thought.

Here I was, shoving not just an enemy, but a fucking *female* ahead of me through camp.

When we reached the intersection of main paths—scattered with hay every couple of days in an attempt to keep the mud from actually sucking off our boots—I hesitated, considering which route was best to take her to my tent.

We were already drawing attention. Neph walking the paths or working alongside them, stopped to look and point at the prisoner. Surprised and curious, they called to their brothers to come see me marching a Fetch by her hair.

Between the scent and sight of a fresh woman, the stories would precede me to dinner tonight. Gritting my teeth, I chose the path that wove between the soldier's tents and the stables. It would take longer, but we would meet fewer Neph and be less likely to incite a frenzy.

Leaning closer to the guard at my right—a young but strong male with amber eyes—I looked around to make sure there was no one else close enough to hear.

"Go see the Handlers. I need an *empty* hound cage brought to my tent immediately—in full working order. If they ask why, or try to delay, tell them the order comes directly from the King."

"Yes, Sir!" His surprise was plain, but he didn't question me, sprinting off in the direction of the stable-tents as I steered the Fetch, ignoring the shocked and amused looks of the men we passed.

I tipped my head at the next guard following at my heels and eyed her so he'd know not to speak openly in front of her.

"Has Jann been advised that I'm back in camp?" I asked quickly.

"Who, sir?" the young man asked nervously. I had to fight not to grind my teeth.

"Find a messenger and tell them that General Handras is personally sending for Jannus the Halfling—I need him in my tent as quickly as possible, delaying only if it affects our efforts in battle."

"Yes, Sir."

Another young man dispatched, another short tug of war with the Fetch who was trying to turn to meet my eye over her shoulder, but I wouldn't allow it.

Somehow I needed to bathe her. And to delay our arrival at my tent so that the cage would already be in place. And then I needed Jann's eagle eye on the entire picture—how the hell to make use of her, to test her insight and ensure it was true, and then to get to the battlefield myself to win this fucking thing when there were *Aethereans* involved.

Fucking *fuck!*

I inhaled deeply to calm myself, then regretted it immediately when I was drenched in the stench of mud and animal shit because we were close to the stable-tents. But as we rounded a corner on the trail and a handful of young guards cheered my name from behind me, a water trough caught my eye.

For the first time since I'd walked into the King's tent, I smiled.

Two birds with one stone.

Sending a glance over my shoulder to the guards still following me, I warned them. "Stand back."

They frowned, but slowed their pace as I wrapped an arm around her waist, lifted her to my shoulder, then took the two steps to the trough and dropped her into it, clothes and all.

Her muffled squeal was quickly silenced by the water. Taken by surprise and fully submerged in the narrow space, it took her a moment to realize her hands were free and she could grab the sides to lift herself out.

Every Neph in sight was laughing by the time she shoved herself up, displacing water in a noisy slosh that seemed too large for her small frame. Waves splashed to join the puddles in the mud when she reared out of the water, grasping for the metal side of the trough and bending, slumping against it, her shaking hands grabbing for purchase on its lip to keep herself upright.

I waited for the deep, wheezing inhale through her nose since the ball gag likely kept her from breathing through her mouth, but there was nothing. Just a bedraggled Fetch, sagging over the side of the trough, strands of her hair plastered to her face, her shoulders heaving... yet no sound.

The others continued to laugh and jeer, the younger ones moving on with their day, unaware of what she was, probably assuming she was just a human slave who'd been captured and brought back for whatever use I would put her to.

Then one of her hands slid off the top of the trough, and she dropped awkwardly against its side, her feet sliding out so that she slipped back into the water and—

I cursed, catching her by her hair as she was about to slide under the surface again and yanking her up to a sitting position. Which was when I saw how wide her eyes were, and how pale her skin.

Her lips, which had been invitingly rosy and plump when she was taunting the King, were now stretched wide over that ball and as white as her cheeks.

I frowned as our eyes locked.

"Time for a bath," I taunted her. Her chin dropped, and at first I thought she was just glaring at me... but then she started scrambling for the gag, but it was as if her hands didn't work properly—she batted at herself, jerking and pulling at the leather strap that had tangled with her wet hair, unable to get it loose.

I growled and reached for her again—she wasn't supposed to take out the gag!—but then her head snapped up as I leaned over her and she grabbed me, shaking my arms, her chest heaving, but her eyes beginning to roll back...

Which was when it occurred to me that she still hadn't breathed.

4. Caged

~ *MELEK* ~

With a muttered curse, as she began to slump forward, flailing, I grabbed for those leather ties and tried to yank them loose—but between twisting them with her hair when I was leading her through the camp, and the fact that both her hair and the thin leather were now wet, it was all hopelessly tangled.

Pulling a dagger from my belt, I shoved her head down. "Don't move, I need to cut it out."

Then I slid the blade under the strap and sliced it cleanly—along with a strand or two of her hair—then let go and stepped back as she spat the gag out, coughed, then sucked in a massive, wheezing breath.

"What the fuck?" I asked her bluntly. "You can't breathe through your nose?"

She was still panting, still gripping the side of the trough like it was a lifeline, but she shook her head.

"Not... not when my nose and throat are full of w-water... you fucking *psycho!*" she rasped.

I grunted. "Well, it's clear that you can breathe now, harpie," I shot back, then reached down to agitate the water, splash it over her head and shoulders, and grabbed a bar of saddle soap that had been left on the fence, rubbing it over her clothes and hair.

"What the—what the *hell* are you doing?!" she shrieked, slapping at my hands and trying to twist away, but her movements were restricted by the narrow trough, and my grip on her shoulder keeping her seat firmly in the bottom of it.

"I'm getting you clean as the King ordered," I muttered. "Take a breath." It was the only warning I gave her before dunking her backwards into the water again, like I was baptizing her.

She gasped, went under, arms flailing, then came back up spluttering and spitting like a cat.

"This isn't a bath!" she hissed.

"It's as close as you're going to get," I retorted, scrubbing her hair and the front of her shirt, ignoring the warm softness of her body underneath that thin leather because she was a fucking *Fetch,* and she had a shriek like a banshee.

Then I held out the bar of soap to her. "Now, do you want me to do your ass and legs for you, or will you do it yourself like a good little girl?"

I couldn't resist the taunt, and chortled when she snatched the soap out of my hand and began scrubbing at her clothes under the water.

"This isn't a bath because I'm still clothed," she snapped, but didn't stop scrubbing.

"You're welcome to remove them if you wish," I offered sweetly. She glared up at me and I stared indifferently back. "Be grateful I didn't give you to the soldiers to bathe. Most of them haven't touched a woman in weeks. There would have been nothing left of you an hour from now."

She scowled, but continued to wash as best she could while still fully clothed and in the narrow trough.

I stayed close, but straightened, folding my arms and watching over her grimly until the trough was full of lather and Fetch dirt, and she placed the bar of soap on the fence with a shaking hand, then turned slowly to look at me again.

"I think… I mean, that's it."

"Very good."

I yanked her up by the back of her shirt and she yelped as half the sudsy trough water came with her. She was still stumbling, trying to find her feet, when I lifted her again and plonked her into the next one to rinse her.

She made a strangled yelp but had the presence of mind to suck in a breath this time as I dunked her again, holding her under for a second or two, before pulling her up and out.

Her eyes were squeezed tightly shut and she spluttered, gasping, gripping my wrists, but she didn't struggle, wisely focusing on preparing for the next dunking.

I grinned and pulled her out of that trough as well, setting her on her feet and grabbing her wrists again, and her hair, steering her through the camp, lifting her back to her feet when she stumbled.

"This isn't n-necessary," she said through chattering teeth after we'd been walking for a moment. "I would just w-walk where you showed me to walk."

"Keep your mouth shut, or I'll send a runner for another ball-gag," I said sourly, *pissed off* that I'd been saddled with this fucking complication at exactly the wrong time.

"You'd like that, wouldn't you?" she snarled. "God forbid someone use clever words against your beefcake."

"I only gag the obnoxious ones," I shot back. "The rest make very different noises." Her face went tight as I smiled. "Be grateful you're in *my* hands, not the King's. He wasn't lying when he said he'd gag you with his member."

"And I wasn't lying about biting it off."

"So, you Fetch eat your males alive, do you? Presumably after the mating, otherwise they're no use to you at all."

"One could argue they never were," she said dryly.

I shoved her a little into the next step.

"Are you Fetch descended from the spiders? I hear the *Jabaya* eat their males. I suppose that would explain why you like the shadows so much."

"Do *not* compare me to those creatures of the dark—" she started, indignant.

"Don't splutter, *Jabaya*. It doesn't become you."

"You laugh now, you fucking devil, but just wait until—"

Rage constricted my chest and I tightened my grip on her hair, dragging her to a halt and yanking her head back so she was bent backwards and looking up at me, her spine arched close to snapping, her eyes wide and teeth bared, glaring up at me.

"One more word and I will get the gag again, and this time if something stops you breathing, I won't assist," I snarled.

She couldn't close her mouth properly because I had her stretched too far back, her breath tearing in and out of her throat. But even though she struggled against my grip, she didn't say anything. And her face went two shades whiter.

With grim satisfaction I filed away the knowledge that something about being gagged—or perhaps the threat of suffocation—was a fearful prospect for her and growled in my throat.

"So you *can* keep your tongue from flapping when you decide to. Good. We have only a short walk until—"

"General! General Handras!"

I looked up to find the original soldier I'd sent running, sprinting back towards me.

"They've delivered the cage, Sir," he said, sliding to a halt at my side, panting, but bright-eyed. "They want to know if you understand the levers?"

"Yes," I growled. "Tell them to leave it."

He nodded, then took off running again and I smiled at his back, then smiled broader as I looked down at her, where she arched awkwardly back over my fist gripping her wrists. Her foot kept sliding out from under her.

"Your new home awaits, Fetch," I spat, then pulled her upright again. "Keep your mouth shut and I might even give you a towel."

My tent was only two minutes walk from where the soldier had found me, in the shade of a large tree that helped keep it cool in the heat of the day and sheltered the ground from rain as well. So soon I was pushing her ahead of me through the tent flap and into the much dimmer interior of my tent.

Normally it was my practice to keep things simple. Easy to pack and move at a moment's notice. So all my things were kept in a very few trunks and chests, each small enough to be moved by one man, alone. But there was a very large bed taking up the back wall of the tent because Gault had insisted that all the high-ranking officers retain beds for sleeping, even though most of our men rolled themselves into furs on the ground at night, and only a portion had narrow hammocks or cots.

But Gault wouldn't be without his comforts, and insisting that the higher among us had them as well obscured his own indulgence. I hated how it had come about, and the efforts the servants were forced to expend to move these things every week or so. But not enough to reject the opportunity to rest on a mattress each night.

Other than the bed, there was a frame of thin, and folding screens for privacy which hid the crates of my clothing and armor. There was a small round basin that sat atop a tall wooden crate with a pitcher of water for washing, a table and two folding chairs just big enough to be used for a meal, a long trunk for my weapons, another for my books and maps. And now, nestled up against the side of the tent that was tight against the face of a sheer, stone cliff so it offered no freedom at all even if she cut through it, was a large, steel-framed cage.

"Home sweet home," I muttered, then tossed her inside and had the door slammed closed and latched before she'd even found her way back to her feet.

~ *YILAN* ~

Melek threw me into the cage so abruptly, I ate dirt and was still stumbling back to my feet and turning to scan the space behind him when a thin towel hit me in the face, followed quickly by a heavy blanket, and... a small pillow of all things.

I caught the plump little square and stared at it, stunned. Why would he—

"Step back. All the way back, I want your ass eating the bars and your shoulders pinned against them."

I blinked and looked up at him where he stood just outside the door of the cage, glaring.

For a moment I was struck by the sheer size of him.

I could stand up in the cage easily. Would barely be able to reach the overhead bars when I stretched. He would have had to duck to get inside and could have rested his hand atop the cage and gripped it without stretching at all.

I swallowed as his chest swelled, and my eyes followed the planes of his pecs up to his shoulders—round as a bull's and just as heavy—the tendons that supported his thick neck, and that jawline, sharp enough to cut glass.

He raised one brow in a wry arch, and it hit me that I'd been standing there, staring at him. I quickly shuttered my expression and backed up against the opposite side of the cage. He waited until my ass and shoulders were, indeed, hard against the steel bars, before he unlocked the door once more and leaned in to place a bucket just inside, before closing and locking it again.

I looked at the bucket, realized that it was intended for my toilet, and had to swallow bile. "Such hospitality," I sneered, then locked eyes with him, wondering if he was expecting me to still stay silent.

When he turned away from the cage, I picked up the towel and started rubbing it against my wet clothing and hair, watching him warily.

"It isn't hospitality. You now have something to lose. And trust me, Fetch, I'll make certain you lose *everything* unless you cooperate."

"I was already cooperating before you tossed me in the horse trough," I pointed out.

He stopped at the base of the monstrous bed at the center of this otherwise almost bare space and started unstrapping and unbuckling. Leather and steel fell to the dirt, to the fur on the bed, all around him, as the man seemed to produce weapons from nowhere... including my favorite throwing knife which I had thought was still sheathed at my ankle under my trousers. But as he slipped it from somewhere in his waistband, he held it up, smiling at me before tossing it onto the bed.

I scowled. He must have got it when I was distracted with the *bath*.

"You can glare all you like. But you're going to discover that I am a male of discipline and honor. And if you carry yourself similarly, you'll remain safe—and somewhat comfortable," he added, nodding at the towel and pillow. "But if you work against me, or make things difficult—if I find out you're lying—I will apply my intelligence and discipline to tormenting you as assiduously as a bee seeking pollen."

"That's an awfully big word, General," I said dryly.

"If you need an explanation to understand anything, let me know, because I want to be clear: If you bring truth willingly, I will keep you fed, clothed, and unviolated. But only if your words prove true. Either you *sing* for me, answering every question I ask and half the ones I don't. Or you spend the remainder of your very short life screaming at the hands of the males outside this tent who do not have my attendance to honor."

"No attendance to honor? Surely you *jest*," I muttered, my blood chilling as my mind conjured just a handful of the things I'd seen in this camp since I arrived. "Your comrades are not simply lacking honor, General. In most cases, they seem to lack simple *reason.*"

He gave me a dark look. "Since you're so astute, no doubt you have gathered that many of my comrades don't have the foresight to consider that you might bite their cocks off... And since you are blessed with *reason,* I'm sure you can understand that even if you were successful in separating them from their members, it would not remove what they may have done to *you* before you got your teeth into them."

I watched him, rage bubbling in my chest when he smiled. But I stuffed it down.

"I take your point. I will answer whatever you wish—if I know it. I cannot be honest if I am expected to create answers I do not have."

His eyes narrowed. "Just like that, ay? Any answers I please?"

"I told your King the same."

He huffed and turned away, muttering so low I almost couldn't hear him. "I would not trust a Fetch anyway… but even less so now. You are far too quick to comply."

"Or I am far too *intelligent* to deny when I have been bested," I said carefully. "And I want to stay alive. Very little in this life is worth dying for."

He arched one brow. "I notice you do not say *nothing* is worth dying for."

"No, I didn't."

He held my gaze for a long moment then, and the roof of my mouth went dry.

5. Lesson Learned

~ YILAN ~

As if he'd made a decision suddenly, Melek tossed the last of his straps onto the bed, then strode back towards the cage, towards *me*. When he reached the bars, he hesitated, then clamped a hand on the top of the cage and leaned down so our eyes were at the same level.

He spoke quietly. Menacingly. "Speak truth: What game are you playing?"

I met his gaze flatly. "This is no game. Though your King does appear to think your army is a toy, and the Continent a child's playground."

"You disrespect my King, you disrespect me. Keep your thoughts on him to yourself, *Fetch.*"

I scoffed. "We are alone, you don't have to maintain the façade with me. The man is an imbecile—"

"One more word against the crown and—"

"You told me to speak the truth! It would be a lie to say otherwise—surely an honorable man like you is not blind to his disgusting, selfish nature?"

He straightened, snarling, ready to launch into me—but then the tent flap twitched and three soldiers appeared, the front one clasping a hand to his chest and bowing his head.

"General, *Sir.*"

Melek shot me a warning glare, then turned to them. "What is it?"

"A message from the front, Sir."

Every part of him snapped to focus like a bird of prey. I was forgotten as he trotted towards them, meeting the first soldier at the center of the tent and snatching the parchment the man held out, ripping it open and reading quickly.

"You two, guard the cage, please," he muttered without looking up while his eyes scanned the paper. "Do *not* get close enough that she can touch you." The two behind the first man came to stand near my cage, both leering, but not speaking.

I watched them warily, but kept my attention on Melek.

He seemed to see nothing but the paper. Frowned, then read it again.

Then he glanced at me and I saw a flash in his eyes that made the pit of my stomach drop. Clearly my comrades on the battlefield had done their jobs.

I smiled as sweetly as he had done when he suggested I unclothe in the middle of the camp.

His eyes narrowed, but he turned his back, beckoning the soldier who'd brought the message to come closer so he could speak below my hearing.

I rolled my eyes, but my sight of him was blocked by one of the others shifting into my field of view, his yellow-green eyes sharp as he leered at me.

He and his brother-at-arms, like all the Nephilim warriors, had the sides of their heads cut short over their ears. But instead of the intricate patterns shaved into Melek's hair, theirs only had stripes that descended to their napes. These two were much younger than Melek. Their fighter's length—the bunch of hair left uncut at the top and back of their scalps—were thin, loose, and still short enough for the strands to dangle around their ears.

They were inexperienced, then. Probably twenty or so, in human terms. Both were bulls—thick and muscular, tall, though not as tall as Melek. Brutes. Their eyes were sharp, but lacked the keen intelligence of his.

They did not lack the edge of lust so common in the Nephilim.

I shuddered, but didn't move away, tensing in ways they would not see, preparing to move quickly if either tried to reach me.

I desperately wanted to know what was in that message, but Melek was keeping his voice too low for me to hear, and the second of the two who'd come to stand near me was leaning closer now. When I looked at him, he licked his upper lip.

"I hear she was caught in the King's tent," he said to his brother at arms. "And she took him. All of him. That's why Melek had to bathe her. She was *drenched* in him."

The first of the two gave a low growl that raised the hair on the back of my neck. "You'd think he'd split her like a cord of wood."

"Apparently not. She must be built for it."

Both of them edged closer as my heart began to beat faster. Surely Melek wouldn't allow them to actually enter my cage?

My heart lurched as I conjured a vision of being trapped in here by these two who would have to hunch to be inside, but who could overpower me physically without even sweating.

There was no room to throw them, and they were each two or three times my weight. I was good at grappling, but not *that* good.

When the first one's upper lip curled up in a sneer and he began hissing about wondering how a Fetch tasted, I threw a hasty prayer to God, but didn't move back.

Come closer, idiot.

Don't come in... but come closer.

I cursed my lack of weapons, my hands clenching around air instead of the hilt of a blade.

"Did you enjoy the King?" the first of them rumbled, giving a menacing half-smile. "You satisfied yet?"

"No," I said bluntly. "Turns out the old adage is true."

"What adage?" the second one snapped.

I tipped my head. "It's not the size of the horn, but how the bull uses it—"

They both sneered and crowded in, muttering promises for how they'd use their *horns,* when Melek's voice cut across their mumbling, sharp with disapproval.

"I said, don't get close enough to be touched!" he snapped.

They both turned, snapping to attention, and presumably about to step away. But as they saluted, I saw my opportunity.

Both had longspears strapped to their backs, blade down and just inches from the dirt.

Because neither of them had stepped forward when they jumped to attention, I snapped one hand between the bars to grasp the spear of the one just an inch above the blade and shoved it into the back of the other's leg.

The first, feeling his weapon jerk, leaped forward—but that only drew the spear blade against his brother's Achilles, snapping it cleanly so that when the first tried to run from the sudden slice of pain, he went down with a shriek.

I wasn't quick enough drawing my hand back, and the jerk of the spear slammed my wrist against the steel bar hard enough to make me hiss, and narrowly missing having the blade slice my palm, as well. But I rolled backwards, deeper into the cage, gripping my wrist and grinning, because the first soldier was screaming like a child, while his brother panicked, whirling between apologizing to Melek who was storming towards them both with a furious snarl on his face, and trying to reach down to help his brother who was rolling on the ground, gripping his leg—the foot flopping sickeningly—and bleeding *everywhere.*

The chaos was short-lived. In moments, Melek had the injured soldier dragged away from the cage so there was no risk of me getting close enough to touch him again, he'd sent the other out of the tent to find a healer, and he was glaring at me over the writhing body of the male on the ground as he issued orders to the soldier who'd brought him the message.

The man wouldn't stop screaming, his eyes wide and his hands and arms covered in blood as he desperately tried to pull his leg back together, but after a few moments of the noise, Melek cursed and pinned the male to the dirt.

"I *told you* not to get close enough to her to be touched. Let this be your warning to listen to your elders and betters. The enemy does not always look threatening, and you have learned that the hard way," he snarled.

"But—my leg! She's—"

"And you will serve out your days as an example to your brothers, with the knowledge that a tiny, irritating woman bested you because you did not listen to those in authority."

Within minutes, the healers arrived, the guards were gone, and the messenger too. I cursed under my breath because I'd missed what Melek said in reply to the message. But suddenly the tent was empty except for me and the General.

He stood near the tent-flap, staring at me, expressionless.

I swallowed.

"Either all your fine warriors are on the battlefield, or somehow your presence there has changed the face of this war, because your soldiers are *for shit.*"

He didn't respond immediately, but stalked across the tent to stand right at the side of the cage, looming, staring down at me with narrowed eyes, his entire massive body poised for violence, his expression *daring* me to try a similar move on him. Which I wouldn't. The sheer, animalistic power wafted off of him like a scent. It took every ounce of discipline within me not to back away.

"Do not make the mistake that idiot made," he muttered as he unlocked the door and my pulse began to race as he swung it wide and beckoned me out. "Come. I have something to show you."

Wary, every sense heightened, braced for pain, I crept out of the cage.

The moment I crossed the threshold of that door, he grabbed my wrist and yanked me out, turning me and pinioning both my wrists at the hollow of my back again as he leaned down, covering me with that massive, brutish body, and growled in my ear.

"This is your one and *only* warning."

Skin prickling where his breath rushed against my ear, I didn't respond as he reached for a small handle on the cage's side.

With a simple tug, the massive cage jumped like a startled animal.

The hammered steel bars that made up the sides flashed. Wide, sharpened blades flipped out from each surface, poised and gleaming for the length of the bars from the floor to the top.

"Are you watching, *Fetch?* It's a very important lesson."

He didn't wait for me to reply, but yanked down on that lever, and those blades—each longer and taller than me, creaked into gleaming arcs of death, slamming like a snapped jaw full of opposing fangs down to the bottom of the cage, slicing the blanket, pillow, and bucket to shreds, wood and girding alike, as easily as if it were butter—then sprang back up to catch those flying pieces mid-air and carve through them a second time.

My pulse slammed painfully inside my skull, thrumming in my ears so loudly I almost couldn't hear Melek's low chuckle. "You would be dead before you saw the hinges engage," he whispered in my ear, his voice a dark rasp of promise. "If you don't want to learn how it feels to be impaled by steel—or by Nephilim prick—you will be *silent* when you are not asked to speak. Do you understand?"

I swallowed hard and nodded, his stubbled jaw scraping against my ear because he hadn't moved away.

For a moment I was frozen, sensing the shift in him as he became aware, just as I had, how closely we stood.

I was chilled in my wet clothes and hair, but his body was so large, the heat seemed to radiate from him, through my clothing, as his quickening breath rushed against my cheek.

Jangling, shrieking fear coursed through me as he rumbled deep in his chest and I felt it at the backs of my shoulders.

Then his thick, calloused fingers gripped my chin and he turned my head, forcing me to meet his eyes over my shoulder.

"I am a man of honor, Fetch. I do not make empty threats. One wrong move—one wrong *word*—and I will have you sliced to ribbons and my brothers will feast on your guts. Keep your mouth shut. Keep your hands in the cage. And do not toy with me or you will learn to your detriment that I say what I mean, and mean what I say."

I blinked, but there was a creak and the world flipped, then I was being dragged backwards, *away* from the cage... and towards the bed.

6. Choose Your Path

~ *YILAN* ~

For a moment that chittering terror screamed in my head. But before I could do more than struggle weakly, there was a scrape, a muttered curse, and suddenly I was plonked bodily into a wooden chair sized for a Nephilim—which meant my feet hung in thin air so I could swing them like a child.

In a blink he had two of the weapons straps from the bed and was wrapping first one of my arms, then the other, to the chair's, from wrist to elbow. He tugged the buckles tight enough to worry me about blood flow.

When I was secured, he took two more straps and spread my legs apart, binding each ankle to one of the chair legs so I was sat awkwardly, limbs spread, tied, and unable to move.

I couldn't even hope to move the chair if I was left unattended. It was massive, and solid. It had to outweigh me by at least fifty pounds.

Melek backed away slowly, eyeing the bonds as if I might somehow produce a blade and slip through them. Despite his size, he moved easily, without the hulking effort of some of the others—including the King. Whether because of his training, or just sheer strength, the man moved like a cat.

I couldn't help a passing rush of admiration for his dominance and power, the presence he carried... and I couldn't help shaking in fear of it, suddenly deeply aware of my vulnerability.

But I kept my head.

The Nephilim were all strong. All physically capable and fierce fighters. But they were not without their vulnerabilities. The primary of which being an apparent lack of discipline and intelligence. Surely this couldn't be the totality of the creatures that had wreaked havoc on the continent over the past few months? The smart ones must be on the battlefield. And yet...

Melek's lips twisted like he was considering something. Then, without a word he turned on his heel and stalked out of the tent, leaving me there utterly alone, though I had no doubt there were guards outside the tent. Still...

I waited, growing chilled in my wet clothing and hair, until that tent flap snapped back, and he entered carrying a platter of steaming food bringing with it delicious scents of fatty meats and roasted vegetables and...

I tried to shift my weight, my tailbone already growing uncomfortable on the wooden seat of the chair, but Melek ignored me, pulling a small table over until it was just feet from my chair, and placing the platter on it, then swinging another of those massive chairs by the back and sliding it into place at the table.

He then proceeded to seat himself and with one short glance at me, focused on eating slowly, methodically, savoring the food as the tent filled with the cloud of its scent.

My stomach growled audibly. Melek acted as if he didn't hear it, but I noticed he ate even more slowly, taking time to lick the fat from his fingers between bites, lips smacking.

I just stared at him the whole time, not pretending I didn't wish to share the food. What was the point? We both knew this was torture. Which was exactly what he'd intended.

Then, finally, when he'd literally scraped the plate clean, he looked up and met my eyes as he lifted one of the bones that he'd stripped clean, snapped it cleanly between his teeth, and sucked the marrow from it.

"This is what I'll do to you if you give me any reason. Any at all," he said quietly, then repeated the process with the other bone.

I didn't respond.

I also didn't doubt him.

When there was nothing left for him to consume, he poured himself a large mug of water and downed it, then placed the plate and cup outside of the tent flap before gathering a quill, ink, and parchment from one of the trunks at the side of the tent, and returning to the table.

When he'd settled himself and organized his things on the table, he licked the end of the quill, dipped it carefully in the ink, then finally looked at me again.

"Now," he said. "Unlike my King I will not grow bored. Start with the Aethereans and their motives for joining the others when it is not even their land, and we'll move on from there…"

An hour later, still strapped to that chair, I was sweating.

He was right. He was not like his King at all.

Not dull.

Not easily drawn.

Very sharp. Very insightful.

He saw through any of my carefully chosen words and would pursue the question, digging into the details until I was forced to give up every nuance—or admit when I did not know.

For the first time, I questioned the path I'd taken. This man would not be easily manipulated. But as the day wore into night, and night into the early hours of morning, I didn't flinch. I was committed now. There was little choice but to continue… and possibly fail.

God forgive me.

"Sleeping, Melek? *Really?*"

The voice was booming and warm with laughter.

I jolted awake, wincing against the crick in my neck and the ache in my tailbone because I was still strapped to that hard chair.

There was a low, rumbling growl, then a graveled, *"About fucking time."*

Melek, who'd been asleep in the bed, shoved out of the furs and stalked across the tent to meet the new Nephilim, who was strapped and armored, with temples damp and hair ringed with sweat as if he'd just taken off a helmet. The two clasped arms, clapping each other's shoulders with the kind of resonant slap that was the only type of affection strong men would allow themselves. Or so I thought.

The new male, sunny and good-humored in his countenance, a bright contrast to Melek's dark brooding, yanked Melek closer and thumped his back so hard it sounded like drums calling soldiers to war.

But I had a brief glimpse of an unguarded smile from Melek over the man's shoulder before they parted, and then both turned to look at me.

I tried to straighten. I'd slumped against the bonds in my sleep and now both my hands were numb. But I couldn't move enough to relieve any of the pain, so I just raised my chin and stared the new man down.

And then I smiled, because the man was smiling at me. And he was quite possibly the most handsome man I'd ever seen.

The light was too dim to be sure of his hair color, but it was clear he was lighter in both hair and complexion than Melek. As he took in the way I'd been bound, he raised one brow and tipped his head.

"I do love a woman who looks good in leather," he said.

The comment from any of the earlier soldiers would have sickened me with their lusty leering. But this man was different. He was warm and playful in his tone. Not threatening.

"That's good," I croaked. "Because I've always appreciated a man who was good at knots."

He affirmed my instinct on his nature by throwing back his head and laughing, then winking at me when I smiled. I was pleased by his easy humor.

"Don't let her fool you," Melek growled from behind him. "She has teeth—and she's been very clear that she isn't afraid to use them."

The sunny man glanced at him, then turned his regard back to me, thoughtful. "I wouldn't let that discourage you *completely,* Mel," he said thoughtfully. "I once took a horse that was a feral beast because it was cheap. Everyone before me said it couldn't be tamed. And it's true, it took a great deal of time, but once I did…" He locked eyes with me. "That animal was the best ride I've ever had."

I snorted, struggling to contain a delighted laugh as he raised his brows in a suggestive waggle.

Melek shook his head and didn't even grin. "Best of luck, Jann. Do let me know how you'd like me to honor you in memorial when she's sliced you open like a piece of fruit. She already hamstrung one of the youngsters. But by all means, give it a shot. Maybe you can domesticate her."

It took me half a breath to realize who this man had to be, but when I did, my jaw dropped and my eyes went wide.

He looked away from Melek's warning and caught my expression, arching that handsome brow again.

"What is it?"

"You're Jannus, the Halfling?" I breathed.

His smile got broader and he turned back to Melek. "Apparently my reputation precedes me."

"Don't give her *anything,*" Melek growled. "Much as it pains me to admit, she is very clever. She'll extrapolate from anything you offer. Keep your mouth shut."

Jannus the Halfling—the only living Nephilim descended from two half-bloods, a male and female pair, both born to human women as a result of unions with fallen angels. His great-grandmother was the only known female Nephilim of royal blood. Every other half-blood ever born was male. At least, that was what the history books said. And as far as we knew, the Nephilim records didn't contradict the position.

The famous half-blood hadn't lived long past adulthood—legends conflicted on exactly *how* she had died. I suspected the King at the time had been jealous of her fame and desirability. But there was said to be a curse on his bloodline. Each generation only ever having one child, most of whom died young, but not before producing an heir. A *male* heir.

Jannus, at thirty-five, was the longest lived in his immediate family line, and not yet a father. As I took in the sight of him—a living legend—he caught my scrutiny and stared back with a considering smile. That little flame low in my belly flared when his nostrils flared, as if he'd caught the scent of me.

I blew out a breath. "I have a theory about your bloodline," I said cautiously.

His brows rose. "Please share, honeycakes. I can barely contain my excitement."

"Honeycakes?" Melek muttered, staring at his friend. "She's as bitter as snakeroot."

I ignored him, biting my lip. I didn't miss Jannus's eyes dropping to my mouth. "Perhaps as long as you don't wet your prick, you'll live forever?" I asked him breathlessly, unable to stifle the smile any longer when he blinked, then threw back his head and laughed again.

"Dear God, she's a *spicy* pepper, isn't she?" he boomed at Melek.

"That's one word for it," Melek muttered, which only made Jannus laugh more and slap his shoulder again. But Melek shot me a glare to keep my mouth shut, then waited for his friend to stop laughing before he spoke low and hard.

"Thank you for coming, Jann. I am in need of your insight."

Jannus took a beat to hold my gaze before turning to his friend, his expression dropping into solemn attention. "I'm your servant, Melek. You know that. What's going on?"

"I am going to be forced to stay in camp for a time," Melek started.

All humor and heat fled from Jann's countenance as he stared at Melek. "I mean, I will be glad to have you close, of course. But is this really the time? We're still debating the route through the swamp and there's conjecture among the strategists about how they've managed to evade you this long."

"Fortunately, I can help with both of those things—or rather, *she* can," Melek growled, tipping his head at me. Jann's brows popped up again, but Melek didn't stop. "She's been through the swamp to get here. She knows every step."

I sighed. "I didn't bring an army through."

"Remember our *arrangement,*" he muttered with a bare glance at me before turning back to Jannus.

I glared. "I told you. I cannot tell you things I do not know!"

Melek turned on me. "Oh, I suspect you have more than an idea. And we will find out when we question you—you may know more than you realize."

I huffed. "I will not be held responsible for misguiding you when—"

"If you'd like to get loose from the chair and curl up on the ground with a blanket and pillow, you'll *speculate* about which way to take them through, Fetch."

Jannus looked back and forth between us, but I ignored him, my heart beating too quickly again.

Damn. *Damn.*

I took a deep breath. "I'll need maps."
Melek smiled grimly and Jannus eyed him warily.
"Those can be arranged," Melek said.
My stomach sank.

7. The Route

~ MELEK ~

I picked up the chair with her still on it and turned it to face the end of my bed since I didn't have a table big enough to spread out multiple maps. Jann grabbed the rolled parchments from the trunk in the corner and began spreading them out on the end of the bed.

The Fetch tilted her head, frowning slightly as each was unrolled and pressed flat.

When Jann had finished, he stepped back to stand shoulder to shoulder with me. We both folded our arms and watched her examine the maps together.

Unsurprisingly, her scrutiny didn't last long then she turned to look expectantly at me.

"Perhaps you'd like to share with me where your troops are positioned?" she asked dryly.

Before Jann could answer, I put a sharp elbow into his ribs. "Tell her nothing that is not already public knowledge. Don't tell her what you know, or don't know. We need everything confirmed without her interference if we're to know if she's telling the truth."

She turned her head to glare at me from her seat. "If I don't know your position, how am I supposed to advise you on my *guess* for the best route through the swamplands?"

"Tell us your best choice—or choices. We'll determine which would best suit our position," I growled.

She stared at me flatly for a moment before she opened that mouth. "I have revised my assessment. You *are* as stupid as your King—"

Jannus spluttered in an attempt not to laugh. I shot him a glare.

"—first you want me to *speculate* on bringing troops through the most dangerous wetlands on the continent, then I'm supposed to know *all the ways?* Without numbers or positions? Did the Fallen intentionally exchange brains for brawn, or was that a curse of God for your ancestor's rebellion?"

"Melek *is* very strong," Jann said quietly.

I shot him a withering look.

Her eyes warmed when she looked at Jann and went cold when she gazed at me.

"I don't understand... Have you truly just... *overwhelmed* everyone to this point? I cannot believe the Tuskarrians aren't putting up a fight if your strategy is simple brute strength. Then again, if this is the mental sword you wield, no wonder you aren't getting anywhere. The Zaryndar are going to flay your skins from your bones the moment they have your—"

I kicked her chair so it hopped and pivoted so she was almost facing me, then leaned down over her, gripping each of the arms and making myself as big as possible to loom over her, seething.

"You were not asked for your opinion on our intelligence, or the King's. You were asked to suggest a path through the swamps. My advice, which I have no doubt you will not listen to, would be to set that clever, obnoxious mind of yours to highlighting the risks of any plan you propose. If I lose *one* Nephilim to an ambush on the back of your advice, not only will I kill you slowly, but I will raze your land, making certain every one of your people hears that *you* were the one who brought my vengeance down on them."

She paled, but her eyes never left mine, and she did not shake. "You set me up for failure, then threaten to punish me when *you* are not adequately prepared."

"Then make sure you do not fail. I'm certain with your *superior intellect*, you'll figure something out."

"We've taken Noctharrow Haven, but haven't entered the swamps yet," Jannus said quietly from behind me.

I hissed and whirled on him. "I told you not to—"

"Please, Melek. I would like *some* sleep tonight. And if she's as knowledgeable as you think, she could save us weeks if we approach it correctly. Besides, we'll check the routes. She won't fool my scouts... even if they are simpletons," he added quickly, winking at her over my shoulder.

She gave a little huff of husky laughter, and I rolled my eyes.

"You may be surrounded by idiots, but I am surrounded by children," I sighed to her.

"Well, since your King is a toddler, it's hardly surprising," she said with a shrug, as if I'd been serious. I ground my teeth, but Jann pulled me back a pace and stepped up to her chair.

"Look… uh… what was your name?" he asked carefully.

"Yilan," she said after a moment, as if he'd shocked her.

"Yee-lawn? What a beautiful name."

She shrugged. "It's a family name." But she smiled.

"Lovely… well, look, Yilan, I know Melek storms around like a cat that got thrown in the bath, but the truth is, he's not *always* stupid. And sometimes he can even be quite kind and insightful *if you don't taunt too much.* The trick is to watch for the vein on the side of his forehead. When that starts pulsing, it's best to ease off."

Yilan rolled her lips together as if she were stopping herself from speaking, but she was smiling brightly and her eyes twinkled like Jann's when he was enjoying a joke. She leaned towards him as much as the bonds would allow. "What does it mean when he grunts? Is he trying not to laugh, or is he truly angered?"

"Oh, that's just gas," Jann said.

"Enough," I growled as Yilan *giggled.* "Both of you," I added with a glare at my comrade. "You aren't the only one who would like to sleep before dawn, Jann. Stop falling for her tactics. She's only deflecting and delaying. Keep your mouth *shut—"* I said quickly when he opened his mouth to answer. "No one is going to speak now, but our… guest. Who will speak of the ways to both approach *and* pass through the swamps safely, or I will slit her throat so that I can return to the front."

She looked sullen, but reluctantly turned to look at the maps again, sighing and leaning forward. "Can you free me so that I can show you points on the terrain? It will speed this up a great deal."

Jann stepped forward, but I didn't trust her. I put a hand up to stop him approaching her, then started unbuckling the leather that bound one of her arms.

She sighed with relief when that hand was free, rolling her wrist and hissing as the blood flowed back into the hand.

Then I picked up the chair and shoved it back around and right up to the end of the bed, until her knees knocked the footboard.

"Start talking," I muttered.

"My other hand—"

"Start. Talking," I repeated through my teeth.

She sighed, but leaned forward as much as her bound arm would allow, her eyes darting left and right over the maps, her lips pursed.

"If you've taken Noctharrow, then my guess is you're riding the line between Tuskarria and Zaryndar—which would have been a great strategy for their caution if they weren't already working together," she muttered.

Then she turned and looked at me, scanning me from my bare feet to my crown, her face thoughtful as if she were measuring me.

"My *guess* is that the Tuskarrians are giving you the physical fight, and the Zaryndar are using their magik to slow you... and so far, your enemies have been far more united in their defense than your men are in their attack. Your progress across the flatlands lulled your ranks into a false sense of security, and now they're ill-disciplined and responding slowly... arrogant and unwilling to admit they've been bested. You're scrambling—"

"We are not scrambling," I ground out. "But... our progress has stayed... for now."

She tipped her head at me. "So, you can be humble when it's needed. Well done, General. Perhaps you do have a soul after all."

I rolled my eyes, but she turned back to the maps, chewing the inside of her cheek. "You need not tell me where it happened, but I need to know: How many times have you attempted to take the gain? How many times have they turned you back?"

Suspicious of a trap, though I couldn't see it, I looked a question at Jann. Should we tell her? Was there a way she could take more from that simple piece of information than I could see?

He shrugged and tipped his head towards her.

I sighed. "Three times," I admitted, though it made my skin crawl. "Only the first was a route. The second and third did not make us *scramble*, but we have not gained ground."

She nodded as if I'd only affirmed what she believed.

Then, her eyes still darting across the maps, she reached out to point at a place right on the borderlands of Tuskarria and Zaryndar. "The ravine," she said.

Rage swelled my chest. "What a fucking waste of time this has been," I muttered, turning from her, pissed at myself for believing she'd take this seriously. I turned to Jann, ready to instruct him to rebind *and* gag her, when she spoke again.

"They will never expect it."

"Of course they won't expect it, because it is a death-trap, and I am not stupid!" I roared at her.

She merely raised an eyebrow and shook her head slowly.

"Not if you handle it correctly. You and your people are far too accustomed to simply showing up and expecting your enemies to cower like nervous pups. The Tuskarrians won't stop fighting until they cease breathing, and the Zaryndar will keep evading you until they can bring their magik to bear and actually wound you. And don't believe that they won't work together—letting the Tuskars battle to wear you out, then bringing the wizards up in the rear to finish you. They may not have it in them to conquer you, Melek, but they can turn you back. And the rest of the world will take notice of that."

"I am *aware—*"

"Bullshit. You're scrambling whether you're ready to admit it or not. You haven't made progress because you've assumed you can whittle their numbers down in the skirmishes, then just walk across the swamps when they're clear of vermin," she snapped. "But you're wrong. The population counts on the Zaryndar alone are in the hundreds of thousands, and they will never actually engage. It would be like fighting ghosts. It would take you *years* to kill enough of them to just waltz through their land, and in the meantime, you're *also* fighting Boars who will willingly die just to bleed you. And *both* are being coordinated by the Aethereans. Your strategy would have worked faster without that, but with the soulsuckers in play, you're screwed. You'd be old and gray before you took the wetlands… and then you'd still have *us* to deal with."

She gave a small, wicked smile. "You want my honest, unvarnished assessment of the best path through? Well, here it is: Your current plan is the waste of time. Aim for the ravine—and expect it to take time. But that mile of precious progress will open a wedge between their peoples and put you in control of where and how you meet in battle. And if you really surprise them, you'll have *them* scrambling, Aethereans be damned."

I shook my head. "You really do think I'm stupid. The ravine is a channel. The ground between the cliffs isn't just wet, it's a mire which works against our weight and size compared to the Zaryndar. Even if it held off the Tuskars, we'd be stuck before we made it through—"

"It's worse than that. The wetlands within the ravine are scattered with sinkholes that even your bodies would disappear into and never return. Meanwhile the tree canopy is so dense, you barely see the sun. You can be attacked from above and below and never see it coming," she said sweetly.

I ground my teeth. "Then why—"

"Firstly, because they would never expect it. If I had to gamble anything on this war, it is that both the Zaryndar and the Tuskarrians believe the risk of you approaching via that route is so small, they have left only a smattering of guards and runners in place to alert them to your appearance. And because they know your progress would be so slow the runners would bring word to the ranks on both sides before you could make it through."

"Which is precisely why—"

"But you can fly."

"Not through a narrow ravine, between trees and archers. We would be picked off—"

"The land atop the cliffs on either side is the driest and clearest of any part of the wetlands. If you could take that, you would not only be on dry, solid ground, you would have the highest position, forcing them to fight *uphill* if they come for you. And unable to see you from within the ravine's depths. There is some risk if they get an Aetherean up there to watch for them, but those cowards don't like sunlight. And they won't be willing to scale the cliffs without protection from the Tuskars.

"You do not need to take the entire swamp. You only need to remove the guards and runners that are there to alert the others. Take those without raising the alarm, and you can fly to the top of the cliffs. With Tuskarria on one side, and Zaryndar on the other, they will be forced to fight you separately—"

"Splitting our forces as well!" I pointed out, though I was beginning to see that perhaps this plan wasn't *quite* the suicide mission I'd assumed.

"Battle is your strength. Get them to face you on higher ground and you will win, and you know it. My guess is that once they realize what has happened, they won't even try to fight. They'll be too busy rushing their forces to the wetlands at the base of the ravine *inside their borders*—but again, you'll have scaled the cliffs and can simply follow them all the way down. They won't be able to meet you on flat ground until you're almost at the Shadows of Shade."

I saw the barest flash in her eyes at that statement—the Shadows of Shade was a thick band of fog, reportedly almost five miles deep, that covered the land from coast to coast and was so dense, even sunlight didn't reach through.

It was the protection of her land and people, the Fetch. They walked the shadows were undeterred by the darkness and lack of visibility there.

But we, of course, would not be.

"So your plan is to help me defeat our mutual enemies, then position me for death on your borders?" I asked dryly.

She didn't even hesitate. "I have given you the route you needed. If you can't beat those armies in outright war, then nothing I have to offer will help you."

I stared at her, but she didn't waver.

Jann, at my side, was remarkably quiet, which meant he was thoughtful.

I glanced at him, but he was examining the maps, a frown creasing his forehead. It was an odd expression for him. I'd seen the man smile while being treated for a stab-wound to the ribs.

The Fetch had sat back in her chair, her eyes were still on the maps, but it was clear that she was smug. Certain.

I wanted to snap my teeth, but I couldn't deny that she had accurately predicted our current position *and* struggle. And I was catching the vision of what she proposed.

"Start from the beginning and speak as if I *am* an imbecile. Show me. Step by step on the maps how you see this being achieved. And when you're done, start again."

She tipped her head up to meet my eyes and smiled. "Don't worry, we'll do this as many times as it takes for you to catch on, Melek," she said sweetly. "I'm a very patient woman. Especially with simple minds. It's not your fault that God gave you a blunt instrument to work with."

Behind me, Jannus cleared his throat to cover a laugh.

But I didn't give two shits if she mocked me—if she really was giving me the keys to finally win this war.

"Start at the beginning," I growled. "And don't stop until I speak."

She took a deep breath, but she nodded and turned back to the maps, pointing with her free hand.

"You'd need a force large enough to fight, but not so large that you march slower than a man alone. There's a trail that runs parallel to the road from Noctharrow and you'd be expected to take that if you were splitting forces to meet the Tuskars…"

8. The Voice of Angels

~ *MELEK* ~

Two hours later, I rewarded her by untying her bonds and putting her back in the cage. She groaned when her hands were released, working them carefully, opening and closing her fingers and rolling her wrists without a word. I left her to herself in the cage while I stepped outside with Jann to discuss details where she couldn't hear us.

Before he pushed through the tent flap, he looked over his shoulder at her, smiling. He opened his mouth like he might farewell her as a friend, but he caught my frown and closed it again, though he chuckled.

"Do you believe her?" I asked him without preamble when we reached the glowing campfire twenty feet from the tent, keeping my voice barely above a whisper so she couldn't catch it.

Jann's brows rose. "I believe the strategy is realistic, but risky. An enemy never moves the way we expect. With that said... it's far better than anything we've come up with so far. The question is how to avoid the sinkholes while we're still on the ground and stalking the guards and runners. We can't afford to let any escape."

It was the same thought I'd had. So extremely risky—and yet, if it worked... it would save lives *and* time.

"Do you think she's setting us up to be defeated by her people?" Jann asked.

I snorted. "Of course she is. The question is, has there been a specific ambush planned, or does she just know the terrain enough to know what would disadvantage us in meeting the Fetch. She seems to have a great deal of trust in the Shadows of Shade…"

We talked through all the questions that remained—and for which we had no answers—then I sent Jann off to share the idea with our strategists.

"…tell them, if we're going to do this, we *must* have taken the ground before the Covenant Days of Peace. We need them tired and weary, not rested and sharp."

Jann nodded, clasped my arm, pulled me into a quick hug, then stepped back.

"Don't let her get under your skin, Melek. She's toying with you. Play back."

I grunted and farewelled him, before walking back to the tent, feeling suddenly very heavy and hulking and far wearier than I wanted to let on. But I pushed the selfish thoughts of rest and peace away, because they benefited no one.

As I took the final steps to the tent and braced myself in anticipation of the Fetch's cutting comments to come, I was surprised to catch a very quiet, but very beautiful refrain riding the night-chilled air.

I hesitated before I stepped into the tent, cocking my head, unwilling to believe the lovely sound came from the source I suspected. But sure enough… in the near-silent night, a lone, feminine voice rose and fell in a stunning, but quiet, almost husky melody. And to my even greater surprise, her words were a love song.

…lay me in the arms of peace.
Lay me in safety, in the shade of the trees.
Feed me at the table of my enemy
Let not the shadow of death take me.
For your hand is power
And your heart beats for me.
I am safe, I am safe, in these arms.
The arms of peace—

She broke off the moment I flipped the tent-flap back. She had seated herself against the back of the cage, pulling her knees up to her chest—to keep warm, or just as protection? I didn't know, but she was still working her hands, opening and closing her fingers, and rolling her wrists.

I took these details in with a glance, then turned away and refused to look at her, or let her know I was listening.

A moment later she hesitantly started singing again, though even quieter this time. I pretended to ignore her, busying myself with finding another blanket and pillow, a new bucket since her cage was now littered with the pieces of the earlier ones I'd offered her.

I swallowed at one point, frowning, surprised by the melancholy surge in my chest.

She had a strange but beautiful voice, and the eerie, raspy way in which she curled her tongue around the words strummed something inside me.

She stopped singing when I approached the cage, her large eyes scanning up my body until they locked on mine.

She was already pressed to the back of the cage, which meant there was no need to give her instructions to that effect, so I just let the warning rest in my eyes as I unlocked the door and threw in the blanket, pillow, and bucket for her.

She caught them easily, eyeing the bucket with distaste, but not commenting until I was already relocking the cage.

"Thank you," she said carefully, her teeth clenched as if the words hurt her to speak.

"I told you—deal with me in honor, and you will be rewarded. Work against me, and you will die."

She didn't respond but looked at the pillow and blanket in her lap.

"Still… thank you," she said carefully.

I shrugged and stalked over to the bed, throwing myself into its soft embrace for the couple of hours I had left before breakfast.

My body was well-trained to grasp sleep whenever possible, so I slipped into the dream immediately. A dream of shifting shadows, wicked smiles, whispered threats, and yet through it all that voice rose to dance with the clouds, singing of peace and love and safety in that eerie rasp that was somehow beautiful, frightening, and welcoming, all at once…

~ YILAN ~

I was woken from a deep sleep plagued by nightmares to the sound of marching feet and voices in the tent, speaking to Melek.

Startled and disoriented, I leaped to my feet in a defensive stance, aware only that I was caged and surrounded by huge, male bodies. But when none of them reacted to me, I blinked and the memory of the day before came rushing back.

Melek, only half-dressed in leather trousers, but with a bare chest and feet, stood at the end of his bed, arms folded across his massive chest. He barely glanced at me before returning his attention to the soldiers standing in front of him.

There were four of them this time. The first two, clearly older and more experienced, spoke quietly and with an efficiency of words.

But the two behind them surprised me.

One was a young lieutenant, trying very hard to be professional by submitting to the authority of the elders while attempting to hide his awe at the sight of the famous general—who was ignoring him. The other was very young. Barely twenty by human standards, I suspected. His eyes—pure gold—were wide, and his expression open and almost childlike. He beamed at Melek until his roaming eyes took me in and widened even further.

He stared at me like a child would, and I stared back, smiling in response when he smiled. My heart squeezed, because as soon as he was facing me and I could meet those incredible eyes, I understood him, and a part of me was deeply shocked.

I hadn't been wrong about the childlike nature. Those eyes were pure and simple. Quite beautiful… and a little empty.

He'd been standing at attention alongside the other young soldier, but when I smiled he beamed and started towards me. His body and gait were all healthy, vigorous man. Yet his eyes… his heart… were something else entirely.

I liked him immediately and feared for him in this brutal place because I knew what he was, and that meant he was desperately vulnerable here.

"Hello," he whispered as he got close to the cage. "What's your name?"

My smile was genuine. "I'm Yilan. What's yours?"

"Gall."

"It's nice to meet you, Gall," I said sincerely.

His smile got wider, but as he opened his mouth to respond, Melek obviously noticed and growled from the other side of the tent.

"Gall, stand back. She's a prisoner. She's not safe."

"But she's very polite!" he said, pointing at me with the short-spear he was holding so the steel tip almost brushed the side of the cage.

My heartbeat sped up, but I didn't move.

"What have I told you about enemies, Gall?" Melek growled and shot me a warning look. "They will pretend to be your friends until they have a chance to betray you. She is an enemy. You need to trust me on that."

The young man's shoulders slumped. He frowned as he turned back to face me, his eyes searching mine as if he was looking for the dragon within me.

"I'm sorry, I have to do what he says," he said quietly, but earnestly. "Thank you for being nice to me though."

"I'll always be nice to you, Gall. I have a sister who... reminds me of you. I am not *your* enemy."

His lips twisted and his brow furrowed as he scratched the back of his neck. "Melek says that's exactly what an enemy would say," he said.

I nodded. "Melek is right... most of the time. And I *am* Melek's enemy," I admitted with an apologetic shrug. "But if you don't try to hurt me, I won't hurt you. I swear it."

"Swear on what?" he asked, suddenly suspicious.

I grieved for a moment, knowing what kind of hurt must have happened to mold that sweet heart to suspicion.

"I swear on—"

"Gall!" Melek barked. "I said stay back!"

He looked over his shoulder to hurriedly give Melek reassurance, twisting his body but not stepping away, and that spearhead clattered against the cage bars.

With him facing away, I saw my moment.

I leaped forward, grasping the wooden handle of the spear and yanking it straight from his grip and into the cage, accidentally knocking his knuckles against the steel. Then, as I scrambled back and away from the bars, I whipped the spear around to point towards the four, huge Nephilim now rushing towards me.

9. Humble

~ YILAN ~

Melek bellowed and Gall cried out, shocked by the pain, and by the loss, his eyes sad when he looked at his hand and then at mine, and realized I'd stolen his spear.

Melek stormed over to him, yanking him back two steps and immediately lecturing him, snarling and pointing at me as he barked a reprimand.

Poor Gall's brows pinched down over his nose and he dropped his head in shame as the General flayed him with his tongue. I tried to give him an apologetic look—to reassure him that I meant him no harm. But the other soldiers were rushing forward, teeth bared and cursing as Melek dragged Gall away from my cage.

The oldest of them was already working at the lock and issuing orders to the others to back him up.

I was still squatting low, but had the spear pointing up and held strong, ready to stab any of them that came at me before they could get hands on me.

"Wait—no! Do *not* open that cage!" Melek bellowed as the soldiers descended on me.

Everyone froze, including me. I was breathing hard, but my stance was spread and balanced, and the spear was just the right weight.

When the soldiers froze, it was clear their leader was furious, but he relocked the cage door and stepped back. "You're right of course, General," he said quietly, then turned to one of the others. "Go call one of the archers. He won't miss from this close—"

"No," Melek snapped. "Let her keep the spear," he said darkly, now between me and Gall, and tipping his head at the others to put space between them and my cage. "No one can get into the cage without risk, but she can't get out either. And she knows the moment she looses that she'll be undefended, and I'll snap her neck," he growled. "She's not going to let it go," he said, then smiled wickedly at me, his eyes dark with promise.

"But, General—" the Lieutenant spluttered.

Melek lifted a hand to silence him. "No one feeds her as long as it is in her possession," he instructed. "Let her surrender and offer it. Let her *choose* to do the right thing. Until then, she will starve."

I swallowed hard, already somewhat sick with hunger because it had been a full day since I'd eaten. I'd been looking forward to any crumb they might have fed me this morning.

As Melek refuted the protests of the others and assured them he was perfectly safe in here with me even when I was armed, poor Gall just stood there, Melek's grip on his shoulder to keep him from moving, staring at me like I'd hurt his feelings.

While Melek let him go with a fierce warning not to move from that spot, and ushered the others out, I watched Gall and waited until they weren't listening to me.

"I'm sorry. I didn't mean to hurt your hand," I said quietly. "I just needed something to defend myself. The men here, they're... quite brutal," I said, eyeing him to see if he would still trust me.

Gall's throat bobbed and he nodded. "I know how that feels," he said. Then his chin rose, and his hands clenched to fists at his side as he looked towards the tent flap where the others were disappearing and Melek stood with his back to us, his stance very obviously tense and unimpressed.

When the others were gone, he turned on his heel with a sharp glare at me, then a slightly softer, but still angry expression for Gall.

"Son, I have told you—"

"I know I shouldn't lose the spear, but she should have one," Gall said, lifting a hand towards me. "She's a woman *here,* Papa. She needs protection."

I blinked, shocked. This was Melek's *son?!*

"That's not—"

"Why don't you protect her?" Gall said, his tone growing frantic. "You said we should always watch for the safety of those weaker than us!"

"Yes, but... that isn't—" Melek spluttered.

If it had been anyone else present, I would have thrown back my head and laughed. But I understood Gall more than either of them could know. And I knew his big, soft heart was pounding in his chest right now as he faced yet another moment in this dark world that he didn't understand.

"You said—"

"Gall, *listen,*" Melek said, keeping his voice low, but firm. "She is an *enemy.*"

"She apologized to me."

"She wants to manipulate you—"

"I would never hurt him," I snapped, locking eyes with Melek who turned to glare at me. "Never," I said just as firmly as he had. "As God is my witness, I would slit *your* throat in a heartbeat. But him? He's safe from me unless he tries to kill me first."

Melek's eyes narrowed, but Gall lifted his hand towards me again. "See?"

Melek gave a low rumble in his chest and a *very* unimpressed look at me, but then he raised his hands towards Gall. "Okay, okay. I'll... I have an idea. If you're so sure of her, Gall... why don't you use your free hours to help me care for her? Then you'll get to check each day that she's *safe,*" he said with a *very* ironic look at me.

Gall's face brightened. "Like a guard!" It was such a strange experience to hear that deep, masculine voice speaking with such childlike delight.

"Yes, sort of."

"I would like that!"

"Good. Then the first thing I need you to do is to go find a waterskin for her, full of water. She hasn't had a drink yet this morning. So that is your task. You go get her water and I'll watch her until you get back, okay?"

"Okay!" Gall said, rushing towards the tent flap. "I'll be back soon, Yilan. Don't worry!"

I couldn't help it. I had to smile at him. He waved then disappeared outside.

There was a moment of stillness then, when neither Melek nor I moved, and we both stared at that doorway.

Was he grieving, as I was, that these simple, beautiful minds had to be taught to fear the world?

I sighed, but then Melek turned to me, clawing a hand through his hair, his jaw tight, and his eyes a dark promise of violence.

"I would never hurt him," I said quietly. "I meant that."

"You'll forgive me if I don't believe a fucking word that comes out of your mouth. But *he* will, as long as it's spoken kindly—and half the time when it isn't. If you so much as curse in his direction—"

"My little sister is... similarly affected," I said carefully and Melek's teeth snapped shut. "She is precious." I swallowed hard. "I am here to fight for her safety."

His lips thinned, but he stopped barking at least.

"I understand the risks they face. I will do my best not to harm him even with my words. Ever."

"He has already forgiven you for the spear," Melek ground out.

"I know. And I've told him I'm sorry I hurt his hand—I meant it."

"That means exactly nothing to me when you stand here armed—and at the cost of his official reprimand. The Sergeant will not be kind. He is a soldier, no matter his simple mind. He is expected to maintain a soldier's conduct. He will be punished for this."

I swallowed hard. "I'm sorry."

"Not enough to give up the spear."

I shook my head.

Melek snarled at me. "Fucking Fetch! I will take every welt on his hide out of yours."

Shit. But I nodded.

The tent flap twitched then, and Gall rushed back in carrying a waterskin and a wooden cup.

He was beaming.

"Here you go, Yilan!"

He rushed straight to the cage door and pushed the waterskin through the gap in the bars, then leaned down to put his hand through the gap, holding the cup, so that he could sit it on the ground without tipping it over.

It would have taken a split second to grab that wrist, pull him against the bars and plunge the spear into his throat, and Melek and I both knew it.

I didn't move.

"Drink! You need to drink if you haven't had water. You'll get weak without it."

Melek dropped his face into his hand as his son plastered himself up against the bars, urging me to drink for my own protection.

"Perhaps you should step away from the bars, Gall?" I said carefully. "And then I'll drink. Thank you for taking such good care of me."

"You're welcome!" he said brightly, then stepped back, blinking as he realized what he'd done. He rushed back to stand next to Melek, looking anxiously back and forth between us, clearly hoping Melek hadn't noticed.

I waited until he was well away before moving to the door of the cage. Still holding the spear I picked up the waterskin by its neck, then the cup, before scuttling to the back of the cage again and squatting. Holding the spear across my thighs with my free hand, I hurriedly poured a full cup of water and drained it. Melek watched me, glaring but silent.

All too soon, after complimenting the boy on his care, Melek sighed and sent him to speak to the Sergeant.

"…I'm sorry, Son. But it's a breach. If I don't send you to him the others will hear of it and—"

"I know," Gall said, his face sad and head down, jaw tight with frustration. "I wish I remembered things like that before they happened."

Melek sighed and put a hand to his shoulder. "You will. The day will come, it will be instinct for you. I promise."

I winced, all at once deeply grateful that my sister would never be expected to learn these kinds of restrictions, and deeply grieved that although Gall would learn most of the rules with time, he would likely never stop making small mistakes.

When Gall was gone, Melek turned away from me without a glance and prowled over to the upright crate at the side of the tent. He pulled a large bowl and pitcher out of a chest, and poured water into it, then began cleaning himself, then shaving in a small, speckled mirror that was hung from the tent pole.

I waited for his condemnation, but he didn't speak. Didn't even look at me in the surface of the mirror. As if I wasn't there.

When he was dressed and had strapped on his weapons, he started for the door.

"Why have him give me water?" I asked quickly before he reached it. "If you really wanted to torture me—"

"Because it is a job he won't fuck up, which makes him feel good," Melek ground out. Then he met my eyes over his shoulder. "And because it would kill you too quickly to go without it." Then he smiled a wicked, predatory grin. "I will see you humble yourself, or suffer, Fetch. And I will swear *that* on any god you choose."

Then he snapped the tent flap aside and disappeared outside leaving me grieving… and hungry.

10. Soulless

~ YILAN ~

Over the following two days I learned that when the General took it upon his very capable shoulders to torment someone, he was a maddening bastard.

I spent that entire time in the cage, hollow on the inside, weakening on the outside.

Yet, not once did he threaten, or growl.

Not once did he attempt to take the spear, or negotiate with me.

The prick just got the hottest, richest food by the plateful and brought it into the tent several times a day.

It started with a breakfast of sizzling hot sausage, honeycakes, sweet fruit and an accompanying mug full of rich, sharp kafk. I would have groaned. Kafk was my favorite drink in the morning, though usually taken with cream and honey. I watched miserably as he pulled the small table to the center of the tent and placed the plate there, dragging a chair to it and tucking in—but not like a monster. No, this asshole savored every bite, and licked the fat and juices from his fingers, then sat back with a satisfied sigh to drink the warm kafk while staring at me.

"Hungry, Fetch?" he asked casually, as if he were being a good host.

I kept my eyes away from his scraped plate, ignored his smiles, and made rude gestures to his back when he eventually turned away.

Lunch was a plate piled high with roasted pork and fire-seared vegetables, heated applesauce, and a hot cup of cider.

When he set aside the now-empty plate to sit back in his chair, he raised the cup of steaming cider and smiled smugly.

"Hungry, Fetch?" he murmured. Then burped.

I held his gaze until his smile broadened, then looked down at the spear laying over my thighs.

It's worth it, I told myself, though my clenched jaw had begun to ache.

Dinner was the hardest—and the largest meal that took the longest for him to consume. This pig sipped and savored *two* bowls of a thick, potato chowder, flavored with bacon and onions. Then he slowly peeled the entire skin off a chicken carcass, tipping his head back to stuff the bounty into his brutish maw, the salted, crispy skin crackling between his teeth as he chewed with a delighted smile. When he'd swallowed that treat, he reached for the carcass that had been slow-roasted to such tenderness, the meat literally fell from the bones.

Had a more evil bastard ever walked the earth?

When he picked a drumstick off the carcass and a piece of the steaming hot meat fell into his lap and burned him, he jumped and hissed. I laughed, delighted.

His eyes snapped to mine. Yet instead of growling and scowling, he smiled.

I watched warily as he got up from his chair and walked towards me with the drumstick.

The scent of the food had filled the tent, and my stomach growled audibly as he squatted on the other side of the bars, lifted the drumstick to his mouth and bit off a mouthful, chewing slowly, then wiping a trickle of fat off his chin with his bare knuckle.

The asshole was still smiling when he swallowed.

"Hungry, Fetch?" he asked slyly, waving the mostly bare bone.

"Not for my own demise," I replied rather more sharply than I should have. His smile broadened, but before he could taunt me further the tent flap twitched aside and Gall entered, his eyes low, and his jaw and cheekbone red and swollen.

I frowned as he walked straight to Melek, his stiff gait making it clear there were many more bruises and tender spots on his thick body under his uniform.

My heart ached for him, but his jaw was tight as he marched to Melek's side and saluted, one hand to his chest.

"I have taken my punishment and was told to report to you for... duties," he said thickly.

I wanted to put a blade through the heart of the male who'd beaten this poor child—for he was a child, no matter the size or development of his body.

Melek, clearly thinking the same, stood and put a gentle hand on his shoulder.

"Well done, Son," he said, his voice almost as thick as Gall's. "Are you hungry? I have food."

Gall nodded once, tightly, his hands clenched at his sides.

They hadn't replaced his spear, I noticed.

Clearly Melek made the same observation. "He didn't arm you?" he growled.

Gall's jaw went even tighter as he shook his head. "He said I had not earned the right to carry arms, so... so you are to give me duties befitting my... my intellect."

And then he blinked several times, quickly.

I wanted to slice the cock off the man who'd insulted this pour soul and feed it back to him covered in thistles and hot pepper sauce.

"Sit down, Gall," Melek said sadly. "Your duty tonight is to feed yourself, and rest."

But Gall stiffened. "I have to pay for what I've done. You can't go easily on me, they'll know!"

Melek's lips thinned, but he nodded. "Even those under discipline need to eat, Gall. Sit down. I will give you duties after the meal."

He shot me a warning look then, as if I might make some cutting remark.

I would feed Melek his own entrails if he thought—

"Where is her food?" Gall said suddenly, following Melek's gaze.

Melek's jaw flexed. "She has already had hers," he said after a moment.

Shocked that he would lie to his child, I left my gaze unguarded when my eyes snapped to him. And Gall saw it.

"Papa! She's hungry! Have you given her water, even?"

"No," Melek ground out, speaking quickly before Gall continued. "That will be one of your duties tonight. Eat up so you can fulfill them."

"But—"

"Soldier, attend!" Melek barked.

Gall immediately snapped to attention and saluted.

Melek sighed heavily. "At ease."

Gall relaxed but eyed his father cautiously.

Melek clapped a hand to his shoulder again. "Son, you *must* learn to fight as assiduously for discipline as you do for compassion. She is being punished—and not without reason. The pain in your body was inflicted by *her—*"

"No, Papa," Gall said fiercely. "My pain was inflicted by the Sergeant because *I* failed. You told me never to lay blame on others for actions I chose! So, don't you do it either!"

Melek blinked, opened his mouth, then closed it... then raised his hands in surrender. "You're right," he said calmly. "I'm sorry, Gall. You're right."

His humility in dealing with his son stunned me.

Gall nodded, his expression softening immediately. "Thank you."

"You're welcome. Now eat. Then go get the Fetch some more water, okay?"

Gall smiled. "Okay!"

He then dug into the food with such gusto I prayed a few splatters of the soup might be thrown far enough to reach me. I would have licked them off the bars. Sadly, he wasn't quite that brutish.

When he was done, Melek gave him orders to take the plates and clean them, then bring my water.

"I can do the water first—"

"You will take the orders you are given and deliver on them, Gall," Melek snapped.

Gall stiffened, then nodded quickly. "Yes, yes, I will. Of course. Thank you, Sir."

Melek sighed as his son hurriedly gathered the dirty dishes, then darted out of the tent, almost at a run before he'd even reached the flap.

He slumped when Gall was outside and rubbed his eyes with the heels of his hands. His weariness and care for his son was apparent and thawed my frigid heart—only slightly.

"He is a good man," I said quietly.

Melek dropped his hands from his face and turned on me, suspicion written all over his face. "You could not possibly—"

"Did you not hear me? My sister is the same way. I know their hearts. They are beautiful and soft, and they do not deserve the harshness with which others deal with them, either as bullies, or in impatience. You're doing well with him. The fact that he can actually function as a soldier at all is a testament to how hard you've worked with him."

Melek's gaze went dark. "I haven't had nearly enough time with him. And his... lack in comparison to his peers is becoming more and more apparent every day."

He looked towards the tent flap, and all that steel strength and arrogance left him as if it had drained off his skin like water from a bath.

He was slumped, looking weary, and miserable.

"I knew you were not the sharpest blade in the drawer," I teased carefully. "But I am surprised that he is yours. Was he deprived of air during birth like my sister?"

Melek didn't move or respond at all for a few moments, and when he did, it was to turn and look at me, his eyes narrowed as if he were measuring me.

But then, as if he gave up, he sighed and just shook his head. "He is not my son by blood. But he is every bit my child. I rescued him from... from a refuse heap as a toddler, where he'd been scavenging for food. He had been left to die, and I couldn't watch that happen. So I took him in. I hired women to watch over him when I worked and hid him from his true father as best I could. Hid him long enough that they never laid eyes on each other until Gall was several years older. I don't even know if his father recognized him by then. If he did, he has ignored the boy ever since."

I couldn't believe what I was hearing. I knew that in some societies—especially among nobles—it was considered shaming to have family with these kinds of issues, but... "Does Gall remember him?"

Melek's jaw tightened. "I don't know. I think so. He seems to do what he can to avoid him." Then his eyes snapped back to mine and his face went fierce. "But no matter how he came to be here, I would die to protect him, and I will *not* hear anyone suggest anything other than that he is mine. Not a word. Do you understand?"

I nodded, but I was stunned.

The General had adopted a son... who was *lacking?*

He had to have a soul. There was no other explanation—

Gall hurried back into the tent then, carrying another waterskin and brought it straight to the cage, beaming at me even with his thick lip and swelling on his jaw.

"Drink up, it will help fill your stomach," he said quietly as he pushed the waterskin between the bars.

I waited until he'd stepped back before inching forward to grab the skin, then scuttling to the back of the cage and guzzling the water straight from the skin, pausing only to breathe.

When I'd swallowed most of it—my stomach now distended and threatening to throw it back up—I sat back, breathing deeply and slowly.

When the nausea passed, I met Gall's eyes and smiled. "Thank you," I said.

He gave a strange smile. "You are nothing like what I thought a Fetch would be," he said.

"What did you think I would be?" I asked him, genuinely curious.

"I don't know, but... not so... *lovely.*"

I blinked, touched and slightly moved by the incredible compliment. "Gall, *thank—*"

Melek growled. "I told you, don't let an enemy deceive you. They can be lovely—until they suddenly aren't."

Gall turned to look at him, opening a palm towards me. "But she *is* lovely."

"You are the lovely one, Gall," I said.

He frowned at me. "I'm a male. Males aren't lovely."

Melek rolled his eyes and shook his head. "Enough talk of lovely. Come, Gall, we have duties to discuss. First I need you to run a message..."

I grew drowsy listening to Melek's deep, quiet voice drone as he listed several tasks for Gall to complete. But then the younger man left and Melek turned to me, his expression angry.

"What?" I snapped.

"If you hurt him or, God forbid, try to seduce him, I will cut you from throat to—"

I leaped to my feet, holding the spear prepared to throw. "You say one more word and I will kill you and consider my life a worthy cost." I was right at the bars, glaring at him just a few feet away. He stared at me, his eyes flat... but curious as well. I shook my head. "The *Great* General Melek may be blind, but *I* know the difference between an enemy in name, and an enemy in truth. And that boy is no enemy of mine!"

Our eyes locked, clashing as surely as swords or spears.

I did not back down. I did not lower my gaze, or the spear. He had deeply offended me and cheapened his son's precious, innocent heart.

"You don't like being accused of possessing the wiles of a woman," he said slowly, as if the idea were surprising to him and he was trying to hide it.

"No, you idiot, I am insulted that you believe I would consider such a heinous act against a *child.*"

"That is not the body of a child."

"Clearly you have heard nothing I've said—I understand him! My sister is the same! No matter his size or development, his mind is immature—and will stay that way."

Melek nodded. "That is true."

"The way he sees the world is beautiful. You would throw shame or perversion on that? How is it possible that guileless heart has not been corrupted by *your* filth?!"

"You wouldn't know a pure heart it if was served to you on a platter."

"You bastard—just because you cannot recognize humanity doesn't mean I'm incapable of it. That child is *pure.* You and your people are the ones who would defile him, not me, nor mine!"

Melek muttered a curse and turned away from me, his eyes casting towards the tent flap, then scanning the sides as he turned as if he saw through the canvas to all the gathered, dark Nephilim beyond and… and it *worried* him.

"Of course he will be defiled. We are all defiled by this world as we mature. But I *loathe* that for him."

"Wait… Melek, you're *agreeing* with me?"

He whirled to face me. "You speak true words I will agree with them—but that does not mean I trust your motives in saying them!"

Oh, dear Lord…

I sat back on my heels and let the spear drop, point to the ground, though I didn't let go.

"You love him," I breathed.

Melek's brows pinched. "You find a man's love for his son… shocking?"

"No!" I laughed humorlessly. "I find a Nephilim's ability to love *at all* shocking."

"Then you are not nearly as intelligent as you think you are," he muttered. "Of course I want the best for him. But... he is soft. Not a fighter–except in compassion for others. And that truth is growing harder and harder to hide."

I blinked. "You actually believe it's not already apparent to... well, everyone?" I asked, trying to keep the stunned disbelief from my voice.

He rolled his eyes. "No, of course not. I didn't mean the rank and file. I meant his f—"

He cut off abruptly and every one of my instincts perked like a starving wolf who'd heard a twig snap.

I frowned. "You must know this isn't the place to mold a soft heart. Why, if you love him, would you bring him here?"

Melek's expression was one of frustration and disgust and weary resignation. "I am his father in... in heart," he said reluctantly. "Not by blood." Then his eyes snapped back to mine. "But he is *mine.*"

Stunned by yet another layer of this man, I made myself plant a hand on my hip and just stare to cover for the whirlwind of thoughts in my head. I blinked more than once, trying to—

"What?!" he snapped. "If you must spew your vitriol, do it to me, not to him! I will not have you—"

"His eyes are gold," I blurted.

"So? Mine were also when I was born. That proves nothing—"

"No," I said through my teeth. "Don't start lying to me now. Your eyes are the bright green of a new leaf—on a kind day!"

"They are now. But when I was born, and even as a youth—"

"Bullshit! The yellow eyes are the sign of the irredeemable. If you were born irredeemable, you cannot change that—it is impossible!"

Melek frowned. "Who is spouting that drivel?" he said, though I saw the flicker in his eyes. He had to force himself to hold my gaze.

I let my lower jaw jut forward and pointed with the spear. "You said you were a man of honor—of course I should not have believed—"

"I am not the criminal here," he snapped, that vein at his temple that Jannus had mentioned, standing proud.

"No, just a liar," I scoffed.

"I am not lying!"

"The eyes are the window to the soul, Melek. Your *son* has the eyes of fallen angels. He is *soulless—*"

"YOU SHUT YOUR FUCKING MOUTH!" he roared, his face turning beet red, and the vein on his temple pulsing visibly. His body swelled and he took two storming steps towards me with such ferocity that I stumbled back and whipped the spear back up, holding it in both hands, prepared to defend myself if he tore into the cage.

But he drew up short of the door, teeth bared and eyes ablaze, chest heaving with his panting breath.

"You speak *one word* against my son, and I will show no more mercy."

"This is *mercy?!*"

"SILENCE, BITCH."

My mouth snapped closed and I took an even firmer grip on the spear as my shoulder blades came up against the back of the cage, even though I hadn't been aware that I was moving. I drew up short, watching him warily as his chest heaved with his breath.

"Just... be silent," he rasped, then turned and stormed out of the tent.

I watched him go, my heart pattering far too fast in my chest, and my mind spinning with the implications of it all.

The General had a son who was not his son.

Someone in this camp that the General needed to keep happy was truly the boy's father.

And... whether that father refused to see it, or Melek tried to hide it, apparently the other male did not know or perhaps believe his own son's limitations.

But why would a man care about a son he did not claim, who was claimed by—

And then it all clicked into place.

Golden yellow eyes.

Melek's fierce protection.

An absent father, yet one that needed to be pleased...

There was only one man in this camp—probably in the entire Nephilim Kingdom—who had the power to remove that boy from Melek. And that was the King Himself.

I blew out a breath, genuinely stunned.

Gall was the King's bastard? How had they kept *that* silent all these years—even from *us?*

11. Hungry?

SOUNDTRACK: *Devil Knows* by Armen Paul

~ YILAN ~

Two days later I was slumped against the back of the cage, swallowing the nausea that twisted my guts every time I smelled food.

It had been three days since I'd eaten, and now Melek was about to bring another hot and juicy meal to the tent. I honestly thought I might weep. My stomach felt hollow. My heart beat too quickly. My limbs were heavy.

When Melek returned, it would be to savor yet another meal in my presence, smiling smugly all the while.

God, help me.

I couldn't let him win.

I tipped my head back against the bars and took advantage of the empty tent to lift my voice in song, in tongues, in prayer.

Care not for my tears,
I shed them for thee.
Care not for my wounds,
I would die in peace.
Your heart carries me.
Your breath lifts my wings.
Do not take me,

Do not take me.
I lay down my weapons
Hands open to peace.
Do not take me,
Do not take me.
Though I lay in the shadows—

The tent flap twitching aside was the only warning before the night air rushed in, carrying with it the scents of fresh, flaky fish, creamed potatoes, and something I couldn't identify but it smelled delicious.

I think I actually groaned.

Melek ignored me completely.

This ritual with the food hadn't changed, but his demeanor since I'd called Gall soulless had been gruff and distant. Even colder than before.

Instinctively, as he stalked into the tent, I tightened my grip on the spear. But he ignored me completely, sliding the large platter onto the table and settling himself in the chair.

As he dove into the food with gusto, my stomach growled and I cursed.

"Hungry, Fetch?" he rumbled, but the words lacked the warmth of humor that he'd given them the first day.

Tonight, they were *only* a cruel taunt.

He did look at me though, which I didn't think had happened in the past two days.

I met that smug gaze with a sneer. But said nothing.

He shrugged and went back to his meal.

I could no longer ignore the food. Now, when he ate, I watched like a forlorn child. I knew it was pathetic, but I had to see every bite. I had tried ignoring him and it only made my mind conjure far more than was actually there.

In the hours between meals, when Melek questioned me or was having a meeting with interesting information to glean, I could drink water and forget my hunger... sometimes.

But this morning I'd woken feeling not just hungry, but shaky and weak.

The danger was not that I would starve to death, but that I would starve to such weakness that I could not defend myself if anything were to happen.

I prayed daily for *something* to happen, to break this stand off. But so far... nothing.

Melek was only halfway through the plate of perfect, white fish and what appeared to be buttered green beans, when the tent flap jerked aside again and Jannus entered, speaking immediately.

"Melek, it's news from—"

Two strides into the tent, he hesitated, looking at Melek seated at that table in the center of the tent, and then at me. I tried to smile, but for the first time Jannus didn't flirt, he frowned.

Melek, apparently unconcerned, opened a greasy hand towards the other side of the table. "Pull up a stool. I have enough for t—"

"Has she eaten anything? Anything at all?"

Melek shot him a look. "Are you blind? She still has the spear."

"Seriously, Mel? This kind of petty discipline isn't *you.*"

Melek's eyes were back on the fish as he tore a piece of the filet off to consume. He shrugged. "She will be fed the moment she relinquishes the *deadly weapon* that she stole," he said casually, though his chewing was decidedly forceful after the statement.

Jann's mouth opened like he'd argue, but then he glanced at me again, before his brow furrowed.

I stared back at him, uncertain what he was thinking.

But it didn't matter because he broke the gaze to stride to the side of the tent, grabbing a heavy stool in one hand, heedless of its weight, then dropping it at the other side of the table.

He straddled it and leaned over the table towards Melek, his eyes blazing with a strange light, but his smile was back.

"The first steps have been taken… and her *guesses* were right. My scouts found the guard camp. There's roughly two dozen spears, and then an additional ten runners positioned a mile deeper into the ravine. One of my trackers even followed a runner from the patrols to their camp inside the ravine, so we have at least a partial path through the sinkholes.

"We used your strategy for the approach, and there are already three hundred Nephilim within an hour's march of the ravine—undetected."

Melek went still, looking at his friend, his brows high. "Already?"

Jann's teeth shone, his smile was so bright. "Tomorrow, I expect to hear that we hold that precious half-mile in which the land narrows to the ravine, *without* raising alarm. And if we do, it will be days, Melek. *Days* until we're taking the runners—we're only waiting now to be certain we know their numbers and none will escape to warn their leaders. Then we'll take them all and fly to the clifftops unhindered."

"Jann, that's—"

Jann's bright face suddenly went dark. "And it's thanks to *her.*"

Melek went still, staring at his friend.

I was shocked—first by Jann's fierce defense of me, and then that he didn't soften at all as Melek stared him down.

"That is excellent news," the General said eventually, his voice wary. "Keep me updated."

Jannus shook his head. "Really, Melek? That's all?"

"What else would you expect?" he growled in return, then bit off the lengths of three green beans.

But Jannus just sighed.

~ *MELEK* ~

After my meal and some careful questions, I followed Jann out into the night, unconcerned about leaving the Fetch alone because I would stay near the tent so no one could enter without my knowledge.

But the moment we were far enough into the dark that she wouldn't hear, I grabbed his shoulder and pulled him around to face me.

"I don't know what game you're playing, but do *not* defend her in her presence like that again. You only embolden her when I need her weaker, not more determined."

Jann shook his head. "You're being cruel."

"I could have let the archers come and kill her. Or slit her throat with my own spear in her sleep. I'm cruel for giving her reason to *surrender* the weapon?"

"You're being cruel, taunting her. You preach dignity for prisoners of war to the ranks, then do *this?* She can't best you, Melek. She is no true threat—why treat her like a warrior when she's little more than—"

I bristled. "You are empty-headed if you believe that woman isn't just as dangerous to you as any warrior."

Jann scoffed.

I growled a warning. "In truth, she is *more* so—because she is underestimated by—"

A swell of horns and raised voices rose from a campfire among the tents.

Jann and I both startled, then relaxed when we realized some of the men were playing music and singing, beginning to dance, while others cheered them on.

I turned back to Jann, preparing to continue, only to find him frowning beyond me, towards the tents.

"Remember those days, Mel? Young, and so sure of ourselves. Even with battle on the horizon there was always a song to sing, or a woman to chase..."

"I was never much for chasing skirts," I said gruffly, even though I knew what he meant.

Life was very different as a soldier than as a leader.

One followed, the other... well, *led*. And that meant that all those lives, all those hearts and minds were our responsibility.

Add to that a King who was ignorant of the intricacies of war, and who had to be managed else he'd create more problems than he might solve...

Well. There hadn't been a lot of singing or dancing for us in the previous two years.

"Forget the Fetch," Jann said suddenly, clapping my shoulder. "Let's go sing and dance again."

He started towards the noise, but I hung back shaking my head.

When he turned, obviously about to cajole me, I lifted my hands and shook my head. "It's not because I wouldn't, Jann, you know that. But... let them relax. If I'm there, they feel like they have to be careful."

Jann frowned and I was reminded how much he was doing that lately, and how unlike him it was. "But—"

"You go, they won't mind you," I assured him. "I need to get back to the Fetch, anyway. Her eyes lit up when you talked about the runner's camp. I'm going to ask her what she knows."

Jann's lips went thin, but within moments I had him convinced that I was too tired to dance, and he should go without me. I started back up the path to my tent before he could protest.

I did hum along with the music as I walked, even allowing myself a small smile. It would be nice to sit in the tent tonight and read.

If Jann was right and we would take the Ravine within days, then there were only a few days beyond that before I would be *needed* back at the front.

I should rest while I could.

So I hurried back to the tent, that glowed yellow in the dark from the lanterns lit within, hesitating before I reached the door, wondering if she'd be in there staring at the food—or perhaps trying to use the spear to reach it.

I decided if she had, I would give grace, and ignore her disobedience. Unless she taunted me.

So, grasping the canvas door and pulling it aside, I was smiling—but I froze before I even stepped into the tent.

The Fetch was on her feet in the cage, the spear held against her forearm for quick use. But it wasn't what she was focused on.

She was... undulating.

It took a moment to realize that she moved in time with the music. But the refrain in the night was bright and jolly, while her movements were much slower and...

I swallowed hard.

She had her back to me, her hair swaying around her shoulders, but her hips...

Her hips seemed to have a life of their own, able to roll and extend in almost disparate movements from the rest of her, as if her waist lengthened. She rippled like water, her body flowing as easily as her hair. And with her back to me, the rounds of her ass were presented, rolling and bobbing like a taut peach, hanging in the wind, ready for plucking.

The roof of my mouth went dry.

Then she raised her arms, one hand curled gracefully over her head, the other clutching the spear, and yet somehow, she made it look like a part of the dance. But that position pulled her shirt up, revealing a slice of skin above her leathers, the hollow of her spine as it rolled in the dance.

A very beautiful, very feminine, very *startling* dance.

Which was when I realized I was just standing there, staring at her—at the exact moment her undulating, coiling dance shifted her slightly towards me and she turned her head to find me gaping like an innocent lad.

She froze for a second and I saw a flash of fear in those large eyes.

But just as I bristled, she came alive again, turning her body and catching the music, *rippling* in that inexplicable way, as if her spine had no substance and she were a serpent.

Then she glanced at me over the other shoulder and smiled.

"Hungry, General?" she asked slyly.

I blinked... then a moment too late, growled.

When her tinkling laugh reached my hot ears, I humphed and turned on my heel, storming back out to join Jann after all.

But even when I accepted his welcome, and those of the half-drunk soldiers around the fire, even when I finished dancing myself and just sat, enjoying the music and singing, a mug of ale on my knee, staring into the fire... even then, the flickering, rolling flames reminded me of nothing as much as her warm, rippling body.

12. Swallow Your Pride

~ YILAN ~

I barely slept that night. With Melek gone and the camp in high spirits, I worried I might find myself visited in the night. But Melek never returned, and in the early hours of the morning, still sitting with my back against the bars and the spear across my lap, I must have dropped off.

At the snap of the tent flap, I jerked awake, blinking, heart pounding, and disoriented.

The rush of adrenaline made me strong for a moment. But when I realized it was just Melek returning, looking very much worse for the wear, the fizz of energy drained from my body along with the slowing of my pulse until I wondered if I would be able to lift the spear at all. All my limbs, even my head, felt heavy.

Melek ignored me as he crossed the tent and went straight to the trunk where he kept his clothing. He began unbuttoning his shirt, cursing as his thick fingers fumbled the small buttons. It was natural to follow him with my eyes—the man was dangerous. But with every moment he continued to ignore me my anger simmered hotter.

I scanned him with a grimace. His hair was messy. The strands falling from his warrior's length were tangled and twisted... as if hands had plunged into it, pulling it half from the leather tie and twisting it...

He finally got the shirt unbuttoned and snapped it back off his shoulders, stretching his muscular arms back to pull the sleeves. When he whipped the shirt off and leaned forward to put it in the trunk there were scratches on the back of his shoulder.

Then, after a moment's hesitation, he began unbuttoning his leathers.

I blinked as he shoved them past his hips, baring muscular buttocks that a woman could sink her teeth into. But then he continued to bend, to push the leathers to the floor, and I caught sight of the heavy, swinging testicles of a *bull*.

A shriek of alarm sang through my core as he straightened, unashamed of his nakedness, folded the dirty clothes with short, efficient movements, then dropped them into the trunk and turned to walk to the bed.

I hadn't meant to look. Wasn't even curious—well, not much. But it was impossible to miss when he turned, both arms bent up as he worked to pull the leather tie from his tangled hair so that his upper-body arched, every muscle and... body part distinct in the light of the lanterns he'd never blown out.

At the sight of him in all his glory—golden skin, scars, muscles, and manhood... my breath stopped.

And then he did.

It took seconds for me to realize he'd stopped walking and was just standing there, watching me gape at him.

"Hungry, Fetch?" he purred.

Fear jangled in my veins, and I lashed out without thought.

"You should take more care sowing your seed with such abandon," I sneered. "The last thing this world needs are more soulless."

His smug smile went cold, and he took a threatening step towards me. "If you cannot speak sweetly, Fetch, do not speak at all. The King has an entire trunk of ball-gags that I am not afraid to use."

I snapped my mouth closed, but my rage roared higher in my chest, burning behind my ribs.

Fucking arrogant *fuck*.

Then, the bastard just folded his arms and stood there, feet shoulder-width apart, displaying himself, one brow arched in a challenge.

But the movement of folding his arms made his length swing and my eyes were drawn down to look. I yanked my gaze back up to his immediately, but he was smirking again.

"Seems like there's a compliment brewing in your eyes, Fetch."

"If you believe that, you do not know me *at all.*"

He huffed and shook his head, but then I saw the prickle go out of him. His shoulders dropped along with his smirk as he turned for the bed again, muttering a curse and raking a hand through his hair again. The length fell down his back in a tangled mess.

"You know, just because you've fooled Jannus doesn't mean you have fooled me also."

"Your brother-in-arms is compassionate—a rare quality in your kind. I would *never* make the mistake of thinking you were the same."

He growled and turned on me again, but instead of storming to me with rage as I expected, his brow furrowed, and he moved towards me with caution.

"You could eat. You know that. Hell, I would serve you *myself* if you would just bend your neck and give up that spear. But *no—*"

"You say that as if I am a petulant child. We both know if you were in my shoes, you wouldn't release it either!"

"What shoes? You are caged! Even if you threw it now and killed me, you'd only be dead at the hands of the next Neph to walk in here!"

"But they won't have to kill me since you're going to starve me, right? You sadistic pig," I spat, tensing when his eyes widened.

The Nephilim had an intense disdain for pigs. I'd heard the word was a terrible insult among them, but never imagined—

"Pig?!" he snarled.

"I've watched you crunch bones!"

His lips twisted as he prepared to flay me with his tongue. I watched the rage wash over him and instinctively pressed back against the bars, eyes darting for an escape that was not possible as he stormed towards me, naked and furious, every inch of his massive body poised for violence.

He lifted a hand and I flinched, yanking the spear up, ready to let fly... then saw him shudder. Then freeze.

There was a moment that he just stared at me, his face still twisted in rage, then the light went out in his eyes. I heard him mutter, *"What am I doing?"* Then he closed his eyes and shook his head as if he shook off the rage.

He started to turn away and I slumped, stunned to see him take such a leash on himself—but then he whirled back. I tensed again as he strode up to the bars of my cage, though without the edge of anger he'd had a moment before.

Then he pointed at me. "For all your judgment and sneering, if our roles were reversed, I would lay money that you would be more ruthless towards me than I have been with you."

"Bullshit. My prisoners would *always* be fed, though nothing rich, it's true." Then I smiled. "It gives them more strength to endure torture."

He opened his hands. "Then we understand each other. I stand by my word, Fetch. If you surrender the spear, I will bring you food myself."

I pressed my lips tightly to stop the offers flowing off my tongue. Then, as we watched each other, I swallowed and pushed my pride aside. "Does your *punishment* extend beyond food?"

"Not yet. We'll see."

I squirmed and his eyes narrowed. He tipped his head in curiosity. "What is it?"

I looked down at the spear and cleared my throat. "I will have need of... resources, within a couple of days."

He didn't respond, and when I let myself look up, his expression was confused. "What resources? You already have a blanket and pillow and bucket... do you think I'd hand you horses?"

I rolled my eyes and squirmed again. God, I'd forgotten that the Nephilim had no women to speak of... But there was no point dragging it out. The situation wouldn't change.

"I am female, Melek," I said through my teeth. "In two days, I will begin my cycle and bleed all over... well, everything, unless I have some supplies."

His brows shot up and his head snapped back. Then he scratched the back of his neck. "Oh, yes... right... Um..."

If I hadn't been mortified myself, his discomfort would have been glorious.

He cleared his throat. "Uh, how much time until..."

"Approximately two days."

He nodded. "Right. I'll make sure one of the women servants visits tomorrow, she can discuss what you need and they'll bring it."

I hadn't expected him to just... give it to me. I'd thought it would be a negotiation. Or some kind of leverage. I blinked.

"I... thank you."

"You're welcome."

I stared at him, fighting the urge in my chest to soften.

He sighed and folded his arms again. "Yilan, you know you can't possibly win this," he said quietly. *Normally.* As if I were a person, not a prisoner. I was stunned. I didn't think he'd ever used my name before. "Give me the spear, and I'll get you a fucking *banquet."*

"No."

He shook his head. "You stare down your nose at me for my pride, but cling to your own as if it sustains you. It will *not.* Your body weakens—and your mind will follow soon. We both know that. Surely it would be better..."

He kept talking, but something brushed the back of my neck, a prickling instinct, and I stopped listening to his lecture and scanned the tent.

It was still dark outside—the midnight dark just before dawn. There was no sound. The camp was quiet. And he was here... so, what scratched at my senses?

"...need further insight into the—"

"Hush," I snapped, pushing onto the balls of my feet so I was in a crouch rather than a squat and no longer leaning on the cage. I gripped the spear tighter, with both hands, listening. Looking. Scanning. But there was nothing, save instinct.

Instincts I had learned to listen to years ago.

"Do not *shush* me, I am *trying* to help you," he snapped. "There must be some way—"

"I said, *hush!* Shut up and use those battle-honed instincts because something is afoot—unless you want it proven *again* that I am superior?" I whispered, letting my eyes scan the tent slowly, but there was nothing.

I kept looking back at that tent flap, but the only movement was the air fluttering the loose canvas...

Melek prickled. But stopped lecturing me. *"What?"* He asked through gritted teeth.

I shivered. "I can sense... something... someone is close. Who would be out at this time of the night?"

His hands clenched to fists at his sides, but he turned, frowning, to scan the tent behind him. "There will always be movement. There are Nephilim all over the camp, and always patrols—"

"No, no. Not your hulking flesh. Something walks the shadows tonight," I whispered.

He followed my gaze as I swept the tent again, frustrated because there was *nothing*. But relieved when Melek's frown deepened and he didn't dismiss me again. Instead, he trotted to the side of the tent where he'd undressed and discarded his weapons, picking up one of the spears and holding it prepared for battle. Then he crossed to the doorway and used the point to push aside the flap just barely, to peer out.

After a few moments, he shook his head. "Don't move," he muttered, then slipped outside in a surprising show of stealth. For such a large man, he moved light and quick.

I waited barely breathing, listening. I thought I heard his passage once, when he was at the end of the tent, behind where his bed was placed. But then nothing.

Moments later the tent flap pushed aside and he strode in, frowning. "Nothing. There's no one out there. Were you just trying to distract me from—"

The shadow seeped in behind him, barely making the tent flap flutter, so subtle I almost missed it. But as he came striding towards me, I leaped to my feet.

"Melek, *behind you!*"

13. Living Shadows

SOUNDTRACK: *Looking at the Devil* by Seibold, Neutopia, and Leslie Powell

~ *MELEK* ~

I whirled, bringing the spear up instinctively, yet barely brought it to bear in time to stop the dagger flashing towards my back.

With a grunt, I whipped the handle of the spear up to push that blade up and away, but my adversary's movements were quick.

I'd barely blocked one blow when another came and there was never a moment to bring my own blade to bear, to stage an attack and put my foe on the defensive.

Once, twice, three times I defended against a new slash—with only a hairsbreadth of space before that blade would slide between my ribs, or across my shoulder.

Yilan was hissing warnings, but there was no space in my head to even take in the words as every instinct for combat I'd ever honed as a warrior, every defensive reflex, took over. Somehow, impossibly, I kept that blade at bay, but everything in my head *screamed* that something was wrong.

With a long-handled weapon I should not have such trouble defeating a dagger—yet somehow, impossibly, I couldn't *quite* see my foe.

He had the form of a tall man—though trim and wiry—still a foot shorter than me. But it was as if his every existence was shrouded in shadow. Even when he moved, I couldn't keep eyes on him, my gaze sliding sickeningly past each time I tried to focus and anticipate his next move.

I took a step back to give myself more room to maneuver, to bring the spear head to bear, but found myself still defending a volley of stabs and slashes. If I was even half a second slower on any of them—

I had the presence of mind on the next defense, to turn my wrist, and as I blocked, in that split second that my spear handle connected with his blade, I twirled and flipped the spear, sending it in an arc that rang against the assassin's wrist.

There was a hissed curse, and the flash of that dagger flying through the air, the light from the lantern gleaming on it.

I smiled and took a firmer hold on the spear, ready to take action—then was forced to shove it aside to block a second dagger he'd already drawn and stabbed straight for my throat.

What the hell was he, and how did he move like a striking snake?

"Focus on the weapon, not on him—he can't affect that!" Yilan

There wasn't time to think, but I tried to do as she said, and kept my eyes fixed on the blade rather than trying to read the adversary. And for a time it worked.

We circled the tent, grunting, thrusting our weapons, the clanging of my spear against his blade singing in the night air more than once. But he *did not slow.*

There were excellent fighters among the Nephilim, and I had been honing my already superior skills in battle for months.

Yet, this was the first time in years I felt truly pushed to my back foot—not just in danger, but losing the fight.

This enemy moved like a snake, and made no mistakes.

While I had been awake for most of two days, and just spent an entire night in dance and play. I was weary, and taken utterly off-guard. And my foe was... *something I could not understand.*

I snarled when he feinted, sending the blade towards my throat again—only to drop it and slash for my guts the moment I lifted an elbow too high.

Yilan gasped as I was forced to throw myself backwards bodily to avoid that blade. Something caught my heel and I was falling, thudding to the earth and rolling immediately, feeling the rush of air at my neck and shoulder as my adversary dove with that blade just a blink too late to plunge it into my throat—but not too slow to slam a foot down on my fist where it clamped around my spear.

With a bellow of pain, I released it and rolled to stand, crouching, defensive—but weaponless, and with that... *thing* coming at me.

I could not see his face, shrouded as it was in that inexplicable darkness, but I heard his hiss of triumph, and then the voice that sounded like the crumble of rotting flesh seemed to ripple along the ceiling of the tent. "The *great* General Melek, finally bested. Let the world take note."

I sank deeper in my crouch and prayed for mercy as he leaped for me, blade high and flashing straight for my chest—

"MELEK!"

It happened faster than a blink.

I dropped to roll towards the cage at the same moment Yilan threw me her spear. It clapped into my palm the same moment I unfurled to come up on one knee with the spear angled up just as my foe descended—and it took him straight in the throat.

I felt the force of him impaled on it and snarled as he froze, arms akimbo, while I gripped the wooden handle of the spear, thrusting it up and forward with all my strength to make *certain* his spinal cord was severed, feeling more than seeing the moment his body gave because of those blasted shadows.

But then the shadows blinked out of existence, and for half a breath I knelt, bracing the spear, gaping at a very normal looking human man, his eyes wide with shock.

He dropped the dagger and both hands came to the spear as he instinctively fought to pull himself off it.

But I growled and did not give, and a moment later, his hands went limp, his shoulders dropped, and his eyes rolled back in his head.

His body shuddered, and then he was deadweight on the end of my spear.

I didn't move immediately, still kneeling there with the butt of the spear braced on the dirt, watching this creature, waiting for the deception.

The only sound in the tent was my heaving breath.

Then, finally, just as I accepted that I'd won, that he was in fact dead, a foul smell filled the tent.

From the place right in his throat where the spear pierced him, black decay began to crawl through his veins and across his skin—and he began to crumble into rot.

With a startled cry I yanked the spear back—and he broke apart, his disintegrating carcass falling aside as he slid to the dirt. The rancid stench of putrefying meat filled the tent as his entire body blackened, shriveled, then desiccated right in front of my eyes.

"What...?" I breathed, pushing to my feet and stumbling back, coughing against the acrid vapor rising from the lump that was all that remained of him.

But there was no answer.

Seconds later he was gone... the only evidence that he'd existed were his shirt, leathers, and that dagger making a wrinkled pile on the dirt.

Even the vapor was gone.

I stood in an empty tent, staring at the crumpled pile, wide-eyed, heart pounding, but hands empty at my sides.

"What the *fuck* was that?!" I breathed.

I hadn't expected an answer, clawed both hands into my hair, and startled when her voice reminded me that Yilan was also there and had witnessed that whole scene.

"A Shade," she whispered. I snapped my head to look at her and our eyes locked—and I saw reflected in hers the same horror crawling in my veins. She broke the gaze to look at that pile of clothes and swallowed audibly. "That was a fucking *Shade,* Melek."

14. The Puzzle

~ YILAN ~

I shook like a leaf in the wind, unable to take my eyes off the vacant shirt and leathers crumpled in the dirt.

A Shade? They were *real?*

Shades were legendary, stories used by Fetch parents to scare their children. For a people who walked the shadows, we brought light. But none of my people denied the draw of darkness. We were all raised on the tales of the Shades, men who sold their souls to the Dragon. Their bodies were infused with shadow so they could hide easily, camouflage in even a sliver of shade, and so go unnoticed.

They rarely slept, barely needed to eat, and were the Devil's assassins.

Or rather, the assassins used by the agents of the Devil.

I'd never been certain they were real. But I'd just seen proof.

Melek let go of the breath he'd been holding and took a step back, brushing his skin as if the rot from that thing might be contagious, then he looked at me and went still.

His eyes dropped to my empty lap, then cut up to my eyes.

"You gave me your weapon," he said hoarsely.

I swallowed. "If I hadn't, you'd be dead."

He nodded slowly. "And that would seem to suit you."

"Not if there's a Shade loose in the tent," I pointed out, trying to keep the tremor of fear from my voice.

He didn't respond, just stared right into my eyes as if he measured me for truth. Then he blinked and looked over his shoulder sharply.

"What? Did you see someth—"

"Hush," he hissed, hurrying to the trunk where his clothing was stacked and pulling on a pair of clean leathers and his boots. "Stay quiet. Only shout if you sense anything else," he muttered as he picked up his second spear and darted out of the tent.

I nodded, but he was already gone.

Taking a deep breath I sank to the dirt, turning my attention inwards, analyzing that prickling instinct that had been screaming such alarm just minutes earlier, but now...

Now there was nothing.

And that would make sense. Shades were so rare, surely there wouldn't be two?

But that turned my thoughts to who might be capable of *bringing* a Shade in the first place—and why they would target Melek. Who would have the power to find, or even make one? It would take a very powerful wizard. Someone with direct access to the power of the Dark.

Like a pureblooded Nephilim.

I remembered that moment when it had spoken, its voice a shivery crumble of rot and decay... and its words seemed familiar...

"The great *General Melek..."*

My mind was taken back to the King's jibing remarks on the day I was taken.

"The great *General Melek may be blind, but..."*

And then my instincts prickled again, but this time not with the sense of impending danger, but with the satisfying *click* that only came with the clarity true insight brought.

The King was jealous of his General—as well he should be. I'd listened to murmured conversations among the ranks. I'd observed the willingness with which the others followed Melek... and their wariness of their King.

They feared Gault. But they *admired* Melek.

And then I remembered Melek's own wariness—his concern about the King being unhappy with the mental state of his bastard son.

Apart from an enemy that wished to remove this weapon from the King's grasp, there was no one else who had reason to want Melek dead. But that had been no normal assassination attempt. That had been an attempt to rob Melek of his soul… if he possessed one.

The Zaryndar had powerful magik, but they shied away from the Dark. And the Tuskarrians were giants, but they possessed no magik.

It was said that in order to bend a Shade to their will, a person had either to give their own soul as sacrifice, *or* that the orders must come from the highest of the Devil's agents here in the land of flesh.

Would there be an agent closer to the fallen Lucifer than the King?

Certainly not in the flesh.

But did that brutish male have the strength of will and discipline to work the Dark?

There were too many questions and not enough answers, but after a few minutes of turning the questions over in my mind and turning circles, I realized there was still no sound near the tent—and no Melek.

Nerves fluttered in my belly, and I got to my feet.

"Melek?" I hissed quietly. If he was close to the tent he'd hear me. "Are you safe? Have you found anything?"

But there was no answer.

Shit.

My stomach growled and my hands were shaking. I realized I was utterly alone. If Melek didn't return, my only recourse would be—

The tent flap snapped aside, and he strode in, bringing a cloud of delicious aromas with him—sausage, fried potatoes, honeycakes, sweet fruit, rich kafk…

My stomach clenched as he approached the door of the cage, his chin low and eyes on me.

I took a halting step towards him, hope screaming in my chest—but he growled a warning.

"Stay back. All the way to the back. And do not move."

Mouth watering at those fragrances, I nodded, but even when my back was against the cage bars opposite the door, I found myself swaying closer.

"Please—"

"Stay back until it's locked."

He had to juggle, placing the goblet on the ground near where the cage would open. I almost wept when he unlocked the cage door and placed that platter on the ground *inside*, then reached back for the goblet and placed it next to the platter.

When he finally closed the cage door, I was quivering.

The moment that lock slid home, I leaped across the cage and onto the food, grasping sausage in one fist and a handful of the potatoes in the other—both foods steaming hot, because he'd picked them up from the early breakfast preparations.

They were burning my hands and my mouth, but I didn't care. I chewed like a savage, stuffing myself.

Mouth full and belly clenching, I swallowed hard as I realized I was crouched on the ground and Melek still stood on the other side of the door, watching me.

While I chewed the next mouthful, I reluctantly dropped the food in my hands onto the platter and picked it up, needing an arm under it to keep it level. Then I grabbed the goblet in the other hand and hurried to the back of the cage, settling cross-legged, with the platter in my lap as I dug back in. I alternated bites of precious food with mouthfuls of the sharp kafk that desperately needed cream and sugar, but I didn't care.

Melek watched me, his expression unreadable. "You need to slow down or it might come back up."

"That would just let me eat more," I said around a mouthful of sausage.

To my delight, Melek chuckled.

He didn't say more as I ate like a fiend for minutes. But finally, stomach stretched tight and churning a little bit, rumbling so that I worried he might be right, I put the platter aside and reached for the kafk again. I held the warm goblet in both hands, letting the steam rise so I inhaled it and sighed, as happy as I'd felt since the day I was taken.

"Feel better?" Melek asked carefully.

"Yes, thank you."

"You're welcome."

It was a strange, polite exchange. I took a sip of the kafk, eyes on him, waiting.

"I didn't give you the spear so you'd feed me."

"I know. That's why I fed you."

My eyes drifted to the platter at my side, cooling now but still half-full of sausage and potato, and I'd only eaten one of the honeycakes.

I picked one grape from the bunch, letting the sweet juice burst on my tongue and sighing happily, before I returned my attention to him.

He stood on the other side of the cage, an unreadable expression on his handsome face that mildly worried me.

"Who wants you dead?" I asked him carefully.

He snorted. "Who doesn't?"

I tipped my head. "Your enemies *are* many... but sending a Shade? That is... intense."

He shrugged, but he looked towards the tent flap uneasily. "Any number of Kingdoms have reason to want me dead—including yours," he pointed out.

"But any of those—including mine—would want to claim your death. To make the *other* enemies tremble."

"Perhaps," he said without commitment.

"Melek... you have to consider who would go to such lengths— who has the *capability* to go to such lengths. Even the rulers of nations wouldn't have easy access to the kind of power—"

"Why?" he asked sharply. "I beat the thing—with your help," he admitted, shifting his weight. "It's done."

"Is it? The person with the kind of power to bring a Shade against you can bring many other things as well."

"And I will meet them when they come," he said abruptly, his jaw going tight.

"Melek, I'm not trying to scare you, I'm trying to help you—"

"You did help me. And I am truly grateful—and will remain so. However... it changes nothing." He locked eyes with me.

I took a deep breath and picked up another grape. "I just think the risk of ignoring—"

"I ignore *nothing,*" he growled. "You're asking me questions I cannot answer. I will not speculate. Nothing is gained."

"Unless speculation leads you to the truth. Take your King for example—"

"Do not start pushing me to treason again," he muttered, shaking his head. "I am grateful for your assistance, but that will not change my mind on this score."

"I'm not pushing you to treason, you knucklehead! I'm telling you; I walked the shadows of this camp for *days* before you took me, and I saw it. I saw that—"

"You name yourself a shadow walker, speak treason, and want me to ignore the fact that you knew what the Shade was? Perhaps *you* are my assassin?"

I rolled my eyes. "That makes no sense—and I walk the shadows, I do not *serve* them. There is a huge difference. In any case, my point is true: The Nephilim follow *you,* not your King. If you deny it, you make yourself a liar."

He grimaced. "Of course they follow me—we are at war. I am the leader that offers them confidence—"

"Bullshit! A true Ruler is both admired and followed willingly! Their people—including their military leaders—serve because they *choose* to. Your people are following you... and you serve the King, so they do as well. The moment you declared yourself they would abandon him—"

"Go back to your eating, Fetch." His eyes blazed, but his tone was even, despite being gruff. "Do not make me gag you. Please. I want to recognize the good you've done tonight, but if you insist on this poison, I will have no choice. Just... please. Be silent on this point."

I sighed and stared at him, but the pleading in his eyes was real.

Shrugging, I threw up my hands. "Fine."

"Thank you. Now sleep while we can. The sun will be up soon, and my day will begin. I have set patrols nearby. We should not be interrupted again."

I almost pushed then. But he caught the shift in me and his eyes flashed a warning.

When I didn't speak, he nodded once, then moved around the tent to blow out the lanterns before walking over to the bed where he stripped down and slid between the sheets with a weary groan.

Still picking at my food and sipping at my kafk, I wrapped myself in my blanket and stared into the darkness to watch the sunlight slowly make the sides of the tent glow while I set my mind to consider the puzzle and solve it.

Because Melek might be unwilling to see his King as the villain in this story, but I was not. And I found I suddenly dreaded the consequences to *all* of us if that brute succeeded in removing Melek from this earth.

15. Order Received

~ YILAN ~

The following day was difficult. I couldn't sleep and took advantage any time Melek offered kafk throughout the day, along with plates of hot food that fed more than my stomach.

He was true to his word and brought a female slave for a brief, murmured conversation about the things I would need when my cycle began. And though it wasn't my first time on a strategic foray that I had needed to alert a male to my situation, it felt... different here.

At least Fetch men were accustomed to mothers, sisters, wives—even friends—who were female. The Nephilim seemed to see women as nothing but chattels, slaves to meet their needs. *All* their needs.

The legend was that a good many human women died in childbirth when bearing Nephilim because the males were so much bigger. Some even died before the labor, bleeding to death, their bodies torn internally by their own offspring.

The darkest stories told of Physicians trained to cut the child out when it became clear that the mother couldn't deliver naturally—at the cost of the mother's life. It was whispered that any female who'd been strong enough to carry a Nephilim to term was extremely desirable in their society. The males fought over her. She would be kept in luxury—and would lose her freedom from that day on, provided for lavishly... as long as she continued to bear young. But more often than not, the women died, either bleeding out, or simply unable to deliver. And the Nephilim didn't care, because there would always be more women.

Surviving Nephilim young were far more rare.

I wished I could speak with this woman to find out how she had come to be here and whether these awful tales were true. But with Melek there and his sharp ears... I made do with thanking her for her help and telling her that should she ever be nearby and wish to share a kafk with a prisoner, I would enjoy the female company.

She smiled, but only nodded. I didn't hold out hope.

I didn't miss the way her eyes followed Melek around the tent, or her bright-eyed smile when he thanked her, though it seemed that he did, keeping his eyes down on his papers. He had stayed in the tent as we spoke but busied himself writing messages at that little table. He didn't even look up when he sent her away with his gratitude.

So, as darkness descended on that day I should have been easing towards sleep. Especially when Melek went to bed early. But I found myself unable to sleep deeply. I woke at any little noise in the night, including the moment a small mouse slipped into the shadow of my pillow on its way through the tent.

The second day after the Shade's attack the exhaustion truly hit. I was still very hungry, though no longer with the gnawing ache I'd been experiencing before. I'd definitely gained strength from the food Melek brought at each mealtime. Especially since the portions were Nephilim sized. Even in my greatest hunger I couldn't possibly fit it all in one sitting. So, I'd kept the breads and fresh fruits aside to nibble at between meals.

But even with the food, I was anticipating my cycle and lacking sleep. On top of which there had been so many dangers... my senses did not want to ease. My mind did not stop conjuring potential threats. And so, my body did not relax.

Thank the Father I did not have a mirror to see how dark the circles under my eyes had become. I saw enough unease reflected in Melek's to know that they must be bad. But he didn't speak of it, for which I was grateful.

We'd just finished breakfast when Gall arrived. I was surprised to see that his bruises had already almost faded, and the swelling on his face was gone. These Nephilim healed quickly.

Dammit.

"Hello, Papa! Hello, Yilan!" Gall said brightly as he strode into the tent, not unlike Melek when he was focused.

He was still weaponless, still being sent to Melek daily for "duties." But I couldn't help but notice how much happier and more confident he was here with Melek than when he'd been with the other soldiers.

I wondered if Melek would manipulate this event to shift him to permanent *assistance.* I hoped so.

"Morning, Son," Melek said, still picking at his breakfast.

"Hello, Gall. Good morning to you," I said warmly, winking at him when he beamed at the dirty plate at my side.

He'd been extremely pleased the day before to learn that I'd given up my spear and was eating again. Which was touching.

I found it interesting that Melek didn't tell him *why.*

"What duties do I have today?" Gall said, coming to a stop next to Melek's seat, his empty hands dangling at his sides.

Oddly, Melek glanced at me before answering his son. "I have need for a set of screens—similar to those I use," he said, tipping his head towards the folding screens at the back of the tent. "But they must be short enough to fit inside the cage with our… guest," he said dryly. "That may be difficult to find."

"I can do it," Gall said confidently. "And I'll get her a new waterskin too."

I was already receiving kafk, and sometimes cider or water with my meals, so a waterskin was far less important now, but I just smiled at him when he looked at me.

"Very good," Melek muttered, taking a final bite of his honeycake, then wiping his hands on his thighs as he stood. "We'll need to—"

"Sir, please pardon my interruption, I have a message from the King."

We all turned as a tall, young Nephilim, much thinner and trimmer than any I'd seen before, entered the tent saluting Melek who hurriedly tugged Gall behind him and gestured for him to stay quiet.

The boy was wide-eyed and stiff, shrinking, as if he wished to hide behind Melek's bulk.

Did he know the King was his father? Or was he only nervous now about anyone because he'd been punished?

"The King sends an urgent message, Sir," the messenger said quickly, eyeing me warily. "He has determined that it is important for both him and you to be seen at the battle front. To *inspire the ranks* as we embark on this critical maneuver. He readies his beast so that you can travel and return immediately and says you should do the same."

Melek didn't react in the slightest. Not a blink, not a freeze. He didn't miss a beat, though I knew he *had* to have at least a few misgivings about this. He only nodded and sighed. "Very well, please tell the King I'll be ready in an hour—"

"He said thirty minutes, Sir... *sorry,*" the messenger added under his breath, his eyes apologetic on Melek.

The messenger apologized to the General for the King's pleasure?

And Melek didn't believe these men followed *him?*

I shook my head in frustration and Melek caught the movement. As if he heard the thought, he shot me a glare but said nothing.

"Very well, thirty minutes. I will be ready. Please take the message to the stable-tent before returning to the King. I'll need my beast groomed and watered right away, while I prepare things here."

The messenger ducked his head and darted out of the tent, his long, loping strides evident even in this small space.

The moment the messenger was gone Melek turned to stare at me, his face grim.

I stared back. "Interesting timing. Separating you from the ranks—"

"Gall, please go find Jannus and tell him that unless he has orders from the King Himself, he is to find cover for all other responsibilities and come here to my tent. Immediately."

Gall hopped like he'd been poked, running out of the tent with barely a *Yes sir!*

Melek waited until he was gone before turning to face me. He stood in front of the cage with his arms folded in a posture that I was growing to understand he used any time he wished to assert his dominance.

"If you speak against the King in the presence of *any* Nephilim again, I will gag you. Without warning. But particularly in front of Gall. He may be slower to learn, but he is not unaware of political... currents. His worry, if he believes I am present for something that is *wrong,* could end in a hurried, unfiltered word to someone else, at an inopportune time."

I blinked. I knew exactly what he meant and hadn't thought. "I'm sorry. You're right. I wasn't—"

"No, you weren't. Do not do it again."

I nodded, but didn't drop his gaze. "Still… we are alone now, yes? Please don't try to make me believe that you can't see the *coincidence* of timing? He's getting you alone with him, and presumably, his most loyal guards two days after an attempt—"

"The only *coincidence* is with the timing of our attempt to split the Tuskarrian and Zaryndar ranks. I should have been at the front for this entire time. And trust me, Gault is far more intelligent than you give him credit for. He is filthy and selfish, but he sees far more than he comments upon, has great restraint with his tongue when he chooses to—and yes, is capable of *great* cunning. Those who underestimate him, do so to their own peril."

I blinked. Melek's eyes were locked on mine—and not angry.

Was he saying that he refused to speak about my suspicions because he believed the King was listening?

Was he saying he didn't disagree… but was playing his own hand close to his chest?

Or was he staring me down because he was a stubborn fucker?

"And yet… on a trip to the front he demands *your* presence to… inspire?" I said cautiously.

Melek smiled grimly. "Both of us. Together. Calling the ranks to battle—a historic moment if we pull it off, wouldn't you agree?" he said quietly.

I nodded as the image came alive in my head—Melek, the General who had led them to victory across the continent, until this point… sitting in the shadow of the King, who called them to a new strategy.

"A false hero," I murmured.

"No, Yilan. A *King*. Leading his people, exactly as a King should."

"Still. Apparently, your mere presence is *inspiring?*"

Melek huffed and began to turn away, towards that screen in the corner. "I need to change into my armor. I suspect you'll be reminded how *inspiring* my presence can be," he rumbled, flashing a self-satisfied half-smile at me over his shoulder.

My jaw dropped but he was already disappearing behind the screen as I scrambled.

Had Melek just… flirted with me?

Or was that a jab designed to make me feel small—a poke at the way he'd caught me watching him when he was naked?

I snorted myself at the torrent of *not-small* jokes that cascaded through my head, and wished Jann were there to appreciate them. They were wasted on Melek who would only be complimented.

"Melek?"

Speak of the devil. Jann jogged into the tent, his expression serious and concerned, especially when he found me watching, but no sign of Melek.

"I'm here," Melek growled from behind the screens. "Are you armed, Jann?"

Jann looked down at the spear he was gripping and frowned. "Of course. Why? What's—"

"I've been called to the front. I need you to watch over the Fetch and Gall for me. We should be back late tonight—we're riding— but if we are held up…"

He let that thought trail off.

Jann looked at me, his brows high in surprise. But then he grinned. "Go with confidence, Mel. I'm sure I'll figure out what to do," he said, with a boyish wink.

I rolled my eyes but smiled with him.

He was delicious. Not at all my type, which was what made the flirting fun. I was certain he meant it even less than I did.

Then Melek emerged from behind the screen, still buckling the armor apron over the bulge in his fighting leathers and the roof of my mouth went dry.

He'd changed into thick leathers that hugged his massive thighs, a tunic of chainmail with plate armor over his *jewels,* and molded, reinforced leather braces at his shoulders and wrists. The wide weapon straps that crossed at the center of his chest were bristling with blades, and the twin gleam of his metal spear heads rose over his shoulders, echoing the rise of folded wings the Nephilim were rumored to have, though I'd seen no evidence of them so far.

Melek's countenance was somber as he checked his weapons, then eyed Jann. A warrior preparing to fight.

I was struck, suddenly, by the *vision* of him.

I knew the legends of his prowess and cunning. I knew the victories he won, and the carnage he'd left in his wake. And still, despite knowing how crucial figureheads were to a force, I had mocked him that the King suggested his mere attendance might inspire.

I hadn't doubted he would inspire confidence in his men. But in that moment, the world around me disappeared as I saw what I'd caught in him the first moment he entered the King's tent when I was hidden there: the sheer *presence* of him.

"…chance to talk to some of the Captains about how to minimize the advantage the Aethereans are giving them. I don't want to overplay that and knock the confidence of the rank and file but—Jann, are you listening?"

I blinked as Melek's eyes cut to me, then to Jann and he arched one brow.

Wrenching my gaze from Melek, I found Jann watching me watch Melek and smiling suggestively.

I glared at the sunny Nephilim, whose smile just got broader.

"This isn't the time for a fucking *joke,"* Melek growled. "Jann, I need you to attend—can you think of anything else that I need to use this time for, since I'll only have hours. And I need you to stay here and watch her, and Gall as well. I don't know when he'll be pulled back to the shifts, but for now they keep sending him to me— don't give them reason to draw him back. I'm sure they're sick of dealing with him and it would be better to keep him here where at least he can be out from under the eyes of—"

"You said I was always useful."

My heart screamed with empathy for the faint, pained tone in that precious voice.

All three of us snapped our heads to find Gall standing just inside the tent flap looking… *so sad.*

Melek's eyes widened, and he lifted his hands. "Gall, I wasn't—"

"You said I was *always* useful. You said I am *strong,* and—"

"You are, son. We've spoken before about how others misunderstand. You know that. I was only—"

Gall's eyes welled with unshed tears and my heart cracked for him. "You said they were sick of dealing with me. Are you sick of me, as well?"

"No, Gall…" Melek rushed forward, putting his hands to his boy's shoulders. I covered my mouth with my hands, simultaneously wanting to rush to Gall's side and slap Melek for his thoughtless words.

In fairness, it was clear from Melek's stricken expression that he'd slap himself if he could.

Hug him, I thought. *Don't just grip him…* hug *him.*

But Melek kept Gall at arm's length, holding him by the shoulders and leaning down slightly—though not far—to be eye to eye with his son.

"Gall, we have spoken in the past about how the soldiers view... all of this. I was only referring to that."

Gall's forehead was lined, his brows pinched together. His expression was one of a wounded child. My heart went out to him.

It was so hard to see him standing there—a big, bullish young man whose body held all the muscle and vigor of an accomplished warrior and yet housed the heart and mind of a child.

Life was already confusing to that kind of mind. Add the disparate nature of his appearance and the world would be greatly confused *by him*. My sister also suffered similar misunderstandings whenever new people were introduced since she looked like a normal young woman and acted with grace and kindness. She, at least, did not have to comport herself among the filth and aggression of soldiers.

But Gall...

I wanted to weep for him, seeing him watch his father scramble to explain his words. The transparency on his face—the clear wound, the fear, the fading hope.

They spoke for a long minute, Jannus watching them, also worried, but remaining silent. Eventually Gall looked down at his hands and shrugged.

"I understand."

Melek sighed, knowing as I did that Gall had learned enough to know he was supposed to hide his fear, his hurt.

"Do you, Gall? Because I'll be gone until tomorrow. I don't want you to worry—"

"I understand, Papa. I do."

Melek stared at him a moment longer, then nodded.

I mentally urged him again to offer a hug, an embrace, some kind of tangible comfort that did not have to be *interpreted*. But Melek only slapped his upper arm, then ruffled his hair. "Good man."

Then he turned back to Jann, and though I could see the tension in him, it was also clear that he'd determined there was nothing more to be done for Gall at that moment.

16. Give You My Word

~ YILAN ~

I wanted to scream, but I knew drawing more attention to Gall's confusion and fear would only make him feel worse, so I kept my lips tightly closed, but watched him closely. And when he remembered me and turned to me—fear in his eyes that he'd been witnessed to be weak—I offered the softest smile I could manage and winked when he smiled back.

His throat bobbed and his eyes were still red, but he lifted his chin and made himself stand there, waiting quietly for his father to leave.

Everything happened quickly then. Jann and Melek consulted briefly, Jann wrote a couple of notes, then Melek clasped forearms with him, then Gall, and turned for the door.

For a moment I forgot he was the enemy. For a moment I saw only a warrior shouldering the burden of carrying a nation and my heart went out to him as his eyes lingered on his son.

But then he turned to the doorway and caught me watching and his face went tight.

Yet, he didn't speak to me.

Instead, he addressed Gall. "I need you to watch the Fetch *closely*. If anyone attempts to order you to other issues, you have orders directly from me, and me from the King, that you are to guard our prisoner. It's a very important job, do you understand?"

Gall's jaw tightened and he nodded once. "I understand. I won't let you down."

Jann and Melek met eyes then and understanding passed between them. But Melek hesitated, then pulled one of his spears from his back, hefted it for a moment, then strode back to Gall.

"Hold this for safe keeping," he said quietly, handing the legendary spear to his son.

Gall's mouth dropped open and his eyes went wide. "Papa, you can't—"

"I don't go to fight, Gall. I go to inspire. I will be back within a day, probably less. Until then, I need you to use every skill you have to keep her in that cage, fed, watered, and safe."

"I will—of course. But—"

"No buts, Gall. You carry that for me until I return, then you pass it back to me. Understood?"

Gall swallowed audibly. "Yes. Yes. I do."

"Good man. I trust you, Gall."

Then Melek turned on his heel and strode out of the tent at pace, on his way to the King. So he missed the question on Gall's face as he watched his father stride away.

But I did not.

When Melek was gone, Jann sighed. "I need to send a couple messages, and make certain I have cover for my duties. You stay here and watch over her until I return, okay, Gall?"

Gall nodded, still staring at the tent flap where his father had disappeared.

My heart panged.

Jann caught my eye over his shoulder, and I nodded.

I would fight tooth and nail against any of these creatures. But I would never take advantage of Gall's trust.

Melek may have appointed his son to bolster his son's confidence, but he could not have appointed a more effective guard for me.

There was a fleeting question in my mind that perhaps he knew that, and maybe this had all been a very intentional decision on his part, but I discarded it. Even if Melek was that calculating, it didn't change where I found myself. Which was in the position to protect and strengthen this precious heart.

So, as Jann left the tent almost as quickly as Melek had, I just watched Gall.

He stood there for a long moment, his eyes distant and his expression sad. Then, when he realized he was doing the wrong thing again, he blinked and approached the cage with a heavy sigh.

He turned his back to me when he reached the cage and began to settle down—sitting on the floor, cross-legged. But his father's spear was longer than he was accustomed to handling, and he had to turn it awkwardly to position it over his thighs. Then he realized it was pointed away from the door, which was less effective in the event of an attack. He maneuvered it until it was correctly pointing at the entrance and resting on his thighs.

He sighed heavily again and leaned back against the cage.

My heart squeezed. I could disarm him in a blink from here, but I wouldn't. It just reminded me that—

"Did you mean it when you said you weren't my enemy?" he asked quietly, not turning his head to look at me. His head was dropping, his chin low, as he stroked the etched metal of his father's spear in his lap.

"Yes," I said simply. "I meant every word."

He did turn his head to meet my eyes over his shoulder then. "Will you give me your word that you won't steal my father's spear because if he lost that it would... it would be bad."

I inhaled sharply. "Gall... I will never take another weapon from you, unless I need it in defense of my own life—and even then, I will return it when I'm done. You have my word."

He nodded. "Thank you."

Then he turned away again and looked down at the spear. And his posture was so full of grief and frustration—exactly the way I had seen my sister hunch when the world hurt her—that I wanted to weep.

"Gall—"

"I'm your guard. I don't think we're supposed to talk," he muttered.

I sighed. "Well, I understand. But if you ever want to talk, I will listen, okay?"

He nodded again, but didn't look at me.

The minutes that followed were some of the worst since I'd stepped foot in this camp. I was washed with grief, missing my sister, my family, but frustrated and sad for Gall too. And for the men around us who didn't understand what he needed and were trying to force him into this mold in which he did not fit.

But even as I began to rant in my head, planning all the ways I would curse Melek for not truly comforting the boy, and for putting him in his position, Gall only sagged more.

Jann still hadn't returned.

The first time I heard Gall's breath catch my own tears spilled over my lashes.

I took a step towards him, stopped myself, then cursed and hurried to where he sat with his back against the bars of my prison.

If it were my sister, I would verbalize her feelings for her—make the whole situation less confusing. But I didn't know if Gall would be wounded by the admission. Yet, I *needed* to help him.

With a sigh, I knelt, leaned into the cold steel letting my knees press against his broad back, and reached between the bars to wrap one hand over his head and slide the other down his chest. I couldn't fit my head through the gap, but I could rest my forehead on his hair.

There wasn't even the *beginning* of a warrior's length growing at the back of Gall's head, I realized. Which meant he hadn't yet made his first kill, so his fellows didn't measure him as a true soldier.

My heart broke all over again, and when he tensed at my touch, whipping his hands down to brace on the ground as if he'd stand, I only hugged him harder.

"I'm sorry you got hurt, Gall," I whispered. "I'm sad too. We can be sad together."

He froze.

Then he sighed.

I held him, breathing into his short hair and holding him as I would my sister if we were in this position.

And after a moment, he relaxed.

And then he lifted his hands to hold my arm that was clutching his chest.

I felt his chest hitch and closed my eyes, tears sliding down my cheeks. "You are a good man. If they can't see that, that's because *they* are wrong," I whispered fiercely. "One day I will introduce you to my sister. She would understand your heart, Gall."

"Women don't like me," he muttered.

"She would," I insisted, cursing whatever women had refused to look beyond his Nephilim*ness* to his gentle heart. "Her name is

Istral, and if I cannot introduce you, when I next see her, I will tell her about you, Gall."

I felt his body slump, and I squeezed my eyes closed, praying he'd believe me.

"Don't tell her how big I am. It scares girls," he whispered back.

I did weep then, for this poor boy and his life and his heart. And for me, and my sister and the world that could be so cruel.

And because... fuck.

Sometimes life just sucked.

We stayed that way a long time, but eventually Gall wiped his eyes and straightened his head, almost smacking me in the nose because he hadn't realized I was still leaning on his skull.

"Thank you for being kind to me," he said, then pushed to his feet. "I know I'm not supposed to let you touch me. But you're nice and I was..."

"It's okay, Gall. I won't tell anyone."

He looked at me gratefully. Then cleared his throat and took his father's spear and leaned it against his shoulder. "I'm supposed to be your guard until Jann comes back, so I'm going to do that now."

I blinked, then nodded, biting my lip when he started walking back and forth—marching—in front of my cage, his eyes fixed on the middle distance.

I sighed and settled myself at the back of the cage, praying Jannus would return soon and distract Gall from his determination to be a good guard.

And I hoped he'd bring lunch. It was a little early, but a girl could hope.

I must have dozed off, lulled by the steady beat of Gall's feet on the dirt, but when I snapped awake it was with every instinct alive and alarmed.

I gasped and leaped to my feet—startling Gall who jerked aside and immediately whipped the spear down and towards me.

I was impressed. It seemed he *did* know how to handle a weapon. I supposed it made sense that it was something Melek could train him in consistently.

Then I realized that Jann wasn't there, and Gall was still marching.

"Gall," I breathed. "How long have I been asleep?"

He shrugged, uncomfortable. "All afternoon," he mumbled.

I blinked. "Has Jann returned and left again while I've been asleep?"

Gall shook his head, his forehead pinched to lines of worry. My heart sank and nerves twisted my guts. But there wasn't time to discuss it as I scanned the tent looking for whatever had made my senses prickle.

My first thought was that another Shade was making an appearance and adrenaline jolted through my veins, but a moment's consideration revealed that I didn't feel the shadows as I had the night before.

Whatever was near wasn't a supernatural threat, but a physical one.

"What's wrong?" Gall asked, looking around, following my gaze.

"I don't know, but you should keep your hands on that weapon, Gall," I said quietly, still scanning.

Then a shadow passed over the tent flap before it moved. I prayed it would be Jann. But my heart sank to my toes when more shadows joined the one. Then the flap pulled aside to reveal a young but very tall Nephilim, his face clean shaven and handsome, but with sly eyes.

When he saw that the tent was empty except for Gall and me, he ducked back out, then a moment later *four* young Nephilim entered the tent, eyes bright with cruel delight.

"Hey, Gall... whatcha doing?" the leader of them asked casually.

Every instinct screamed.

Gall frowned but he relaxed his stance, letting the butt of the spear drop to the dirt as all four of them walked towards him, their eyes bright with mischief.

No. *No no no nononono.*

"I have to stay here," Gall said immediately, making me think these young men had forced him to go with them before. "I'm the guard. I have to keep her here until Jannus comes."

The young men looked at each other, grinning, and my senses shrieked.

"Jannus got called by the King to attend with Melek, so they won't be back for *hours.*"

Gall blinked and his eyes swiveled to me in surprise.

Unwilling to let these young bucks see me taken off guard, I folded my arms and glared at them.

"Well… then, I really can't leave," Gall said a moment later, turning back to them. "I was given the orders by Melek and he said they came from the King."

"The King isn't giving orders to a drong like you," the leader sneered. "And even if he did, it's fine because they aren't here. We can all go for a little walk—it'll be good for her and means you don't have to stay here all night. Right?"

Confusion flickered on Gall's face. "No, I don't think… I mean…"

"C'mon, Gall, while the cat's away, the mice will *play!*"

I could tell Gall didn't have a clue what they meant, but the lascivious look on the young men's faces made me very, very nervous.

"Gall, remember your instruct—"

"Shut up, bitch. Gall doesn't have to listen to you—he's a Neph. And you're a fucking *woman.*"

"A smokin' woman though—and stronger than our others. She might survive a breeding," one of the others commented, peering over his friend's shoulder.

I wished for a blade to plunge into his throat to shut him up.

The leader tipped his head at me and smiled. My blood ran cold. "I mean, I doubt it. Plus, Fetch stink. But still…" He walked closer and Gall hurried to put himself—and Melek's spear—between the male and me. But the young warrior just shoved him into the arms of his friends, who teased and cajoled to convince Gall that they were there to have *fun.* I swallowed hard and stifled a shudder as their leader approached the bars and ran a finger up and down the length of metal as if he were touching me. "What do you say, *Fetch?* I could fill you better than any Fetch male ever would."

"Don't… don't try. Don't open the door, she's dangerous," Gall said uncertainly—not entirely sure if he was lying or not. "She has to stay in the cage."

"We won't tell if you don't, Gall," the young Nephilim said in a quiet purr. "After all, we're friends. We keep each other's secrets, right?"

He turned and looked at Gall, whose brows pinched as he looked back and forth between them and me, licking his lips nervously. "Yeah," he said finally. "Friends. Friends keep each other's secrets." Then he looked at me with hope in his eyes.

My heart sank as I started to sweat.

17. Proud King

~ MELEK ~

As darkness fell on the continent, Jann and I were still riding across the plains, half a field from the King because Gault's Khalrion stallion was snorting, wanting to challenge mine.

My burnished copper beast shook his head, rattling the muzzle and stamping with his front feet as his long legs ate up the ground back to the camp.

I slapped the side of his neck and made the soothing hums that would help him ease.

Riding Baelor was very much like riding a horse, but the ranks always eyed us warily when the King and I rode. The Khalrion are only half horse with the barrel, head, and neck of a thickly muscled stallion, though broader and taller than any of the purebred animals. They were also half lion, their haunches thick and legs ending in clawed paws like a lion, with a menacing tail lashing their rumps.

And of course, the teeth. Even the Nephilim who grew up with the creatures shook in fear when a Khalrion opened what looked like a wide horse's muzzle to reveal the fangs of a predator.

Nephilim had been breeding these beasts for centuries, though only the richest and most powerful males possessed them.

Like us, they were a hybrid. We neutered all but the biggest and strongest of them, otherwise the herds would tear each other apart. Usually only Royal bloodlines of Nephilim could own the stallions, but Gault had rewarded me Baelor when we crossed the borders of the Kyrion Vale, having defeated the centaurs.

At the time he said my efforts against those beasts deserved one of my own, and the Khalrion were the closest we could get. The Centaurs were the original model for the creatures, after all. Proof that a true hybrid could be achieved. But the centaurs were capable of reproduction, while the Khalrion, created by the fallen angels with the dark power they possessed, were always male.

I didn't know what sex magik the Fallen had used to combine the two species, but there was no denying that the beasts were fierce, strong, and—when well trained—extremely useful both in battle, and in travel.

On foot, even fresh, it would have taken us half a day from the camp just to reach the front. But on the backs of these creatures, we'd made it all the way there, spent three hours meeting with the Captains and *inspiring the ranks*, and now were almost back to camp in eight hours.

If not for the fact that Gault had suddenly insisted that Jann accompany me when he'd brought a message for the Scouts as we were leaving, I might have found the day a pleasant break from the usual grind of war planning and *Fetch management*.

But I'd been relying on Jann to keep Gall focused... and even as I reassured myself that Gall *wouldn't* make a mistake and free her, the woman's words about the King having the power and motive to send the Shade wouldn't stop echoing in my head. All day, from the moment I swung into the saddle and bowed to my King, my mind saw shadows around every corner, every expression, every decision of Gault's.

Especially when we were at the front and he made such a point to keep me behind him.

I caught a dark look from Gault when the battalions cheered louder after seeing me appear in his wake. But they'd received his speech with great enthusiasm and cheered him highest and loudest at its end.

I hadn't been able to meet alone with the Captains as I had hoped, however, because Gault had kept me at his side. Luckily, with Jann there, he could run messages and questions back and forth between us.

All in all, it had been a helluva day after very little sleep—and a threat on my life. I couldn't wait to return to my tent, and my bed.

Even thoughts of Yilan's cat-eyes on me seemed welcome—until I observed the thought and decided my exhaustion was muddling my mind.

The moon was high and almost full as it rose, casting everything into shades of silver and steel. The forest was approaching which meant we'd reach camp in minutes.

I caught Jann's look from the side and nodded. "Go ahead," I said. "Make certain he's gone, just in case." It wouldn't be the first time Gault came to find my tent. "Tell Gall to keep his head down and stay in his bedroll, even if the trumpets are blown."

Jann nodded once, then dug his heels into his beast's side—the entire entourage were riding Khalrion geldings at the King's insistence. After all, we'd be too slow if they had to stay on foot.

Half an hour later, my focus was on keeping Baelor calm as Gault brought his stallion closer so we could enter the camp together.

Gault smiled and handled his stallion easily, enjoying the flash of his spirited animal against the relative calm of mine.

The ranks had clearly been prepared for our arrival, because they lined the edges of the track we called a road that led into and out of the camp.

Gault raised his chin to them, receiving their adulation with a smug smile and a patronizing wave.

He did cut an impressive figure—the largest of the Nephilim astride the largest Khalrion stallion, and a cloak that made his shoulders even wider than his beast's swirling in his wake. Even the dirt and dust of travel on his skin didn't mar the image of a fierce, vital ruler.

And of course, the gold of the pure, angelic blood shining in his eyes.

Only those within two or three generations descent from the Fallen possessed them, and they glowed in the dark of night like tiny suns. An unnerving sight to the uninitiated.

Inspiring to those who knew those eyes were on their side.

With his chin high and body pulsing with vigor, the gold and precious jewels of his royal garb shining in the light of moon and campfire, I had to admit, if Gault *was* feeling threatened by my sway with the ranks, he was playing it well.

Halfway through camp, riding in Gault's wake, and trying to keep my waving and acknowledgement of the men as subdued as possible, I heard my name barked over the roar of the crowds and turned to find Jannus popping out of the line of Nephilim to march alongside my beast.

I frowned, looking down at him, my blood chilling when I caught the expression on his face.

"What is it?"

He glanced at Gault's back ahead of me, then back to me. "It's worse than we feared."

I almost kicked Baelor to a gallop but forced myself to keep my head.

Jannus was grim, but calm.

Gault, obviously noticing Jann, turned in his saddle, looking a question at me over his shoulder.

"Just an issue with some of the guards," I said as casually as I could. "Some of them are... celebrating too soon. You know how the young can be."

Gault snorted. "I do." He looked down his nose at the ranks lining the road.

"I can take care of it, but I'd rather you didn't move too deep into the camp, Sire, until I can be sure it's taken care of. I don't want to risk a frenzy—I can't afford to lose guards to their stupidity and your obviously superior strength."

Gault huffed, but he was still smiling and enjoying the adulation of the Nephilim ranks. "Whatever you need to do, Melek, just do it. Take care of the children. Eat. Sleep. It has been a good day. I plan to wash and end the evening in my tent with my girls."

Relief coursed through me that he wasn't going to come after the Fetch—or Gall—tonight. But even as I nodded and saluted him, my blood cooled further.

Whistling for two of his Handlers to ride forward and take Baelor for me—even muzzled the beast could be trouble if he wasn't dominated—I swung off Baelor and threw his reins to the first of the two handlers to reach me. Then I followed Jannus, ducking back into the crowd, pushing through them to dart into camp.

"The tent is empty," Jann said the moment we were sure we wouldn't be overheard.

I almost stopped in my tracks. *"What?!"*

"Both Gall and Yilan are gone. Completely gone. And no one saw him come get dinner."

He hadn't been joking about it being worse than we feared.

I blinked once, cursed twice, then made myself focus.

This wasn't a crisis. This was a battle. This was strategy. And I would win.

"I'll change while you get food and your weapons—we can't grow weak now. Meet me back at my tent in five minutes. We'll split up and search. I don't believe he would free her. But she may have manipulated him into taking her somewhere she believed she could fight her way free."

Jann kept nodding as I hurriedly laid out the plan through gritted teeth, then peeled away towards the main cook-tent to grab supplies and send a message for a tracker. If we couldn't locate them in minutes, we'd have to bring someone in to follow the scent trail from the cage.

Fuck.

Fuck!

I shoved the tent flap aside, rushing into the dim tent—no lanterns lit. But there was enough moonlight to make the roof and side of the tent glow. I didn't take the time to light a lantern, especially since we might need to get Gall and Yilan back here under cover of dark.

FUCK.

I was stripping before I'd taken two steps, throwing my armor onto the bed to be stored properly later, I grabbed my black calfskin leathers from the trunk and pulled them on. Soft and dull, they were the best for furtive activities at night and would remain comfortable on my weary body.

One quick scan of the tent revealed that my second spear wasn't here either. I prayed Gall hadn't lost it to Yilan, though I doubted she was strong enough to wield it effectively.

Moments later, dressed and armed, I stood at the center of the tent when Jann appeared, having also changed and carrying hot rolls filled with sliced beef. We both tore into the food, quickly and carefully discussing who would take which routes through the camp, and what questions we'd ask, and of whom.

But my mind was spinning.

Why would Gall have taken her out of the cage? She must have manipulated him.

Curse me for believing her wide-eyed, earnest assurances that she understood him and wouldn't take advantage.

Curse the King for insisting Jann come with us.

Curse that fucking Fetch for putting the questions in my mind about the King setting me up for...

No.

One problem at a time. Right now, I *had* to locate Gall and Yilan. There was no other option.

"You go north and east," I instructed Jann quietly. "I'll go south and west—he has some hiding places in the forest. If he perceived danger, he may have taken her to hide…"

Jann and I quickly determined who would cover which territory, how to leave signs for each other in the event that one of us didn't return, and agreed to meet at my tent again in ninety minutes. I prayed that one of us would have found the pair before then.

I clasped his arm, thanking him for his help. Then we left the tent and split up, Jann to follow the paths into the camp proper where he would ask careful questions to identify where they'd been seen—*if* they'd been seen. While I darted around the tent and followed the lay of the land deeper into the forest that hugged the foothills of the mountain above and kept my eyes peeled for any sign of their passage.

In truth, I'd left the questions to Jann because he was less suspicious to be seen talking throughout the camp, but also because I suspected Gall wouldn't have just marched her through the camp, even if he thought it was right to get her away.

Gall always tried to be alone when he didn't have responsibilities and couldn't be with me. Everywhere we camped for more than a day he'd find some dark spot or quiet clearing to be alone and breathe. He called it Being Still. I knew he'd found more than one spot within a mile or two of this camp where we had now stayed for weeks, but I hadn't taken him up on visiting with him. Now I cursed myself for not taking the time when I was in camp before. I was sure if he thought he had to protect her he'd take her to one of those places.

One thing I could be confident of with Gall, if there had been a threat, if he'd taken her away, he would be found or he would bring her back.

But what if she'd tricked him?

My heart hammered as my mind spun with the consequences if Gall was the one to lose her—consequences to me and to him. But I couldn't focus on the problems that had not yet arisen. I had to give all my attention to solving what I knew: Both were missing, and this left us all in great peril.

I was only minutes from the tent, slipping deeper into the forest, when the deep roar of a male crowd rose. My first instinct was to dismiss it—but as the voices rose higher, a feminine shriek cut through and I froze. Turning my head towards the camp I realized that the roaring wasn't coming from behind me, but from my left.

Deeper into the forest.

Cursing, I began to run.

18. A Cry in the Dark

~ MELEK ~

A minute later I was creeping up on a clearing in the forest, grateful I'd had the foresight to wear dark clothing and bring my weapons.

Ahead, through a gap in the trees, I could see a crowd of young Neph, milling, talking, cheering, laughing. If I'd happened on them, I would have thought they'd come out here to drink. I drew close enough to see but kept myself out of sight in case I'd been wrong about what I heard, there was another ripple of laughter.

"Gall's gonna become a man!"

"Hey! You'll get to show her your *warrior's length,* Gall!"

My heart sank as a cluster of the males leaped aside, laughing and tussling with each other.

What were they doing with him?

The worst occurred to me, but Gall wouldn't. I knew he wouldn't. He still had the mind of a child.

And yet… if they showed him the way?

Where the fuck was the Fetch?!

Still staying back and undetected, I tried to slip further around the group, seething that I could be even this close to so many so-called soldiers in the dead of night, and not one of them was watching their surroundings, or aware of my presence.

Their backs remained to me. No one even checked over their shoulders.

Idiots.

There were shouts, cajoling laughter and rising taunts. But the Neph were so large I couldn't see beyond them to be certain of what I suspected.

I was forced to slip back into the forest and leap up to grasp the bough of the largest nearby pine, pulling myself up onto its broad branch so I could see beyond them.

And what I saw made my blood run cold.

A hundred feet away, Gall stood facing the crowd, my spear in both hands and leveled, his head snapping left and right, his lips peeled back from his teeth—like a cat cornered by a pack of dogs.

And beyond him, a small, lithe shadow crouched, one hand on his back, her eyes wide and expression grim.

Yilan. Looking like a prey-animal under the eyes of wolves.

I gritted my teeth as Gall's attention was taken by one of the leaders, calling to him, *daring* him to drop the spear—and meanwhile, one of the others slipped out of the crowd from Gall's right and darted forward.

There was a hissed, *"Gall! Watch out!"* and he whipped around, bringing the spear around with handy speed and some skill despite the fact that the weapon was longer and heavier than he was accustomed to using.

I would have been proud as he stabbed it towards the interloper, but one of the young leaders stepped forward putting his hands out to stop the others.

"Calm down, calm down, Gall. I told you; you've got nothing to be worried about. We're *friends,* right? Remember?"

Gall's determined expression faltered, and my heart panged for him. He was still half-crouched with the weapon readied. He was trying to protect her from whatever it was these younglings thought they would do with her. But the Siren call of *friendship* was being weaponized against him.

And it wasn't the first time.

I'd thought everyone had grown up enough, that we were beyond these games. But clearly I'd been wrong.

Fuck.

"She's... She's not mine. She belongs to Melek."

"He won't care," the leader pointed out.

"Or know," his friend added.

"I think he will," Gall said, his forehead puckered.

Then, because Gall had turned towards her slightly, everyone moved, and I caught a clear gaze at Yilan's face—her darting eyes and obvious terror.

And yet...

There was no one behind her. She had a clear escape, but she hadn't run. She was leaning into Gall, moving with him even when he moved quickly. She appeared to be guarding his back. Her lips moved, though I couldn't hear what she said.

Reassurance to my son?

Or manipulation?

Had she created this conflict to find opportunity to flee?

And yet, if that was the case, why hadn't she run yet? They'd obviously been out here for some time—no one was feeling uncertain or self-conscious. In the distance I could hear the cheering and rollicking in the camp. So, these young ones had obviously decided they were safe to get up to mischief.

And in truth, this wasn't a scenario that would be discouraged by most of their leaders. Something Gall and I had discussed many times—that my honor kept me from behaviors many others encouraged.

Gall was an idealist. A kind heart. Compassionate. But still *male.*

I couldn't know how he would be swayed with time. I was grateful that he had remained strong so far. But I could see the uncertainty in his expression, and the thought of where this could have gone with a little more time left me nauseous.

I would stop it. The question was how to do so without drawing attention to Gall's failure—or my protection of her.

"Look, Gall, brother, she's a *woman.* You know why God made them, right?"

Shit.

Gall nodded. "Yes. God made them for our babies. Melek explained—"

The snorts and guffaws made me want to snarl.

"Right, right, so... did he tell you *how* a girl gets a baby?"

Gall went still and he swallowed. "Yes. But..." he trailed off, frowning.

If the situation hadn't been so dire I would have dropped my face into my hands and groaned. Gall was at a strange place in his life—his adult body driving him to things his developing mind didn't understand. I had explained. More than once.

His interest swung wildly between embarrassment and fascination, depending on the day. It was, in part, why I'd warned Yilan against attempting to seduce him. I worried he'd misread it.

The leader who'd been keeping Gall's attention stepped forward casually—just like a friend talking. But another of his friends had slipped around the back of the crowd and emerged at the furthest end in the opposite direction that Gall was now facing.

"So, let us show you, Gall. You need to become a man so you can be part of our club. And she can make you a man, Gall. You know that right?" their leader said slyly.

This had gone too far. I slipped off the branch and dropped lightly to the ground, creeping closer as my head spun, trying to find the way into this without casting suspicion—

"No. She's not for us. She belongs to Melek," Gall said stubbornly.

"Except, he's not here. And she's—"

The leader's friend darted out quietly while Gall wasn't paying attention and leaped towards Yilan.

She saw him coming and gasped, twisting out of his grip, pulling at Gall's shirt from behind.

He reacted instinctively, whipping that spear around with a cry—and catching the male in the arm, slicing his bicep with the edge of the spearhead that I kept razor-sharp.

The youngling yelped, but he was well-trained—he twisted, and dropped, rolling back to his feet gripping his arm a moment later, but no longer laughing. He was cursing now, bellowing and hissing through his teeth as blood seeped out from under the fingers of the hand he had clapped to the wound.

And just like that, this was no longer a party, but a *fight*.

Twenty young Nephilim, all trained, all bored, all humming with unspent energy, sexual tension, and the instincts of creatures that were told to take what they wanted, when they wanted it.

By God's mercy, everyone was so surprised that Gall had actually wounded the man, a ripple of shock washed through the crowd. And Gall himself.

His eyes widened and he stared at that blade, now smeared and glistening with his comrade's blood.

It was the only hesitation. Then they all realized what had happened and all hell broke loose.

The leader roared forward, calling curses on Gall—who swung the weapon, thrusting and stabbing. He screamed at them all to stay back, while Yilan stayed at his back, her face a mask of horror and weariness.

She had no weapon. Not even a blade for eating. And because Gall had been disarmed by the sergeant, apart from my spear he wasn't carrying any extra weapons she might have taken to help.

And so, she was left with one protector holding a single spear. And no matter his size and training, he lacked the confidence and ruthless nature of those he faced.

As the Neph descended on them with a roar, I tore forward, praying I could intervene quickly enough. But it all happened too fast, while I was still running to reach them.

The Nephilim came at the pair from both sides at once, and even though they were forced to dart back and away in the face of that blade, it was seconds before one of them drew Gall's attention so he turned, and while he was off-balance, their leader slipped in behind him and grabbed Yilan.

She screamed like a fighting cat, clawing and raining blows— landing one hard enough to make him flinch and let go of her arm.

I was tearing forward, but too late, too late.

I almost tripped when she didn't even hesitate, but launched herself at the males encircling Gall, screaming at him to *stop listening and* fight!

But even as she reached the Nephilim trying to disarm him and he roared, swinging the spear to try and fight for her, two got behind him and pulled him off his feet. The leader jumped after her, catching her around the waist, and grabbing her wrist to wrench her arm behind her back. And this time, even when she fought, he didn't let her go.

His comrades rushed Gall, disarmed him and held him back. Their leader spat something ugly about *female vessels* and used brute force to haul her off her feet, turning her to catch her flailing arms.

"Settle, *bitch,* or this will hurt more than it has to," he snarled.

Bringing his superior weight and strength to bear, he whipped her around, pulling both her arms back mercilessly and locking her wrists with one of his hands, while he plunged the other down the front of her shirt and gripped her breast.

There was a surge among the males watching.

Gall roared, screaming her name when she shrieked and twisted, trying to free herself. But the leader held her so tightly and threw her down with such force, her arm twisted grotesquely, her shoulder flexing in a direction it was never designed to do.

She screamed in pain and fell under him.

He was on her in a moment, panting and calling for Gall to watch, that he'd show him how to make a baby, and calling for the others to come taste a Fetch.

The crowd sucked in around them just as I burst into the clearing with a roar. Heart pounding, I bellowed the only thing I could think of to make them stop.

"UNHAND WHAT IS MINE, YOU FUCKING *WORM!*"

19. It is Done

~ MELEK ~

All the young Neph who'd been watching with such lascivious delight a moment earlier whipped around at the sound of my roar and fell aside like flesh opened by a blade.

I passed through the gap, tackling the fucker who had her on the ground and was scrambling at his own leathers, trying to free himself—but not in time.

He was lucky I didn't wrench his cock *off* when I got hands on him.

He released her the moment he saw my face, his hands going wide half a blink before I ripped him away from her and tossed him bodily into his comrades, so he took four of them out.

"What the fuck did you do?" I snarled, standing over a weeping Yilan, pointing at Gall—who was immediately released and shoved forward, stumbling and almost falling at my feet.

"He was playing with her!"

"He told us she was there!"

"It was just a game, sir."

Gall had almost lost his feet when he was thrown forward. Now, he crouched in front of me, his eyes wide, sweat trickling down his temple as he watched me roar and dominate.

He was *terrified* by my anger.

And he believed it was truly leveled at him.

Apparently, I'd been more convincing than I'd thought, because the others relaxed a hair, standing straight and starting to nudge each other.

To distract them all, I stepped forward, swiped my spear from the hands of a young Neph who'd been staring at me open mouthed, then whipped it in a circle, sending a few of the others back a hurried step or two as I turned, scanning all of them, letting them see every ounce of my anger and domination over them.

"A few hours…" I growled, turning to meet eyes with each of them. "I am gone for *a few hours* and you *pups* cannot keep your dicks to yourselves even that long?"

"Sir, Gall said—"

"I don't give a fuck what one soldier said when you are gathered as a legion and know better."

Most of them shrank under my eyes. But the leader, clearly startled and embarrassed by how easily I'd tossed him aside, was scrambling to reassert himself in the eyes of the others.

And he was a clever fuck.

"We meant no disrespect, General," he said slyly, still panting. "Please… show us. She's yours. And strong. Strong enough to survive a breeding, right? Show us…" he insisted, and the sick light in his eyes resonated with the nausea in my stomach because I knew these young males had witnessed a woman taken against her will before.

Every Nephilim had.

Avid, they all leaned in, waiting for me to laugh and finish the job this fucker had started.

Nerves twisting in my guts, I smiled at them like a cat on a mouse, and with the spear still in one hand, I took the two steps back to where she was on all fours attempting to get to her feet with only one usable arm.

Grabbing a fistful of her hair, I yanked her head back, internally wincing at the pain it would no doubt cause her shoulder but keeping my expression fierce for these *children.*

"She is mine to do with as I please," I snarled, eyeing all of them and ignoring her gasps of pain and shock. Then I brought the spear up to point, swinging it slowly so that it leveled at each one's heart as I met eyes with him. "I don't share with grunts. And I don't want your dirty pricks in her. Get your own," I growled.

There was a groan of disappointment, and some taunting of their leader for assuming I'd play his game. His eyes darted from his comrades—who he relied on to bolster his strength—to me and he licked his lips. But then he smiled and my blood turned to ice at the conniving, sinister light in his eyes.

"Then bleed her. Fucking kill her—she got out. She almost got loose. That's a killing offense for an enemy. Slay her, General. *Slay her!*"

"I don't take orders from children," I snapped. "And there is no breeding with a dead woman, you imbecile."

Some of them laughed and taunted him, but many were panting, eyes bright with bloodlust and leaning forward.

I growled, the hair on the back of my neck standing up. We Nephilim were most often our own worst enemies. Most of us were born out of violence then raised in a brutal culture that rewarded aggression. Although there were calm, thoughtful minds among us, in our culture strength ruled. That light in their eyes was a warning—the fallen power within coming forward.

My rank wouldn't protect me from a well-placed spear, and even I couldn't fight this many at once if the bloodlust hit and they worked together.

I couldn't let the blood frenzy grip them, so I pretended indifference to the danger, yanking Yilan to follow me as I began to walk straight back through the crowd, using the spear as a warning against any attempt to hinder me.

As I passed where they still held Gall, I paused and glowered at him. "It was your job to keep her for me. Yet I find her pawed and dirtied? You will come with me to account for your failure!" I snarled, my heart weeping for the fear shadowing my son's eyes.

The males cheered and taunted Gall as his head dropped and he slunk up behind us. I used the moment when their attention went to him to pretend to lift her and sniff her as if for the scent of other males and murmured in her ear.

"Grip my hand with your good hand as if you're trying to stop me hurting you. Make it look like a struggle. I'll follow your steps."

She whimpered, and for a moment I thought she hadn't heard me, but sure enough her good arm came up and she grasped my wrist, writhing as though I were shaking her head and pulling at her, when in truth it was her movement that I just allowed my arm to follow.

Perfect.

As I stormed away, hauling her with me and Gall following us, that little prick spoke up again, lifting his voice.

"But what will you do with her, General? Will you kill her, or breed with her?"

They all turned to me, going quiet, waiting.

I cut one look over my shoulder and flashed them a dark grin.

"I won't kill her…"

They groaned, but I only smiled wider.

"…I'll *own* her."

A ripple of cheers and laughter, some ugly taunts, and a few questions rose in the air behind me, but I kept walking a steady pace. Unconcerned.

Just the General who'd interrupted some young Nephilim getting above themselves.

Nothing to be worried about.

Nothing important.

And definitely *nothing* to see here now that I was pulling her away.

They didn't follow immediately, so I picked up the pace as soon as we were out of their sight—and then, when I was certain we were alone in the forest, I swung her up into my arms and began to jog, whispering instructions to Gall to run ahead and find very specific supplies then bring them to the tent.

"You do not come to my tent until you've found *everything,* do you hear me, Gall?"

"Yes, yes, of course, Papa," he said in a small voice that made my chest pinch. But I shook it off. I needed him to feel defeated. I needed him *scared*. He couldn't act. He definitely couldn't lie. So, he needed to believe he was in desperate trouble. Then, if anyone asked him what he was doing he would tell them I was in a rage and he was serving me as punishment.

When we got closer to camp, he peeled off, murmuring that he'd be back as soon as he could. Then I started to run in earnest.

I had a soldier's medical pack in my tent, but he wouldn't remember that. And I needed him gone for a time.

"Almost done, don't worry," I muttered, but I wasn't even sure she heard me.

Yilan held her useless arm against her body. Her face pale and her eyes squeezed shut against the pain.

Then I was darting along in the shadow of that rocky lee behind my tent, then flipping the tent flap aside to hurry inside—no lanterns. No warning to anyone that I had returned.

I hurried across the tent and lay her on the bed, checking her eyes, her pulse, and made a hurried examination of her body.

I was sickened to discover that her shirt was ripped down the front, and the buttons of her leathers torn loose. That little fucker had pawed her far more than I realized.

She lay on the bed, shivering, eyes glazed and face pinched against the pain, her lips moving so quickly on breathy, whispered words, it took me a moment to make out what she was saying.

"…don't be scared, Gall. You were right. You were right. Don't be scared…"

Oh, dear God.

I dropped my chin for a moment, knowing she was in shock and probably not taking anything in. But there was no time. And improving her pain would help her come out of it faster.

I took a deep breath and set my jaw, gripping her face in both hands.

The moment I touched her, her eyes cut to my face and her entire body went rigid with tension.

"Yilan, listen. Your shoulder is dislocated. I need to reset it. It's going to hurt a great deal, but only for a moment—do you understand?"

She nodded quickly and licked her lips once, her eyes bright with fear.

I prayed she took in the words, that she would remember that I'd warned her. But there was no more time to waste. I had a hunch that those young Neph had followed at a distance and would be curious about what the General was doing with the Fetch.

I suspected if we didn't have an audience already, we were about to. And they needed to be certain of what they were hearing.

I grunted and sent up a quick prayer for clarity. Then, with grim determination, I gripped the bad shoulder in one hand. Yilan cried out and I let myself give a low growl. I leaned over her to get the right angle, positioning my other hand on the bad arm and rotating it slightly, humming low and warm as I did so.

She cried out again when I leaned my weight on her and I cursed wickedly—and heard a snicker outside the tent.

So, my instincts had been correct.

Dropping my chin so my lips brushed her ear again, I whispered. "Make any noise you need to."

Then without any further warning, I braced the shoulder to immobilize it, and turning her wrist, I yanked the arm to reposition it correctly.

Yilan shrieked and I roared as if I'd taken her in truth.

Then, as she slumped into unconsciousness, I continued to roar and grunt rhythmically, praying the sounds covered my footsteps as I rushed to get my soldier's medical satchel, then stripped her shirt off to wrap the shoulder with the long, clean linen we all carried for battleground first aid.

She was bare under the shirt. It wasn't hard to rumble approvingly—much harder to wrench my gaze away as I hurried to find a clean shirt.

But then I realized her leathers were dirty, torn, and sweaty.

I tore those off too and threw them on the ground with another low rumble of approval, praying that the witnesses outside understood what they were hearing.

Then, grabbing one of my long sleep shirts, I tugged it up her bad arm as gently as I could, then rolled her towards me to get the shirt behind her.

To lift her without hurting the bad shoulder I needed to put a knee onto the bed and half-straddle her to tug the shirt under her back.

It was in that moment that the tent flap snapped aside, and Gall rushed in—sliding to a halt at the sight of me bent over the Fetch on my bed, his eyes wide and afraid.

"GET OUT AND GUARD THE DOOR!" I roared at him.

He startled and turned so quickly he almost lost his footing before running back out of the tent still gripping the supplies I'd asked him to bring.

My heart broke for him—for the fear and confusion in his gaze. But the whole incident would affirm the story I was building for those fuckers and their lust outside.

So, while I was crouched over her, I moved as much as possible while pulling that shirt around her back, ensuring the bed creaked several times before I gave a gargling cry.

When I was done, she lay on the bed, unconscious, wrapped in my clean sleep shirt.

I was panting, I realized. My heart thudding uncomfortably in my chest—and not from lust, though there was no denying she was a beautiful woman.

It was fear, pure and simple that made my brow sweat.

But again, it was something I could use.

Disgusted with myself, and simultaneously grateful that the course of events would further the story I was building, I turned away from her to remove my weapon straps, pulled my shirt out of my waistband and tore through the buttons, let the two sides of it fall aside, Then I unbuttoned the top of my leathers as well, before stalking back to the tent flap.

Shoving it aside, I found Gall standing outside, his shoulders hunched up around his ears, his arms curled around the things he'd brought, that I had requested.

A few shadows melted away when I appeared, but that was just as well. It meant they were listening.

"Give me those," I snapped, silently praying that Gall would forgive me the next day. "You stand out here. You don't move. You don't let anyone but the King Himself inside until I change the order. Do you understand?"

Gall nodded hurriedly, not meeting my eyes. I stepped out of the tent so anyone watching could see my disheveled appearance and sweaty brow. I grabbed the satchel and linens in his arms and yanked them from his grip, growling as I turned and snapped the tent flap aside again and disappeared inside.

And then, as I stormed back to the bed, to her pale, still form, I realized it was done. For better or for worse, it was done. Tomorrow morning the entire camp would believe I had claimed her and taken her for breeding.

I stood back a moment, breathing hard, taking in the sight of her—dirty, messy, but untouched. Laying on my bed, in my shirt, her black hair splayed over her face, and her pale skin almost glowing in the dimness. She looked so small and so fragile... And it hit me.

That had been close. So close.

I took one shaky step back, then another, until I could get a hand on the chair and pull it closer.

I sat down hard.

So fucking close.

20. Fear Not

~ *YILAN* ~

I did pass out when Melek reset my shoulder.

But I came to while he was bandaging me and clothing me with gentle hands, muttering curses in the moments when he jostled my shoulder. At first I didn't open my eyes because of the pain. But then I didn't want to let him know I was aware because I was terrified and exhausted and *so relieved he'd gotten me away.* I just… needed a moment.

But then he growled at Gall, and then he left me on the bed and sat in the chair and was quiet. I didn't want him to see me cry, so I didn't move. I acted as if I was still unconscious.

I guess at some point I fell asleep.

My dreams were uneasy, broken visions of being in the hands of those monsters—but every time, Melek arrived just in time and relief coursed through me before I sank into darkness again.

I woke up with sunlight making the tent glow, my body warm and dry, and with a lovely, comforting scent filling my nose. But I was hurting too. For a moment I was disoriented. The cage bars were overhead, but closer. And I wasn't laying on hard dirt, but something that creaked when I moved my leg. A cot?

I blinked and looked down at myself—I was in a long, white shirt. The cuffs rolled up many times to shorten the length. My legs were covered by dark leggings made from soft cotton.

Suddenly, a male throat cleared nearby, and I jerked to look. I tried to push up to sit, but my entire right side screamed in pain when I put pressure on that hand to lever myself up.

I ended up curling up slowly, awkwardly, gripping the edge of the cot in the other hand, breathing heavily against the pain and shaking my head when Gall stared at me, worriedly.

"I'm fine. I'm fine. I just forgot about my shoulder when I woke up," I said, though the pit of my stomach now roiled with nausea against the pain.

"Are you okay, Yilan?" Gall whispered, his eyes wide, forehead lined with worry. "That was horrible. And you—"

"I'm fine, Gall. I promise."

It took a minute, but I got myself up to a sitting position, my legs swung over the side of the shallow cot and feet on the ground, so at least I could brace to stand if I needed to.

Then I just relaxed and breathed for a moment, praying the pain would ease.

Gall looked at the tent flap like he was afraid someone was about to walk in.

He was armed again, I noticed. And staying a few feet back from the cage.

I smiled and nodded at the spear. "Thank you for helping me yesterday. You were very brave. And I see you're armed again! That's great, Gall—"

"You don't have to pretend, Yilan. I know what he did. And it was… it was *wrong.*"

I thought he meant the young Nephilim who'd come in here, pretending to be his friend, and who'd prepared to rape me.

I shivered at a flash of memory of his brute strength, his calloused hands pawing my body—

I flinched but shook the memory off and cleared my throat. "It was scary, Gall. But I got away. I'm safe now. And I'm very grateful for—"

"No! Don't try to honor him when he did not honor you!" Gall hissed vehemently. I stopped, blinking.

He thought I was honoring his friend?

But then Gall's eyes shadowed, and he shook his head. "They all do these things. They are beasts. He always told me it was wrong. He *taught me.* Then he did it. And to *you!*"

That was when I realized Gall believed Melek had raped me.

Oh shit.

I blinked and raised my good hand to soothe him because I needed to figure out what was going on here. "Gall... wait... how long have I been asleep?"

"All night and now it's almost lunch. Yilan, I—"

"Gall, step outside. Do not allow anyone in without announcing them first," Melek growled, striding into the tent, hands clenched to fists at his sides and his jaw tight. He didn't look at me, but locked eyes with Gall who stood facing him, his hands fisted as well. And, alarmingly, he didn't immediately move. It was the first time ever I saw Gall hesitate in taking an order from Melek.

He bristled and raised his chin, his eyes dark and accusing. "Don't you hurt her."

Melek just glared at him, his jaw jutting forward until Gall swallowed and gripped his spear tighter as he finally moved. He walked past Melek, letting his shoulder bump his father's as he passed, and turned his head to look at me. "I will be right outside," he said quietly, then stalked out of the tent.

I watched, stunned. But the tent flap drifted closed behind him and then there was nothing.

I turned to find Melek also watching it, a worried frown on his face.

"Melek, why didn't you tell him?" I whispered.

His head snapped towards me and our eyes locked. My breath stopped.

He looked older, suddenly. His forehead creased and his eyes sunk deeper under his heavy brows. And there was a storm in his gaze.

"You fought for him," he said hoarsely.

I blinked. "What—"

"Stop, Yilan. Just... please. Speak to me as if... as if we are not enemies." Then he cleared his throat and leaned closer, pointing away, in the direction we'd been last night. "I saw you. You were about to be raped and killed. But instead of running away when you got loose, you ran to fight for Gall. Are you truly... truly that courageous, or simply stupid?"

I dropped my chin, but couldn't break that gaze. "F-fear not the creature that can kill your body... fear the God who can condemn your soul."

Melek's frown got deeper. "That isn't an answer."

Because I wasn't going to give him one. So, I turned the tables. "Anyway, you saved me—"

He tensed, raising his hands quickly to shush me and looking back towards the tent flap. "You cannot speak of—"

My heart was beating faster and faster. Using my good hand, I gripped the side of the cot and pushed to my feet, wavering a little, but I steadied when I widened my stance. "I remember, Melek. I was shocked, but not—"

"The shoulder will heal," he said in a normal voice, louder. Easier to hear outside the tent. "But you need to rest it for a few days. No more picking fights with young bucks. Give yourself time to heal but move it gently every hour to keep the joint limber if you don't want to have restricted movement later."

I closed my mouth when he spoke over me, lips pursed. I knew what he was doing. But why?

"Melek, why did you—"

He dropped his voice to a hiss and took a step closer. "They were insolent bucks who should be neutered. They needed to be stopped."

"But... you saved *me* from them. And Gall thinks—"

Another step and he could have touched the cage if he reached out, but instead he only leaned in glaring, and muttered through his teeth. "If you say that out loud one more time, I'm going to gag you. No one can know. *No one.* You understand?" Then he glanced at the tent flap and the shadow of Gall there.

I shook my head. "No, I don't understand. He's blaming you—"

"It cannot be avoided. Gall cannot act. He cannot lie. He cannot *protect* with his words. He must believe it—then there is no doubt others will believe it too."

My jaw went slack as I stared at him.

He *wanted* everyone to believe he'd raped me? Why?

"But..."

"There is no *but.* Leave this alone!" he growled, then turned his back on me. I was about to argue when I remembered the King with his *bayan* girls, the haunted looks of the slaves here, and the way the woman slaves had watched Melek with eager, hopeful eyes.

And it all came home to me… of course…

For a Nephilim to rape a human woman was only natural. Normal. It was how the Nephilim had come into being—human women raped by angels—and so it was what they *did.*

But for a Nephilim to *save* a woman? And a sworn enemy, at that?

In this culture, that would be reason for suspicion.

I closed my mouth, swallowing hard as I put it together in my head.

I could understand him wanting the young Nephilim to believe that he'd *taken* me—that he possessed me. But Gall?

Then his words echoed in my head again.

"Gall cannot act. He cannot lie. He cannot protect *with his words. He must believe it—then there is no doubt others will believe it too."*

Of course. Of course. I saw what he meant. My sister could be the same: Honest to a fault, and confused when others read more into her words than she'd meant. Or when they were offended by what was simple truth.

And now Gall… surrounded by brutal Nephilim who took what they wanted and protected no one unless it benefited them to do so… They would see Melek's protection of me as some kind of weapon. Some kind of tool.

Or some kind of treason.

Melek sighed heavily and ran his hand through his hair as he stalked to the other side of the tent to remove his weapon straps and jacket.

"He will get over it. He always does," he muttered quietly a moment later, while I stood there watching him. "He will forgive me."

My stomach clenched at the force he put behind those words, as if he were arguing with himself, determined to convince his *own* heart that they were true.

Gall… good, simple, beautiful Gall, who would forgive an enemy for stealing his weapon because she was kind.

But would he forgive his *Papa* for violating the very same kind woman?

I wasn't so sure. And clearly Melek wasn't either. Which made my stomach ache.

I didn't know what to say, so I just watched him half-strip, then throw himself down on the bed and pick up a book, ignoring me.

At least, that's what he wanted me to believe. I had no doubt his skin was just as prickled as mine, his senses just as attuned to my movement as mine were to his when I pretended the same.

I waited until he'd been quiet for some time though, to make sure he wouldn't offer more.

Then I sighed and walked back to my cot to sit.

"Thank you, Melek," I said as softly as I could.

He didn't take his eyes off the book, but his lips twitched at the corners for a moment. "So, you can bend your neck when you need to," he commented airily as he turned a page.

I snorted, but didn't answer. Then realized the reason I'd been feeling like something was off in my cage was because there had been screens located and placed around my bucket—and all the things I'd asked that woman to bring were neatly stacked in a basket next to it.

It was such a simple thing, such a practical gift, and yet it touched me right at the center of my chest. A pang that made my throat close.

Fuck him and his insistence on not talking about it.

"Why did you do it, Melek?" I asked hoarsely.

He didn't look up from his book. "Because... I fear I could not have *borne* it," he rasped.

My heart stopped beating, and my jaw dropped. A moment later his eyes rose from the book to meet mine, but his face was blank. Expressionless. He didn't move or speak again. But he didn't look away either.

And before I could figure out how to respond to *that*, Gall pulled back the tent flap and announced flatly that Jann was outside and said he needed to speak to Melek.

There was a beat. A bare moment. Heartbeats before he answered, and I saw the flash of a shadow in his eyes. My breath stopped.

But then he tore himself away from the gaze and swung his legs off the bed, getting to his feet, and muttering.

"Send him in."

And the moment was lost.

21. Strange Peace

~ YILAN ~

The days that followed that moment were... strange.

Strangely peaceful.

Strangely tense.

Melek was busy. When he wasn't already gone from the tent, Jannus came for him several times a day. Gall was posted as my guard with instructions to keep the tent entirely free of *visitors* unless Melek ordered otherwise.

This new routine meant there had been very little activity in the tent, and even fewer dramas... unless you counted Gall growing more and more silent and sullen around Melek—which broke my heart.

Everyone believed the endless guarding was a punishment for Gall—including Gall himself. I hated it, but also found it a relief because it meant no more groups of young Nephilim showed up to manipulate him. And that meant, even if Gall was upset or angry, he was at least safe.

I knew that was why Melek had done it. And I wouldn't breach his instructions. But it made me ache every day knowing this might have been the most peaceful and easy *task* Gall had ever been given if he wasn't harboring anger and confusion towards his father... because of me.

I prayed for wisdom to see how to soothe him, and a way to smooth the path between the two so that Gall could forgive him. But no opportunities were presented in those days.

I slept a great deal.

Between my cycle starting, the fighting, the injury, and the general lack of sleep for the weeks prior, I found that whenever I wasn't eating or speaking to someone my body constantly dragged towards sleep.

It was easy to give in to because Melek was quite clearly burdened with a great deal and avoiding any conversation with me beyond instructions. Even when he woke in the mornings, or returned to the tent at night, he kept to himself. He would call in Jannus or Gall to speak if he lingered over a meal. Or, if he did have a free hour, he brought out his book and ignored me.

I might have been offended. I might have feared he resented the situation he found himself in on my account and was scheming to get rid of me. But more than once, I caught him watching me.

Our eyes would snag, and he would turn away immediately, his face a blank mask, as if I were only an inanimate object his gaze had passed over.

But his body always stiffened at the brief connection.

After a few days of this, I began to mirror him, tensing when he was there, but afraid when he was not. The moment he walked into the tent my stomach would flutter, fizz with a bubbling kind of anticipation—though I could not have said what my body thought was to come.

The moment he would leave, after that first breath of relief because my nerves disappeared, a crawling kind of dread would climb my spine and would not leave me until he returned.

It was insane. Confusing. And very unsettling.

But after five or six days of sleeping whenever I could, forcing myself to ignore Melek when I could not, I was rested and growing rest*less*.

I needed to move. I needed something to engage my mind.

I needed a purpose.

So, it was with that fidgety, agitated spirit that I finished eating my lunch a full week after that dreadful night.

There were crumbs of the bread left on the plate, so I gathered them and sprinkled them in the corner of the cage, then placed the plate next to the door where Gall would remove it later.

The only time Melek had spoken to me with any kind of levity had been three days earlier when he'd seen me spread the crumbs and he took a moment to tease me about inviting rodents into his tent—was I trying to get him bitten?

But before I could respond, there had been a messenger and he'd left abruptly. Then he was in a black mood again when he returned hours later.

But even though that little memory made me smile, now I found myself with nothing to do, no one to talk to, and a body that no longer yearned for sleep.

I had been careful to keep my injured joint mobile, swinging and rolling it every hour or so, increasing the activity a little more each day. I thought perhaps to try pull-ups on the cage roof that day, but the moment I jumped up to take my own weight on my hands the joint screamed.

Too soon.

I sighed and began jogging a small, tight circle around the cage just to keep my blood pumping.

But then there was nothing left to do. And so, once I had caught my breath again, since I was still alone, I began to sing.

I crouch in shadows, but still your heart beats for me.
I am safe.
I lay in the arms of danger, but you do not leave.
I am safe.
I am safe in your arms.
Safe under your eyes.
Safe with you.
I am safe.
The shadows do not touch me.
Danger does not claw.
I am safe.
Rest with me, and find
I am sa—

The tent flap snapped aside and Melek strode in, his expression dark and his body lined with weariness. I opened my mouth to greet him, but to my surprise a small army of serving women followed in his wake, along with two young soldiers struggling under the weight of a very large bath. It was oval shaped at its base, but the rim was irregular, with one end higher than the other. All of it large enough for a massive Nephilim to sit comfortably inside.

I watched the soldiers drop the tub to the dirt, then turn. My heart flinched when the women behind them dropped their heads and jerked aside to let the males pass, their postures making it evident they feared being touched or hurt.

Once the two soldiers were gone, the line of slaves continued to file through, each carrying a large pot or pitcher that steamed. One by one, the women walked to the tub to empty their vessels—some glancing at Melek from the side while others avoided all eye-contact—then turned and exited the tent in single file.

They were as efficient as the soldiers that marched towards the battlefields.

But then one of them broke from the rank to slip up to my cage with a small smile. I recognized her as the woman who Melek had brought to speak with me the week before.

"Are you well, Yilan?" she asked graciously. "Do you have any further needs?"

"No, thank you," I said, smiling at her. "My courses are done. I am grateful for your thoughtfulness, though."

She ducked her head. "Please tell Melek if you have any further needs, I'm happy to fulfill them, even if it is during my rest hours."

I was about to thank her profusely—slaves had so few hours of rest that for her to offer to give them up was truly a gift. But then her eyes drifted to Melek and I saw her... *yearn.*

Ah.

That explained it.

I gave a little huff. "I'll remind him... when the time comes," I said quietly.

She nodded absentmindedly as she stepped into the line with the others, glancing one more time over her shoulder towards Melek.

Oblivious to her admiration, he stood over his clothing trunk unbuttoning his shirt, his face a cold mask, his eyes fixed on nothing as if he stared through the canvas wall.

What happened today? He seemed even darker than usual.

Had Gall said something?

It took some time before the last of the slaves poured her tall pitcher into the bath. The steaming pool, filled deep enough to submerge a Nephilim body, sloshed up the sides of the tub, nearly overtaking the rim.

She walked over to where Melek still stood, holding his belt and frowning at it. She curtseyed, then cleared her throat hesitantly when he didn't notice her.

He startled, as if he'd been deep in thought, then turned to face her, nodding when she indicated the full tub. "Do you have soap and a washcloth?" she asked him carefully. "Do you need assistance? I could scrub your—"

"*No,*" he said quickly, biting the word off so hard she flinched. He took a deep breath as if he was catching himself. "Thank you. I'll send Gall when I'm ready for it to be taken away."

She curtseyed again, which was odd, but then she turned and scuttled out like she was afraid. I watched her leave without really thinking, then turned back to find him shoving his leathers down, pulling them off his feet and folding them quickly to lay in the basket he used for the launderers.

Then he turned, entirely bare, and walked with a heavy sigh to the bathtub.

I quickly averted my eyes and kept them down until I heard the water splash and a deep groan of relief from Melek.

I looked up, surprised to hear such an emotive sound from him, to find him leaning against the high back of the tub with his head tipped back, eyes closed, and his arms resting along the rim on each side.

He was the picture of a troubled man in repose, his face no longer tight, but... pained.

I frowned. "Melek—"

"You have a beautiful voice," he rumbled without opening his eyes. "This has been a trying day. Would you... would you be willing to sing?"

I didn't think I'd ever been more startled by a request from a male—and startled again by how self-conscious I suddenly felt... and the warmth that bloomed in my chest at his compliment.

I almost teased him. Opened my mouth to tell him that we hadn't negotiated the terms of my release, and so I was not his servant. But the way he sighed and the lines on his face...

I cleared my throat. "I... I'll try," I said. Then repeated the song I'd been singing before.

I crouch in shadows, but still your heart beats for me.
I am safe.
I lay in the arms of danger, but you do not leave.
I am safe.

I am safe in your arms.
Safe under your eyes.
Safe with you.
I am safe.
The shadows do not touch me.
Danger does not claw.
I am safe.
Rest with me, and
I am safe.
Do not fear for me while your arms hold me close.
Do not fear the dark while your eyes watch.
I am safe.
I am safe.

He sighed more than once during the song, and when I let the last note hang in the air, for a moment I thought he might have fallen asleep.

But then, without opening his eyes, without moving, he spoke.

"We should have taken the ravine already," he said, so quietly I could barely hear him and no doubt to ensure that no one else would be able to either. "If my instructions were followed, we would have. But I believe... I believe our *Commander* grows greedy."

I blinked. It was the first time he'd spoken to me by choice all week. I swallowed hard.

"Greedy for... what?"

"We possess the land leading into the ravine already—there was one scout sent out, and our trackers avoided him easily. So, if they were to try and push through the Ravine, we would have them."

"Then why haven't you taken the rest? Is it the sinkholes?"

"No," he growled. "We have followed runners and mapped three paths through now. No, it is not that. Instead, we sit on our asses, risking discovery every day because the *Commander* has decided that more troops are needed, that the easily hidden three hundred spears we had were no longer enough. He demands we *more than triple* it so that when we advance into the swamp, we will have an actual force ready to fly the cliffs and descend on *both* armies. Which would be excellent... if it didn't delay our movements by a full week in order to bring the ranks across the plains and into the ravine without being spotted," he snarled through his teeth.

Dear *God*. "You're being set up for failure," I said.

He didn't open his eyes, but I saw his hands grip the side of the bath. "I don't know."

I sighed, shaking my head. "Melek, I know that he is—"

"There is no point speculating. I have done what I can to ensure the safety of our ranks, and our victory. All that is left is to wait and see."

I frowned. "Then why—"

"There are more pressing matters tonight," he muttered, then waved one hand towards the tent flap.

Ah. "Gall," I sighed, nodding. "I meant what I said when I offered to smooth that road. Without undermining your story, I have been trying to... help him soften."

Twice I'd had a chance to actually speak with Gall. Only a few minutes each time.

He wasn't ready to listen about *anything* to do with that night.

But Melek shook his head against the rim of the bath, his eyes still closed. "Nothing can be done. Nothing *should* be done. Nothing about this can change. Don't try."

I took a deep breath. "But... you don't deserve his ire. You deserve his admiration."

Melek's eyes opened. He blinked at the tent ceiling twice, then lifted his head and looked at me, his expression stunned. "Did you just... compliment me?" he asked incredulously, with a wry twist of lips.

I rolled my eyes, but nodded. "You said to speak truth. I am. I hate seeing him hurt, and... and I hate seeing it hurt you."

I still had my chin down, but I lifted my eyes to look at him from under my brows, wondering if he would grow angry again and stop speaking.

But he just stared at me, his face blank. Unreadable.

Except... something crackled in the air. Something I didn't understand. Something I wouldn't allow myself to think on, because it *could not be.* But my breath quickened.

Then he jerked his eyes away, shaking his head like he shook off some kind of fog. Then he pushed himself to sit upright and reached for the soap and the rag he'd left on the other side of the bath. Plunging both into the water, his jaw set and eyes down on his task, he began to wash himself.

And I found myself unable to look away.

His movements were efficient, strong, and confident—the quick, thoughtless movements of a soldier at a task he'd done countless times before.

He stretched high first one hand, then the other, revealing snatches of coarse hair in his armpits, coiled muscle on his arm, and rippling lines down his ribs and sides as he scrubbed. His expression remained troubled as he leaned forward, reaching over his shoulder to scrub the back of his neck and upper back in a move that, for a moment, made him vulnerable if someone were to aim for his chest.

And I found myself imagining *tsking,* telling him to give the rag to me. Then plunging it into the water, and adding soap before leaning on that glistening shoulder to reach in and scrub his back... those shoulder blades, that dip that ran the length of his spine, those rippling muscles in his back...

As he twisted and curled his body, contorting to reach difficult places, more and more of him was revealed.

I grew so lost in the vision in my mind of the other ways those muscles might contract and his body might twist, that my throat went dry and *my* body began to thrum—deep in my belly, high between my thighs...

My breath grew shallow.

Had there ever been a more masculine, more alluring male form? If so, I had not seen it.

And that was a problem.

That was a very big fucking problem.

22. Torment

SOUNDTRACK: *Going to Hell* by Bryce Savage

~ MELEK ~

I felt her eyes on me and discovered that I was not the slave to self-discipline I had always striven to be.

Had I ever scrubbed my arms three times before?

No.

Had I ever worked harder to reach the center of my back, or been more assiduous about cleaning my chest?

Never.

But then, I couldn't remember ever feeling eyes on my skin that blazed like the sun. The heat of her gaze warming me so that I began to sweat.

Which of course meant I would need to wash again.

Then her breathing grew shallow and my body began to tighten.

I grit my teeth against the rush, but could not stop it.

My dreams had been invaded by her ever since that night—the night she'd fought for Gall. The night I'd had her naked and vulnerable. The night I'd touched her warm, soft skin, and stood over her in the dark…

Every night since then she had invaded my dreams. Against my will, my sleeping mind conjured visions of her joining me in my bed. Uninjured. Not coerced. And definitely not an enemy…

On the nights I didn't wake tight and throbbing, instead I gasped awake in a cold sweat from nightmares of her being taken by those fuckers, or being unable to reach the two of them in time and Gall dying in the fight for her.

I was exhausted from fighting *myself.*

But as I bathed here in my own tent, under her eyes, I stopped fighting what I knew to be true: Something in me had shifted—weakened! And no matter how I tried, I could not move it back.

For a week I had stayed away from her. Refused to acknowledge her. Refusing to indulge myself in the slightest.

But tonight, I had finally lost the struggle with Gault about our battle choices, and I found myself even weaker.

Weak to temptation.

Weak to indulgence.

Weak to *her.*

Even in bringing the bath I'd known I was testing her. Teasing. Gauging whether she was as tormented by me as I was by her.

I thought the answer was... *not quite.*

But not, *not at all.*

When I heard her breathing grow quicker—shallower, I got so hard it ached. I had to swallow against the urge to simply stand up, stride over to that fucking cage and pull her out of it, strip her naked and plunge into her.

God, she'd hate me forever.

And so... I bathed. And prayed for mercy. And self control. And—

The cage, the tent, everything *practical* disappeared. I turned to find her standing several strides away in nothing but my sleep shirt, her bare legs hinting that she wore *nothing* but that long cotton.

Her head was tilted and her lips pulled up on one side as she reached for the buttons.

The shirt was so large on her that the first button nestled right at the center of her chest, between her breasts. Her smile got wider as her small fingers slid it free and the two sides of the shirt fell apart revealing a scant inch of that pale, unblemished skin and the barest crescent of the soft rounds of her breasts.

Then her hands drifted down to the next one.

And the next.

And then the last. The shift fell open—baring *all* of her, except her breasts—but she only reached up to the collar and pulled it wide, sliding it back, off her shoulders until all that cotton dropped, fluttering as it rippled over her ass then fell to the dirt behind her.

My nostrils flared as she started towards me slowly but steadily, her eyes never dropping mine until she reached the side of the bath, then scanned my body.

I felt that look like fingernails clawed along my jaw, down my neck, over my pecs, and then lower… and lower.

And her breath got faster again.

"Not a lot of room left for me," she whispered as she leaned down to take hold of the edge of the tub.

It was large for her. She was forced to lift one leg carefully, then the other to step in, placing her tiny feet to the sides of my thighs. And just as her second foot reached the bottom, she wobbled and clapped a hand to my shoulder to help herself balance.

Except I caught her arm and we both froze. Not breathing.

There was a single, silent moment that we stared. Then I threw my scruples aside like unwanted rubbish and pulled her down into my lap to straddle my thighs.

Not nearly close enough.

I growled and grabbed for her ass with both hands, pulling her forward against my straining cock so that we were brought together. When she tilted her hips as she found her balance, she slid against me.

She bit her lip and I groaned.

Our eyes never strayed, even when she reached for the soap and cloth, even when she wet them both and made the cloth soapy… and especially when she began to wash me. Starting at my neck, her small hand fit high under my throat as her thumb drew the cloth along the line of my jaw.

Her eyes never left mine, but they glazed over and her lower lip went slack as I pulled her hard against me again and this time indulged in my *own* hip roll, pressing my length against her.

I hadn't even tried to control myself. My breathing was harsh and heavy, hot in contrast with the cool air of the tent.

Then she looked down to see me there, between her legs, thick and full and *wanting,* and her eyes got wider.

I growled, sliding a hand to her jaw, my fingers curling around the back of her neck while I traced her cheek with my thumb.

And just as I was about to pull her closer, to take that soft pink mouth, and the rest of her too, she shook her head slightly—but started using both hands to bathe me. Soaping them to so they were slick, she ran them all over my chest, then down… over my abs. Then she ran her tiny fingers along the paths between my muscles that were even more defined now, because I wanted her so badly my stomach clenched as hard as my teeth.

And then, just as my pulse began to vibrate in my skin, she bit her lip, soaped her hands again, and reached for me.

The position meant her upper arms pressed her breasts together and towards me and I almost came at the sight of her soapy, slick, little hands, cupping around me, sliding up and down, and her breath short and quick fluttering against my wet skin and her breasts *right there.*

I groaned and dropped my head back against the bath, gritting teeth against the *immediate* need for release. But she didn't stop.

Her eyes were wide and her hips rolled—I suspected she didn't even realize she was seeking her own pleasure against me. But she didn't stop, up and down, slowly at first, softly, teasing my flesh until I hummed with need.

I didn't lift my head but dropped my eyes, watching the way I pressed up between her legs—and then her hands.

I imagined tipping her forward and thrusting between her beautiful breasts.

Then I imagined grasping her hips, lifting her, and pulling her down onto me, impaling her with a roar.

But I did nothing—one hand on her, the other gripping the side of the bath as my body tensed and shivered, and my orgasm beckoned. I closed my eyes again, trying to fight it off. But then my legs began to shake, and her breath became a pant. And when I couldn't resist and looked at her again, it was to find her watching herself touch me, her nipples hard points and lower lip slack.

My orgasm detonated at the base of my spine, and I did roar then. Grabbing for her hands, keeping them tight on me as my breath froze and I pumped twice, three times... then I shuddered and slumped, releasing her hands as my head clunked back against the rim of the bathtub.

But she moved with me, leaning forward over my body, her hands sliding up my chest, fingers lacing behind my neck, holding herself close to me as my body twitched and jerked in the throes of that orgasm.

"Yilan—"

Her nose almost brushed mine, her eyes locked in, shining as she smiled.

"Thank you. For saving me. That was... thank you."

I blinked and everything *practical* reappeared—the tent was back, my bed, my clothing trunk, the cage… and Yilan—still fully clothed, sitting on her cot and staring.

And to my horror, I found the hands on me were… mine.

What the—?!

Grabbing for the soap and cloth, trying desperately to swallow back my panting breath, I blinked again and again.

It had been so real. So *visual.* How—

Then I froze.

The Fetch.

It was said they could speak to each other in their minds. Said that they could turn eyes away without their owners knowing their minds had been changed.

But I had assumed that was only rumor. Similar to some of the more ridiculous stories that haunted the Nephilim.

I snapped my head around to look at her, uncertain whether I was angry or afraid.

Her eyes were wide… and her cheeks were red.

I swallowed hard. "Did you… was that—?"

"Thank you. For saving me," she breathed. "That was… thank you."

Then, as I sat there stunned, she laid down on the cot, pulled the blanket over her bad shoulder and rolled herself up in it with her back to me.

I gaped for a moment, confused and turned on and…

And suddenly fucking furious.

23. Curiosity

~ *MELEK* ~

"Don't you turn your back on me," I snarled, my chest, already tight from the shock and arousal, now constricting against the fire of rage. "What the actual *fuck?!*"

She jerked a little, like she'd been able to roll over, but her shoulder must have hurt, because she hissed, then slowly leaned up on her good arm before pushing herself up to sit, then turning to face me, pulling that blanket around her.

Her chin was low and she looked up at me warily from between the black curtains of her hair. "I wasn't turning my back, I was just—"

"How the fuck did you do that? You can just insert thoughts in my head? Just make me see things?"

"No! No... Melek, it wasn't... Not like that. It was... I can form visions... show you things your mind would conjure, or-or that you *want*—"

"Don't fucking tell me what I want!" I shoved out of the bath, heedless of the water splashing into the dirt and sliding down my body. "I didn't *want* that! I didn't ask for that! You're lying!"

"No! I'm not!"

As I stalked towards her, Yilan's eyes got wider, but her expression got fiercer too.

"Fucking Fetch and your fucking mind games. Is that why you're here? To turn my head and—"

"No! I can't put anything in your mind that you're opposed to receiving!"

"Bull*shit!* I *never* wanted *that!*"

"Are you lying to yourself? Or to me?" she asked quietly, still keeping her chin low even though I now stood dripping at the bars, looming over her.

I was breathing heavily, arms at my sides, hands loose, but ready to grab for that fucking cage—for *her!*

But she just stared. I caught the little bob of her throat, but she didn't look away.

"I cannot create false awareness," she said warily. "I cannot make you see the real word as if it isn't there. I can... *show* you things. But I cannot create your thoughts. Those are all yours."

"Influenced by your mind-fuckery and—"

"All you have to do to stop me or any of my kind from... *showing* you anything is resist," she said carefully. "If you don't resist... *well...*" she shrugged, and a tiny light of amusement lit in her gaze.

I glared. "I don't believe you."

"I cannot enter your mind if you defend it, Melek," she said blandly. "And even when I can, all you have to do is push the image away if you don't want it."

"So you say, but—"

"Try it," she murmured.

I was about to open my mouth, to demand that she never again enter my head, when another image appeared there—an image of... *me.*

It was her memory. The moment I'd entered the King's tent, striding into his presence then kneeling. And although I knew the memory was true—I remembered that moment, knew she was showing me the truth of what I'd done and what I'd said—the vision was... colored differently.

Breathless.

Awed.

Nervous.

"You can see that it's from me. You know that. Push it away, Melek," she said quietly.

But it took me a moment, because there was something I didn't understand: An inkling in her memory of *hope.*

Was the memory colored by her own thoughts and feelings in that moment? Or was she merely trying to soften me so I wouldn't be so angry?

I didn't know, but I sucked in a deep breath, took hold of myself, and pushed the images away.

And sure enough… they were gone.

Vapor blown on the wind.

Relief coursed through me—but was immediately followed by suspicion. Had she only let go of the control so I'd believe I could make her do it?

"Fetch are not evil, Melek," she whispered. "We are not puppet masters—not in that way. I can give you images, show you things. But you can deny it at any time. And the more opposed you are to receiving what I show you, the harder it is to make the connection at all. If you do not want me in your mind, simply decide so. Like holding your hands over your ears—my whispers will not penetrate."

I rolled my jaw, considering her words.

They could be blatant lies. But I didn't think so.

Over forty years on this earth and I had learned to trust the instincts God gave me. They'd led me through battle, helped me navigate tense political conflicts, even friendships…

Then I blinked and focused on her properly.

She was still sitting, holding her injured arm carefully, chin down and eyes up on me. There was no guile in her expression.

There was some fear.

"Why?" I asked her bluntly. "If… why would you do that? Was it truly simple gratitude? It seems an odd way to… *thank* me."

She cleared her throat and dropped her gaze to the floor. "I may have… overstepped," she murmured, grimacing. "But you should know it… I could not… I *would* not have contact with your mind in that way if I did not trust your… restraint."

Restraint. Of course. She'd been abused, threatened, on the cusp of violation and I had saved her.

It was a strange response, but not uncommon. I'd seen it in men on the battlefield—winners in the end, but having walked the line of death, it was as if every emotion, every drive were heightened.

Desire became need, and need became survival.

In the wake of battle, I had fallen into the arms of a woman more than once myself.

And those moments were nothing. A drive. A need to *feel*.

I stared at her, still unwilling to trust, but cautiously accepting that perhaps I understood what had just happened more than she did. And that understanding gave me compassion for what she had been through, but also left me a little... sad.

"I will not violate you, Yilan. I would kill you first."

"I know," she said simply.

I nodded. My anger beginning to pass, though my unease did not.

"Rest assured—for yourself and your men—that is not easily done. Fetch do not enter the minds of those without the gift easily. We must be close, and as I said, all it takes is your resistance."

"But if you seduce, or intrigue, or *anything* when their defenses are down..."

She nodded once. "It is a tool. But not flawless. And it... drains me."

I narrowed my eyes. "Then why? Why for such a...a flippant purpose, if it wasn't an attempt to draw me into deception?"

Her expression was strange, half-frown, half-fear. As if her thoughts turned inward in alarm. And when she answered, I was once again left stunned.

"I was curious," she said, squirming slightly, not meeting my eyes. "And I did have a desire to give you... something for your help."

"That is not the kind of thanking I need," I growled.

"I know. Which is why it was easy to gift it," she said simply.

And what was I supposed to say to that?

24. Covenant

~ *MELEK* ~

An hour later, I lay in the dark, my body weary but clean, and relaxed from both the heat of the bath, and my climax. But my mind raced, replaying those moments in the vision, though I would never have admitted it.

Much of it had gone in ways I would never have created for myself—my fantasies would be *far* more erotic. And yet...

And yet there was something about those simple touches from those small hands that had left me shuddering harder than any tumble ever had before.

I still suspected she was toying with me.

Except, I really hadn't *felt* her playing games. Not like the flirting she did with Jann. And her discomfort when I asked her why...

But if she wasn't teasing or manipulating, then why?

Curiosity, she said. About me? Or any Nephilim?

It was true some women sought us out. Our physical size and strength—even the brutality of my brothers was an aphrodisiac for some.

The thought that perhaps Yilan wanted me left me warm... and *deeply* uneasy.

And if it was her in my mind, the fact that she'd chosen not to pleasure *herself* too was confusing and left me nervous. The memory of her words in the vision that she'd then echoed in truth came to mind.

"Thank you. For saving me. That was... thank you."

I didn't like how that felt.

After the first time I'd watched a woman torn apart in a Nephilim frenzy, I'd always sworn I'd never let myself lose control in that way. Restraint meant that while my sexual exploits were satisfying, they were rare. And *always* with a consenting adult.

Sadly, over time I had learned the hard way that some women would give themselves not out of desire, but gratitude. Seeking protection in the arms of a male they thought would keep them from others—not because they desired them.

Was that what she was doing? Drawing me closer to assure my protection?

She already had it. Did she not realize that yet?

I didn't know. But I found, as I slipped closer and closer to sleep, that I deeply, deeply hoped it was not simple gratitude.

And if my mind had truly been open to that, I fervently prayed that it was nothing more than a moment of weakness. Because no matter what she might want, this... whatever it was that now crackled between us... it simply could not happen.

At least, that was what I told myself as I finally gave in to sleep. Because any other thought was far, far too dangerous.

~ *YILAN* ~

Melek was gone the next morning when I woke up.

I wasn't sure how to feel about that. Or rather, I didn't like that it felt like a rejection.

I'd only given him a vision. None of it had actually happened. But I found my body thrumming with pleasure as if it had.

And *that* made my heart shrink. If I *had* given myself to an enemy with such abandon, it was an offense to the crown.

And yet, I hadn't.

But I felt like I had.

And I felt like I maybe *wanted* to. But I never would.

Well, *never* was a strong word.

And yet...

I groaned. Running circles in my head like the circles I ran in the cage to keep my body strong would get me nowhere.

As the day drew on and Melek still didn't appear, my tension grew wondering if he was avoiding me. He'd been furious last night. Clearly off-balance.

My mind conjured the moment he stood over the cage, naked, body gleaming wet and dripping... and that fire in my belly flared alarmingly.

I hurriedly pushed the thoughts away, just like I'd told him to do the night before. But the restless simmer wouldn't leave me.

Where was he? Why leave me *now?*

But I would sleep that night with no answers because Melek was gone all day until the very small hours of morning. And when he returned, he did nothing but fall into bed clothed and sleep for a few hours before leaving again, instructing Gall to stay with me.

Then he walked out and he didn't even meet my eyes.

Nerves fluttered like butterflies in my stomach. I turned to Gall, hoping to find a way to reassure him without breaching Melek's order not to tell him any secrets. But Gall was sullen and quiet.

He was very attentive to my needs though, so on one of the trips when he brought me a fresh waterskin I tried to get him talking.

But even though he was sweet—checking to find out what I needed—he also wouldn't meet my eyes.

"Gall," I said at one point. "You don't have to be worried for me. I'm fine."

His jaw went tight and his golden eyes finally lifted from the dirt to meet mine, but then flicked away almost immediately. "You got hurt. And it was my fault. You don't have to make me feel better. I'm not a child anymore. I can take it."

"No! Gall—"

"It's okay, Yilan. You just rest and get better. I'll make sure you have all the things you need."

"But, Gall, it wasn't your fault those men—"

"Yes. It was," he said through his teeth. "They confused me and I made a bad decision. And you got hurt. And Melek—" He bit his father's name off with bared teeth and turned quickly away from me, shaking his head as he marched towards the tent entrance.

"Gall, don't go! Come talk to me."

"No. It's dangerous," he mumbled. "I have to stand guard and not let anyone in. Except *Melek,*" he said bitterly.

My heart broke, but he was gone, pushing through the tent flap. I knew he'd set himself a task and wouldn't be turned from it. It would stress him if I tried.

So, I fell back onto the cot, sighing in frustration, waiting for Melek to return. We *had* to figure out a way to tell Gall so he didn't carry that.

But Melek was nowhere to be seen. And Gall remained guarding outside the tent.

There were a couple of hours when it rained that he came inside, but he spent the time marching back and forth in front of the cage door to *prove his attention.*

And after a gentle attempt to speak with him again clearly stressed him out, I stopped trying.

My frustration and uncertainty grew for two days. Apart from singing, I had nothing to do, and no one to speak with. I had only my own mind for company. And my mind was not an easy place to be just then.

Two days. Two days where I cursed myself for the indulgence of interfering with Melek's mind like that, for revealing the truth of my power—and for finding him attractive enough to have done so in the first place.

By the third, it became clear that he wasn't just busy, but intentionally staying away from me.

I *had* to convince Melek to relax with me again—and between us, we needed to find a way to let Gall be at ease.

On the third morning I woke and it seemed that nothing had changed. Melek's bed was empty just as it had been late the night before when I went to sleep.

The morning sun beamed against the tent from the east, casting Gall's shadow over the doorway and the silhouette of flickering leaves and branches across the ceiling.

It seemed it would be another boring, frustrating day.

But then a distant *hum* caught my attention.

My instincts alerted, like pricked ears. I sat up, but couldn't quite place the sound. Occasionally I caught a raised voice, but it was too distant to make out the words.

When Gall came in minutes later to see if I wanted breakfast, I asked him.

"Is something going on in camp today?"

Gall's brows rose. "Didn't Melek tell you?"

"Tell me what?"

"It's the Covenant Days of Peace."

It was? I had already been here for how long? Of course. Holy *shit...*

Traditionally, the Days are a time of recognition for blessings, and for peace negotiations. Five days—first day, to fifth day—during which every people on the Continent rested, feasted, and called truce in battle.

It is a time to remember the Covenant of God with Man and the peace treaties between peoples of the past. A time to reflect on life as it would be without conflict or competition. And intended to motivate all to *seek* peace.

The rest of the Continent celebrated the Days, yet I'd never been sure the Nephilim did. But the way I heard Melek roar at Jannus that morning outside the tent about how *this was exactly what he'd been working to avoid* indicated that, apparently, they did. And Melek was not happy that they had not taken the ravine before this.

Even though the Covenant didn't technically begin until midnight, that hum of anticipation increased throughout the day, and the strains of music and echo of raised voices began in camp early in the afternoon.

By late afternoon, the camp was awash with the sounds of men dancing, playing music, and from the sound of their horrendous off-key singing, mostly drinking.

Even Gall's expression was a little lighter when he came to check on me throughout the day.

But the true surprise was the moment Melek appeared, just before dinner time. And it wasn't simply to pick up a weapon or dig through a trunk, then leave again with hurried instructions to Gall.

When he pushed through the tent flap it was with a platter of food in each hand and his head turned back to call Gall over his shoulder. "Gall! Fuck midnight. Everyone else is already resting. Come eat!"

He strode to the center of the tent where he'd left the table chairs set up and plonked the platters down.

Gall pulled back the flap to peer into the tent, his brows high and expression uncertain. "I am guarding, Papa—I mean, Sir. The others—"

"Apart from the perimeter guards who cannot leave their posts, there is not a single, sober soul in a five-mile radius—including the King, and our enemies. There is nothing more to be done. What will be will be... Please, Gall. Come sit with me, Son. These are the

Covenant Days—the days to remember blessings, to seek peace, and… and to forgive sins. Please. Eat with me?"

I held my breath—and suspected Melek did too—as Gall stared at him, perplexed and obviously tempted, but a frown still pinching his brow.

He opened his mouth once, then closed it. Then stared at his father.

There was a moment that passed between them then, a pleading on Melek's face, and a soft uncertainty in Gall's, that made my heart squeeze.

When Gall looked at me, I nodded, then tipped my head towards the table. "Eat," I murmured, forcing myself not to clap with relief and hope when Gall finally stepped inside, his expression still uncertain.

And even though it meant that I had to wait for my meal, I sat there in the cage happily for over an hour, watching the two eat. At first it was just two warriors diving into food like pigs at a trough. Melek ate with gusto, but watched Gall the whole time, who also ate heartily, but kept his attention on his plate and avoided eye-contact with both his father and me.

But as their plates began to clear, Melek sat back in his seat and stared right at Gall, whose shoulders hunched higher and tighter towards his ears with every passing moment, until he finally took his last mouthful and pushed the plate away.

"Thank you for the meal father, I'll—"

"You'll stay here and talk to me, Gall. It's time."

Gall stilled, hands on the edge of the table like he'd been about to push out of the seat. He swallowed. "I don't want to talk."

"We need to. Remember? Bad feelings don't go away until you say them out loud. Plus, it's the Days of Peace. I want to be at peace with you, Gall. Can we do that?"

Gall's shoulders hunched higher. But he didn't speak.

Melek sighed. "Gall, I'm sorry that you had a difficult day when I was gone. I didn't mean for you to have to handle her on your own. I was irresponsible in not sending someone else when Jann had to come with us. As your leader, I put you in a place that was too tricky for anyone in your position, and I'm sorry."

Gall lips twisted. He kept his head down like he was trying to keep his eyes off of Melek. "I'm sorry I listened to them when they said they were friends," he mumbled quietly. "I'm sorry you had to stop them…" but then he trailed off.

174

Melek sighed again. "Gall, I'm sorry you saw things that upset you. Do you remember the conversation we had about war? About how sometimes bad things are necessary to stop worse things from happening?"

Gall's head snapped up and his eyes met Melek's. His father just stared at him calmly, waiting.

I bit my lip, inwardly cursing that he didn't just tell Gall the truth. But I understood. My sister thought in similar ways to Gall. And even though she understood secrets, and attempted to keep them, she was very poor at hiding facial expressions. Words she thought were veiled were often far clearer than she realized. And if she was frightened, or angry, she might blurt things out without thought.

So, I knew *why* Melek thought it was too risky for Gall to be told the truth. But I desperately wished it wasn't so.

"That wasn't just bad," Gall insisted, dragging me back to their conversation. "You always taught me—"

"And I taught you true, Gall. Everything I said was true. I'm asking you to trust me that *in this instance only,* what you saw was necessary."

"I don't... *I don't understand,"* Gall said through his teeth, his hands gripping the edge of the table so hard his knuckles turned white.

I wanted to weep. It was obvious that Gall *hated* admitting that.

Melek's face softened as well and he leaned forward, elbows on the table. "I know, Son. I do. But this is like... like when I receive battle plans and I can't share them, even with the soldiers. Not until the time is right. This is just like that. I cannot explain right now. But I will. When the time is right. I promise."

Gall blinked. "You promise?"

"I promise. You have my word that when I can, I will explain all of this."

Gall's Adam's apple jumped. He stared at Melek with a mixture of fear and hope, then finally he nodded. "Okay."

I felt my body relax at the same time Melek slumped and muttered something under his breath that I thought was *Thank God.*

He pushed out of his chair and stepped up to Gall's seat, pulling his son out of the chair and into an embrace so tight that it brought tears to my eyes—and Gall's.

It was easy to see when they broke apart that Gall was still uneasy, but in the childlike way his precious heart had, it was also clear he'd decided to forgive and trust.

I was suddenly washed in a deep longing for my sister. For her intense hugs. Her bright smile. Her hilarious observations about life that she had no idea were funny. And... for home.

The Covenant Days of Peace...

Thoughts of everything that should have been happening in *my* life came crowding in, but I pushed them away. Because there was absolutely *nothing* I could do about it. But as the two men stepped apart and gathered themselves, settled back into their chairs and began to talk, I allowed myself the feelings.

I allowed myself to feel the loss. I allowed myself to miss my loved ones, and be grateful that events had spun out of our control. And I allowed myself to feel the relief—and the self-disgust for it. And then, a very, very tentative hope for the future.

A future that was now very foggy. In part because of the man who sat in front of me, now eagerly asking his son the questions they hadn't discussed for the past ten days.

In the spirit of the Days of Peace, I made a resolution that no matter what happened when I was finally free, I would not forget this moment. I would honor these two men in my mind for their kindness and strength. And no matter what happened in future, one day I would tell Gall the truth about his very honorable father.

25. Dinner for Two

~ YILAN ~

I lay there on my cot, happily drowsing for the next hour as they continued to speak and reconnect. Although I was hungry, I didn't want to interrupt this precious reunion.

I must have fallen asleep, because it was entirely dark outside and the lanterns had been lit when a clanging sound woke me with a jolt.

I sat bolt-upright—my shoulder giving a zing of pain and my heart racing... then galloping when I looked around to find Melek standing just outside the cage door, staring at me with a strange look on his face.

The *open* cage door.

When our eyes caught his forehead pinched. I blinked and breathed, heart racing, trying to figure out if I was dreaming or—

"I still don't trust you," he muttered.

I swallowed hard and nodded.

"And yet, I find myself in the mood to give a certain *fuck you* to... those around me." He clawed his hands through his hair and raised his chin. "It is the Covenant Days. I seek God blessings at all sides. And He blesses those of us who seek peace and offer hands to enemies on these days."

My breathing got shallow. I nodded again because I wasn't sure what to say.

Melek took a deep breath then folded his arms. "Give me your word that you will not flee, or harm me or Gall, and you can join me at the table. Unbound," he said.

I blinked and looked past him to see a new, fresh platter of steaming food sitting on the table.

"Your dinner," he added.

"I—"

"Give me your word, Yilan. Before God."

I stared at him, shocked. "I do. I mean, I will. I mean—"

"I know what you mean," he muttered as he stepped back, opening an arm towards the table, leaving room for me to walk out of the cage.

I had never been more stunned. "But... *Why?*" Was it a trap?

He sighed. "Yilan, it is the Covenant Days of Peace. I am reunited with my son. You are safe. And there is nothing that can be done about the struggles in our lives for another five days. God will bless me for blessing my enemy—which *definitely* includes you," he said with a wry look. "Even you aren't heathen enough to break the Covenant, surely?"

"Is it after midnight?" I asked, pretending to consider his proposal. "After all, if it isn't, I technically wouldn't be *breaking* the Covenant—"

He growled, and it startled a laugh out of me.

Then we both went serious.

I stared at him and he stared back and neither of us spoke for a time, yet that *hum* was in the air.

"Where's Gall?" I murmured.

"I gave him the Covenant Days off. He's gone to be alone which is his favorite thing to do when he's confused, or had a bad event."

I was reminded again, then, of my own life. My own *plans*. I found myself washed in grief and tension, compassion... and relief.

The Covenant Days.

I had a life—had had a life—before I was taken here. My people celebrated the Covenant with great abandon. And I had had plans for a great celebration at this time.

My chest tightened and it must have shown on my face because Melek's face went serious.

"What?" he asked.

Nothing I could speak to you about. I shrugged to hide my discomfort. "I suppose I just assumed the soulless wouldn't honor such a life-giving covenant," I said slyly, then grinned at him.

Melek rolled his eyes. "Perhaps just for these days we can stay away from references to the *soulless?"*

"I don't know," I said seriously. "I mean, peace? Certainly. But I'm not going to *lie* for you."

He growled, and it made me giggle, and then I was cautiously walking out of that fucking cage—no hand clamped on my arm, or in my hair. No imminent threat. Nothing. Just a table and a meal and a huge General sitting across from me as I looked at him suspiciously.

"Did you poison this?" I asked, only half-joking.

He huffed. "Only one way to find out."

"That's not reassuring."

"I said I was going to bless my enemy, not *indulge* them," he muttered, one brow arched high.

So, I took the seat and had dinner with General Melek Handras. Or rather, *I* had dinner, and he sat with me.

It was… a surreal experience.

Melek had a bowl of grapes in front of his seat and he ate them one by one as I dug into the meal and tried to tell myself this was actually real.

Our talk moved from Gall to the war. Then a jibe from me that I could confidently help Melek defeat our neighbors because the Nephilim would never survive the Shadows of Shade led our conversation to the differences between our people and how they would celebrate the Covenant Days.

That subject turned my mind back to the stark realities of how differently this night would have been spent if I hadn't been here with Melek. And that was… uneasy.

Melek must have sensed that I was shying from something.

"You don't speak of your own traditions much," he said quietly, watching me closely as he popped another grape into his mouth.

I took another mouthful of the juicy beef dripping in gravy before I answered.

"There didn't seem to be much point."

He gave me a skeptical look, but didn't press the point.

"Are you married?"

I shook my head, then watched him, alarms jangling in my head as I realized I didn't know. "What about the *great* General Melek Handras? Has he a mate back home awaiting his return?"

He shook his head without hesitation. "No," he said emphatically. "I wouldn't wish a soldier's life on a mate. Our only females are humans. They are... fragile."

I raised an eyebrow, but he didn't correct himself. But it did give me an opening to ask him about the women among them, which I'd been curious about from the beginning.

"How do they come to be here?" I asked carefully. "The women, I mean. Is there a human population among the Nephilim, or—"

"They are mostly slaves," Melek said, his eyes dropping to the grapes. He took another and chewed it before continuing. "Generations of slaves. And more taken when they're needed. We have males as well, though very few."

My blood went cold. So, the rumors *were* true. "You really do steal human slaves from Meyrath?"

It was the nation on the western side of the Raven Peaks, a nearly impenetrable mountain range that acted as a natural fence along the Nephilim's border, both a warning and a protection for the rest of the continent. The high, freezing summits were nearly sheer cliffs. Only the Nephilim could cross because they could fly. But they rarely did.

Or should I say, rarely *had*.

Legends were recounted by the parents of every culture of the Continent, terrorizing stories of the Nephilim flying over the Raven Peaks, then descending on disobedient children, stealing them and taking them back to Ebonreach—their nation—to be slaves.

"I don't take slaves," Melek said firmly. "And I don't encourage it in others. But my people... yes. Women are enticed, seduced, even paid. But many are just... taken."

I suddenly lost my appetite. "Breeders," I said through my teeth.

Melek's eyes snapped to mine, a warning there, but he nodded slowly.

"Fucking *pigs,"* I muttered under my breath, stabbing the beef again, just for something to do with my hands.

"They aren't *all* taken against their will—"

"Even one is too many," I hissed. "And you have *generations?* Could you imagine if you were taken by a—but no, wait, what am I thinking. There are no other peoples that out-weigh the Nephilim.

No wonder your young think they can take a woman and ride her like a horse stolen from the neighbor's barn."

Melek's jaw rolled. "I don't condone it, Yilan."

"You do—by sitting here, you do."

"No, I—"

"Stop living in denial—"

"I cannot change the ways of my land—I can only show the right way!" Melek growled, leaning towards me, furious.

I met that fiery gaze and pointed my knife at him. "You *faked it* so they'd leave me alone. *That* is the example you set—"

A low puttering growl rippled through the room and my heart began to race.

"You would have preferred I take the risk that they frenzied and overpowered *me* to take you? Because that's where that was heading, Yilan," he said firmly, meeting my eyes unapologetically.

"Sick," I hissed, shaking my head and trying to hide the way my hands were beginning to tremble. "This entire society is just… *sick.*"

"Not *all* of us."

I huffed. "Don't think I'm going to *congratulate* you on simply abstaining from something monstrous that shouldn't happen *anyway.*"

Melek's eyes went flat. "I work hard to teach my men to take only the willing—"

"And yet, over forty years old and never married because of the risk to a woman when you leave her home?"

He gave an impatient huff, but shifted in his seat, as if his thoughts made *him* uncomfortable.

"Our cities aren't the same as a war camp. There is more… restraint. But from a weak woman's perspective, it's dangerous enough. Especially left unguarded. Unless I found the One God intended for me, a true mate, I wouldn't bring a woman into all of *this*. For obvious reasons," he muttered, his eyes flicking up to mine—an admission—then back down to his grapes.

I was still furious, but I knew I needed to keep him talking. He was growing tense and almost finished his grapes. I couldn't let him decide he needed to lock me back up. So, I forced myself to let the subject go.

Sort of.

I huffed. "I suppose no decent human female would accept your brutish pawing unless she'd been forced into a marriage contract anyway."

Melek snorted, but then shrugged. "We don't use marriage contracts."

"Oh? What do you do—swoop in from the sky and kidnap them, show them your *snakes,* and see if they don't faint?"

He gave me a flat look. "In our tradition marriage is rare. But when a woman is found to be a twin soul we speak a vow, then join bodies to complete the bond. It's far more binding than signing a piece of paper."

I froze with my fork halfway to my mouth.

Melek frowned and looked quickly around the tent. "What? Is something wrong?"

"You believe in soulbonds?" I squeaked.

He frowned deeper. "Of course. Don't you?"

"Yes, of course. But the Shadekin—the Fetch... we aren't descended from the irredeemable."

His eyes shuttered at that, so I rushed on.

"We also speak vows to acknowledge the bond," I told him hurriedly. "But we wrap a cord around our wrists and make love while bound together to symbolize the bond of our souls. It's said that the longer a Pair stays tied together after that first lovemaking, the stronger their bond will be."

His brows rose. "You don't use contracts either?"

"No. Anyone can write a word to paper. The soulbond is..."

"Eternal," he ended for me.

My breath stopped.

I wasn't sure whether to be offended that he seemed as shocked as I was that we were so closely aligned on this.

"Did you... are you... have you found your soulbond?" I blurted, then wanted to shovel the words back down my throat.

A moment later, he shook his head. "No."

Why did I feel relief? This monster should not inspire *relief* in me!

But then his expression went blank. "You, Yilan? Are you bonded?"

I shook my head. "I have never found the male who tied my soul in knots. Not that it would matter... would it?" I swallowed hard. "Would you keep me here, Melek, if I had a soulbond out there waiting for me?"

He didn't answer.

My mouth went dry.

Neither of us moved and I wasn't quite sure how all the air seemed to have gone from the tent—nor how we'd gotten to this place. Or what it meant.

Why was he staring so intently?

Why was I?

Still nothing had passed between us when suddenly a high, pure chime resonated through the air and was met by a roar from the Nephilim ranks in every corner of this mile-wide camp.

Midnight. The Covenant Days begin in earnest.

And still we were staring. I couldn't move. The hair on my arms rose. I couldn't tear my eyes from his—and yet every instinct within me screamed that I *must*.

But it was Melek who spoke first.

"The chime... the Covenant Days have truly begun." His eyes never left mine. I nodded, but didn't speak. He cleared his throat. "We have a tradition in our people that when the Chime rings each night, we offer a wish to God. A prayer for... for a gift."

We had a similar tradition, but I couldn't find the words to tell him.

His Adam's apple bobbed. "Do you have a wish for the peace season, Yilan?"

I nodded.

He blinked, but still didn't look away. "What is it?"

For a moment my mind *spun* with images from that erotic vision I'd given him—a total indulgence. A horrific breach of my integrity... and I had yet to regret it. But even as images of those moments flickered in my head I couldn't wrap my tongue around them. Couldn't make them real. Because we walked a cliff-edge. I didn't know how it had happened, but I knew it was real and I couldn't—no, *wouldn't*—be the one to step off the edge.

"Yilan?"

"Yes?" I breathed.

"What is your wish for the Days of peace?"

I swallowed to wet my throat, then croaked. "A bath."

And then Melek fucking *smiled*.

26. Quiet Night

~ YILAN ~

"Quickly—hold my belt, step in my steps, and make *no* sound," Melek breathed in my ear, then hitched up the strap on the long, soft bag that hung over his shoulder and slung across his chest, leaving his arms free.

We were crouched behind a rock nestled beneath a small tree, just at the edge of camp. The Nephilim around each of the fires that circled the camp and cast shifting shadows from the trees were supposed to be the only sober Nephilim left—except Melek himself.

And these two did appear to be sober—standing, leaning on their spears, bored and resentful, looking back over their shoulders towards the camp where the noise from the revelers was growing.

Melek froze when one of them looked towards our rock, but he was only scanning the dark. Then he sighed and told his companion he was going to take a piss.

When both the guards were distracted, Melek took off silently, bent in half yet running fast enough it was difficult for me to keep up—and still his steps were *silent*—staying in the shadows of the forest, following the lines of the dark, but moving farther and farther from the camp proper, until we crouched under a copse of trees fifty feet away.

Melek waited only seconds, then grabbed my hand and dragged me deep into the forest, looking back over his shoulder now and again, but otherwise heading steadily east.

When we'd been walking for a minute, he cast one last look over his shoulder, grinned into the dark, then slowed his pace and let go of my hand, which suddenly felt very cold.

A few minutes later the trees opened up and Melek drew to a halt. I stepped up beside him and sucked in a sharp breath.

We stood at the tree line. From here the land dropped away to a soft, sandy shore on a lake large enough that I couldn't see all of it, because it spread too far out to the right and left, the trees began to block it from sight.

In the dark, the water seemed like rich black metal, yet the moon was high and bright, and it glittered on the surface that was almost glassy flat. Only the tiniest ripples here and there to make the reflection of the moon's light waver.

"Melek…" I breathed. "Thank you!"

He chuckled as I ran straight down the steep shore and into the water, shrieking when the cold hit my heated skin, then clapping my hands over my mouth and freezing where I stood, where the water was still only just past my knees.

Slowly, I turned back to look at Melek who still stood in the shadows of the trees, unmoving, looking over his shoulder, then around at the night.

"No one is coming," he said in a low rumble a moment later, and I let myself hurry forward again, gasping when the freezing-cold water splashed up to drench me, but I couldn't have cared less. It had been *weeks* since I'd had more than a wet cloth to clean myself. Weeks since Melek dunked me in that trough—and that had come days after my last bath before it.

It was heaven to turn and let my body fall backwards into the water, submerging completely, blowing air bubbles from my nose as the ripple and hum of the water closed in around me, then breaking up and out of its cool surface, gasping at the air—and against the cold—but ecstatic.

"Thank you, Melek!" I whisper-shouted. "Thank you!"

He was walking down to the shore, but keeping watch for me as I wallowed and splashed and swam underwater.

Soon it didn't feel so cold. And then Melek gave a low whistle, so I stood up—just in time to catch the small block of soap he'd thrown to me out of the air before it thunked into my chest.

The General had excellent aim.

But I was too happy to be grumpy. Walking deeper into the lake until I could half-sit and submerge myself underwater to the neck. Then I took off my sopping clothes and scrubbed first myself, then them.

Some time later, wrinkled and happily exhausted, I made Melek turn his back and watch for anyone approaching while I got out of the water and threw my clothes over a couple of bushes to dry and wrapped myself in a Nephilim-sized towel that was large enough to wrap me from my neck to my ankles.

Then, when I was dry, I sat down on the lakeshore where the sand gave way to grass and listened to the tiny lapping of the water on the pebbles and stared up at the stars and felt like I could breathe for the first time in weeks.

Melek came down to the shore and sat just a few feet to my left, staring out over the water… and he looked relaxed as well. The set of his shoulders not quite so tight. His jaw not flexing.

Neither of us spoke for some time, and with the sound of the celebrating Nephilim distant enough to be ignored, the silent night and quiet ripple of the water was quite soothing. I found myself growing drowsy, eventually laying back on the grass and lacing my fingers under my wet hair.

"This is how life should be," I said quietly. "Just… quiet. Easy. No pressures. All noise in the distance. Don't you think, Melek? Or does your soldier's heart need the fight to feel alive?" I asked, considering some of the comments I'd heard from Turo, the General of the Shadekin, my people.

"I would give anything to never fight again… to have every day like this," Melek answered a moment later.

I sighed happily. "Me too."

My eyelids began to droop, but I was still awake when he spoke again.

"Enjoy your freedom, Yilan. May God bless you this night," he murmured the benediction. Not a whisper, but keeping his voice quiet.

"And you," I responded by rote, then blinked, realizing what I'd said.

Melek grinned, but didn't tease me, just continued staring into the beautiful dark.

~ MELEK ~

It was the strangest night I had ever lived.

It had been an indulgence to take her out. If I was honest, the idea had been one big *fuck you* to Gault for interfering in this war. At least, that's what I'd told myself.

But here I sat, not simmering in bitterness or resentment, but… resting.

I sat in the middle of a warzone, yet at peace. My body relaxed in a way I hadn't felt for *years*.

My comrades celebrated the peace, feasting and drinking just a mile away, and yet there was no part of me that wanted to join them.

Instead, I sat on a peaceful lakeshore, in the dark, with my *enemy*. And I couldn't remember a moment I'd felt more at ease.

It should not be. And yet, it was.

As Yilan slipped into a soft, easy sleep, I stared out over the water and let myself just breathe. The noise of the camp grew dim and distant as I sank deeper into my thoughts.

Watching her joy at being in the water had done something to my insides. But seeing those clothes come off had taken my mind back to that vision. Even though any hint of her skin was hidden from me by the moonlight on the water so I couldn't possibly tell if what I had seen was how she truly looked, my body tightened just knowing she was huddled there in the lake without a stitch.

I'd had to take my guarding duties very seriously to keep my eyes averted.

Then, when she was pruned and shivering, she'd finally admitted defeat and told me to turn my back so she could get out.

I heard her watery steps, heard the splashes, heard the tinkle of water dropping from her skin to the shallowing lake as she walked out—and my cursed mind conjured images of water flowing from that shiny, jet-black hair, down her shoulders, to her chest… the droplets trickling off her collarbones and down, diverted by the plump of her breasts so it trailed between them and—

I cursed under my breath and pushed the intrusive images away, growling and shifting my seat because the tightness in my body was becoming an ache.

But then a Nightcaw screamed and flew across the moon, and my eyes followed it until its silhouette disappeared against the surrounding forest above. And when I looked away, it was to her.

She'd fallen asleep, curled into that towel as if it were a blanket, her wet hair dark and shiny in the night, fanned out over the grass. The towel as almost as tall as her. She gripped the edge in her fists and tucked it under her chin—between that and her tiny stature, she should have looked like a child. And yet...

She lay on her side, her knees drawn up so her feet were covered by the towel too, making her even smaller. And yet...

And yet, her shoulder rose in a point that sloped down to the curve of her waist, then rose again sharply to the round of her hip in a deeply feminine shape that had never failed to draw my eye since the very first time I'd been blessed to see it as a young man.

Even with the meals she'd missed, even with the weight she'd lost, there was no mistaking her for a child.

And there was no pretending that her form did not affect me.

Yet, though undoubtedly a woman, she was still young. Twenty-five? Twenty-seven? Perhaps. It was harder to tell with humans. They aged differently.

I wanted to turn from her, to ignore the discomfort in my chest and *other areas* that seemed a constant companion now, but I also recognized the urge for the fear that it was and made myself see her. Made myself ask the question.

Why would God bring her here? Why bring her to *me?* Was she simply a temptation? A test? Or...

I wanted to shy away from any other explanation. But I had learned the hard way that avoiding thoughts because their conclusions might be difficult was the fastest track to regret and self-destruction.

So, I made myself ask.

Consider.

Confront.

Why would God bring her here? And to me, personally?

She was so young. We saw the world so differently. We understood *life* differently. We aimed for different goals. *Opposing* goals.

She was my enemy.

Why would God bring me a woman who sought to destroy me and my people?

Everything in me went still and cold as I caught the thought that had been whispering to me for days and that I had so tirelessly ignored.

No.

It could not be.

Surely?

She could not be intended for me.

She must be the vengeance on my people! Or... or the siren, lulling me into a false sense of security in order to lower my guard and—

Yilan shifted in her sleep, squirming and resettling, murmuring to herself as I stared at her like an asp crawling across the grass towards me, reminding myself she was a *Fetch*. A spy. An assassin.

She was the enemy. *Not* the rising sun of my heart. *Not!*

And then she sighed.

And then, as her body settled more deeply into sleep, she smiled.

I remembered her fierce protection of Gall, and that vision, and...

Something in my chest broke open, staring at her there in the dark. As I scanned her from head to toe with terrified eyes, my heart ripped in two—half of me driven to lift her, shake her, demand that she release me from this... this *death sentence*, to kill her and remove the threat... and the other half roaring at the world that she was *mine,* to place my body between her and this war that would destroy her, to cover her, to *possess* her and the world be damned if they thought my strength would be anything but a weapon to her protection, because she was precious, she was needed, she was *mate.*

A low, strange rumble began to curl in my chest. My chest that was pumping, squeezing, *shuddering.* My breath coming fast and too thin.

I was trembling.

Stunned.

Mate.

Soulmate.

Soulbond.

The other half of my soul... *if I possessed one.*

Whatever lived deep in my chest had come alive, even as I sat there, shaking my head, denying it.

I couldn't breathe.

It *couldn't* be.

She couldn't be.

Yet, everything in me sang that she *was*.

God help me.

27. Why?

SOUNDTRACK: *Lost* by Ghost Nation

~ YILAN ~

I woke slowly, not immediately aware that the bath hadn't been a dream. But the towel was cold where it had been wet against my skin. I shivered and came awake, blinking at the dark trees before I sat up quickly, mind racing, body tensed, clutching the towel to my chest and...

And there was no one on the shore with me. No one at the edge of the trees.

I was alone? Where—

The sound of displaced water rippling behind me tugged at my attention and I turned... but for a moment there was nothing.

It was still darkest night. The water black and gleaming like liquid metal, but the moonlight sparkling on its surface wherever it bobbed and rippled... Then suddenly it rippled a great deal twenty feet offshore.

The sound I'd heard of water moving must have been the moment Melek submerged.

Now, I froze at the sight of him, back to me, rising like a God from the lake, water sluicing from his head and hair—the length of which slicked down his spine. The water washed down his body leaving it gleaming in the moonlight, shining and wet, as he gasped at the cold and a shudder rocked through him.

Then he just... stood there, not quite waist-deep in the black, his hands extended and flat on the surface, his hair shining, reflecting moonlight like the flat of a blade. The muscles of his back seemed carved from marble, rippling and bunching with the slightest move. When he stilled, the water lapped at the hollow of his back, where his buttocks began.

For a moment I was taken by the sheer *beauty* of him. It was overwhelming. But as the water trickled away and I continued to stare, slowly I became aware of his scars.

So many.

Some simple, fine lines that seemed silver in this light and would be easily missed.

Others, ugly puckers and bunches, marring the incredible perfection of his back and shoulders.

It brought tears to my eyes.

He looked the way I felt: Battle weary. But strong.

And as the events of the previous days came back to me, one by one, I was washed in a rush of *understanding*. Understanding him. Feeling understood *by* him.

I had never experienced that before.

With only one exception, the men among my kind had always either admired me from afar—too weak to approach with intention—or sought to dominate me. Conquer me.

In either case, it seemed like they saw a prize, not a person.

But Melek...

I was suddenly, undeniably *sure* that he saw me. And moreover... that I saw him.

I knew he was a great General, a leader, and a great achiever.

He was also stubborn, given to dark moods.

And he was a father. *By choice.*

He had a heart that filled that broad drum of a chest to bursting. A heart so large and tender, he was forced to protect it at all costs.

I *understood.*

I did not want to understand.

There were pieces of him I *refused* to understand.

His shoulders rose and that back expanded as he took a deep breath. Then I watched, mouth dry, as he dropped into the water again, submerging entirely... and when he came up, this time his back was obscured *by a pair of massive wings,* feathered and black as night, but gleaming—glossy in the water.

He ducked into the lake again, rustling those wings that had appeared from nowhere, then stood, his body braced and strong as he stretched them out until they shadowed the water for a dozen feet either side of him and I couldn't inhale.

He was... awe-inspiring.

I'd always heard the rumors that the Nephilim had the power to call up wings, but I'd never imagined they would be so breathtaking.

Those wings shifted something in him—he held himself differently, his chin higher, his hands clenched. He flapped them once, twice, three times and they snapped like a sheet shaken out, the surface speckling with the tiny droplets sent raining back to the lake, and rippling with the air currents he blew up.

He turned his head, extending the right wing as if for examination, and his face came into profile—the hard line of his jaw, his brows rugged but not heavy. His expression firm. Certain. *Assured.*

This was his truest self.

This was what I'd seen in him from the beginning.

The intelligence and foresight. The maturity and self-restraint. The sheer strength.

Then his chest expanded again and he raised both wings high, stretching them as he arched his back, the moonlight highlighting the gleam of skin and feathers. He groaned and something about that sound—so full, so masculine—vibrated in my belly and I sucked in the breath I'd been waiting to take.

Melek heard my sharp intake and turned quickly, wings rustling in preparation for flight.

But our eyes locked.

And even at this distance, he pinned me with that gaze.

Neither of us made a sound, but the air hummed, that undeniable electricity crackling from his gaze, straight to my heart. From his body to my soul.

I leaned forward, bracing, prepared to leap to my feet and throw myself into that water... then all at once, I was reminded.

Who he was.

What he did.

Who he served.

How *impossible* it would be to be near him.

And all that energy building within me combusted to white-hot rage.

"Why do you do it?" I spat the words like venom.

Melek's face was an emotionless mask. "Do what?"

"You are strong, intelligent, honorable, *powerful.* And still you serve that petulant, hedonistic *child* of a King?" I hissed.

He turned, expression fierce, his wings snapping and water spraying from them again, pattering to the lake's surface. "The fact that you use those words shows how little you know him—selfish he may be, show me a royal that isn't! But call him stupid to your own demise. That male works to be *underestimated* by his enemies—and they always regret it. He is not stupid in the slightest. He is incredibly cunning, strong, and trained. He allows no one to see the sheer strength and fury that he possesses until he has need to use it—and then he *destroys* whoever stands in his path."

I got to my feet. "I bet he couldn't destroy you! Look at you! You're *magnificent.* Why do you hide the fullness of what you are, what you can be, and cower in his shadow?"

"I do not cower!" he snarled. "I lead!"

"Lead straight into his sweaty palms and wet prick," I seethed. "Lead his kingdom to victory and place the crown that should rightfully be yours on his head again, and again!"

"It is not rightfully mine!" he roared, slapping the water as he began marching towards me, the water roiling around him but seeming not to slow him in the slightest.

I scrambled to my feet, clutching the towel around me.

"Of course it is! These men follow you, not him! *You* are the one who has earned their trust. You are the one who makes them feel safe and sure so that they forge into battle with confidence—and win!"

"They win because we are blessed by God, not because of me—"

"Bullshit! If there is any blessing it comes to you and so they follow in your wake."

He'd made it to the shallows and was still coming for me, furious, rushing towards me onto the shore, water flying from him in every direction. I stared him down, refusing to take a backwards step as he stormed all the way up until he stood over me, toe-to-toe.

He was only more impressive up close—vital, furious, *male.*

And deep, deep in the back of my head a little voice whispered that, unlike the other men in my life, he did not restrain himself from me. That he came at me as an equal. Not making himself less. Not challenging me more softly than he would any Nephilim.

He measured me strong enough to take him in his full strength.

I swelled, lifted my chin, and stared at him down my nose though I had to tip my head right back to meet that hot, furious gaze. And I let my eyes blaze just as brightly.

"You think God chooses *that* perversion and self-indulgence?" I hissed. "You think that is God's will?"

"Of course my people live outside of God's will—we are the offspring of the rebels—"

"And yet, here you stand with honor and a soul! And you lead—and they follow. Why? Why do you continue to hand your power to that heathen every day?"

"Because the power was *his* birthright, and if God holds any delight in me, any blessing, it is because I serve him as I should!" he growled.

I shook my head but did not drop his gaze. "Then we do not serve the same God."

"Of course we don't!"

I narrowed my gaze at him, knowing he felt as I did that we certainly did.

"My God would exalt a man like you." I poked his chest. "Integrity to his word, protection of the weak, love for those who could never match him. My God would urge *that man* to lead his people to the honor and integrity he holds. Not turn a blind eye to the perversion and debauchery. The brutality."

"I do not turn a blind eye—I saved you from it!" he harshed.

"Exactly! You contradict your*self*. So, which is it, Melek? Are you a man of God, a leader of honor, and a warrior for truth, or are you the lapdog of that piglet?"

"My God says serve even the emperor who is unreasonable."

"What a fucking cop-out."

His eyes narrowed and his lip curled back from his teeth. "So easy for you to say, so easy to judge—you, a simple thief, a spy, an *assassin*. No responsibility or burden beyond your own hide! I have observed before how quickly the lowborn judge those of us who carry the future on our shoulders. It is easy to sneer when your steps affect only *you.*"

"You know nothing about my life!"

"Oh, of course, Yilan, you're the only one with insight, the only one who observes. No man could possibly know a crumb of you unless you spoke it clearly and slowly first, right?"

"No, they couldn't—" I snapped. "Because men are obstinate pigs, dragged through their lives by their pricks and their stomachs."

He just stared at me then, raising one brow in a challenge to that, and I *knew* he was thinking of that fucking vision that *I* started.

I spluttered, searching for the right response, but Melek, eyes glinting, just leaned in until our noses almost brushed. "Do you want to know what I have observed?"

"This should be stunning," I muttered sullenly, folding my arms over the towel so his chest wouldn't brush mine.

His eyes narrowed. "I observe a woman who *provokes* with the mouth of a soldier, yet shies from the act even at the height of arousal. I see a woman who would slit the throat of a man without a backwards glance, yet offers crumbs to a rodent and yearns to befriend it. I see a woman who will fearlessly spit in the face of the most powerful General on the continent, yet win his friends with flirtation and cutting humor."

I snorted. "I'm still waiting for the part where I have no integrity and deserve your derision."

He stared back at me, stern and... disturbed? "That is precisely the problem, Yilan," he said, his voice suddenly deep, calm, *unhappy*. "I'm still waiting for that too."

It was the last thing I'd expected from him and it stunned me to silence.

We stared at each other and the hair on my arms stood up as I realized how close he was. How large. How strong.

He could snap me like a twig if I didn't keep out of his grasp.

And yet he stood here, challenging me with words, waiting for an answer, not bringing his brute strength to bear.

My breath was shallow and quick. My mouth dry. I licked my lips and my heart jumped when his eyes dropped to my mouth and grew tortured for a moment.

"You are an enigma," he said hoarsely. "You are a Fetch. I do not understand you, and yet..."

I couldn't breathe, because I knew. "Yet?"

His brows pressed down, pinching over his strong nose and he searched my eyes. He opened his mouth as if he'd reply—but then only muttered, *"Shit."*

Without warning, he took my face in his hands and kissed me, a low, tormented groan rolling in his massive chest as he gathered me in.

28. Under the Dark

SOUNDTRACK: *I'll Make You Love Me* by Kat Leon
and Sam Tinnesz

~ MELEK ~

I didn't have the thought. I never made the decision.

One moment I loomed over her, arguing my point even as my heart ached—she couldn't feel the bond? She'd described how they formed one, but did Fetch even sense bonds or did they merely stumble into them?—and then I stopped being angry and then something in her eyes softened and then her face was in my hands and...

She stiffened and gave a little gasp when my mouth landed on hers, but I hadn't even had time to plead with God to keep her there when her body eased and her back bowed, her little hands dropping the towel as her arms snaked around my waist and she arched against me... *hugging* me.

Kissing me.

And... dear God, her *mouth.*

Those wide lips, so given to sly smiles and wicked delight, suddenly soft under mine.

That tongue, so quick to lash or reprimand, now velvet and slick.

My hands slid into her hair, taking grip, holding her there as a jolt of need rocked through me and I shuddered with it. Every inch of me trembled. My *soul* sang.

Mate.

Soulbond.

The One.

Holding her in my kiss, I tilted my head and fought a battle with myself—with a tongue that wanted to delve and tease, yet also yearned to speak the words.

Mate.

Mine.

I took the kiss deeper, fighting not to overwhelm her, but overwhelmed myself as I shook with the force of the feelings coursing through me, lighting my blood, igniting my body.

It could not be. *It could not be.*

And yet, it was. There was no question. No doubt.

Mate.

Impossible, unstoppable *mate.*

Mine.

She was *for me.*

And though I was near certain she did not sense the bond, something within her responded, because she whimpered as her hands slid up my back, my sides, my chest, then around my neck, pulling me down as she arched her back and tried to press herself against me while I was folded almost in half to reach her mouth. The towel slipped and fell. I caught it at her back, but the sides opened between us, revealing her as both of us stopped resisting and I lifted her.

She clung like a barnacle, legs around my waist, arms looping my neck, her body plastered against mine as I gasped her name and dove back into that kiss, walking her further up shore, into the trees, to the spaces where sunlight reached during the day to grow a thick blanket of grass, but moonlight wasn't strong enough to touch it.

I was forced to break the kiss as I lowered her to the grass, throwing the wide towel down so there was some cushioning—but she only buried her face in my throat and scraped my jaw with her teeth so that my blood caught fire and roared through me.

The moment I had the towel spread enough I lowered her to it and took her mouth again, everything in me crying for her—my body aching for her with such a fire, I trembled from head to toe.

And when I pinned her to the ground, covering her, plunging one hand into her hair, the other dragging up from the back of her thigh to her waist, she caught fire too and suddenly we were clawing at each other, the kiss growing aggressive, teeth clashing in its intensity.

There was a moment when she threw her head back, gasping my name and I dove for her throat, sucking and laving that delicate skin with my tongue, growling when I tasted the sweet honey of her. She fisted both hands in my hair and held me to her, her breath hot and quick, her hips rolling, seeking me and every one of my senses came alive—skin prickling, heart thudding in my ears like ritual drums, fingertips trailing fire because her skin was *hot,* and everything in my chest building pressure, coiling, expanding, ready to explode with sheer need.

I was hard as steel and shuddering every time she rolled her hips, my instincts screaming that I need to pause, to speak, to *know her mind.* And yet my hand dragged back down to the back of her soft, soft thigh and pulled her leg up, hooking her knee over my hip and opening her to me. Then I dragged myself along the slick seam of her, my breath releasing in a harsh rush when she whimpered again.

At that sound, the two sides of my nature, the twin drives, went to battle.

Every animal instinct in me roared for dominance. And every ounce of my honor—my *love,* she was my *mate!*—demanded restraint.

I groaned and flexed my hips, pressing against her harder than strictly necessary, but was rewarded by her gasp and the tightening of her fingers in my hair.

I had never forced a woman in my life. And was not forcing her.

But she was so small. And under my care. And she'd been violated just days ago by that bastard.

I needed to stop. Needed to check in. Needed to find the control to—

Almost tearing my hair from the roots, she clawed her fingers from my scalp, down my neck, and into my back, her head tipping back, mouth open and eyes squeezed tightly closed as I kissed down to her throat again, then rocked against her… and almost took her.

The most beautiful little gasp broke in her throat and her hand clapped to my back. But then she went still under me.

"M-Melek, I—"

There was a tremor in her voice.

Curled over her, one hand cupped over her head, the other holding her knee over my hip, I froze.

I was breathing so hard, her hair fluttered in the wind of my exhales. I'd sucked so hard on the sweet skin of her neck that it was going to leave a mark—and the animal in me wanted to growl in approval so any who saw her would know. Yet I knew to them it was nothing. Merely a confirmation of my claiming. They wouldn't think twice. Wouldn't know—or care—what might run under the surface between us.

Fisting my hand in the towel under her, I grazed her neck with my teeth, then made myself push back just far enough to meet her eyes.

My chest was a bellows for my heaving breath—and she panted too.

For a moment we just stared.

Her beautiful eyes were wide as she searched mine, a look of pure awe on her face.

"Melek... I have to tell you—"

There was a smattering of snaps and cracks like a great weight falling into a bush, followed by a chorus of howls and laughter.

We both startled and looked off into the forest in the direction the noise had come from.

Reality slapped me in the face like I'd been doused in a bucket of ice water.

We were both naked and curled together in plain sight if anyone followed the trail down to the lake, and the Nephilim were reveling.

Drunk, young, fit, lonely and fueled by recent rumors of her rape... they'd frenzy in a heartbeat if they caught sight of her.

"I'm getting you out of here. *Right now,*" I graveled, my voice deeper than I ever remembered it.

There was another crunch and more laughter, closer this time. I didn't wait for her response. I shoved to my feet, pulled her up, grabbed the towel and threw it over her shoulders.

"Don't move," I hissed, pushing her behind a nearby shrub as I darted back to grab both our clothes as fast as I could move.

Keeping my wings tucked tight against my back, I dove back into the bushes where she was crouched, clutching that towel around her, just as footsteps, laughing voices, and muttered curses broke the peace of the lakeside.

One of them howled and I muttered a curse, turning my back to her as I snapped my wings out, then back, covering her with the raven dark of them.

It was too much to hope that they hadn't heard my wings rustle the bushes. Of course, they assumed they'd been followed by one of their friends, so as they called and rushed towards us, I turned my head and hissed through gritted teeth.

"Don't speak. They won't see you through my wings."

She stiffened, but wisely kept her mouth shut as the bushes shook, then parted just two feet from where I crouched—which was when the danger to my mate became undeniable and I roared to shake the trees.

29. My Enemy

I was shaking—brimming with want, my body alight in a way I'd never experienced before. As if every touch, every kiss, every brush of his body lit a new flame that burned away any thought or drive in me beyond *more.*

But when he shoved me into those bushes and tore away leaving me cold and shaking, I was forced back to reality—and the fact that we were about to be discovered by a group of young males just like those who'd almost raped me.

Then I shook for an entirely different reason.

He was back in seconds, his wings high and wide, hissing at me that he'd hide me, but that just left me crouching there, helpless, as the bushes in front of him parted and young, *drunk* Nephilim faces appeared like the faces of baby coons popping out of a hollow tree.

Then Melek *roared.*

They fell backwards, scrambling over each other to get away as he stood, his wings spread and so thick I couldn't see anything except the beautiful, scarred back of his massive body—which meant they couldn't see me either.

"Leave us!" he snarled, the words puttering off into a growl as he took a prowling step towards those young idiots.

Those strong, drunk, and *numerous* young idiots. Even Melek couldn't beat a dozen of them if they combined efforts.

Could he?

"Oh shit!"

"Sorry sir!"

"Is there a *woman* in there?"

"You question me when *you're* supposed to stay within the circle of fires?" he snapped.

"We were just going to swim—"

"Shut up!"

And then Melek growled. The sound was so menacing, my blood ran cold. It was a harsh reminder that he was, at his core, a *creature.*

"Go. All of you. Back to your tents and your drink. I will forget I saw stupidity, but not rebellion."

For a moment, no one moved and my heart froze. The young Neph obviously emboldened by drink and the thrill of celebration, sized up their General.

But then the one at the front dropped his eyes and his posture shrank.

"Yes, Sir," he said, though there was an edge of tension in his voice. "We'll go."

He slapped his friend on the chest and they both turned, the others behind them following suit. I started to take a breath, but then the one at the front looked over his shoulder and grinned wickedly at Melek.

"Enjoy the Fetch, Sir."

Then he took off after his friends, all of them laughing and whooping as they crashed back through the forest.

Melek stood before me for the length of several short breaths, unmoving. Then suddenly came alive, whipping around, sweeping me up into his chest and running into the forest at a different angle than the young ones had taken, his jaw clenched and eyes on fire.

I squeaked in shock, but clung to his neck, though the reality of... well, everything was starting to set in and an uneasiness churned in my guts.

"We have to get back to my tent, *now."*

"Melek, what's going on? They left. Do you think it was a ploy? That they'll try to ambush you?"

"No. I think they'll run back to camp and tell anyone who will listen that I have you out here. And there are many, *many* older, stronger warriors in this camp that have been lonely too long. Under the influence of drink, they might see challenging for my female as a fun start to their Covenant Days."

I clung to him harder. "Surely they wouldn't... I mean you could beat any of them—"

"Your faith in me is gratifying, Yilan. But even I couldn't take four or five of our strongest fighters if they came at me together."

I blinked. "They'd challenge you for a female *together?*"

He nodded once, his lips peeling back from his teeth as he spat, "And after they won, they'd take her together, as well."

I stiffened and his hands tightened on my hip and back.

"If we are not under their eyes, they will be distracted. And they would never have the courage to challenge me sober. Do not fear, Yilan. I will not allow it. My female will never face—"

"I am not *your* female!" I hissed.

His head jerked back like I'd slapped him. His eyes dropped to meet mine for a split second, but he ran on.

"Regardless," he murmured a few steps later. "I'm going to get you back to the tent. If any of them come out there to hunt us, they won't find us. Problem solved."

We had to sneak past the guards again, though Melek came at the camp from a different angle this time and the guards in this spot were even less attentive than those we had ducked earlier.

When we were almost back to the tent, as we passed the campfire twenty feet from its door, Melek slowed to a walk, panting lightly from the run, while I panted more from fear.

Fear of these creatures who would take women as if they were little more than possessions? Or fear of Melek? Fear of being raped? Or fear of... what had been happening before we were interrupted?

I wasn't sure which was more terrifying.

No. That wasn't true.

Melek... Melek was by far the more frightening prospect.

The General of our enemy. Arguably, the most powerful man on the continent. A Nephilim—a rebel against God and humanity.

Intelligent. Cunning. And *honorable?* With a *soul?*

It had to be true. The soulless King's response to his own son only demonstrated that.

The sheer power of Melek, the way he owned a room. The way my heart would stop when his eyes locked on mine. The way my heart pounded when his mouth was on mine.

The way the world disappeared with his body on mine.

My blood on fire—

Flinching inwardly, I sucked in a breath and shook my head.

His grip tightened on me.

"They haven't followed, Yilan. You're safe."

I squeezed my eyes closed and gripped harder against the urge to take his face in my hands and kiss him—and that was the final straw.

Melek was the *most* dangerous of creatures: A compelling, powerful, leader of a man. A man who called me in darkness *and* in light. And if I allowed it, he would draw me away from *everything* that had ever mattered to me.

And everything that was supposed to matter, as well.

"...Very little in this life is worth dying for."

He arched one brow. "I notice you do not say nothing is worth dying for."

"No, I didn't."

I did not know why God had put me here. I did not know why *this* man called to me like no other had before. But I knew the purpose I had been given. The responsibility I had to *my* people. And loyalty to an enemy *could not fulfill that.*

My heart flinched within my chest.

It hurt.

Unaware of my thoughts, Melek turned me sideways as he ducked into the tent, letting the canvas flap pull over his shoulder as he marched into the dark interior and once again did not light a lantern, gave no indication to anyone outside that we were here.

He reached the center of the tent and stopped suddenly, still panting. Then dropped his chin to look at me, his eyes piercing, even in the dark.

Neither of us spoke.

Melek gripped me at the knees, and behind my back. My entire body trembled. My heart swelled and pushed towards him and I fought.

I gritted my teeth and *battled.*

And when Melek set me back on my feet, I shrank from him.

He froze, his eyes locked on mine.

"Yilan—" he reached for me and I took another step back, dropping my eyes to my feet, grief blooming in my chest when he stopped himself coming for me. "Yilan, I know it's been frightening, but I would never let them hurt y—"

"You are my enemy."

I *felt* him flinch.

When he spoke again, his voice was hoarse. "God tells us to love our enemies."

"Not like *this.*" But still I didn't move. I had said the words, and they were true. But still I didn't move.

I needed to move.

He was not going to move away. It had to be me.

As if he'd heard the thought, he inched closer, eyes on me, his body hesitant, but firm. *Taking* space to be close to me and that fright, that alarm, the part that feared him for what he could be, not what he was, pulled away.

I took one step back, and his breath caught.

Another, just beyond the reach of his long arms, and he opened his mouth.

I took the last three steps in a rush, turning to slip into the open cage door, then grabbing and pulling it closed in front of me.

He took two long strides to cover the same space, and gripped the bars of the cage over my fingers, his jaw tight. "Yilan—"

I resisted when he started to pull it open, and shook my head. "Lock it, Melek," I whispered. "You have to lock it."

He stared down at me, his brows pressing together, his forehead lined. "I am a man of my word, and I meant the words: I will not let them take you. You are safe—"

"I know. But that changes *nothing.*"

I had to draw the line. Had to make myself hard, because he was not and I couldn't fight that.

"Lock the cage, Melek."

"Yilan, do you... have you looked within yourself? Do you sense—"

"I sense that we are enemies, our peoples are enemies, yours are the enemy to the God I serve and you refuse to lead them into change so... I cannot choose you and your people over me and mine, Melek. I cannot. *Lock. The fucking. Cage.*"

He leaned back, his expression suddenly very heavy. His cheeks pulled down, shoulders slumped, and his eyes flickered with shadows—but he never broke eye contact as he reached for the lock and slammed it home, returning me to prison.

I thought he would give in to his anger and storm off, but instead he leaned in again, his nose only inches from mine.

"I will never let them have you," he whispered and the intensity in him, the power wafting from him made me shiver.

"You are far more frightening to me than them," I croaked.

His eyes narrowed. "Truly, Yilan?"

"Truly."

He huffed. "I do not deserve that. I have *proven* that I will protect you."

I didn't reply, because he was right. But that was *exactly* what made him so dangerous. Couldn't he see?

I held his gaze, and he held mine and then he shook his head, drawing slowly back, his upper lip beginning to curl back from his teeth.

"Do *not* judge me for defending myself against an enemy!"

"Oh, I don't," he muttered as he stepped back. "I just hadn't picked you for a coward."

Then, after landing that blow, he turned on his heel and marched to his bed, leaving me shaken and weary, begging God to remove the weight of grief that suddenly appeared on my chest.

But my prayers were not answered.

30. Dream a Dream of You

~ *MELEK* ~

We were in the water together. Deep in the lake. And this time there was no one coming to interrupt.

I'd picked her up and carried her out because the water would close over her head while I was only chest deep. It was a precious moment, to hold her to me, her flesh warm in the cold water, one hand under her ass, the other free to... roam.

She had laced her fingers behind my neck and wrapped her legs around my waist, her ankles locked at my back. Her eyes never left my face.

And then, when I had us deep enough, I released my wings and used them to keep us buoyant, drawing my legs up, so she could sit in my lap without having to hold on.

"You're so strong," she murmured, but there was an edge in her voice—a tang of fear.

I stroked her hair back from her face. "Strength is an asset when it's applied to your protection."

She nodded and smiled, leaned in and kissed me—and then let her hands drop down to stroke me.

I shuddered into that kiss when she took hold of me, those little hands so soft and small compared to mine. But just when I might have let my head fall back and given myself up to her touch, I caught her wrists and blew out a breath, staring deep into her cat-like eyes that were wide.

"Yilan," I said hoarsely. "I love your touch. But I need more. I need you."

A strange look came over her then. She smiled as if I'd pleased her and leaned in to kiss me briefly but deeply... then sat back. "I know."

Reaching for her beautiful face, I pulled her back into the kiss, my chest thrumming, sighing her name and trying to find the words to reassure her, to insist that she not deny what was between us.

Mate.

Soulbond.

Mine.

"Yilan—"

She'd plunged both hands into my hair and was kissing me back with vigor, with enthusiasm. Yet, small noises broke in her throat— fearful whimpers.

As her body told one story, the sounds she made told another, leaving me uncertain, pulling away, until she gasped, "No!" and pulled me back in.

Yet, when our mouths met, there was that fearful cry again.

Did she fear my size? Fear that I'd hurt her?

Fear breeding with me?

The thought that she was my mate and so might bear my young was a rush—quickly followed by a wave of fear.

So many women died giving birth to Nephilim young. Being a soulmate didn't protect from the sheer size of Nephilim babes in relation to their mothers.

The dark thoughts made me hesitate, but she whispered, "No, don't, Melek." She curled one hand at the back of my neck and pulled me in, reaching between us with the other and stroking me again.

She still made those sad and fearful whimpers, but her touch, her kiss—everything grew heated.

She breathed almost as heavily as I did, her nails digging into the back of my neck. The water rippling as we began to rock together, her stroking pushing me closer and closer to release.

"Yilan... oh god," I gasped.

That little cry broke in her throat again and I reached for her, ready to stop her, but she shook her head and took me in both hands then, breathing my name with a plea.

And then my body was cresting that wave, ready to crash over the peak. I spread my wings for balance as my back arched, grabbing for her to keep her close as I bowed and let my head fall back, jaw dropping, and everything in my heart rushing out of my mouth.

"Yilan…"

"Melek! Please!" she cried.

"YILAN, dear God—you hold my soul, my… MATE!" I roared, the water rippling and sloshing as my body jerked and shuddered towards—

I woke with a start, sweaty and throbbing for release, panting, but every instinct at alert.

I was blinking, ears perked, the hair on the back of my neck standing straight up, and for a moment I was disoriented, coming out of the dream, uncertain what had been real and what was only my mind.

Was she toying with my mind again?

But then I heard her whimper my name and that plea—not one of need, but of fear. And my blood ran cold.

I leaped out of bed, searching the shadows, looking for the enemy… but found only the cage… and Yilan curled up like a child on the cot, shaking and whimpering.

"No… no…" she gasped in a small, broken voice that tore my heart to shreds.

"No… Melek—help me! Please!"

Her head shook and she lashed out feebly with one hand as if she was fighting for freedom, and it clicked.

We'd both been dreaming—but hers wasn't like mine.

"Yilan, wake up! It's a dream!" I tore across the tent, yanking back on the lock and scrambling into the cage to reach her, shaking her, pulling her upright, holding her as her head shook and she shrank from whatever she saw behind her closed eyes. "Yilan… *Yilan!*"

Her eyes flew open, so wide they were white all the way around, and her body jolted. She reached for me as if to push me away—but when her hands landed on my chest she froze, her eyes darting, blinking, as the dream faded.

Squatting next to her cot, I held her face, made her see me, whispered that it was a dream, and pleaded for her to come back to see that she was safe, that I was there, that she wouldn't be touched…

And then she blinked. And finally, her eyes focused. She locked on me and blinked again and I stroked her hair.

"It was a dream. It was a dream, beautiful. Just a dream."

She frowned hard, then tore her eyes away to look around the tent, obviously needing to see that we were truly alone, before turning back to me. And then her eyes welled, and her chin trembled.

"You're safe," I whispered. "Just breathe. You're safe."

My heart broke for her as she slumped, curling her body up, dropping her face in her hands. She covered her mouth to stifle a sob, then tipped forward right into my chest. Into my arms.

The relief that washed through me when she sank into me was intoxicating in its intensity. For a moment I just held her.

But then another sob broke in her throat and she trembled, and I closed my eyes, my heart squeezing and swelling in equal measure.

Then I cursed and gathered her to my chest as I stood as tall as I could in the cage, then carried her out, holding her as tightly as I dared.

When I reached the bed, I loosened my hold, intending to lay her down, to get her a drink of water, or something. But she inhaled sharply and clung to my neck, trembling in waves.

Whatever she'd been seeing in her mind had obviously been dark. She was terrified. I couldn't let her go.

So, I crawled up onto the bed and laid down, still holding her, curling myself around her and bringing my wing over her to cover her completely from view as she sobbed against my chest.

I stroked her hair and reminded her that I was there. That she was safe.

And that I would not let any of them touch her. Not once.

Never again.

As her shoulders shook, her tears wet my collarbones. I wrapped my arms more tightly around her, and sighed, finding a new clarity in myself.

I would protect her. There was no doubt. But that didn't change the fact that if anything were to happen to me, she would be left vulnerable.

We both knew it.

She was haunted by dreams of events that were not unrealistic in this camp. And as much as I despised it, I could not deny that truth.

So, as I lay there, whispering her safety, my jaw got tighter and tighter, until I was resolved.

Enemy she might be, but she was also mate.

Ignorant of the bond, for certain. But that did not remove it from existence.

I'd always vowed to myself that if I ever found the twin to my soul, I would keep her from the worst of my people.

Now, here we were.

Which meant it was up to me to make her safe. Not just protect her from the harm that already existed… but make her safe.

She could not be safe here.

The thought was a cold, hollow echo in a cavernous space.

She could not be safe here… *even with me.*

The truth of that statement stabbed as surely as any weapon. But I was not a General for nothing.

As her sobs turned to hitching breaths, then to the slow, steady breath of sleep, I considered, and measured, and planned.

And determined that there was no choice but to find a way for her to get out of here.

Without me.

31. Morning General

~ *MELEK* ~

I woke with a start the next morning, my entire body jolting with alarm when the tent flap snapped back with no warning.

Yilan is in bed with me.

I sat bolt upright, throwing the furs aside to cover... nothing. I blinked, looking down at the empty space next to me to see that the hollow left in the mattress where she had been laying was empty. Jann was striding into the tent and—

"I see you rise as reliably as the sun, Captain..." Yilan's tone was suggestive, and made even more provocative by being husky from sleep. And crying last night.

I blinked and looked at the cage, to find her sitting on the side of the cot, her feet on the floor and elbows on her knees, like she'd just woken and was taking a moment before she stood.

Her head was turned toward the sunlight that had followed Jann into the tent and she squinted against it, her hair sticking out in every direction as Jann chuckled and let the flap drop and returned her to shade.

"Good morning to you, too," he said warmly.

An ugly burst of possessive jealousy detonated in my chest so my voice was harsher than I'd intended when I spoken.

"What the fuck are you doing here so early on a peace day?"

They both looked at me in surprise, Yilan's eyes puffy, Jann's a little wide.

"Early? The sun has been up for two hours, Mel," Jann said with brows high.

Shit! I tossed back the rest of the furs and leaped out of the bed, then caught myself as I remembered it was a peace day and most of my duties would be set aside, at least in theory. Which was why no one had woken me. Even the servants were on minimal duties.

I rubbed my eyes with the heels of my hands and took a deep breath. I needed to *think*.

Yilan had been free, and hadn't run. She had put herself back in the cage.

I turned to look at her and adrenaline coursed through me again when I caught sight of the unlocked door.

Jann couldn't be allowed to notice.

"Let's start again," I said gruffly, moving across the tent to find my leathers and drawing his eyes away from the cage. "Good morning, Jann. Peace to you."

"Peace to you as well, Mel," he said jovially. "Late night?"

"Too late."

"You're getting too old for those kinds of shenanigans."

"And you're not?"

"You've got at least five years on me. I will forever be more virile than you, brother."

I snorted, buttoning my leathers then reaching for my weapon straps before hesitating. This was supposed to be a time of recognized peace. Within the camp, I often went without my spears.

But then I remembered that moment the Shade came at me—I would have been dead if Yilan hadn't seen him first and warned me…

After buckling my weapon straps, I slid two large daggers into the sheaths on the shoulders. That way I wouldn't be unarmed, but also wouldn't be obviously bristling with weapons.

"I'm hungry," I said. "Have you had breakfast?"

"I was just coming to ask the same of you."

"Perfect. Let's go."

Jann's brows rose and he turned to look at Yilan. "Are you sure? Gall is still asleep and I thought you'd told him—"

Following his gaze, I caught eyes with Yilan who hadn't moved from her seat, but was staring up at me with a strange intensity on her face.

The cage was unlocked.

I couldn't lock it in front of Jann without drawing attention to that.

If I left, she'd be free—if she wished to be. She'd had a chance to escape twice now, and hadn't taken it. But perhaps this morning she'd only woken as Jann was approaching and…

And did it matter? My thoughts of the night before came swimming back, turning my heart into a deadweight.

She could not be safe here… even with me.

I'd turned the problem over in my mind for hours, but always ended up right where I had started: She could not possibly be safe here. Even with me. The pressure around her would only increase. And the moment something happened to me, or I was taken away for other duties, she would be devoured.

My only options were to endure her inevitable death, or to help her escape. Which meant there was only one choice. I would not be party to the death of my mate, whether the bond was completed or not.

But I also hadn't thought I'd be taking action on that this quickly. My soul shivered at the idea of losing her already. I'd only just found her! Yet, it could not be denied that I had made the decision in logic and analysis, in the dark of night. If God opened a door, it was foolish not to walk through it.

"I'm sure," I answered Jann, who was frowning between us. "If she can release herself in the few minutes it takes me to eat, then she's as smart as she claims, and deserves to be free," I said, praying she heard the true meaning of my words.

Yilan's brows popped up and I tore my eyes from her, gesturing to Jann to go first out of the tent, but hanging back, walking slowly so that he preceded me out of the tent by several paces.

The moment Jann was outside, she hissed, "What are you doing?!"

Stepping closer to the cage as I headed for the door, I whispered to her. "We'll be twenty minutes. Use it."

"Melek—"

"There's no time to explain. But you're too vulnerable here. Just go."

Her eyes went wide, but I turned on my heel—my ribs creaking, my heart screaming, my soul twisting like a dagger in my chest.

My feet were so heavy it seemed my boots were made from lead. But I forced myself to keep walking, to keep my eyes on that tent flap and the freedom it now symbolized.

Freedom for her.

Torment for me—but what choice did I have? She was my mate. I couldn't keep her imprisoned. And the moment I had my back turned, any of these males might come for her. I couldn't fight *two* wars.

If the King wanted to see me humbled, well, the loss of the prisoner would do it. And if that meant she was finally safe...

It felt as if two hands gripped my skull, trying to force my head to turn back, to look at her, to drink her in before I stepped out of the tent. But I braced myself and kept my eyes ahead, slipping out into the sunlight, nodding at Jann's questioning look as if I hadn't understood what it meant, then striding forward and away. Towards the campfires. And breakfast.

And the rest of my life with a gaping hole in my soul.

The communal eating area at the center of camp was usually bustling with Nephilim at any time of day. We were an army with patrols and duties around the clock. Our kitchen never closed. There were multiple fires, multiple stations at which a Neph could be served hot food. And a large area full of tables, stools and even stumps of wood to be used as seats for when things were really busy.

But this morning the dining area was almost empty. In the thin sunlight of an autumn morning, there were only a handful of Nephilim awake and eating, spread out at the many tables and stools. Which meant it was quiet. And not nearly distracting enough.

I started questioning my decision to free her the moment we made it to the campfires. The servants—heavy-lidded and mumbling, dragged from their beds to make the meal—served us, then dropped back to their seats next to the fires.

So, Jann and I took a table in the middle where no one else would hear our conversation.

222

He spoke lightly of the events of the night before, describing pranks, drunk stupidity, and amusing anecdotes I didn't really follow, but made myself smile when Jann laughed.

I kept finding myself looking off to the right, in the direction of my tent, wondering if she was already gone.

It was the perfect time to attempt an escape. The guards would be few, and tired. And focused on any attempting to get in to camp, not out of it. With her skills in the shadows, she could probably turn them in circles, or slip past without them even realizing she'd been close—

"Mel!" Jann snapped.

I blinked and turned back to him. "What?"

Jann arched one brow, looked pointedly down at my untouched plate, then back up to me. "I thought you were hungry?"

I was. But not for food.

"Sure, sure," I mumbled, dropping my head and digging into the food. "I was just distracted. I guess I'm a little hungover after all," I lied.

I thought I did a fairly good job of engaging with him from that point. But my thoughts never stopped turning to her and where she might be. I managed to stay away from the tent for a full thirty minutes, but by then we'd both finished eating and Jann was talking about washing up.

Shying away from any mention of bathing, I clasped his arm and bid him to have a peaceful day, then turned to the trail that would eventually take me through the camp and back to my tent at its edge.

"Mel?"

I stopped, just one pace away and turned.

Jann was staring at me strangely. "Aren't you going to take her some food?"

Shit. "Yes, yes. Of course. I'm just—"

"Are you okay?"

"I'm fine. Just tired, as I said," I muttered, clapping his back in thanks as I hurried past him, back to the fires to get another platter.

He watched me for a moment, but I pretended I didn't notice as I asked a servant to dish a plate for her and took it, turning back to the trail and raising my chin to him as I passed between the tents and out of his sight... then slumped.

Surely she had to be gone by now?

My heart panged, and my steps dragged. But I had nowhere else to be. And I needed some time to plan my strategy for telling Gault she'd escaped.

By the time I made it to the tent, my body felt heavy and I was considering covering her cage and going back to bed to buy myself some time and rest before all hell blew up.

Then I pushed the flap aside and stepped in... and Yilan lifted her head from where she sat in the cage *reading one of my books?*

I blinked, my breath catching.

She smiled. "Is that pork? I could smell you coming."

"What are you doing here?" I hissed, hurrying to the cage— only to find it locked. I frowned. "How did you—"

"Melek, we can discuss when or how I might leave. But... I don't believe my purpose here has been fulfilled. Not yet," she said carefully, standing but staying away from the cage door as I opened it and stepped in to hand her the plate.

She took it in both hands because it was large for her, then looked up at me, her eyes shining and serious.

All that screaming pain that had been stabbing at me since I'd thought she would be gone flipped into warmth and hope. Had she sensed the bond? Was she going to—

"Thank you for... for comforting me last night," she whispered. "But we must be more careful. I'm still the enemy, Melek," she finished quietly. "The Covenant Days will end and then..."

That weight bore down on my shoulders again and I frowned at her.

But she just took the platter over to her cot, sat down, and started eating.

A moment later I sighed, stepped out of the cage, and locked her in again.

"You're welcome," I said, then turned away to make my bed and sort out my whirling thoughts.

32. Plans vs. Plans

~ YILAN ~

Melek stayed in the tent most of the day. I didn't want to think about why I felt relief at that.

He'd been so busy the past couple of days, I was surprised when he didn't rush out to another meeting, but lay on his bed with a book. Then even more surprised when Jannus appeared to tell him that the Council was meeting and Melek replied that they should come to the tent.

Jannus was clearly shocked as well. His brows climbed nearly to his hairline.

"Mel… are you sure?" Then he glanced at me.

I gave him a flat look back and he winked, which was cute.

Melek ignored us both. "I can't leave her unattended. I don't want to call Gall in. And… it's the Days of Peace. Tell them we'll meet here. Hell, tell them all to bring something to drink."

Jann shrugged and marched back out of the tent. I was staring at Melek, who had gone back to his book. But a few seconds later he spoke without looking up.

"What?"

"Nothing," I said, raising my hands and sitting back on my cot. "Nothing at all."

But it wasn't nothing. He'd been meticulous about keeping me away from their discussions of the front and their next steps. Even silencing messengers who started to relay anything to do with strategic movements, or questions for him.

"Your lips are thin," he said absently.

I blinked. "I'm sorry, what—?"

"Whenever you're stopping yourself from saying something, your lips press thin and you tilt your head. So, what is it you want to say?"

I gaped at him, but then the first of the Council arrived and he was immediately distracted, clasping arms, greeting, offering benedictions of peace, and hearing stories from the night before.

I noticed that he didn't share any of his own.

Twenty minutes later there were four of them, and they waited for the fifth.

Jannus was just relaying a story about a prank he'd seen some of the ranks pull on their Lieutenant the night before—something to do with horse dung and boot polish—when the tent flap twitched and the temperature in the tent dropped. At least, that was how it felt when I turned to look at the man who entered.

The other two Nephilim who'd entered were warriors—one younger than Melek, one older. Both big, burly, and clearly fighters who'd earned their way through the ranks, just as Melek had done. They had spoken easily and loudly and stood with the casual grace that only men of immense strength and capability possessed.

The man who entered the tent next was an entirely different creature.

He wore a thick, hooded cloak so dark blue it was almost black. It was voluminous and dusted the ground as he walked so it seemed he had no feet. The sleeves were long, and widened at the cuffs. With the hood up, the cloak swallowed his entire frame.

When he first stepped into the tent, everything about him was dark—only his eyes peered out of the shadow of his hood, glowing with the bright, golden light of the Nephilim born within just one or two generations of the fallen angels.

He was still Nephilim. Still tall and imposing. But leaner than the others. And very obviously older. Gnarled and wrinkled, like an old tree.

He was steady on his feet, and his eyes were bright, but there was something disturbing about the way he moved. If he had been a warrior, his fighting days were long gone.

As the others looked up to greet him, he threw back the hood to reveal his face and my blood ran cold. Though his hair was lush and thick, falling in waves around his shoulders, it was gray throughout and framed a lined face, pocked with old acne scars. His eyes stared out of deep shadows cast by protruding brows, the sunken caves matching his hollowed cheeks. And his skin was gray.

"Hever, thank you for joining us," Melek said with a grim look.

All the joking and smiles from the others ceased immediately. As Hever crossed the space to join them in that queasy flow, their faces grew stern and their eyes dropped to the map on the table around which they stood.

"I apologize for the delay," the man rasped, his voice quiet and wheezy, like wind whistling through a canyon. But there were no more manners. No one commented as he joined them. His eyes dropped to the map Melek had spread on that table, and he began to examine it immediately, frowning.

There was no extra room on that little table, so the others were on the bed to be retrieved if needed.

"Is one thousand spears enough?" he asked Melek hoarsely as he put a finger to the map.

I saw Melek swell and hold, stifling his frustration. I didn't know who this man was, but he was clearly someone Melek believed he had to please.

"Three hundred was enough to take it," Melek said through his teeth. "A thousand—if they aren't discovered—will hold the high ground easily until the rest can reach the peaks and—"

"The King believes we should move the additional ranks now, during the peace. Place them ready. Not just hold the summits of the Ravine, but make an immediate advance."

"I have explained, there will be no advance if we do not win the swamplands first and get our ranks to the highest ground *without discovery*. We already risked everything to wait. It is too risky to move during the Covenant when they are not distracted by battle, so all they will be doing is watching."

The three other males watched Melek and Hever like two wolves about to fight for dominance.

Hever's eyes never left the map when he spoke. Melek's never left Hever. There was a very strange dynamic here that I didn't understand.

But I understood the battle strategy and Melek was correct.

Every army would enjoy the Peace. And expect their enemies to be moving during that time, even if they didn't attack.

Without battle to take attention and resources, focus would turn to scouts and trackers. Not to mention that those at the mouth of the ravine were now sitting ducks. They could only *retreat*. Yet, it would take only one scout to catch a glimpse—or to disappear because the Nephilim caught them—to raise the alarm, and then all their element of surprise would be lost.

Archers appointed at the ravine would pick the flyers off before they did more than clear the canopy of trees. And the Nephilim ranks would be lost in the hundreds.

Rage simmered in my chest, along with an even deeper certainty that their King was doing this on purpose—setting Melek up. Most likely to fail. But there was a small chance they would get through, in which case the King's commands would be celebrated as *his* clever decisions, not Melek's.

I should have resisted, should have stayed out of it, but I couldn't. I couldn't let Melek continue to waver and deny—at least outwardly—the danger he was in if his foe was his King.

So, I sent him a vision. Not one to consume him as I'd done when he was in the bath, but a suggestion. Relaying an idea.

It was simple—first an image of the Nephilim, crouched and advancing on the Ravine—and being discovered. Then an image of them holding the high grounds, and cheering *Gault.*

Melek's eyes never moved from Hever, but he stiffened, then rolled his shoulders and stretched his jaw like he was making room for his rage.

I listened to their discussion and didn't interfere again, but he was too careful about not looking at me. It was no surprise when the others eventually left—with no actual change to the plan—when he took his time packing away the maps to give them time to be well away from the tent before he turned on me, his eyes dark and face tight.

"What the hell game are you playing?"

"I'm trying to help you. We both know sometimes it takes an objective eye, looking in from the outside, to see the true picture—"

"Objective? Yilan, you name yourself my enemy. You speak treason on my King!"

"I'm trying to *help you*—"

"Why?" he rasped, then came at me, stalking across the tent like a predator ready to pounce. "I didn't ask for your help. Why should I believe that's what you're doing?"

I shrugged, trying to disguise the squirm because I knew what he was really asking and I wasn't going there.

"If you Nephilim defeat our neighbors for us, we will only have one battle to fight to win the entire continent," I said casually, though my Kingdom had no intention of going to war, except in defense of our own borders. "You kill all the others, we have only one enemy left. You."

"The strongest one," he pointed out.

"Perhaps."

He reached the cage and put a hand to the top of it, leaning in as he huffed. "We have routed most of the continent, and in these battles our biggest obstacle is the landscape, not its people. Soon we will take them as well. What possible evidence could you account to suggest otherwise?"

I didn't answer him, because he was right. But it aggravated him.

His jaw went tight and he leaned in, muttering at me through the bars. "I am not stupid, Yilan," he said quietly.

"Debatable," I said lightly, teasing.

But he bristled. "I know you let me see you that first day. Now you're helping without being asked. You kissed me in the lake—"

I leaped to my feet. "*You* kissed *me* at the lake!"

"And you kissed back!"

I folded my arms. "Still—"

"Look, that isn't the point," he growled sternly. "The point is, if you don't want me and won't have me, why help me? Why give yourself up, only to help? Is *all* of this a... a manipulation, Yilan? Do you plant thoughts in my head and feelings in my body? Are you deceiving me even beyond the things I know?" He was growing more and more agitated, gesticulating as he snarled. "Why did you cage yourself again? What game are you playing?"

"This is no game," I said seriously.

"No, game, yet you're playing with fire."

I raised my chin. "God is in the fire with me."

His eyes narrowed. "What were the words you used? Oh, right... *What a fucking cop-out.*"

I tensed, but at that moment a messenger called from outside the tent flap, asking Melek if he could enter.

Melek stared me down a second before answering, then bid the man to enter.

It was the young, lanky messenger again, looking a little intimidated. His eyes widened when he found Melek glaring at me through the bars and obviously already upset.

He swallowed hard as he saluted his General. "Sir. The King has heard of the... the battle plan and requests that you bring the Fetch to him."

Melek went very, very still at that, his eyes still fixed on me in a blazing scowl. But I knew... I knew how the nerves hit him in that moment. Because they hit me too.

Adrenaline in a sharp, electric jolt. And not the good kind.

What did the King want with *me?* And why now?

33. Bound to You

~ *MELEK* ~

I sent the messenger back to Gault with assurances that I would have her there as soon as I could do so safely.

The moment he took off, I started pacing, raking a hand through my hair, my head spinning.

Why? Why now? Why *her?*

I'd almost believed Gault had forgotten she was here. He hadn't mentioned her during our entire trip. And the few times her presence had been raised, it was only to debate whether the information she'd supplied could be trusted.

So why now?

I feared I knew the answer, but would not allow it to be so.

He would have heard the rumor. His Advisor, Hever, ran an entire network of eyes and ears that started in the ranks themselves, and extended out across the land. I *never* lied to Gault, rarely omitted anything I knew, because there was never any telling when he was asking a question not to gather information, but rather to test whether I would be honest with him.

"Melek—"

"You should have run when I gave you the chance," I growled. "If you disappear now, he'll know I let you loose and we'll both be dead."

"I wouldn't—"

"Be quiet, I need to think."

She sighed and for a flash I wanted nothing more than to *throttle* her. She was my mate, my soul, and she was *blind.* Now the greatest threat to her wellbeing that existed had called for us and there was no avoiding it.

Whether Gault had designs to remove me or not, he did not entertain delay, or games.

I needed to have her there within the hour. Sooner.

Shit.

I turned and paced the tent, cursing as I considered plan after plan, and discarded them all, because there was no way around this. Now that his attention was on her, the only choice was to bring her.

But I was bringing her as an enemy. As an asset. As *leverage* to him.

Fuck!

There was no choice. I was caged just as surely as she was, and just as helpless. Probably more so.

Yilan might believe that the men in this camp would follow me, but she was a spy, and a manipulator. She functioned in a place of deception. I knew a soldier's mind. The discussions between those in the ranks were often nothing more than bluster. Ideas. Wishes. There was a *massive* difference between dreaming of a different King, and putting their bodies and futures on the line to crown one.

And besides... I'd never sought a throne. Always been grateful I wasn't burdened with one. I was a male of action. To be constantly in company, to be forced to stand as figurehead in pomp and formality... God, if the boredom didn't kill me, the machinations would.

Part of the reason for my success had come in my early decision to speak the truth. I was surrounded by deceptive males who always assumed my forthright words and acknowledgement of my struggles was a strategy. When I had been young and working my way up the ranks, my rivals assumed I knew far more than I let on, and was confident of victories I hadn't even aimed for yet.

They stepped carefully because they saw my forthright nature as an indication that I had resources or knowledge they didn't. They read my confidence as arrogance, and my questions as manipulations designed to lull them into false security.

They defeated themselves. Handed me victories.

And yet...

Gault was a different creature.

"Melek..."

I shook my head and kept pacing, thinking, planning. If Gault only wanted to interrogate her himself, to check on me, he wouldn't have me present. If he was calling for me to bring her, he wanted me to see or hear whatever it was that he planned to do or say. It had to involve me somehow.

That left only one possible conclusion: He knew we were connected and was going to use her against me.

Either I had somehow, unwittingly, given away the bond. Or he'd heard the rumors that I claimed her and wanted to take her from me.

Nothing else made sense.

Shit… *Shit.*

"Melek!"

I turned on her, scowling and her head snapped back when she saw my eyes.

"You should have gone when I gave you the chance."

"There is no point discussing what should have been. We are here now. You have to—"

"I have to take you to him, is what I have to do. The question is, how to do so with even a chance for both of us to live through it."

She blinked and her eyes went wide. Then I turned away, looking at my trunks, mentally cataloging the resources I had, considering what this could be. How Gault might approach it. And what options were open to me.

I would *not* surrender her.

I *could not* challenge my King.

Which meant there was only one option left.

I started towards the trunk in the corner, flipping the lid and digging through it until I found the scarves I'd been searching for. Then I stalked over to my weapons and flipped through my blades until I found the smallest, thinnest of them.

When I returned to the cage she was watching me warily. And when I flipped the short dagger, catching it carefully by its blade to offer the hilt to her, her eyes widened.

"Take it. Hide it," I growled. "If you need a belt, I can offer you one, but it would likely be too bulky—"

"I don't need a belt," she said faintly. "But do you have a sheath?"

I nodded and trotted back to find the smallest sheath I owned, then gave that to her as well.

She slipped the blade into the sheath, then reached around her own back, pulling up the back of her shirt—my shirt. She was still wearing my old sleep shirt with the sleeves rolled up. Thank God it was thicker cotton and long. Then she tucked the sheath into the hollow of her back and pulled the back of the shirt down over it.

I growled. It wasn't a fantastic placement—the shirt was long and would take precious seconds to raise if she had to go for it.

"Which is your dominant weapon arm?" I asked her quickly.

"I don't have one."

I raised one brow skeptically.

She raised one back. "I'm not lying."

I tilted my head and pressed my lips thin so she'd know I was suspicious. "Which hand do you *prefer* to use?"

"My right."

I nodded once, then opened the cage, ignoring the surprise in her eyes. "Then give me your left," I muttered. "You're coming with me, bound to me."

Her head jerked back. "Bound? Why? You could hold me—"

"Because I have to stop you escaping, *obviously,*" I said dryly. "Next time I tell you to run, Yilan, you do it. If you'd listened earlier, I'd be the only one in danger right now."

She didn't respond, but she did take a deep breath, then stepped forward and offered me her left wrist.

I looped the silk scarf around it once, then tied that end off with a non-slip knot, before twisting it, then binding the other end to my wrist, so our hands rested back-to-back. Our knuckles brushing.

The twist between us would offer rotation—she could turn her hand without mine changing position, and visa-versa. But she was bound to my side as surely as any cuff or chain.

Unless she got that blade loose and cut through it.

"But… that's *your* right hand," she said as she watched me tie us together.

I smiled grimly. "I don't have a dominant hand, either," I said.

Her eyes cut up from our hands to meet mine and she arched a brow just as I had a moment earlier.

But neither of us spoke. And a few moments later I was pushing the tent flap aside to lead her out into the sunlight… and into the den of the lion that might very well devour both of us.

34. An Audience with the King

SOUNDTRACK: *I'm Not Afraid of the Dark* by Oshins and Anna Graceman

~ YILAN ~

We stood in the center of the King's lavish tent which was three times the size of Melek's and filled with a full suite of furniture, including the armoire I'd hidden behind for days. Rich rugs covered the dirt floor, and a battery of slaves lined the walls, including guards at the door and several women dressed provocatively, but keeping their chins low and their eyes on their feet.

It turned my stomach.

Melek offered the benediction of peace, and the King nodded to accept it, but didn't return the favor.

"Do you want a drink, Melek?" the King said, his deep voice resonant with disdain as he snapped his fingers at one of the slaves, and she rushed to a sideboard to begin pouring whatever Gault usually drank.

Melek shook his head. "I drank as much as I wanted last night," he said. If we hadn't been under the King's eyes I would have gawked at him for the manipulative words.

Deceptive fucker.

Gault waited until he'd been served a goblet full of what looked to be red wine. He stroked the woman's breast as she handed it to him, and gave her a disgusting smile. But she gave nothing away, only nodded once as she offered the cup, then waited for him to be done and dismissed her with a wave of his hand before she moved again.

I thought of what she and the others must endure at his hands and my stomach churned.

"Did you enjoy your night last night, then?" Gault asked Melek, as if there'd been no break in their conversation.

"More than I should have," Melek said sincerely.

Even as fear coursed through me, I tensed with the urge to *laugh*. I recognized it as a hysterical response. But where was Jannus when you needed him? We could have had such a field day with that if Melek and I weren't standing here, knees trembling, awaiting either my demise or his. Or worse.

I prayed fervently that this was only the King toying with Melek and nothing more sinister.

"I met with the Captains this morning as you suggested," Melek said as if Gault had asked. "I believe our current plan is—"

"I didn't bring you here to discuss the strategy. I agree. It's time to move," he said quietly.

I blinked, but kept my eyes fixed on his hand on that goblet. I found his golden eyes unnerving.

"Oh. Good," Melek said. "Then what—"

"This is an... interesting way to bind a prisoner," Gault said, raising his goblet in the direction of our tied wrists. I would have assumed he was disapproving, but he smiled, and his tone was all suggestion.

Melek huffed. "I gave the guards the Covenant Days off. I have to keep her close."

"Hmmm, close. Yes," Gault murmured, his eyes gleaming. "I take your point."

Melek began to frown, but then the King turned to the two guards that stood either side of his door—not having been given the days off—and beckoned them closer.

"I need to speak with the General. Take the prisoner outside and—"

"Sire, I have to disagree. She is... very slippery. I don't usually allow her out of her cage at all. She has already almost escaped once, and that was with the cage. I can't let her out of my sight. I will not put the burden of her on a male who has not had my experience with... stifling rebellion."

Gault's eyes narrowed.

Then Melek smiled at him, a sly, predatorial smile I hadn't seen from him before. It chilled my blood. "Besides. I find I've grown rather... attached. There's something quite satisfying about making an enemy submit."

Gault snorted. "So, I heard. I'll admit, I didn't remember her enough to understand the appeal, but now that I see her..." he trailed off, his eyes raking down my body and making my skin crawl.

I kept my eyes on the wall of the tent behind him and refused to react. But I *felt* Melek tense.

"To keep her here while we speak, though..." Gault added with a sharp, questioning look at Melek.

"She is an asset for now, then she'll be removed," Melek shrugged. "As long as she's at my side, she's no risk."

Gault tipped his head. "It seemed odd that you chose to lay claim to a *Fetch*, but then I suppose she's been quite useful to you. And she is strong. She could likely survive a breeding."

Melek took a beat to agree.

I was starting to sweat.

Gault waved his hand as if to push away a thought. "Very well, I suppose what I have to say won't give her more information than she could have anticipated on her own anyway," the King said, taking another mouthful from his goblet before continuing. "Now that we are positioned and our enemies will be rested before our advance, I want you there in person to lead that charge."

Melek went still. "Gault—Sire, to get to the ravine would mean marching during the peace."

Gault nodded. "Marching is not attacking. And you'd be alone—feel free to take a small guard, of course. Even if our enemies know you've moved, they won't be able to accuse you of taking action. You will not attack until you lead the ranks. And we will not do that until after the Covenant."

I was shaking with both fear and rage.

Melek was the most prominent figure in this war. If he left the camp at a time there was no other movement on the plains, scouts would see him. And even if he could be hidden before he actually moved to the Ravine—a big *if*—they would still know something important was happening. Messages would be sent. Strategies employed. He would be watched. *Everything* would be watched.

"Gault… if this was what you wanted, I should have stayed when we went before. We could have taken a decoy to ride back with you—"

"I have only just decided that this is needed."

Melek swallowed. "But the Fetch… Sire, she's a huge asset. But as I said, she is slippery. I wouldn't trust her to anyone else. She's in that cage, or tied to me—"

"You will win this. Once you have, she'll have served her purpose."

Melek went quiet. He couldn't argue with that without revealing something the King would not like.

I didn't even bother to hide my fear. These men discussed my death. It would only be natural that I would fear that. But my deepest fear, the one that made me grit my teeth against letting them chatter was—

"You go to the front. Leave her with me. I'll take her until you've won and we're certain of victory. We both know she won't betray her own people no matter how much she wants to stay alive. You take the ravine. Then I'll slit her throat because she's no longer needed and join you for the final advance."

And then he looked at me, and *smiled.*

Melek barely blinked. He didn't twitch. Didn't swallow. Didn't even *hesitate.* "If you're certain you want to deal with her—she has a sharp tongue as well as great skill—"

"I'll keep her gagged. One way or another," he said, his eyes locked on mine, his voice puttering off into a low rumble that made me brace and raise my chin.

"Of course," Melek said as if it was no big deal. "If you're sure, then I'll need another day or two to make certain she's hidden nothing and our final plan is foolproof. Then I'll travel at night to try and avoid the eyes."

The King shrugged. "Take whatever time and travel you believe is needed. I trust your judgment. But when you go, she stays with me."

Then he stared at Melek and waited. And I couldn't breathe.

It wasn't a request.

By their traditions, everyone believed Melek had taken me— laid claim to me. More than once. In their eyes, he *owned* me.

Gault telling Melek to hand me to him meant he'd make me the King's property. He was the only male I knew of who outranked

Melek, and therefore, the only one who could make the claim as an order, without an outright challenge.

And if Melek were to resist, it *would* be a challenge.

You did not challenge a King without staging a coup, intentional or not. And we all knew it.

Melek hesitated a bare second, before dropping his chin and thumping his free arm to his chest. "Of course. But if I'm to do this, I need to move now, Gault. There's a lot to do before I'll need to travel if I'm going to make it in time."

Gault nodded, his expression unchanging as his eyes returned to me. "I look forward to victory," he said absently, then licked his lips.

I wanted to scream. But thankfully, Melek only bowed, then whipped around and dragged me out of the tent. He moved so quickly I was pulled against him and bounced off his arm and side until I found my balance.

When I was back on my feet and steady, I was still having to stop my teeth chattering.

And Melek was so tense his entire body felt like steel.

35. A New Understanding

~ YILAN ~

"You should have run when I gave you the chance," he insisted as he dragged me through the camp.

"We couldn't know—"

"Of course we could! Do you really believe I would just release you on a whim? That I hadn't thought that through?" he hissed.

I halted suddenly, turning to stare at him. "You knew the King would decide to take me?"

"Of course not!" But before he continued, his eyes cut up the trail and he jerked me into motion again, closing his mouth with a snap and warily watching the trail ahead between the tents where a line of women carting water and other resources had appeared, walking single file, their heads down and eyes on the feet of the woman in front of them.

The first in line looked up fearfully when we moved... then when she saw Melek's face her shoulders sagged with relief and she dropped her eyes again.

The little exchange was so telling that it brought home to me what a blessing it had been that the King put me in Melek's capable—no, *honorable* hands, and not some other Nephilim. I'd known that in my head, but I was washed with some potent relief of my own as he tugged me forward, ignoring the women.

As we walked, he ground his teeth, eyes blazing, daring anyone who looked to find anything but a fierce General dragging a prisoner through the camp.

But I didn't miss that he had kept away from the main tracks that were wide and passed the central stable tents and other busy areas. And he walked so quickly, eating up the distance with his long, angry strides that I had to trot to keep up with him.

"Melek," I started when we were alone on the trail again. But he interrupted me.

"Not now," he muttered, continuing to tug me along. "Wait until we're at the tent."

I sighed, but kept up with him, letting some of my fear show so that if anyone saw us they'd think he was about to punish me and I was afraid.

When we finally made it to the tent, Melek blew out a breath he must have been holding. But he didn't slow. He marched me straight inside, pulling the arm up where we were tied and muttering as he worked at it while we walked, tearing the knot free before grasping my wrist and tossing me into the cage, slamming the lock home before turning away and stalking over to his clothing trunk, wrestling with the knot on his own wrist as he did so.

"Melek, this just makes everything clearer. You must do it now. It's time."

"Time for what?" he muttered, putting his teeth to the knot on his wrist to finally pull it free and tug the scarf off with a snap of the silk.

"Time to lead the coup. To take out Ga—"

I wasn't sure I'd ever seen such a massive body move so quickly. One moment he was crossing the tent with his back to me, the next he was at the cage door, throwing it wide, grasping my hair in one fist and clapping his other hand over my mouth, looming over me, glaring with such fury my relief fled to make room for sheer terror.

His eyes were flames of rage as he stared down at me. Then, without letting go of my mouth, he slowly lowered his head until his jaw brushed mine and his breath fluttered in my ear.

"If you ever again say those words out loud here, where a listener could hear, I will slit your throat myself." He lifted his head only far enough to meet my eyes, his nose almost brushing mine. "I am not a traitor, Yilan. I *cannot be* a traitor, do you understand?"

Was he saying…?

I blinked and he slowly let go of my mouth, but he kept that hand fisted in the back of my hair. When he'd freed my mouth his eyes dropped to my lips for one moment, then he wrenched them back up to my eyes and nerves jangled through me.

Was it time?

Yes. It had to be time.

I had to trust him…

"You serve one. Does that not matter to your precious honor?" I whispered.

"A King cannot be a traitor to himself—"

"He can betray his people. And he does. Putting his own needs before theirs *always*. And they know it, Melek. They *know*. They already have no loyalty to him. They follow *you.*"

"You're lying, trying to get me—"

"No, I'm not. I've been listening to them for *weeks*. I've checked and double checked. Even found some evidence that he was behind the Shade, though I can't prove it—"

"Bullshit. Jannus isn't close enough to him to have heard anything, and none of the others would speak to you about him—"

"They weren't close to me. I was close to them. Without their knowledge."

He went still, his eyes searching mine, back and forth. "When?" he grunted.

I hesitated, not because I didn't have an answer, but because there was no going back from this moment. If I told him…

"Yilan, if you hold even an *ounce* of respect for me, you will answer me. *Right now*."

I swallowed hard and nodded, my hair tugging against his grip. "Let me go, and lock the cage," I said hoarsely.

His eyes widened slightly and his head jerked back a hair. He stared at me for a breath, but then obviously made a decision, because he let me go and stepped out of the cage, still watching me.

"Lock it," I said.

He reached for the lock and slammed it home, but his eyes never left mine.

"Step back."

His eyes narrowed, but he did as I said and took a wide step back, then stood with his feet shoulder width apart and folded his arms, his jaw rolling.

It was the middle of the day and the shadows were dim, but the sun glowed more brightly on the front of the tent, than at its back, and there was a deeper shadow across the back of the cage where he'd left the screens up for my dignity.

"Just... don't panic," I murmured as I stepped behind the screen and he passed out of my sight... and me out of his.

And then I walked the shadows at the back of the tent, holding tightly because it took a great deal of strength and was easy to lose myself in such a dim shadow.

He didn't catch it, because he was so focused on the spot where I'd disappeared behind the screen.

When I was behind him and he still hadn't noticed, I cleared my throat.

And then I was gratified to see the great General Melek Handras leap with the alacrity of a cat—and a yowl not too dissimilar, either.

36. Tell Me True

~ *MELEK* ~

I stared at that screen in the cage, my wits scrambled and mind spinning from Gault's maneuvering. I knew what she was implying, but it had to be a trick of some kind and I was watching for it, not for her, but for the movement of the cage or the screens or—

Ahem.

I almost leaped out of my skin, whirling, reaching instinctively for one of my blades before I'd even returned to earth, every hair on my body standing straight—and every instinct shrieking alarm when I found her standing demurely behind me, her hands clasped in front of her, and her chin low, but eyes up on me.

And only *slightly* smug.

"What... the actual... *fuck?*" I breathed, then I blinked as it came to me. *She was making me see her.*

I growled and folded my arms. "This is another of your visions. A very good trick, Yilan, and one that you'll probably need to use to escape now, but—"

"No, Melek. This is real."

Her face was solemn, her knuckles white where she clamped her hands together, and I realized she was stopping herself from shaking.

"Walking the shadows is... I am very adept at it. While you slept at night I walked the camp and listened and spied and..." she lifted her hands and kind of shrugged. "I'm not lying to you."

I gaped at her, empty headed. Utterly speechless.

It was a trick. It had to be—a manipulation of my mind.

"I can tell you that Gault has his own spies. They aren't as good as me, but they're good. He also knows the men follow you. And he's growing more and more jealous. All these efforts to show himself up next to you, to set you up for failure... they are not by chance. And they are not for any other purpose. He knows. And he's working against you. I'm *certain* the Shade was his, though it is the one part I cannot prove. He is... You were right that he is not stupid. But he is made foolish by his own pride. And his gluttony for power. He is already King. He already conquered most of the continent. And now he's coming for you. You cannot let him win. If not for yourself, then for the rest of us."

Unable to take my eyes from her, certain she would pull another trick, and—despite myself—convinced that she spoke truth. I shook my head.

She took a step closer to me, then another, until she stood at my toes, her head craned back to meet my eyes.

"I'm telling you the truth. All of it. I vowed to you that I would not break my word, and I haven't. I haven't escaped. And I have not used my knowledge against you. I... I cannot. I could not without hurting myself," she breathed.

She was impossible. She was infuriating.

She was *incredible.*

I couldn't find words. I clawed a hand into my hair and blew out the breath that was making my ribs creak, still just staring at her, yearning to reach for her, and frightened to as well—what if it was an illusion? What if I'd fallen to her in my mind?

"I'm not lying, Melek," she whispered, her brows pinching and eyes beginning to shine. "Everything I've told you is true. I... I am here. I need to know what you're going to do."

I shook my head. "I truly do not know," I croaked.

Her throat bobbed. "What... what do you *want?"*

I was so far beyond anything comprehendible, I just shook my head and groaned. "You."

Her eyes went wide, and the dam broke on my tongue.

"Yilan, I cannot give you into his hands—not for a moment. He is ruthless, brutal, and utterly without conscience. And you... you are my *mate."*

She sucked in a breath and took a step back, but I followed her.

"I saw it that night at the lake, and I think you see it too, but you don't want to. You've been denying the inevitable and it has brought us here. Don't you see? Can't you feel it? Of course you can, I know you can—stop telling yourself it is anything other than—"

"Lust. Lust is not a bond—"

"This is not simple *lust!*" I snarled and she continued to back away from me, but I did not let her retreat. I followed her, snaking a hand around her waist and keeping her there, though she leaned back and her hands came up to my chest as if she'd push me away.

But she didn't.

She just stared.

Terrified.

And I had to know… Was my mate terrified of *me?* Or of the situation in which we found ourselves? Because she had me by the balls and she didn't even realize it.

"Stop *thinking*, Yilan," I hissed. "Stop reacting in your fear and just… *measure this.* If there is truly a soulbond between us—which I am certain there is—we will never be free of it. We can face it together or apart. *But we cannot pretend it doesn't exist."*

"I… this isn't… you can't just—"

Unable to resist, I reached up, cupping her jaw with both hands and opening my mouth against hers—softly this time. Not the deep, demand of lust, though that fire blazed in my belly. This was a question, a taste, a *request.*

Lips open and hovering over hers, I sighed into her mouth and barely traced her tongue with mine.

She sucked in and froze, but did not pull away, and so I did it again.

I kissed her not as a conquest, not even as a lover.

I kissed her as the precious twin to my soul that she was.

And to my delight, she melted against me, her breath short and sharp, but her kiss soft, tentative, *questioning.*

"Yilan," I breathed, *"please."* Fighting myself for restraint, I slid one hand into her hair, and the other around her waist, pulling her against me, pinning her to me, and deepening the kiss.

And, joy of joys, she responded, arching back over my hand on her spine, the skin on her neck pebbling, and opening her mouth.

Her hands slid up my chest to lace behind my neck, her nails digging into my skin, but even that bite was a desperate pleasure.

I rumbled, arching her backwards and leaning over her, unable to be close enough, my body quivering like a boy, desperate with need.

I felt the moment she accepted me, felt the thrill of her body turning liquid in my arms, and the delight of her needy whimper. Felt the shift in my chest, as if a piece of my heart had been nudged aside to make room for something—a warm presence still coyly hidden in shadow. But present now. Making itself known.

I groaned again and dove for her throat when her head tipped back and she let me take her weight—her featherweight. There was nothing to her at all, which was terrifying, and also so fucking *admirable.* She was a little wisp of nothing, yet she kept me thinking, kept me moving, continued to surprise me.

Mate.

Soulbond.

Mine.

She gasped when I nipped at her neck and her nails dug harder into the back of my neck, pulling me closer. I chuckled and kissed my way up to her throat, the corner of her jaw, the nipped at her ear before whispering.

"It has been torment listening to you breathe every night, knowing how close you are and what I would do to you if you were willing."

Her breath caught and she dropped one hand to the side of my leg, drawing her fingers up slowly in a way that set my blood on fire, but also reminded me of the danger that she was in. That we were both in.

I made myself take her face in my hands and lift my head to meet her eyes, staring down at her, pleading with her to trust me. To *hear* me.

"Yilan, you are in danger even I cannot be certain to protect you from. The bond... the bond exists. If he were to take you—or kill you... I could not survive it," I croaked.

She blinked, her eyes, which had been glazed with lust, now wide and wary. She searched my gaze as desperately as I'd searched hers moments before.

"I will not leave you with the King—and that statement alone is tantamount to treason. Do you hear me, Yilan? You *must* escape before I leave. You *must.* Walk the shadows, kill the guards, whatever is needed, you *must* be away from here, and soon. If he changes his mind—"

"I cannot simply walk out of here, Melek," she whispered hoarsely, then cleared her throat, still staring at me. "It takes a great deal of power to move as I just did—I can only do it for short distances. And I am not invisible to anyone who knows how to look. And besides… you push me to accept that there is a bond between us, then insist that I leave you?"

"There is no other choice!" I growled.

"Yes, there is!" she hissed. "You could lead. You could control. You could take the Nephilim in a new direction—"

"God, you don't get it at all, do you?!" I growled, releasing her so that she stood straight, though I couldn't step away, my body wouldn't allow it. "So intelligent, so certain of your path—but so fucking stubborn. Think it through, Yilan!"

"I have! That's why—"

"You draw so much from half a word and a second look, and you stay blind to this? I tried to let you see it, tried to make it clear: I *cannot* defy the King. He is Gall's true father and he knows how much I care about the boy. He knows I would never leave him to… to *this,*" I spat. "The moment he gets so much as a hint that I am working against him, he will take Gall and hold him. He will not kill him. Only torment him—just to get to me."

She blinked and took a deep breath. "I did… I did gather that."

"Then why do you—?"

"It just means we need to take Gall with us."

I jerked. She couldn't mean…? "We?"

She nodded quickly. "We. *Us.*"

I could barely breathe. "So… you sense it? You admit—"

"I sense the most terrifying thing I've ever experienced, Melek," she whispered. "And instead of sending me into a panic, it… it lights up my heart."

God, the joy that coursed through me then was—

"And… it cannot be," she breathed.

37. Vowed to You

~ MELEK ~

I staggered, my blood running cold just as I was about to grab her up. Just as I was about to take her mouth again.

"Yilan… it already *is.*"

She shook her head and her eyes began to well, simultaneously breaking my heart and making me want to roar with rage.

"We have not… nothing has cemented between us. We are not truly tied—"

"Yilan—"

She started to back away, a single tear tipping over her lashes and trickling down her cheek. But I wouldn't let her flee. I followed her as she backed across the tent.

"Melek, it couldn't be. God is testing us. We both know—"

"I know that this is nothing to be *denied*. It exists whether it is convenient or not!"

"But our lives… our roles… this war—"

"If God put us together, then he must have a plan for our future!"

"He does!" she whispered. "And you refuse it."

I froze, but caught her wrist as she was about to step away from me again. Both of us stared in horror and pleading and… pain.

Doubt. Fear. Indignation. It all coiled through my thoughts, tightened my chest.

She stared at me with grief in her eyes and I braced, shaking my head.

This was not just lust. Not simple need.

This was two souls that sang the same song. And *she* was the one denying it!

"Tell me," I growled, pulling her into the circle of my arms and not letting her go. Then I caught her hand with mine and put it flat on my chest, let her feel how she made my heart pound. "Tell me this is not real. Tell me that you will not accept me—*tell me.*"

She stared, shaking her head, her mouth opening and closing, her body tense... but she made no sound.

I could barely breathe, but hope took flight in my chest as I stared her down.

"Yilan... tell me there is no bond. Tell me your soul doesn't *sing* when we touch?" I flattened my hand over hers on my chest and waited.

She stared back at me, that horror and fear roiling in her eyes, and yet...

She slumped in my arms and shook her head. "I can't," she whispered.

I descended on her with a tormented groan, with hands clawed, body shaking. The kiss was deep and brutal and a relief because she clung and clawed and gave as good as she got. And then she pressed herself against me, hooked her leg behind my thigh and gasped my name, and the leash I'd been holding so tightly for what seemed like forever, just snapped.

I was mindless, growling, *devouring* her. Clawing at her clothing, tearing it from her body, hissing when her nails scored my back as she tried to pull off my weapon straps.

Instead, I was forced to let her go long enough to rip the buckles loose myself—and open my leathers to free myself because my need was so great, I worried I would limit blood flow within the confines of my trousers.

There was no sound but our gasping breaths and the rustle and rip of clothing as I stumbled with her towards the bed, bit her lip between my teeth until she gasped, then picked her up and threw her onto the bed.

She bounced. She gave a small, breathless chuckle as she pushed up on her hands to sit, then reached for me as I crawled up after her. Unable to be apart from her for even the seconds it took to find her body, I gripped her hair and pulled her into a deep kiss as I lowered her back to the pillows and settled between her thighs.

But just as she writhed against me and her mouth opened, just as I would have muttered the vows and taken her *right then,* I froze.

She went still under me and her eyes flew open—and I saw the zing of fear there, the immediate question, the doubt—and shook my head.

"I will give no room for anyone to deny this, Yilan. Tell me how your people bind for the vows?"

Her eyes went very wide. She had both hands on my face, gripping me and she stared, breathless for a moment.

"Are you certain?"

All the questions, all the doubts, all the obstacles and complications we would face swirled in my head, but they were nothing in the face of this *conviction* deep in my chest.

She was for me.

She was made for me.

And I would never be complete without her.

"I have never been more certain of anything in my life," I croaked.

She gave a breathless little laugh and shook her head, but she was smiling. Then she looked to the side, found the edge of the pillowcase and gripped it. I frowned, then realized she was trying to tear a strip from it.

Letting my weight rest on her so that she sighed, I reached over her head for the simple cotton and tore it, pulling a strip that ran the length of the pillow, yanking it off, then offering it to her.

She blew out a shuddering breath as she took it, then looked at me. "Give me your wrist."

I offered her my right hand, knowing she preferred her right to be free, and her forehead creased. She stretched up to kiss me, her lips soft and plump and her tongue teasing so that I almost forgot what was happening, but then, after plunging the velvet depths of her mouth, I growled and leaned back again, bracing on my other arm so she could have that wrist.

Breathing quick and sharp, she tied the end of the cotton to my wrist, looping it twice, then tying it off with a complicated knot I'd never seen before.

She hesitated, and looked at me before she put her own hand near mine, and I knew she was considering what we were about to do. The bond that we would forge. The *eternal* nature of this moment.

And, even as desperate as I was, as deeply as I yearned to *fight* for this, I stayed silent.

I would not convince her. I could not take her against her will. I would not complete the bond that way.

She searched my eyes, then used that hand to cup my cheek. "Melek?"

"Yes?" I grunted, terrified she was about to retreat.

She bit her lip. "Thank God that you're mine," she whispered, and as my heart exploded, she laid her hand against mine, looped the cotton around both our wrists in a figure-eight, then tied it off on hers, using her teeth to pull it tight.

There was a strange, still moment then as she stared at our hands and her eyes went wide.

"My mate," she breathed, her tone awed.

I laced my fingers with hers and pulled it to my chest, holding it there so that she felt my pulse against her knuckles, bracing on the other hand to keep my back arched so I could hold her eyes.

And then I spoke the words I'd so rarely heard of a Nephilim offering, and that I had spent most of my adult life wondering if they would ever cross my lips.

My body for your protection.

My voice for your champion.

My blood runs for you, my soul.

My mate.

Behold, you are my beauty. Behold you are my love.

Let me taste with my mouth because your kiss is richer than wine.

Let my body speak the words my tongue cannot form.

Set me as a seal upon your heart, as a seal upon your soul.

For my love is stronger than death, my jealousy fierce as the grave.

I burn for you with fire, the very flame of God.

I am your beloved. I am your mate.

My soul sings for you. My desire is for you.

I give myself in this world, and the next.

Before God… you are mine.

Her eyes welled and she reached up with her free hand, cupping my face as she whispered the words in return.

And my blood began to ignite, like a fuse, burning closer to my heart with every word.

~ *YILAN* ~

Strange things were happening in my chest. I couldn't breathe—didn't want to. My skin crackled and fizzed like fireworks. I'd been plunged from the fear of the King's demand to this incredible, impossible, *necessary* moment and I wanted to weep—but I wouldn't let myself, because I couldn't bear to miss a moment of it.

He was here. He was real. He'd opened himself and my soul stretched for him, battering at me.

I had no idea how this would play out. No way of knowing if either of us would survive this. But I couldn't keep fighting. He'd looked me in the eye and claimed me, and it broke through the last of my defenses.

He was my mate.

And that meant he *couldn't* belong to anyone else. I wouldn't survive it.

And so, with the echo of his whispered words still curling around my heart, I swallowed back my fear and embraced the joy of this moment. Of *him*. And I gave voice to the vows I'd been supposed to speak the day before—but to an entirely different man.

My heart for your safety.
My voice for your champion.
My blood runs for you, my soul.
My mate.
Behold, you are my strength. Behold you are my love.
Let me taste with my mouth because your kiss is richer than wine.
Let my body speak the words my tongue cannot form.
Set me as a seal upon your heart, as a seal upon your soul.
For my love is stronger than death, my jealousy fierce as the grave.
I burn for you with fire, the very flame of God.
I am your beloved. I am your mate.
My soul sings for you. My desire is for you.

I give myself in this world, and the next.
Before God...

I took a final breath as everything within me clamored to finish this, to claim him, to be claimed by him—and yet the roiling storm of what would come as a result of this day would not leave me in peace.

I sucked in a deep breath and Melek's eyes shadowed... and pleaded with me. Looming over me, his thick chest and broad shoulders casting me in shadow deep enough to hide me from eyes...

And I knew I would never be the same. He was possibly the strongest man on the continent—in creation! If we could not defeat these demons together, no one else would bring me through, either. And so, I curled my nails into the stubble on his jaw and let the love I'd been so desperately denying blaze from my eyes, and I took him. Claimed his soul. The words rushed from me in a torrent.

...You are mine!

Like a fire lit to oil, need and love exploded in my chest, igniting my veins and rushing through me to burn every other thought or desire from my body and mind in a single, white-hot flash.

I stopped breathing, my heart stopped beating for a moment as it felt like the explosion within cracked my ribs and bared my chest.

But just when the pain should have begun, just when I was braced there, gasping and stunned, my ribs cracked and heart exposed, something within him rushed for me—fuel to the flame, and soothing ice to the burn.

At every point where our flesh touched his soul rushed from him and into me, coiling with mine, twining, twisting, braiding together, then yanking tight.

We both cried out as our hearts stopped—then rushed on, pulsing, filling, pumping in time and suddenly that space within me that had felt so empty, the spot where something had gone out from me to stretch for the darkness of him was bathed in light.

Mate.

Soulbond.

Mine.

I cried out as Melek bellowed with relief and joy. He gripped my hand so tightly, yanking it from his chest and pinning it on the pillow above my head as he descended like an avenging angel to take me. Forever.

38. Nothing Else Matters

SOUNDTRACK: *Burn* by Corvyx

~ YILAN ~

I had feared this moment, avoided it for years. Fought to keep myself apart from any man that wanted me because deep down I had known that I would lose myself in a bond.

Soulbond chosen by God, or forgedbond chosen by me, it wouldn't matter.

I'd always known that something in me yearned to find the man who would make me surrender. But, before Melek, I'd never yet met the man who inspired that in me. And I'd worried that if I gave myself, I'd surrender to the wrong one.

Melek was a shock. A stunning surprise. Impossible, hopeless, *perfect.*

And when the moment came, for the first time in my life, the fear was gone. Surrender no longer shrieked at me from the dark. Instead, it was light and warmth that curled and beckoned.

Mate.

Soulbond.

Mine.

I could no longer deny it. And so, I gave myself up.

For better, or worse, he was mine and I was his.

Neither of our lives would ever be the same.

As he dropped to cover me, his weight pressing me into the mattress, his free hand cupping the back of my neck and descending with a groan that seemed to start in his toes, I gasped his name and threw my free hand around his neck, grasping the tail of his warrior's length and pulling him to me as all thoughts of any other male were blown from my mind like smoke in the wind... and I gave myself over. Forever.

"Please, Melek," I gasped. "I want you. Just... just be gentle."

He groaned and dove for my mouth, his plunging tongue a tantalizing taste, of what was to come.

"Hold onto me," he rasped. "Don't let go."

I nodded quickly, then threw my free arm around his shoulders, burying my face in his thick neck and clinging as he nudged at me once, then again, teasing, and stealing my breath.

"Yilan—"

"Yes," I gasped. "Yes!"

Still rolling his hips, still sliding against me, still nudging at my core, tainting with the slightest push into me, he leaned up on his elbows and dropped his forehead to mine, our eyes locking, mouths open.

His tongue darted out to tease under my lip as he nudged at me again—an inch, this time—and the first hint of the fullness of him dropped my jaw. Nerves fighting sheer need.

"I'm here," he rasped, squeezing my hand where we were bound, and cupping the other over my head. "Don't leave me."

"I won't."

"Oh, God... *Yilan,*" he groaned, then rocked his hips, sliding up and into me another inch, slowly, his body quivering and his grip on my hand so tight our knuckles rolled against each other.

Pleasure on the edge of pain ignited there where we joined as my body began to stretch, but then he let go of a shuddering breath and pulled slowly out, leaving me trembling in his wake, hollow, *needy.*

"Don't stop," I gasped.

He groaned and dropped his head, taking my mouth, then graveling my name as he dropped his free hand to grip my hip and hold me.

Then he lifted his head, opened his eyes and stared down at me, his warrior's length splaying over his shoulder as, mouth open and eyes bright with need and torment, he quickly thrust into me, filling me, stretching me, breaking through that barrier, reaching the places within me that no man had ever touched.

I cried out, arched, clawing into his back and gasping, overwhelmed with the perfect pleasure of joining with him—but unnerved by that clang of pain that promised more because I knew he still hadn't given me everything he had.

Shuddering, Melek threw his free hand back up to my head, then froze, dropping his face to the pillow next to mine, his shoulders heaving... but he didn't withdraw.

He took most of his own weight on one elbow so he wouldn't crush me, but leaned into me enough to press me down into that mattress. His body rippled as a shudder rocked through him, but he still didn't move.

I was gasping, clinging, blinking as he panted into the pillow next to me, swallowing hard, his hand over my head now fisting my hair and keeping me in place.

"Yilan... are you well?" he croaked a moment later, his voice muffled by the pillow.

I nodded quickly. "I am. I am. I... I want you, Melek."

He huffed. "You have me, beautiful. Trust me."

A splutter of a laugh broke from me and my body tightened around him and he tensed, and it was the *strangest sensation* to feel him within me—to feel him react to my body. To be... consumed.

Melek's fingers tightened in my hair. Then he muttered a curse and pushed up on his elbows again to meet my eyes and I almost wept at the creases beside his eyes, the empathy and concern shadowing his beautiful, bright gaze.

"Catch your breath," he whispered, stroking my hair with his thumb. "Just breathe."

I couldn't look away from those eyes, and I lifted my hand from his back to hold his face, stunned by the incredible intimacy of feeling *joined* with him. How even that small movement let me feel the way my flesh gripped him, and yet moved with him.

My heart pounded, my blood was alight. And my body... my body *wanted more.*

We stared at each other and I wondered if he looked into the depths of my eyes and saw the future stretching out before us as I did.

And then, I smiled. "I want more, Melek," I whispered.

The corners of his eyes crinkled and his eyes lit with joy. "More of what?"

"More of you," I admitted, embarrassed and overjoyed in the same breath. *"All* of you."

He blew out a breath. "Are you certain? It is your first time and—"

"You're my mate," I said, suddenly shy at the admission, and yet unable to look away, and so I was blessed to see his eyes dance. "I want everything."

A deep, satisfied rumble began in his chest, vibrating against my sensitive nipples and I bit my lip, my breath picking up again.

"I don't know why God made you for me," he graveled, still stroking my hair with his thumb. "But I am very grateful that he did."

He leaned in and kissed me again, trembling under my hands, then whispered in my ear. "Hold onto me, Love."

With a little sob of joy, I gripped the back of his neck as he began to draw out of me, but instead of leaving me entirely, he only retreated inches, then tilted his hips and pressed into me again.

A cry broke in my throat without my permission. But before I could even inhale, he did it again, drawing out of me, then thrusting back in, taking another inch, and then another. And even though pain sang within me, it was overwhelmed by the wave of pleasure that every movement ignited in my flesh.

He dropped his head, his breath panting, rushing over my shoulder, beginning to sweat as he plunged deeper, and deeper. With each new thrust I was lost to anything but the sensation of *him*. Of the fullness of him, of the way my body stretched and reached and fizzed with pleasure for *him*. And then he gave a deep cry into the pillow as I felt him reach fully within me, and I was gasping with him. All of him.

He trembled as he drew out of me then, and for a moment I wanted to weep, my body aching to be so fully *with* him again— until he graveled my name and thrust again. Then he didn't stop.

His body, so large and strong, rippled like a snake. That hand, so calloused and capable, stroked my skin with a deep tenderness that brought tears to my eyes. And as he moved and called for me, as he gave in to the whispered cries and tormented groans, my pleasure grew and bloomed, my soul opening like a flower until we moved as one, and it was impossible to know where I stopped and he began.

My head was back, jaw slack, breath tearing in and out of my throat. When he drew out I could think of nothing but to have him back, and when he thrust into me, I could think of nothing but *again.*

Pleasure and need glowed on the horizon of my mind, like a rising sun, glimmering, igniting, turning everything gold.

I was gasping, panting, calling his name, fighting to keep my voice quiet as he picked up the pace and his great body shuddered and uncoiled for me.

He shook and groaned, his body steel, but his touch sweet silk. My name on his lips was a plea, a benediction. And every sound, every sensation pushed me closer to that horizon, made the sun burn brighter, and the wave rocking through me break harder.

I was shaking, whimpering, clinging, stretching within and without—clawing for that promise of pleasure, desperate and unable to think of anything else when Melek pushed up on his elbows, mouth open, jaw slack, eyes locked on mine and he groaned. "Come for me, Yilan—beautiful... *come for me."*

The deep roll of his voice, the desperation in his tone, and the sight of his massive body shivering with pleasure sent a bolt of pleasure through me that reached a place deep inside I'd never felt before.

I shattered.

"Mele—!"

His hand clapped over my mouth as my body bowed and I crested that wave, tumbled into the hot sun, plunged into pleasure that washed from deep within me, through my veins, into my skin, raising every hair on my body and stealing every breath, every thought.

With a gasp and a *"Oh fuck, yes!"* Melek pulled out of me, then plunged back in and pushed that wave higher, deeper, pushing me completely over the top... and my body gripped him so tightly, he was yanked over the edge with me.

The roar that tore out of him was so loud it vibrated in my body as he pulled out and thrust, pulled out and thrust, his body twitching and jerking, completely out of control. As my orgasm eased away, I watched him in awe, so abandoned, so unleashed... for me.

And then, with a groan, he slumped, catching himself as he covered me, clamping that free hand on the pillow and taking his own weight so that he wouldn't crush me as we lay there, tangled and sweaty, both of us panting.

He leaned his forehead on mine, locking eyes with me as our panting breaths mingled, and he stared at me, wide-eyed and trembling.

"Yilan… I… *love you,*" he rasped.

I sobbed. Tears pricked my eyes, though I didn't know why because I'd never been happier. And yet, the moment those words were spoken I could feel the profound shift happening within me—and within him.

The pressure building in my chest. The rumble as if a great weight was moving towards me, picking up momentum as it rolled down on me.

And then, as my pulse throbbed in every part of me—but especially where we joined—and my blood flared and fizzed, and suddenly that space in my chest that had been so tangled and vulnerable, so open and so filled by him, began to contract—first only a tug, a pressure… but pressing into pain and leaving me gasping.

"Yilan, *beautiful!*" he croaked, clinging to me, pulling me against him, our bodies curling together as we were rocked from within—spiraling, rushing power that expanded my ribs, stilled my heart, and threatened to suffocate me.

"Melek—what's happening?" I wheezed, clinging to him.

"Mine," he growled, curling that hand over my head again, covering me with his bulk and pulling his knees up to curl me into the cavity of his body. "*You cannot take her, she is* mine!"

I closed my eyes, trying desperately to inhale as it felt like my body was pummeled, clawed. As if an enemy had descended and threatened to pull me from Melek's grip. His hand bound to mine squeezed and pressed, grounding both of us as he twitched, grunting, holding me as tightly as if he fought for me, as if the unseen enemy tried to tear us apart—and he would not allow it.

"NO!" he snarled. "She is *mine!*" he roared and wrapped himself around me, lifting my hips off the bed, pulling me up into his lap so we could not be separated, embracing me with his free arm and covering me with his body, trembling, growling, flinching as if he were taking blows.

I gasped his name, clinging to him with my free arm, confused and afraid, but utterly unwilling to be apart from him, shaking my head and holding so tightly I feared I would bruise his ribs.

And then, as quickly as it started, that sensation was gone.

We were left, Melek kneeling, curled over me, holding me, covering me, both of us panting.

I could breathe again, thank God.

I wasn't sure how long we lay there catching our breaths and blinking back to reality, but eventually he sighed heavily and lifted his head to look at me, without moving away.

"Are you… well?" he whispered, then pushed a strand of hair back from my face.

I nodded, clamping my hand to the back of his neck. "What was *that?*"

I was almost crushed as Melek took a massive breath, then let it out and shook his head.

"I don't know who you are, or why, Yilan… but Lucifer himself did not want us to complete that bond."

I blinked. "Wait… what?!"

Melek shook his head again and sighed. "I don't understand any more than you do. But that was the power of the dark coming for you." His eyes took on a gleam and he cupped my face. "But I will not let it take you. *Ever.*"

Then he kissed me as if my breath was oxygen.

And I kissed him just as desperately in return. So deeply that my skin began to prickle again.

Melek had just groaned and rolled to his side, pulling me with him, murmuring about needing me again soon when the tent flap snapped aside.

Melek jerked and his wings appeared, one snapping open to fold over me as he pushed up, ready to throw himself against whoever had appeared—but then he froze, his eyes wide and mouth open.

I couldn't see beyond his wing, but I heard Jann's voice clear as day. And there wasn't an ounce of the sunny friendship, or flirty warmth he usually brought into this tent. His voice was dark, hushed, and *angry.*

"Seriously, Mel? You actually took her? *Seriously?*"

39. Mated

~ *MELEK* ~

I snapped a wing over Yilan to cover her and snarled over my shoulder, bracing, my body quivering, readying to take out whoever had appeared. But the figure storming across the tent, drawing his spear, was Jann. His normally bright eyes dark, and his easy countenance twisted into a snarl.

"I knew you had an eye for her, but I never thought you would stoop so low. But that roar—you can't hide that fucking roar, Melek—"

He didn't stop coming, and he was carrying his spear. Every instinct rushed to her protection, and every thought beyond removing the threat disappeared.

Still bound to her, I swept Yilan up and leaped off the bed, one wing curled around her to keep his eyes from her, landing in a half-crouch in front of my best friend, my mate clinging to my side and my wing curled for her modesty. As I raised my free hand for defense, I cursed under my breath. My weapons were laid aside against the wall of the tent, and I couldn't reach them without turning her towards him.

Jann stopped advancing when I landed and took a defensive stance, but his lip curled up in sneer, and he didn't lower the spear.

"Jann," I snarled, low and deep, every ounce of authority I'd ever possessed behind those quiet words. He *would* listen. "You will throw away the weapon in the presence of my mate, or I will make your guts her garters."

Jann froze, blinking, but a moment later his eyes narrowed and he growled. "Mate? You really think I would believe—"

"It's true."

Yilan's soft, feminine voice was soothing in this moment—and her words made my heart leap. But when she pushed the edge of my wing back so she could see him, I pulled her closer—did she not see that Jann was armed?

I could beat my best friend hand-to-hand, I was certain of it. But unarmed, and one of my hands tied to her, it might tip the balance.

Yet, at my side, Yilan was relaxed. She held the edge of my wing aside, like she looked at him from behind a curtain. I got a rush in my chest the moment I looked at her—her cheeks still pink, a tiny strand of her hair sticking to the side of her face.

She stopped when I tightened my grip on her, but her eyes were on Jann, which made my chest squeeze and my lip curl back from my teeth.

"It's true, Jann."

Pulling her to my side, I placed her between my side and the hollow of my wing, boxing her in, shooting a warning look at Jann that would leave him in no doubt of his fate if he were to keep advancing with that weapon.

But Jann had stopped moving, his brows so high his forehead was wrinkled.

He stared at her, stunned. Then looked at me, then back to her. Then he took a step back.

"Mate?" he breathed. "What... *How?*"

"Jann, toss the weapon. *Now,*" I seethed.

My friend blinked, then looked down at the spear he was holding.

When his head snapped up again, it was to level a measuring look at me. I tensed, ready to take him, but Yilan hugged my arm and whispered, "Just give him a second."

Jann's eyes widened when she did that and he shook his head. But a moment later he tossed the spear aside, letting it clatter to the dirt and roll away.

"I knew her flirting lacked heat... but I never imagined—"

"Neither did we," I growled, then swallowed, trying desperately to bring my body back under control. But the new bond—the singing of my soul—had ignited a frenzy in the beast within me. The dark side of my soul that would kill first and ask questions later. I had heard the stories about the Nephilim who found soulbonds, and the resulting carnage when their women were so much as under the eyes of another Neph. I'd always thought it was just males finding an excuse to unleash.

But I had just been a hairsbreadth from killing my best friend. No mercy. I would have *delighted* in killing him if he'd gotten that spear within reach of Yilan. And even though the threat had now passed, my body still quivered and roared for his blood.

And he was one of the good ones.

How the hell was I even going to leave this tent knowing the risk it posed to her?

She was a part of me—physically, spiritually. Even the slightest threat to her would send my instincts into high alert, as if *my* life was in danger.

Because it was, I realized. She was part of me. If she died... I would die.

I inhaled sharply and looked at the place where her little hand still rested on my arm, though I was no longer threatening to move towards Jann. Did she yearn for that touch as much as I did? I thought she did. She crowded close to my body as well…

"Does Gall know?" Jann asked her abruptly.

"No."

"He *can't*," I snapped.

Jann's stunned gaze snapped to me. "He *has to*. Melek, he believes you took her against her will. If he sees you two like this—"

Everything in me tensed immediately, poised for combat. Yilan's grip on my arm tightened as I leaned closer to Jann and pointed at his chest.

"You will keep this to yourself, or I will silence you. Gall is off Being Still and he won't come back until the end of the Covenant Days. But we won't make it that far. Two days. That's all we have. On the third I have to leave, and so will she."

Yilan sighed. But Jann frowned.

"Leave? Why?"

"Gault called us to Audience this morning. Both of us," I snarled. "He's *told me* that I am to lead the attack on the ravine, and I'm to leave her with *him* when I do. Once I win that battle—if I do—he'll kill her."

Jann's eyes widened. "Holy *shit*—"

"I have it handled—"

Yilan scoffed. We both turned to look at her and I swallowed back my bristling pride when her free hand left me and she planted it on her hip.

"You are my mate. I'm not leaving you." From this angle I could look straight down the valley between her breasts. It made my cock twitch.

I gritted my teeth. "You *are* my mate... and I am not leaving you with *him.*"

"So... I will go with you."

Jann coughed as I shook my head. "That's the first place Gault will look when he can't find you. In Nephilim eyes, I *claimed* you, Yilan. He's taking you from me on purpose. He is petty as fuck and already threatened by me. He won't stand for it—"

"So, you admit he's threatened by you?" she jumped in. I gave her a flat look, but she rushed on. "Yet I'm supposed to just leave and let him kill *my* mate?"

"He won't kill me. He'll punish me—"

"He didn't discover me when I spied on him for *days.* And I will have *more* freedom in the chaos of the frontline."

"And greater threat if you are discovered. Our best warriors are there, primed for battle, rested, and *itching* for an enemy to kill. No, Yilan."

She looked impatient. "But—"

"Do not ask me to accept your death!" I roared.

Yilan bristled and Jann took a step back, raising his hands. "I'm going to leave you two to... talk," he said carefully.

I sighed and turned to him, ignoring the shadows flickering in Yilan's big eyes. "I'll be out to get us food soon. An hour, maybe. Can we speak then?"

"Sure." Jann took a deep breath, shaking his head in disbelief, but his shock beginning to wane as he looked back and forth between us, then turned to walk out. He reached for the tent flap, then hesitated and looked at us over his shoulder. "I'll stay close. Make sure no one else comes to the tent."

I sighed. "Thank you, brother."

He nodded, then winked at Yilan, which made me stiffen again.

"Congratulations, both of you. I hope... somehow... you find a way." He gave a small, wistful smile that surprised me. Yilan thanked him quietly, then he was gone. I was frowning. Why was he—

"Melek."

268

I turned back to my mate, unfurling my wing so she just stood next to me, my heart—and my body—swelling in the rush of bathing in her gaze, even if it was disapproving.

"We have three days, Yilan. It's the latest I could justify leaving for the front. At the end of that time, I'll leave you in the cage for Gault to retrieve you. You're to escape the moment I'm gone. I'll figure out a plan for how we can find each other later."

She folded her arms again. "I'm not leaving you. You're *mine*." Even while she was pissing me off, my heart thrummed when she spoke with that possession in her tone. "We will not meet later as enemies. We will stay together as allies. And you will lead this continent in truth. That crown is yours."

Rage coursed through me, right alongside the warmth of her claim and I turned, looming over her, leaning down into her face and hissing the words through my teeth. "Mate or not, you will never, ever speak those words in this camp to me again. Or I will cut out your tongue."

I expected her to argue, to prod me, to force me to silence her. But to my surprise she tilted her head and put fingers to her chin as if she were considering my words.

"But Melek... with no tongue... how would I pleasure you?"

The jolt that snapped through me then—every sense heightened, lust burning in my belly.

I knew I should stay angry. Should force her to give me her word. But the sly smile on her face, and the burning heat in her eyes...

"God help me," I groaned, and dove for her mouth.

40. The Taste of You

~ MELEK ~

The beast within me was roaring to possess her again, but I knew she'd be sore. And the humanity that still held the reins in my heart ached for her. I had to be careful.

So, taking a firm grip on my leash, I kissed her deeply, delving the sweet depths of her mouth with my tongue and growling my need for her. She gave a small, startled laugh when I first kissed her, but within moments she was humming her own need and wrapping her free arm around my neck.

I picked her up, urging her to wrap her legs around my waist while I pulled her hand down and used my bound arm to carry her back to the bed without breaking the kiss.

It was strange to have her sit so high, her breasts pressing against my chest, her mouth level with mine, and her slim arm locked behind my neck.

Strange, and *wonderful.*

Unable to resist, I slid my free hand up her side, then between us to cup her breast that didn't quite fill my hand, but the sensation of its plump warmth, combined with the way her nipple went rivet-hard under my touch, sent a jolt of desire straight from my heart to my cock.

"Shit, Yilan. Do you hurt?" I rasped against her lips, then kissed her again before she could answer.

"I want you, Melek," she breathed back.

I caught that she hadn't actually answered me. But I could feel her body coming alive, and the bond was thrumming between us.

Who was I to deny my mate's need?

When I reached the side of the bed, I tipped her back onto it and she gave a little squeak, but she smiled and her cheeks flushed again. God, I loved the way her eyes sparkled when she looked at me—and how she reached for my chest.

But I needed to touch her, to *explore* her. Our first mating had been so desperate, so frantic... This would be slower... easier on her.

With her laying there on her back, me standing between her knees, I reached for the tie that bound us. "I may need your help with the knots—"

Her other hand slapped at mine where I'd started pinching at the knot and I stopped immediately, looking at her—surprised to see a flash of fear and *insecurity* in her big eyes.

"Can we leave it for now?" she asked carefully, taking my free hand in hers and drawing it away. "It's a... tradition. The bond grows stronger the longer we're bound..." she trailed off, her cheeks heating adorably.

I couldn't help but smile down at her, twining the fingers of our other hand and leaning over her.

"Of course," I murmured, drawing the tip of my nose against hers. "Hell—if it will help, tie my other hand as well. I'll use my body as a shield and go to the grave if it draws you closer," I murmured.

Her eyes widened. "Truly, Melek?"

I blinked. "Yes. I... Yilan, you're my *mate*. My soul is tied to yours. Do you truly believe I would resent my body being tied to you also? I don't even want to speak words that would take me from your side. I cannot imagine that moment... but I know it must be. The only thing that would hurt me more than leaving you would be watching you harmed."

Her forehead crinkled and she reached for my face, cupping my jaw, letting her nails catch on the stubble on my cheek.

"I love you, too," she breathed, her eyes swimming and dancing. My heart *sang* and my body hummed with a rush of need for her. But she wasn't done. Eyes shining, she gave me the most beautiful smile. "My mate... my God, Melek, this is—"

"I know," I said hoarsely, then dove for her mouth, twining the fingers of our bound hands again, kissing her long and slow, pinning that hand to the bed over her shoulder and leaning into her, letting her feel how much I wanted her.

She smiled into the kiss, which only made my heart spin faster. I needed her desperately—but I was terrified of hurting her, taking her again so soon. I had to be certain she was ready for me.

And so, with a warm rumble in my chest, I kissed my way down her jaw, her throat, her neck. Stroking her breast with my free hand and teasing her nipple with my thumb, I licked her collarbone then continued, pulling her bound hand down with me, until I was kneeling next to the bed and dipping my tongue into her navel, then down.

"Show me, Yilan," I rasped against the inside of her thigh, pulling her hand down. I heard her breath catch and she lifted her head. I kissed her inner thigh one more time, then raised my head to meet her gaze, and took her hand, drawing it down to where her flesh was heated and swollen. *"Show me what makes you burn."*

Her eyes widened and her cheeks flushed a deep crimson. "Melek, I can't—"

"Oh, yes you can," I rumbled, smiling and taking her fingers, using my own to press hers to her flesh, rubbing gently, smiling when she blinked and her head dropped back down onto the bed.

"Show me," I whispered. "Please?"

Her chest rose and fell once, then she began to touch herself. Tentatively at first, barely teasing her own flesh. But watching her arousal increase, her body flush, made my desire surge. My breathing got harsher and it seemed to embolden her and she began to stroke in earnest, inserting her finger to wet it, then sliding up and down against that bundle of nerves.

I was gripping her hip with my free hand and felt when her stomach sucked in and her legs began to tremble.

"That's it... that's it," I rasped. "God, you're so beautiful, Yilan."

"Melek," she whispered. Her head fell to the side and her back arched as I watched, riveted, as she teased and pleasured her own flesh.

But at each time her body seemed to respond and her pleasure grew, she'd hesitate.

"Don't," I ordered her, holding her hand to herself when she started to draw it away. "I want to watch you."

"But Melek... I want *you,"* she whimpered. She lifted her head, both our hands on her, but she'd stopped moving. Our eyes locked and there was a silent plea in hers.

"Oh, you will have me, beautiful," I growled, then drew her hand away and smiled.

Grateful that the binding allowed me to turn my hand in opposition to hers, I left her hand resting in the crease between her thigh and stomach, while I gripped her hip. With the other hand, I drew fingers down the inside of her thigh, raising goosebumps there—and making my own breath come faster—then nudged her knees wider, whispering to her to relax.

"Just tell me if it's wrong. Tell me how to make it right," I croaked, then grabbed her other hip as well and pinned her to the bed.

The world disappeared when I tasted her. She gasped and her hips tried to buck, but I held her down, chuckling when she blew out the breath and her free hand grabbed for my hair.

She was already slick, already heated, already *ready.*

Following the example she'd given me, I started at her core and licked up to that nub, teasing it with the tip of my tongue, then holding pressure as I slid back down, dipped inside her, and traced the line back up.

Repeat. Repeat. Repeat.

I began teasing her more and longer, flicking that bundle of nerves several times before dropping away, until she was quivering under me, gasping my name, her bound hand clamped tightly to her own thigh, her free hand fisted in my hair.

"Melek… *Melek, please!"*

I'd intended to bring her to climax first, then take her. But I looked up when she called my name and seeing her laid out like that, her skin flushing, her body trembling, eyelids fluttering, feeling her pull at my hair to draw me up her body, I couldn't resist.

I released her hip on my free side and took myself in hand as I reared up over her, positioning myself. Then, ready to take her, I clamped that hand to the back of her neck.

"Look at me, Yilan," I harshed.

Her eyes flew open and locked on mine, and in that moment I pushed into her, firmly, but carefully, filling her. It was the most thrilling experience of my life to watch her eyes first widen as I took her, stretching her poor body, then roll back in her head when I groaned and dug fingers into her hip to hold her so I slid to the hilt.

Her back arched and she gave a wordless cry, reaching for me, that hand slapping to my waist and nails digging into my side as she pulled me in—and the sight of her, gasping for me, almost tipped me over the edge immediately.

Gritting my teeth, I drew out as slowly as I'd taken her, until I left her body completely.

Her eyes opened and she raised her head again. "Melek—*oh!*"

Letting myself tip forward, I planted my free hand on the bed, using my wrist as a brace against her shoulder, then thrust into her again.

My breath hissed through my teeth as I fought for control. She was already pulsing, already reaching her peak.

"God, you're so beautiful," I croaked, pulling our bound hands up, lacing our fingers and pinning that hand over her head on the bed so I was braced on both arms, looming over her, staring down at her, watching her breasts bounce with every thrust as she climbed closer and closer to her climax, her body trembling, her breath catching at every peak.

"Melek... *Melek...*"

I felt her orgasm hit and groaned, fighting a battle not to come myself as she clamped down on me and her back bowed, her head throwing back and eyes going wide, unseeing, yet locking on mine. For several seconds I thrust into her, drawing as much pleasure from her body as I could without losing my own grip—and she remained arched, keening when her breath released and silent when it caught again on the next wave.

Then a shudder rocked through her and her legs twitched. Her mouth dropped open and she began to pant.

I dove for her, delving her mouth with my tongue in a parody of my body.

She whimpered and kissed me back, her free hand plunging into my hair, taking a grip on my warrior's length and holding me into the kiss as our bodies met and parted again and again.

She was breathless, sweating, small cries breaking in her throat—but still shaking. Still needy for me, and *God help me,* she was the most stunning sight I'd ever seen.

With a growl, I bent myself in half, still pressing into her as I opened my mouth on her nipple and sucked. Hard.

She jolted, my name tearing out of her throat, half in plea, half in admonition—but her back arched and she pressed herself into my mouth.

And when I lifted my eyes, still sucking on her, I caught her lifting her head to watch me, her eyes wide and glazed with need—and my leash snapped.

With another roar that would announce to anyone listening what was happening, I closed teeth on her breast as gently as I could and began to pound, as short and sharp as I could so I wouldn't injure her, but reaching the limits within her, my growing pleasure intensifying with every cry she made.

I tore away from her breast, my teeth grazing her nipple as I let go and she arched again, her body bowing and clenching on me. One more thrust and my orgasm detonated at the base of my spine. I arched my back, gripping her shoulder and pulling her onto me, watching her reddened breasts bounce and jiggle with the force of my thrusts, praying I wasn't hurting her—though I was gratified to see she remained gripped in her own throes in that moment.

And then, with a shuddering groan, I collapsed over her, pulling her bound arm up so I could brace elbows and curl my hands over her head and hold her there as the final waves of pleasure twitched through my trembling body.

Both of us panted heavily, our twin breaths harsh in the otherwise silent tent, our bodies still joined.

When I could breathe again, I pushed up enough to meet her eyes and look down on her.

She was smiling.

"God you're beautiful," I whispered, then dropped to kiss her sweet mouth again.

"You're pretty fucking incredible to look at, too," she chuckled breathlessly.

I stroked her hair back and smiled down at her, rolling my hips just slightly to watch her blush.

"That was…" she bit her lip, her eyes sparkling, meeting mine, then turning away as her cheeks flushed.

"Yilan," I breathed, taking her chin in my hand and turning her head, forcing her to meet and hold my gaze. "That was *incredible.*"

She nodded, joy painted on her face. "Have you… I mean, with anyone else was it ever—"

"Never," I said hoarsely, holding her eyes so she'd see my certainty. "Not even *close.*"

Her smile broadened and she leaned up, wanting to kiss me, but unable to reach.

I met her halfway with a soft, open-mouthed kiss, growling approval at the warmth of her plump lips and teasing slide of her tongue.

When we broke apart I combed her hair back from her face and smiled. "You know, if that's what it's like when we're newly bound... the offer to tie my other hand stands..."

She spluttered a laugh and threw her free arm around my neck, pulling me down into another kiss—soft, sweet, but her breath still rushing.

For a moment there was no war. There was no King. There was nothing but my mate and me, both of us high on the joy of each other and trembling in the wake of the ultimate pleasure. For those precious moments, I was able to forget everything else that we faced, and just thank God in heaven for whatever I had done to deserve... this. *Her.*

And pray desperately that I didn't fuck it up.

41. Behind the Bond

~ MELEK ~

An hour later, my skin still hummed and my heart was swelling, but Yilan slept—deeply. Curled into my side and her body completely slack... her trust in me was so touching it made my chest tight.

But when things had been quiet for so long, Jann obviously thought she was killing me in my sleep or something, because he stuck his head into the tent, jaw tight.

Carefully curling a wing around her to keep her shaded from sight and hopefully muffle any sound so she wouldn't wake, I held up the hand that wasn't bound to hers and motioned him closer, gesturing for him to remain quiet.

I sighed when Jann reached my side, glaring and hands clenched to fists as he stared down at me and my wing that obscured her from sight. I didn't like the anger in him, but I knew we needed to speak, and I didn't want to wake her.

My chosen brother was the most laid back and easy-going Nephilim I knew. He rarely disapproved or took issue with me or my actions. But when he did... he would not let it go until he'd been heard.

So I just watched him and waited. Speculating in my mind about which problem he'd raise first—and what he'd fight for.

He surprised me.

"How does it feel?" he asked finally, his voice a bare whisper, though the edge it in was still rage.

I frowned. "The bond?"

"Yes. And with *her.*" He said *her* as if she were some kind of mythical creature he hadn't thought was real, and he was struggling to articulate it.

Unprepared for this line of questioning, I gave it some thought. "It feels like... like I finally found my home," I admitted.

Jann shook his head slowly. "A *Fetch.*"

"I know."

"Do you?" he asked pointedly.

I met his gaze to find him staring at me with real fear in his eyes.

"Are you *certain* she hasn't pulled some magik, or moved your mind or... something?"

I chewed on that for a moment, because it was exactly what I would have assumed if he were in my position, and I couldn't deny that it hadn't crossed my mind. But... "No, it's not. I did worry about it for a time—I felt the bond before she did. But no. I'm sure. There is... this isn't just a lust for her, Jann."

"Then what is it?"

I blew out my breath. "It's as if she's alive *inside* me. When she feels pleasure, I feel it too. When she feels afraid, it alerts my senses. When she is angry, I'm furious." I was whispering so quietly, my voice cut out at the end when emotion flooded my senses.

He snorted, then rolled his eyes when I gestured for him to be quiet.

"That's just your pride," he muttered.

"No, Jann. It's my soul braided with hers. We are... one."

I held his gaze as he stared, a very odd look on his face. "Then how the *fuck* are you going to leave?" he asked, glancing at the door as if someone might come in.

"What choice do I have? It's leave and save her life, or stay and watch it taken. Or force her to watch me be killed, knowing that she's going to be violated and *destroyed* when I'm gone."

That thought made my blood run cold. Even memories of the way she'd walked the shadows in front of me didn't really soothe that fear. She'd admitted the power wasn't faultless—and could only be used for short distances. If she were in the middle of this camp and they knew what she was doing...

An image bloomed in my head—Gault laughing his ugly, malicious laugh, holding her in front of him and—

280

I flinched and Jann caught it.

"What—?"

"It wouldn't just be death," I muttered, squirming, holding her more tightly under my wing. "It would be worse. Gault would take her in front of me. If he knew, he'd bind me, hold the hounds on me, and rape her right in front of me so I had to listen to her scream—"

I cut off, my voice shaking, my body pulsing between fear and rage.

"I can't do it, Jann. I can't even *risk* it."

"Wake up, Melek. You already are."

God, hearing that was like being dropped in a trough in the middle of winter, when the ice had formed a crust over it.

"Precisely why I have to leave. And so does she," I hissed.

"Yeah, I can tell she's very committed to that plan," Jann murmured.

I scowled. "She knows. She fights because it's all she knows how to do."

"So, she's a warrior for their people, too?"

I shrugged. "Of sorts. A spy. An Adept. She is… like nothing I've ever seen before. She's incredible, Jann. And she loves me."

I didn't miss that Jann didn't affirm that statement. I tried not to bite at him, not to press—if our roles were reversed, I'd be skeptical too. But my hackles were up.

"This isn't a trick," I growled.

"Are you certain?"

"Yes."

"Don't give it any thought at all, Melek. Just go ahead and throw the entire nation's future underfoot. I said, *Are you certain?"* Jann turned, eyes blazing and teeth bared. "Do you *know* that she is not deceiving you?"

I was surprised by the peace in my chest when he asked so angrily. "Yes, brother. I do. This is bigger than both of us. She fought it longer than I did, for these very reasons."

Jann slumped, seeming slightly soothed, but still uneasy. He raked a hand through his hair and stared down at the dirt under his feet.

"So, what are you going to do?" he asked finally.

"Spend every second of the next two days with her, loving her, and convincing her to leave when I do—and not follow me—then fight my way through to her land and…"

I trailed off because I didn't have a plan beyond that yet.

Jann looked at me. "Then what? Surrender?"

"No. I…"

He huffed. "You don't know."

I didn't want to answer.

He dropped his voice again. "You don't fucking know, do you? You're going to line us up at the Shadows of Shade and all you'll be thinking about is finding *her* while the rest of us get slaughtered in the fog!"

"No."

"Yes. God, Melek—even if you don't want it, that's what's going to happen!"

"No, it's not. We're going to make a plan. Find a way to… to ally. Or… I don't know yet, but—" My head was spinning. My heart thudding uncomfortably in my chest. Yilan took a deep breath and both of us froze until her breathing returned to the low, slow rhythm of sleep.

"As long as Gault walks this earth, you will never be King, Melek," Jann whispered so quietly I had to strain to hear him.

I went still, eyes snapping to his face, letting him see the warning in mine. "I don't *want* to be King, Jann. I never have."

Jannus stared, emotion and thought flickering behind his eyes too quick for me to catch. Then he broke the gaze and dropped his sullen gaze to the dirt again.

"I know," he admitted reluctantly. "But that just means we're all fucked. So you better enjoy her while you can."

I wanted to protest, but I was very, very afraid that he was right.

42. Promise Me

~ YILAN ~

It was easier for us to sneak out this time. The guards we passed were drinking and trying to hide it from anyone who might see, so they were more concerned with watching the camp than the nearby trees and shadows.

Melek took me to the lake again, but farther away from the camp this time, so we were less likely to be interrupted by rebellious young Neph.

When we finally broke through the trees, the sight took my breath away. We stood on a small spit of land that extended over that lake. A large, flat boulder at its tip leaned into the shimmering water, but provided a dry platform on which to sit and view the surroundings.

There was a light breeze tonight so the water's surface shimmered and rippled, the moonlight frosting those tiny waves in white. On the other side of the lake, the forest stood guard, black peaks rising before a clear, indigo sky, freckled with stars and the glow of the waning moon.

It was exactly the kind of spot I sought out in the few hours per week I could relax back home.

When Melek had mentioned Gall liked to Be Still, my heart had swelled with understanding.

Yet, I was here *not* alone. And never happier to be in that state.

Melek stood behind me for a moment when I stopped to take it in, his broad torso brushing my back, warming me. It was awkward for him, though, with our opposing hands still bound. He looped his arm over my chest, holding me to him. Then he gently placed the other hand on my shoulder.

"I find I wish for no space between us. Let's sit," he murmured.

I nodded, swallowing hard because I felt the same but hadn't dared to speak it.

When I stepped forward he stayed close, nudging me out to the flat of the rock, then tugging me down to sit between his thighs, his arm around me, our bound hands resting together.

Once we were settled and I was caged in his embrace, I felt his breath on the back of my neck and it made my skin pebble and my heart skip. And the rest of me ache with desire.

"You are braver than me," I said quietly.

He leaned down, nuzzling my hair. "How so?"

"You say what you feel. I feel it too," I said, squeezing his hand. "But... there is always a part of me that shies away. Not brave enough to say it when it's for myself. You're stronger in that way."

He exhaled. "Or less wounded. Have you learned that speaking your feelings invites hurt? Or that they are ignored?"

I went still. Stunned. *"Both.* How did you know?"

He tightened his arm around me. "I watched it happen with Gall. His feelings are as blunt as his words. I watch the way people react to him. And since he can't lie, as he's grown, his only recourse has been to remain quiet when he feels what he fears others will judge. I always know who he feels safe with because he speaks freely of how he feels with them present."

I had a flash of a memory—Gall sitting in front of my cage, weeping. My throat pinched. "Well, then, I am touched. He trusted me with some of his feelings."

"I know." Melek's voice was deep and husky. "It was part of what opened my eyes to what my heart was saying about you."

We were both quiet for a time. I hugged his arm that was around me.

Then Melek sighed.

"Two days, Yilan—"

"Don't."

"Two days," he pressed. "Then I have to leave. That circumstance will not change. We must discuss what happens next."

"I told you—"

His hand pressed against my stomach and his fingers clawed into me. He dropped his voice to an urgent murmur. "I need you to give me your word that you'll leave when I do, and not follow me. And I need you to put that clever mind of yours to a solution for how we will find each other when its safe... how to make it safe."

I leaned back against him, warmed by his strength, shivering at the thought of losing it.

"Melek... you make it safe by winning. Then ruling what is left so they cannot defy you."

A low, frustrated growl puttered in his chest, vibrating against my back. But he didn't respond.

I wasn't sure if that should give me hope, or even deeper fear.

Then he swallowed. "Yilan, I do not know if an alliance is possible, but when the time comes, I will work for it. I will tell Gault that crossing the Shadows of Shade is a death sentence and will undo all that we've gained. If I can convince him to negotiate, do you have the ear of your King—or anyone who ranks high enough to reach him?"

I swallowed. "I do."

"Then the moment I go, hurry home and get word to him. Prepare. Place markers at the edge of the Shadows of Shade..." He lifted our bound hands. "Strips of cotton on tree branches. I'll know if they're torn cotton that they're from you. Leave them places where your people can be reached. We will open lines of communication—"

I closed my eyes. "Melek, you have to—"

"The only thing I have to do is keep us both *safe,*" he growled.

I hugged his arm, trying to soothe him, because I could feel the tension in his body, the way he curled around me, subconsciously shielding me from threat.

I leaned into him. "God gave us to each other. We must trust there is a plan—"

"He gave you to me, made you my responsibility. You have to listen and follow my instructions so that I can sleep at night once you have gone. Please. Yilan... give me your word."

I was breathless. "My word for what?"

"Your word that you will leave and not follow me. That you will go home—take what we've said to your ruler and not try to conquer Gault, or those here. That you will *stay safe.* That we will work together to solve whatever needs solving after this."

I sighed heavily, but pressed back into his chest, hugging his arm to me. "You have my word, Melek."

"For what? Be specific," he muttered.

I leaned my head back on his shoulder. "I will not stay here when you leave," I said reluctantly. "I will not go to the battlefront unless you ask me to. And I will undertake no plan without you," I said, my chest growing tight.

He exhaled, then kissed my neck. "Thank you," he murmured against my ear. His relief was so palpable and his care so obvious, it moved me. My throat grew tight and I squeezed his arm tighter.

For a long time, we just held each other, me in the circle of his arms, under the cover of his body, and his big, beautiful heart. Him, shielding me even from the dark. It was exactly the kind of simple *togetherness* I had yearned for my entire life and come to assume would never be... it washed me in waves of emotion.

When I brushed away a tear, Melek murmured my name, then kissed my cheek when I blinked to dispel the rest.

"Don't cry, Love," he whispered. "No matter what comes, you have my heart. No. Matter. What."

I prayed it was so, prayed God intended it so. I held him so tightly I feared I would cut off the circulation in his arm.

After a few more moments, he cleared his throat. "Would you sing for me?" he murmured.

I was humbled again by the request, and my heart lightened to know that he truly liked my singing.

"Do you like music?" I asked.

"A great deal," he rumbled. "I pray the day comes when we might dance together in Valgorath," he added, giving the word the strange, guttural roll that the Nephilim used when pronouncing their capital city and other ancient words.

I blinked. "The Nephilim dance?"

He huffed, shaking his head. "You think we're nothing but brutes and mindless grunts. Our city is full of... so much humanity, Yilan. A war camp... it is its own world. When you return home, ask your soldiers. They'll tell you: Men at war are... different."

I already knew it to be true, but realized I hadn't applied that to the Nephilim. With their King here in the thick of it, I had assumed this was how they always functioned.

"So this... brutality? This disregard for women that you've described—"

"Oh, that is rooted in who we are, it's true," he said with a dark growl. "But it is not all that we are. Our city is beautiful, and ancient. We have scholars and artists and women who are there by choice. It is not *all* so dark. You would be surprised."

I would be, but I didn't tell him so. He had already proven that he thought deeper and conducted himself with honor. I supposed it made sense that he wasn't the *only* one.

"Sing for me, Yilan. Please?"

I cleared my throat and nodded, casting my mind back for a song that was right for him, and praying no one else who would understand was near enough to hear it.

Hold my heart.
Hold it true.
Leave me not in a world without you.
Hold my hand,
Hold it safe.
Don't let me go without you apace.
For the world is dark.
But your eyes light my path.
For the world is dark.
But your hand is my staff.
So, hold my heart.
Hold it true.
Hold my hand,
Hold it fast.
Hold me now, and tomorrow.
Hold me. Don't let me go.
Hold me, my heart.
Don't let me go.

My voice was growing husky by the last line. I let the final note fade slowly, then sighed.

"Beautiful," he murmured. "Did you sing those words for me, or—"

"Of course."

He gave that warm rumble that vibrated in his chest and made me smile. "I will hold your heart, and your hand, and any other part of your body that—"

I sucked in a breath and tried to whip around to face him, but with our hands bound together and his arm across my chest, the best I could do was to twist and look at him over my shoulder.

"You understood the words?" I gasped.

Melek frowned. "Did you think singing hid them?"

"No! I—Melek... I was singing in the ancient tongue. The tongue of *angels*. Not fallen ones—you could understand those words? How? Who taught you?"

His frown deepened as he stared down at me. "I wasn't aware of another tongue. You were just singing. You've always just sung—was this song different?"

I almost swallowed my tongue. "You understood *all* the songs I sang?"

It was a stunning revelation. The ancient tongue of angels was known and spoken by so few. A supernatural gift to those of pure heart. If Melek could understand it...

"Yilan, is your brain addled? You weren't singing anything different than we speak."

"Yes, Melek I was! And that can only mean... Melek, you don't just have a soul. If you can understand the tongue of angels, *you are called by God."*

"Why do you say that as if it is a surprise?" he muttered. "I've told you from the beginning I walk in God's blessing."

"Yes, but—argh!" I lifted his arm back over my head and turned around to face him, pushing to my feet. Thankfully he followed and stood also, which let me grip his shirt. I had to make him understand how important this was.

His brows rose when I took hold of him, but he didn't fight me, even with the bound hand.

"This only proves my point," I insisted, craning my neck to look him right in the eye and leaning in, shaking him. Or trying to. Moving the bulk of him felt akin to trying to shake a stone wall.

"Melek, don't you see? You aren't just *my* hope. You are the hope of every person in this world. Their *only* hope to be ruled in redemption, not rebellion."

"Not this again," he growled.

"You hear the tongue of angels!"

"If that is true, it is only because I listen to the God who created them."

"And you want me to believe He hasn't opened His hand for you to rule?!"

"Yes, I do," he said, his eyes flat.

"Have you asked the question?"

"No."

"But then how can you—"

"Because I do not *want it,* Yilan. And surely if it was in His plan I would at least desire it?"

I leaned back a hair. "Did you desire me on our first meeting?"

His lips pursed and a warning flashed in his eyes.

"You see! We don't always—"

"Yilan, please. I am *begging* you," he growled, pulling my hands from his shirt, holding them in his, staring at me intently. "You *have* to let this go."

"But if Gall's safety is your only concern, I know we can arrange—"

"Of course that's not the only thing!" he snapped, then caught himself and looked over my shoulder, scowling at the lake and the trees and the distant moon. He breathed deeply, and was clearly working to control himself while I stood between his feet, heart pounding, my chest tight with the frustration of how *blind* he was to his own strength. He refused to see what he was. What he could be!

Then he took a deep breath and brought his gaze back to meet mine. "Listen to me," he said gruffly. "Listen to me carefully: You have to stop talking about this. The risk is too great. You cannot hold on to this notion, because it *will. Not. Be,*" he said through his teeth. "When I am gone, you need to *leave.* Otherwise, Gault will brutalize you, and I could not survive that, Yilan. Do you understand?"

"But if he wasn't—"

"STOP!" he roared in my face, so loudly and fiercely that I flinched.

He bit the word off and dropped his head, cursing himself, and probably me, though he didn't say the words.

"Melek, I only want to see you be everything you can be," I breathed. "And I want that in a world where we can walk hand in hand without pretense."

"So do I." His head snapped up and there was a fire in his eyes that made my breath stop. He raised his hands to my face, holding my jaw, stopping me from turning away from the intensity burning in his eyes. "So do I, Yilan. As *allies.* Not revolutionaries."

My shoulders slumped. "I want that too." *But his King would never allow it.* The words bubbled on my tongue, but his heavy brows pinched together and his eyes begged me.

"Then please... *stop.* We have so few hours left—please, Yilan, I do not want to spend them fighting with you."

I sighed and leaned into his chest, holding his waist with my free hand and letting my bound hand drop. He did as well, but wrapped the other arm around me.

"God, I love you. How did this happen?" he muttered as he lifted my chin. When I raised it, meeting his eyes again, it was only for a moment before he was kissing me with such intensity, such passion, that he stole my breath. "Precious. You are *precious* to me, Yilan," he breathed against my lips. And when I whimpered and clung to him, when another tear slipped from the corner of my eye, he kissed that from my cheek as well.

Then he took my face and held it as he tipped his head back to stare at me down his nose. "Give me your word."

"I already did!"

"I need to hear it again. I need to be *certain.*"

I sighed, but put my hand to his chest and repeated my promise.

"I will not stay here when you leave," I stroked his chest with a trembling hand. "I will not go to the battlefront unless you ask me to. And I will undertake no plan without you at my side," I said with a heavy sigh to fight the way my chest constricted.

"Promise me that you won't risk yourself," he growled.

I blinked. "I won't. I never intended—"

"Tell me! If something happens to me, or if the opportunity presents itself to get out safely, you *will* take it. You will not do as you did before and lock yourself back in to stay near me."

I wanted to cry at the anguish in his eyes, the stress he was feeling.

"You have my word, Melek: I will not lock myself back in. If the opportunity presents, I will not stay here when I could get out. Now you promise me something."

He stared deep into my eyes. "Anything that doesn't involve taking a *crown,*" he said simply.

"Promise me that no matter where the future takes us, how we might be forced apart by this war, you will not give up on me or forget… this…" I whispered. Then I reached up for his hair, grabbing him, pulling him down into a kiss that spoke everything my heart was too fragile to say. All the need. All the admiration. All the ways I ached for him.

And with a groan, he wrapped his free arm around my back and pulled me up onto my toes and into his body, kissing me as if the world would end without it.

Which was exactly how I felt.

43. Need You

SOUNDTRACK: *Devil in Her Eyes* by Bryce Savage

~ MELEK ~

The need for her hit me like I had been tackled. All this talk of separation and planning for being apart from her... I only just found her, yet the time left to us was so short, it felt like a sword pressed to my throat.

Unable to resist, I lifted her up and carried her back into the trees, still delving her mouth. My first thought was to return her quickly to the tent where I could lay her down and love her properly. But when she held me so tightly, wrapping her legs around my waist and plastering herself to my chest, I couldn't wait.

Tearing myself out of the kiss, I rasped. "Yilan, I—"

"Don't wait."

Warmth rushed through me that she knew my thoughts and shared them. But *fire* rode my veins that she wanted me as desperately as I wanted her.

I stumbled into the woods, holding her to me until I could find one of the huge Sacer trees with its wide, flat trunk and smooth bark. Then I made myself put her down, but kept her mouth, kissing her hard, leaning her back against it as I reached for her clothing.

Slipping my hand under the hem of my shirt that she wore—which made my cock tighten further—I hurriedly grasped the waistband of her leggings and shoved them down, while she wrestled with my belt buckle.

We struggled and reached and pawed—she laughed more than once when we fought to be the one pulling our bound hands to each other's clothing. But finally, I got her leggings off and she kicked them aside, just as she finally got my leathers unbuttoned and I sprang free with a low groan of relief.

I looked down at her, prayed my eyes were as brightly alight as hers, then reached for the buttons on that shirt, resisting the urge to just tear them off because we would still have to walk back through camp.

It was an exercise in restraint, but *heaven* when I finally got the last unbuttoned, and the sides fell apart to reveal her lithe, tight body to my eyes. I took our bound hands and clamped mine on the back of her neck, bending her elbow high as she gripped my wrist.

She bit her lip and her hips rolled forward when I reached for her breast, teasing the nipple with my thumb as I leaned into her, kissing her neck and thrusting gently into her other hand where she stroked me.

But then I leaned back to look down at her touching me and instead my eyes were drawn to the pale skin of her stomach and breasts that had apparently never seen the sun. I growled with need and reached between her legs.

She gasped and her hips bucked, seeking more of my touch, but I didn't enter her—not yet. I was still shaking, smiling, because she was already slick.

She wanted me.

"Melek," she panted as I curled fingers against that hot flesh. "Don't tease me." I let a rumble of pleasure roll in my chest and she smiled, closing her eyes. "God, I love the sounds you make."

I rewarded her for the compliment by sliding first one finger into her, then a second, curling them inside her, watching her jaw go slack.

I was beginning to sweat already.

I set to the purpose then of setting her flesh alight, playing, rubbing, sliding, teasing, resting my forehead on her shoulder, but arching my body away so I could watch her body roll and twitch in response to my touch.

My breath was already harsh when I slid fingers into her and used the pad of my thumb on that nub that brought her pleasure, and she cursed. I would have laughed, but I was growing more and more needy—the bond between us thrumming like the plucked string of a lyre. And making music between us just like that instrument, as well.

Exhaling shakily, I stopped touching her and she gave a little growl of protest, but I was already reaching around with both hands to lift her up my body, hitching her higher, trembling when she wrapped her legs around my waist, and pinning her back against that tree.

Then I took her bound hand, lifting it above her head to stretch her, then sliding my fingers between hers and clawing my nails into the tree to pin her hand there.

Stretched as she was, her back arched. Because she was sitting high up my body I could bend, still keeping her hand pinned over her head, and suck her nipple into my mouth.

When I had her gasping and writhing, panting and digging her nails into my back I lifted my head and locked eyes with her when she opened hers to see why I'd stopped.

"Are you well, *Mate?*" I rasped.

She nodded quickly, panting. "I'll be even better if you do that again."

I huffed a delighted laugh, but I was done playing at the edges of this. Her body was trembling and her breath caught every time I rubbed against her. So I took her mouth, leaned against her so she couldn't move, tilted my hips, then let her slide down onto me, shuddering myself with the pleasure of taking her—and with watching her eyes widen again.

She gasped, then stopped breathing entirely when she had all of me.

I forced myself to stop, to breathe, to wait. This position took me deep and gravity pulled her down onto me. Though it made me shake to restrain, I forced myself to stay still, only breathing for a moment, allowing her to stretch and accommodate me.

I groaned as she pulsed around me, leaning back into that tree and tipping her hips, shifting, finding her comfort… and then she swallowed hard and let her head fall back against the tree, eyes still locked on mine.

"Why did you stop," she asked, her voice low and husky so that *I* pulsed within her and her eyes glazed for a moment.

"I don't want to hurt you," I croaked, leaning into her.

Head still resting back on that tree, she stared right into my eyes, lifted her free hand to grip my hair and said in a tight but rough voice, "Let's get this straight: I want everything from you, Melek.

And I want it *real*. I have spent my whole life with the men around me trying to protect me from anything they believe I am not strong enough to bear. And they are usually wrong."

A happy little growl puttered in my chest and I leaned in about to kiss her, but she wasn't done.

She gripped my warrior's length and yanked my head back, still staring me right in the eye. "You give me your word that you won't hold back, and I'll give you mine that I'll tell you if it's too much."

I smiled, *thrilled*. "My mate is fierce and beautiful *and* wise."

"And mine is tastier than honeycakes, so please, Melek, stop trying to protect me from you. You are not what I need protection from. With you I want *more*."

I admired her courage, but still raised a brow, smiling and hitching her slightly higher to draw almost all the way out of her. "Are you *certain*, Love?"

"I'm certain," she rasped.

Her fingers gripped my hand tighter and she rolled her hips, seeking me as I growled and took her at her word, loosing my grip so she dropped to meet me as I plunged into her.

The sudden penetration tore a cry from her throat and her head clunked back against the tree, baring her divine throat. I dove for that, opening my mouth on that delicate, vulnerable skin as I began to plow her, keeping her pinned in such a way that she could barely move. She could only hold on, resist me, and take it.

Her mouth was open, her jaw slack as she keened, wordless, gasping, her hand slapping down to my shoulder and clinging—but she did not retreat, and I reveled in that, dropping our bound hands down so I could hold her ass and move her with me.

"Mine," I rasped. "My beautiful, savage mate."

"Yes," she gasped, letting her chin tip down as I thrust into her again.

"Mine. And *only* mine."

"Forever, Melek. For eternity—oh, *yes!*"

I groaned when she clawed her free hand back into my hair. Riding my thrusts, mouth open, but eyes on me, she yanked my head back and bared my throat. I bellowed when she nipped me there, then latched on, sucking as I picked up the pace, her body jiggling beautifully. Still, she didn't lose her grip.

She was *marking me*.

That thought was so thrilling, my body shuddered and I knew I was tipping towards my climax, but I needed her there too. Grasping her hips, I sharpened my thrusts, pushing her closer and closer, until her lower lip went loose, until she gripped me with the same intensity that I gripped her. Eyes locked and both of us panting, she had me marveling as she clung.

Then, in a moment I would remember forever—just as she began to shudder and tighten on me, she narrowed her eyes and rasped, *"Mine."*

My leash snapped. I roared her name as she tipped over that edge, crying out, her body twitching as she came, clenching down on me as I pumped into her again and again until my climax struck like a ringing gong. I roared until it rolled off into a growl, and then a fierce inhale when I ran out of air. And clung together, jerking, twitching… then finally I slumped against her, my heels grinding into the dirt as I shook and twitched, panting, as she dropped her head to my shoulder, and I buried my face in her neck.

She touched me with every inch of her body.

Our chests both heaved as we tried to catch our breaths.

Then, finally, when I could think straight, I lifted my hand to cup her face—but forgot it was my bound hand. And when I lifted it, I caught sight of the abrasions on the back of her hand from the bark, because of the force with which I'd pinned her there.

"Yilan," I croaked. "You should have told me!"

"Stop worrying like a mother," she rasped. "If it scars, I'll cherish it."

I looked right at her then, shaking my head with disbelief and sheer joy. "You, my mate, are more than I could even have thought to ask for."

Her lips tipped up on one side and she flicked her hair back. "My thoughts exactly," she whispered. Then she kissed me.

I would never have thought kissing a woman could be an act of worship. But I was proven wrong in that moment.

44. Troubles

~ *MELEK* ~

"Melek... *Mel!*"

I woke with a jolt, sitting up, my wings snapping wide to cover Yilan, but she was awake as well, sitting up quickly, her free hand on my arm.

"Melek, I'm coming in. I have to talk to you right now." It was Jann, thank God.

"Just... one minute, Jann," I growled, looking at Yilan whose eyes were hooded from lack of sleep, her hair messy and skin flushed. Her shirt was open and hanging off her shoulders because it was too hard to get on and off with our hands bound and it left all of her bare to my eyes and...

I groaned, tearing my eyes off of her as she pulled the sides closed over her beautiful breasts.

She smiled. "Good morning." Her voice was husky and that just made me want her more. But Jann was outside and my instincts were prickling.

"Good morning," I rumbled, leaning down to kiss her swiftly, then holding her hand to help her off the bed while we were still bound.

I helped Yilan put on her leggings, then grabbed my leathers. I was still buttoning them when I called Jann to come in.

The tent flap twitched aside immediately and he stalked in, his eyes cutting to Yilan once, which made my hackles rise. But he didn't flirt, and his gaze when he turned it on me was dark and grim.

"What is it?" I asked.

"There's an issue with Gall."

I swore. Yilan gripped my hand where we were bound and her eyes got big. "What is it?"

Jann clawed a hand through his hair and stared at me as if I should be understanding something. I frowned. "What—"

"It isn't... I need you to come with me."

"Well, of course, lead the way—" I started walking, Yilan trotting at my side, but Jann didn't move.

"No, Melek you can't take her. The young Neph... they'll frenzy. Things are... escalating."

Shit. Those assholes must have found Gall in his Quiet Place. Dammit! I stopped dead, turning to look at him. He glanced at Yilan, then back at me apologetically.

Shit fuck motherfucking *shit*.

With a heavy sigh, I turned to face Yilan. Her eyes were sad, but she gripped my fingers with her bound hand and stroked my arm with the other.

"Leave us," I ordered Jann. He opened his mouth, but I shot him a look. "Just for a moment—wait outside. I'll join you soon."

Jann nodded and trotted out while I turned to face my mate. "Yilan, I'm sorry—"

"Melek, don't apologize. If it was my sister, I'd be gone in a heartbeat. It had to happen. I'm glad... I'm glad we got this time."

We were both looking at our bound hands. The cotton had lost its crisp white, the creases in the material emphasized by dirt, and the edges fraying. I twined our fingers, aching to see how small hers were between mine, her short nails digging into the back of my hand just like they'd dug into my back last night.

I blew out a breath.

"How do we do this best?"

She took a quick breath. "The best way is to leave the knots tied. We'll need a dagger."

I led her to the side of the tent where I'd left my weapon straps and pulled one of the blades, offering it to her, hilt first.

She took it with a frown on her face, but then lifted our bound wrists and examined the twists of the fabric, sliding between them with the flat of the blade.

"I cut the bond as a symbol of my freedom, and yours," she whispered. "But I hold to it because my soul remains bound to yours."

Then she lifted her eyes to meet mine. A shadow flickered in her gaze as she twisted the blade with a jerk and the cotton gave.

A shriek of pain clanged through my chest and I instinctively grabbed her wrist to stop her. But it was too late. The loops around my wrist and hers loosened. It was the work of a moment to remove the tie completely.

Yilan didn't meet my eyes as she gently pulled her wrist from my grip, then took the cut edge and began to unwrap the loops. Then, so sweetly, she lifted my wrist and kissed the inside of it softly, where red lines of compression marred my skin.

"Yilan," I croaked.

She shook her head as she drew both hands away and took the length of cotton, shaking it out and folding it in half, then applying the knife to it again so she was left with two pieces.

"I will take the half with the knot," she murmured, handing me the other, frayed length and my dagger.

I took it gently, frowning. "What—"

She took the ends of the cotton and began to twist them in opposing directions until the length tightened and twisted like a small piece of thin rope. Then she offered it to me. "Would you... tie it onto my ankle? Like a bracelet?"

Suddenly moved, I swallowed and took it gently from her, then knelt at her feet to tie that simple cotton around her ankle, forced to loop it twice because her limbs were so tiny.

When I straightened, she looked at me, her eyes large. "Keep your half," she said. "However you want to. Just... keep it."

"Show me. Help me... I want to wear it too," I said gruffly, offering her the length of cotton she'd given me.

Blowing out a breath and blinking a couple times, she took it from me and twisted it as she had her own. Then she knelt at my feet and tied it around my ankle. It could only loop once, and it was a good thing she had such little fingers, because there was barely enough left to knot it. But she managed, then laid a hand on my shin for a moment, before she stood.

I didn't wait for her to raise her eyes from it, but slipped a hand into the hair at her nape, cupping her neck, then leaned down and kissed her—slowly, deeply. Not the kiss of passion, but of love. She reached up quickly and gripped the back of my neck as well, holding me into the kiss tightly. When we did break it, neither of us moved away.

I opened my eyes to meet hers. "I'm sorry that my duty required this," I whispered.

She shook her head. "Don't be. It's life. Gall is too important. I want you to go to him."

I nodded again. "Thank you." Then I cleared my throat. "I don't know how long this is going to take."

"I know, it's fine—"

"No, Yilan, it's not. We have to... *you* have to be ready," I said hoarsely.

Her eyes got big as I straightened, still keeping my hand on her neck, not moving away, but looking down at her from whatever advantage my height gave me, and swallowing hard.

"If something keeps me... if something goes wrong, you have to go," I whispered.

Her eyes got wary. "Melek—"

"You gave me your word," I growled. "Do not break it, Yilan."

"I won't, but until I know—"

"There is no time or room for error now," I said huskily. "If I do not return by dark and Jann doesn't bring word, you need to go."

"But—"

"Yilan, please don't make me order it. Please... I pray I will return soon. I pray this is simply youth and vigor caught up in the celebrations. But if it isn't... I *need* to know that you're safe."

Her beautiful throat bobbed and she nodded silently.

"Use your judgment. Use those instincts. Even if it is only hours... if *anything* happens before I return, go. Go swiftly, and don't look back. If I come back and you're not here..."

Her forehead pinched to lines. "No. It's not... that's not what's happening right now."

There was a high edge of fear in her tone, so I pulled her into my chest.

"I pray it isn't also. But I'm telling you, Yilan. Don't hesitate. Do you understand?"

She nodded against my chest, her arms wrapping around my waist and squeezing.

"You promised me, Yilan. You gave me your word."

"I won't break it," she breathed, but her grip on me tightened. "But I am praying that you're back soon and... this isn't goodbye."

"So am I."

Then I lifted her chin and kissed her. And just in case, I held her to me so tight and fast it must have been difficult for her to breathe. Kissing her as if it *would* be the last time.

She gave a little sob, her hands clawing into my hair, and kissed me back with every ounce of intensity and fear that roiled in my chest.

"Melek!" Jann hissed from outside, and I growled.

Yilan and I broke apart, staring at each other.

"I love you," she whispered. "My mate. I have waited for you. I am… I love you, Melek."

God, I was going to weep like a child. "I love you too," I graveled. "If this is it, don't forget to mark where we can find your messengers on this side of the Shadows of Shade."

She nodded, but her expression tightened. "Go," she whispered. "Hurry. Take care of Gall."

I nodded, then stole one more kiss before I straightened and let her go. I whirled to storm to the other side of the tent and grab my weapon straps and spears. To hell with the peace. If these fuckers were hurting Gall, I'd hurt them.

As I turned back, towards the door and away from her, I had to clench my hands to fists to stop myself reaching for her again.

I walked quickly and didn't look back because I didn't trust myself not to rush back to her. Instead, I pushed out of the tent with a snarl.

"Let's go." I started down the trail strapping on my weapons, Jann striding at my side, watching me warily, then looking over his shoulder, back towards the tent.

"She'll be fine," I muttered. "Tell me what's happened with Gall. Is it the same group?"

We had just met the intersection of paths from my tent to the main camp. It split into three at the spot where the natural lee of the hill tapered to nothing. I looked at him to see which direction we should take.

But instead of answering me, Jann cleared his throat, then grabbed my elbow and pulled me off the trail into the shade of a gnarled tree, watching the trails from the camp back and forth as he whispered to me.

"I lied. I'm sorry, Melek—I haven't seen Gall. But—"

"You did *what!?*" I snarled, but Jann stood his ground, his eyes dark and grim.

"*Listen!* You think I would do that for no reason? I just couldn't say the true reason in front of her!" he hissed.

"You can say *anything* to me in the presence of my mate," I hissed. "You have *no idea* what you've done. Fuck! I can't believe this." I turned on my heel, back to the trail to my tent, but Jann caught my arm again. I swung and twisted it in a defensive move that snapped his grip, then turned back on him, teeth bared and rage blazing. He backed away with his hands up in surrender, speaking quickly, but barely above a whisper.

"Melek, there's a rumor being whispered that you're informing for the Fetch. That she's magiked you with lust and... and that the sentries in the ravine have been warned and are only pretending not to know that we're there. That she set this up from the beginning. There are whispers that you're a traitor, Melek. Leading us into a trap. *For her.*"

I stared at him, stunned.

Jann stared back, shaking his head. "I know it's not true, and so do the ranks, but Gault..."

I blinked, my breath growing short.

I *knew* what Yilan would see in this, what she'd say the moment she learned of it.

The King started the rumor. And he would use it as a reason to blame me if things went bad—and it likely would because we had put off our advance for far too long.

In truth, it was remarkable that we hadn't been discovered already.

I knew I hadn't betrayed my people. But it was more than possible that someone else had. Or that they had simply discovered our presence and were playing strategy to lull us into a false sense of security.

Would Gault go that far? Would he risk *all* of us that way?

I prayed not.

He was not as stupid as he played. He had no desire to truly fight for his own crown. He was a fierce warrior, but he'd had no reason to defend himself for years.

I could hear Yilan's voice in my head.

Until now. Until a man showed him up and won a war he couldn't?

I wanted to argue with her. Surely he wouldn't throw away what we had achieved just to undermine me? Would he?

My head spun and my heart clenched. I looked back towards the tent. I needed Yilan's eyes on this—not for her drive to revolution, but because she always saw details, manipulations, implications that I missed.

"Melek—" Jann said quietly.

"This changes nothing," I growled.

Jann went still. "How can you say that?"

I turned on him, glaring my disapproval for his deception, even though I understood it. He was uneasy with Yilan, still not entirely convinced that she hadn't magiked me.

"I say that because it's true. I still have to go to the front. I have to be there to show them that I fight with honor—and to win, if it can still be done." It was true, and I meant it. But God... it made all of it real.

Jann's eyes widened. "But if you're being set up—"

"There's no way to know that until we make the advance," I growled. "And I can still win. Winning this is the *only* way to remove those questions."

My brother swallowed. "But... if—"

"The only thing this makes me think is that I need to take Gall with me," I said quietly, as I surveyed the landscape of this shitshow. "I didn't want to put him in the fighting, but the truth is, he's probably in *more* danger here. If Gault—or anyone else in power—is truly trying to take me down, they'll go for Gall the moment my back is turned. Use him as leverage. I should have seen it."

"You've been... a bit preoccupied," Jann said dryly.

I huffed, but I was still watching him, still angry that he'd forced me to break the tie with Yilan. Though I knew he didn't understand that.

"Do you believe in me, Jann?"

His brows snapped up. "Of course! I warned you because I know it's not true!" Then he looked left and right and dropped his voice again. "I admit I am... uncertain about *her*. Which was why I wanted to tell you alone. But I know you Melek. I know you wouldn't do this. Not intentionally."

I arched one brow. "You think I would *un*intentionally betray the people I led to conquer the entire fucking continent?"

He gave me a flat look. "I think she has you by the balls, and I don't know what effect that has on your judgment."

When I started to growl, he leaned in. "You can get pissy if you want to, but we both know that if it was me, you'd have a *great deal* of concern."

I hesitated, because I knew he was right. In truth, I likely would have interfered a lot more than he had, if the roles were reversed.

"She is true," I snapped, but kept myself from bristling at him. "And now I need to speak with her. And figure this out. Will you help me?"

Jann sighed. "You know I will, Melek."

"I need to find Gall."

He nodded. "I figured."

"I can help search soon, but… could you see if you can find out which direction he left in?"

Jann nodded, raking a hand through his hair. "Sure."

"I need an hour," I muttered. "Then meet me at the fire outside my tent unless I find you first."

We clasped arms, both of us already turning our minds to the next task. And even though I was *furious* that he'd forced me to unbind, I was also grateful for the heads up. When I turned my steps to march back up the trail towards the tent, I turned my focus too. I needed to come up with a plan for keeping Yilan focused on fighting to win, instead of her incessant call to revolution.

These rumors were *not* true. And I would not give any man a reason to believe that they had been.

Of course, there was also relief that I would see her again—and my thoughts turned to ways I might justify having her one more time, just in case. I knew it was unwise to take the time, but I *had* told Jann an hour.

I growled at myself as I reached the flat of land where my tent was nestled against the rock and under the tree, the campfire crackling.

It was habit to keep my steps quiet, to give no indication of my presence in the quiet. I smiled, looking forward to seeing her eyes going wide, and her smile when she saw me back so quickly and it meant we had more time.

I reached for the tent flap with a smile on my face and stepped inside… stopping dead at the sight of Yilan standing, chin high and arms folded, glaring at a tall, male Fetch who loomed over her, his teeth bare and every inch of his stance screaming aggression.

Then both of them caught the flash of sunlight pouring in behind me, and exploded into motion.

45. Fight You

~ *MELEK* ~

Time always slowed in battle. Everything seeming to happen in slow motion in the moment. Yet, when I remembered it later, it would come in flashes—drives, thrusts, jolts of fear. and of triumph.

As the two of them startled like cats, I was already reaching for my spear at my back—it was taking forever to get my arm high to pull it from its loops and bring it down to bear. Meanwhile, the male Fetch whirled into shadow and seemed to disappear for a blink before reappearing five feet to the right, one arm cocked back to the hilt of a sword over his shoulder, the other reaching across his body to the sheath of a longblade under his ribs, defending his heart as he drew the weapon.

As I moved through molasses to bring the spear down and flip it into position, he brought both weapons forward, his lip peeled back from his teeth and a warning cry breaking in his throat.

We both took our first steps at the same time

A high, catlike scream filled my ears, punctuating my pounding pulse in my ears as we both moved—him lifting that smaller blade just a hair too high, leaving me a small target in the crook of his arm where my spearhead could slide between his ribs—

And just as I thrust for it, Yilan appeared from a whisp of vapor, her back to the fucking *Fetch,* both hands high and her beautiful eyes wide as she screamed my name.

I had instinctively committed to the thrust, and bellowed, twisting, turning, my body screaming with the effort to turn it from her, thanking God that somehow she twisted her shoulder just enough to the right that my spear thrust ended in the air, just an inch from her shoulder—then time snapped back to its normal pace.

"—no, Turo, *no!*"

"Yilan!"

I caught my weight and turned onto my back foot, releasing my spear with one hand and hooking my arm around her, pulling her with me as that fucker's blade flashed, curling her into my side and using her weight as a counter-balance to turn us both away from him, screaming as we tumbled to the ground and I held her, the spear against her chest, rolling to come back to my feet a body length away, with her in the circle of my arms and the spear ready.

"TURO, STOP! *I owe him life debt!*" Yilan shrieked, both her hands outstretched towards the Fetch who finally slid to a halt, eyes wide and lips peeled back from his teeth.

Then we were all still, chests heaving, eyes darting... and my heart pounded in my chest like a drum.

"What *the fuck* is going on?" I snarled in her ear

But Yilan still had her hands high and was trying to soothe the other male.

"Turo, listen... *listen to me.* He saved me—more than once."

"Impossible," the male snapped. "This rutting *rapist* has turned your mind."

"No! He is the opposite—I swear it, Turo. He helped me. He claimed me to save me... It was a ruse. A show, to throw the others off the scent and keep them from me. Turo, you have to believe me. Please... *please...*"

The male didn't lower his weapon, but his eyes were bright with vengeance and locked on my mate.

"Yilan..." he said hoarsely. "We heard the roars."

In the circle of my arms, Yilan sagged, but kept her eyes and hands up. "I'm sorry you were... I'm sorry. But you heard what you were intended to hear."

The Fetch's jaw jutted forward and he clenched it so tight I wondered if he would crack his teeth. Then his eyes cut from her to me, and narrowed.

"You will pay for your violation in—"

"NO!" Yilan protested. She tried to push out of my arms, but I gripped the spear and kept her close. "Melek, you have to let me—"

"I have to do nothing but rid my tent of an intruder and protect my—" I growled.

"No!" Yilan whirled in my arms, turning to face me, her eyes so wide the white showed all the way around. She had her hands up again and such alarm on her features, I bristled and took an even firmer grip on my spear. But she shook her head and locked eyes with me. *"No.* He will not kill you—and you will not kill him."

"Don't be so certain."

"Stop!" she hushed, then turned back to point at him again because he took a step forward. "Both of you!"

There was a very tense few seconds where she hissed and tried to pry my grip off my spear so she could step free of my arms, but I growled at her.

"If you want your *friend* to live, you won't move within range of his weapons," I growled, and she went still.

For a moment her chin dropped, then she blew out a breath before releasing my hand which hadn't moved from the handle of my spear.

The Fetch snarled, but she raised a hand towards him again, and took a breath, swallowing hard, before speaking.

"Melek, this is General Arturo… our, well, equivalent of you, I suppose," she said quietly. I could feel the tension in her—and the control she was exerting on herself to keep her voice calm.

"Turo, this is the famed General Melek. And no matter what you may have heard… he saved my life. You will *not* harm him, or I will kill you myself," she said, her voice going hard and clipped at the end.

His eyes narrowed, but he straightened in his stance. He stood there a moment, glaring at me over her shoulder, then he bowed.

"The Shadekin thank you for your service, Melek," he said with a twist of distaste on his lips. Then he looked at Yilan and reluctantly sheathed first the longblade at his ribs, then after another moment and a glance at me, the sword on his back.

Yilan exhaled like she'd been holding her breath too long.

"Melek… please, put your spear away."

I grunted, but she turned her head to look at me over her shoulder, and something passed between us through the bond. It was startling. She'd spoken nothing, but I *felt* her—her desperate need for my cooperation, her ache to be in this together. Then suddenly an image bloomed in my head of her holding my face and speaking hurriedly, quickly.

I heard no words, but I knew. She would explain. I need only wait. She would tell me. And whatever it was, it was deeply important to her.

Reluctantly, I straightened out of my fighting stance and slid the spear back into its loop at my back. But I never took my eyes off that fucker. And I kept her at my side when she looked like she might step away.

"Thank you, both of you," she said quietly then. She stood right between my feet, her back to my chest and clasped her hands at her waist. "Turo, I understand why you came, and I'm grateful. But I'm telling you the truth. I'm perfectly safe here with Melek—the rumors of his honor were true. This is... this has been nothing but a misunderstanding. It's why I didn't call anyone in."

The Fetch's lips pursed and he looked at me, then back at her, but he didn't move. "I remain unconvinced. But I will not breach the... honor of your life debt."

He shot me a glare, letting me know exactly how far he thought my honor extended towards her. My hackles rose.

I was about to bite his head off, but then it occurred to me.

This was another Fetch. A male. Clearly a strong fighter, and highly positioned in their society if she called him *General.*

"You have the ear of your King?" I muttered to him. Yilan tensed.

But he just gave me a flat look. "Do you have the ear of yours?"

Cheeky fucker. "In that case then, your appearance is... opportune."

He didn't respond, but Yilan did, turning to face me again and shaking her head with a warning in her eyes. "Melek, *no.*"

"Yes," I growled, never taking my eyes off of him. "He can walk the shadows like you, and if he's capable as a fighter, there's no better or safer way to get you out of here."

"Melek, I said—"

"You want her gone?" the Fetch said, startled.

I let him see my teeth. "For her own safety, yes."

"I can take her," he said hurriedly. "She's already been here far too long. I can take her. And I will keep her safe."

"Melek!" she hissed.

I looked down at her. "This solves that problem we were discussing," I said pointedly.

"No, it doesn't. It's just a different door—"

I opened my mouth to tell her about the rumor, and needing to take Gall, how I needed to go search, but then the male moved and I was reminded that there was an enemy *in my tent.* I growled.

"I am not going to discuss plans in front of... *him.* "

"Good. There is no need," she said shortly.

Arturo stood in a posture that would seem at ease to any untrained—but I saw the perfect balance, his weight on the balls of his feet, his slightly lowered center of gravity, and the open hands that could become fists, or knifehands in a blink.

I watched him uneasily as I replied to her. "There is every need. And he seems... more than happy to help."

She opened her mouth, but Arturo nodded once. "Yes. Absolutely. It was my mission to bring her out. Our intentions are aligned in this," he said shortly.

Oh, what a surreal moment, as this *enemy* became a light in my world. The answer to my greatest fear.

Yilan spluttered when I addressed him directly, but I had to know.

"If I allow you to take her, are you willing to protect her with your *life?* "

He tensed, offended and his eyes narrowed. "She is my bond-vowed. I would give every drop of blood that runs in my veins to keep her safe," he hissed in an astounding revelation.

It was as if the earth suddenly ripped itself out from under my feet.

It was only by God's grace that I didn't let the sudden freefall show on my face, though my grip tightened on Yilan's arm and she rushed into the silence, babbling, reassuring both of us—but still arguing that it wasn't yet *time.*

And in my mind that image bloomed again.

Her, in my lap this time, holding both sides of my face, speaking quickly, frantically. *Explaining.* And then, as if she heard the questions in my mind, another image—her speaking to this male... his countenance intense and... grieved.

She showed herself drawing away from him and into my arms. And suddenly I could breathe again.

Unaware of what passed between us, the Fetch only stood, watching me, waiting for the verdict.

I cleared my throat and she jerked her head back up to look at me, her eyes wide and pleading...

She did not want me to reveal the bond to this man.

Because he was a danger to her?

Or because she would yet deny me?

A surge of dark jealousy twisted in my chest and I had to make myself release her before I hurt her.

"I have a task I cannot escape," I said as casually as I could. "I will leave Yilan here with her... general." I said through gritted teeth. "When I return, we will all speak again and make a plan to get her out of here safely."

Arturo's eyes brightened. "Yes," he said.

At the same moment Yilan whirled to face me and hissed, *"No!"*

46. Bond-Vowed

~ YILAN ~

"Melek, *listen!*" I hissed. His eyes—dark, yet lit with a gleam that terrified me—snapped down to me. But the warmth, the joy, the *need* wasn't there with it. I grabbed for his arm. "I can get word back to my people through Turo," I rushed on, pleading with my eyes that he give me a chance to explain. "That plan, the... alliance. We can set it in motion even now. Or if you would consider taking the lead—"

"No. Yilan, stop pushing. I am not a traitor to my people," Melek muttered sullenly.

I felt Turo bristle behind me at his dark words, but I stamped my foot.

"You cannot be a traitor to a man who is trying to kill you!" I wanted to *throttle him* for being so willingly blind to the danger he was in.

But Melek leaned in over me, his eyes guileless—and I felt the bond vibrate with the ache of his pain because he didn't understand what Turo was to me and he was afraid. And I *hated* that I'd hurt him. But I never imagined that these two would meet, and there'd been no chance to fill Turo in. Not that it mattered, because despite Melek's honor, it was clear his hackles were up and he was now leaning into his pride.

"I will not be a traitor to God," he seethed. "And to the honor that brings His blessing. Not to mention the *vows I gave to serve,*" he snarled, leaning down right into my face.

I sensed Arturo stiffen behind me and fear jolted through me. I couldn't let them start drawing weapons again!

Melek's eyes snapped to him over my shoulder and I whirled again, turning halfway to glare back and forth between them, *pleading* with God not to allow these two, wonderful, honorable men to hurt each other.

"Fucking *men* and your fucking *egos!* Do neither of you trust me or my judgment in this—or my word? Do you really believe I *want* to get myself killed?"

"Sometimes," Arturo muttered.

Just as Melek grunted, "Yes."

They locked eyes again and I literally growled with frustration. "Men! I swear, you will be the death of me."

"If you don't beat us to it," Melek muttered.

I huffed, but suddenly Turo's voice was blooming in my mind. *'Yilan, what the fuck is going on?'*

'I'll explain later. But for now, we have to create an opportunity rich environment for chaos, Turo.'

Then I showed him what I needed. The plan I'd been forming for days, but hadn't quite had the courage to call into action. But now I was left with no choice.

'You're brilliant,' Turo sent delightedly.

My stomach sank. *'No. Just cunning.'*

His tone on the next words were a warm purr that made me want to scream. *'Brilliant... Cunning... it all lights the fire for—'*

'Not now. This isn't the time!' I snapped back, far too quickly.

As Melek stared at him, thinking, utterly unaware of our exchange, Turo sighed in my head and grew *reasonable*. Which was the *worst*.

'I'm worried about you,' he said softly. *'You haven't told the truth here. I understand that you don't want to speak of it in front of him. I understand that you're surviving and things have been... truly difficult. But do not fear, Yilan. It changes nothing for me. Whatever you need, whatever time it would take to heal, I only ask that you let me replace some of these dark memories with... something better.'*

I closed my eyes for a moment, inhaling deeply, half-wishing he could see the *wonderful* memories that swam through my head in response. But knowing it would only make this entire situation even more dangerous.

Unfortunately, he took my silence as affirmation—and now Melek was staring at me because he'd seen me deflate a little and now he was worried too.

Shit.

As I hurriedly considered how to get Melek to agree that we had time and our plans didn't need to change—yet—Turo was alive in my head, reaching for me, desperate to offer reassurance.

'I will never turn my back on you, Yilan. No matter what these creatures have done to you. I told you my desire for you was never in the pursuit of power, and I meant it.'

'I know, Turo—I do. I'm not… there's just a lot to… explain. And this isn't the time.'

'I am here when the time is right.'

'Thank you. Now please… please just go. Leave, and do as I showed you. Be ready. Always.'

Then I cleared my throat and spoke to Melek. "Let him go. He can take word. We have to prepare. Nothing has changed. He can be ready to help me then. The risk will be no higher—in fact, won't they be celebrating more tomorrow? More chances to slip out unnoticed, right?"

Melek's eyes on me were a strange mix of thoughtfulness and wariness.

Inside, I took hold of that bond, that space within my chest that was *him,* and I embraced it, soothed it, let it pulse and surrounded it in my warmth in return. He *couldn't* believe that I would betray him.

"Let him go, Melek," I said softly. "He'll be nearby. Ready to help when he *is* needed."

Melek looked at Turo then, and something fierce crackled between them.

"If it's tomorrow anyway, you could come with me now," Turo suggested slowly. I shot him a glare and shook my head.

"There is more here than you understand. And all of it good. I will make the call tomorrow when Melek leaves—it will cover us because their attention will be taken elsewhere. Strategically, it's the better choice."

There was some back and forth, but somehow the two had reached some kind of truce. Or perhaps, an alignment of purpose. Whatever it was, within a very few minutes, Turo was reluctantly agreeing to leave me—with assurances that he wouldn't be far once he'd passed on the messages and plan to others, a veiled reassurance to me—and Melek was no longer twitching for his spear.

The worst was the moment before Turo walked the shadows.

I stood at Melek's side, urging Turo to be easy. He prepared to farewell, but his eyes stayed on mine.

'It seems wrong not to embrace you. I want you to be certain, Yilan, that I am not—'

'It would only complicate things,' I sent nervously. *'Please, Turo… thank you for trusting me. We're almost done here. We're so close. Please, just wait for my song.'*

With a deep inhale, Turo nodded, then cut a look at Melek. "She will always be safe in my hands. But anyone who harms her will watch their back for the rest of their days," he said bluntly.

Melek stiffened, but Turo turned and melted into the shadows at the back of the tent. I felt him go, knew he'd only passed out of the tent that way, that he wouldn't waste his power walking the shadows in broad daylight if there were no eyes to see anyway.

When Melek took a breath like he might speak, I put a hand to his arm and waited, knowing it would take some time for Turo to be truly far enough away not to overhear anything that might be said here in the tent.

The moment I relaxed, Melek spoke.

"Is he truly gone?"

I nodded, still watching those shadows at the back of the tent, wondering when I would be forced to walk them out of here myself. Hating that idea. "He is," I said quietly.

I turned to Melek, wanting to lean into his warm strength. But the moment I moved, he took a step back.

I looked up, surprised—then remembering why I shouldn't be as I caught the deep tension and sudden cold on his features.

"Bond-vowed?" was all he said. But the word dripped with rage and suspicion.

47. Hold My Soul Safe

~ YILAN ~

"I had no time to tell him. You appeared bare minutes after he did!"

"And he just stumbled on your location?" he growled suspiciously. "Is it *him* you've been meeting while I slept?"

"No! He knew… they send patrols—my singing in the angel tongue… it's how I've been telling them to leave me here—and he knew that wasn't the plan."

His stony expression didn't change.

I blew out a breath. "He thought you were trapping me. Coercing me somehow. I told him you weren't, but I couldn't tell him about the mating." I gripped his shirt in both hands and didn't break eye contact. "Melek, he has to get in and out of this camp safely. He has to function out there without being taken. And you want him to help me get out… I can't have him… *preoccupied*."

"You didn't tell him at all."

"No, but I will speak with him as soon as we're safe and alone."

Something in him tightened, and his face went harder if that was possible.

But he leaned down and cupped my face with one hand. When he spoke, his voice was a soft growl.

"I know *exactly* what type of *talk* I would expect to have if I had been separated from my bond-vowed and we had both been in danger." His fingers curled in, his nails just a hairsbreadth from hurting on my cheek.

I gripped his wrist. "That is *not* the kind of conversation I will be having with him," I said bluntly.

"You told me you had no mate."

"And I didn't, until you," I said earnestly. "We are—we *were* bond-vowed. Intended. Betrothed. Whatever you want to call it."

"And you didn't think that was worth mentioning?"

"Not when I'd already decided not to take him," I said honestly.

He grunted, his eyes shadowed, but I saw the barest hint of hope in his gaze. "Are you lying to me, Yilan? Making me a fool?"

I wanted to weep, and shook my head. Stepping closer to him. "No. And I never would. Melek, our bond is real and true and... *precious.*"

"And yet, you were promised to someone else."

"I am almost thirty. I am *years* past the age of taking a mate in our culture. It was... I thought I'd never find you."

He just stared at me, but his thumb stroked up and down on my cheek.

I gripped his wrist tighter and the front of his shirt with my other hand. "Melek, there is nothing in this world that I want less than to belittle you. Can't you see that?" I breathed.

He was so tense, the flat plane of his chest feeling like warm steel under my hand.

He stared deep into my eyes, and a low rumble began in that chest. I leaned in harder.

"Please, Melek. I'm not—"

"I have to find Gall today. I have to take him with me when I go to the front."

I blinked at the sudden shift in subject. But he didn't move away from me, so neither did I.

"Why? You said—"

"He is trained to fight, and I fear when I leave—and I *have* to leave tomorrow, Yilan—that someone may try to use him against me."

My head *spun* with the arguments, points, and sheer *facts* that he resisted when he spoke about his King. But as I tried to figure out which to raise first, I hesitated.

He looked so pained. So afraid—but always for me, or for Gall. Even for Jann. His fear was never spent on himself.

It was half the reason I loved him.

With a heavy sigh, I reached up to take his face and draw him down to me. He resisted for a moment.

"Melek, *please,*" I whispered. "We only have hours. Please… believe me. We will both leave tomorrow. But I'm not going until you do."

"I think I believe that you want no one but me," he muttered sullenly. "My question remains of what he'll expect when you are… reunited."

I shook my head. "You know I'd never taken him before. And I won't. His expectations, if he has any, won't matter. Because I'll tell him that I'm mated. I have no qualms over telling anyone that, Melek—when we're both safe. I waited to keep everyone, all of us, *safe.*"

He was searching my eyes as I spoke, but on that last word, he groaned and dropped his head to kiss me, wrapping his arms around me.

He was trembling.

When he kissed his way from my mouth, along my jaw, to my neck, I sighed with relief and let my head drop back, wrapping my arms around his neck.

When he made it to my ear, he nipped the lobe sending a cascade of goosebumps down my side, then he turned his head and whispered, right in my ear.

"You have no clue how it torments me… the thought of you gone and alone. Away from me. From my protection. The thought of other men looking at you—I could kill them just for that, Yilan," he breathed.

"But—"

"But I will not," he rasped. "If he is true to his word—if he protects you, gets you out of here, makes you safe… it is me who will owe the life-debt then, Yilan." He took a deep breath, but didn't move, just held me against him. "If he gets you to your King safely, I will swallow my pride. And when we are reunited, I will bow to him in gratitude. Because losing you… Yilan… *God—*"

I inhaled sharping, turning my head and taking his mouth, whimpering when he gripped my face and held me into the kiss.

He shuddered when I reached for his weapon straps, then his buttons, then his leathers.

His body seemed to rock with waves of tension, then of need.

One moment he'd kiss me deeply, growling for me. The next he'd pull back, his hands tight on my arm, or clamped to the back of my neck, and then the bond would vibrate with fear.

"I'm here," I whispered whenever he tensed. "You belong to me, Melek. And I belong to you."

He groaned and dove in to kiss me again. We undressed each other hurriedly, him walking me back towards the bed.

It was crazy, I knew—there was no time. But it was *necessary*. It could be the last time. I prayed it would not be, but it wasn't even lunch yet and already the threats were multiple. I knew if anything else happened, he'd insist on leaving so that I would go. Fear clutched my heart at the thought.

With a little gasping cry, I pulled him closer. He growled and picked me up, swinging me into his chest and crossing the tent to lay me on the bed, then crawling up after me.

I trembled with need for him, frantic, *terrified* of what was to come and the many and varied ways it could go wrong.

There was no time. No more chances.

And so I begged for him, pulled him to me, reached for him, stroking him and marveling at the thrumming need that sizzled between us, lifting my hips, trying to reach him, whimpering when he didn't take me immediately.

There was a gasping moment when I thought he would. He'd settled between my thighs and pinned me to the mattress, he kissed me as if I was water in the desert. And he rumbled in his chest in the way that teased me from within.

But then, just as his hips began to roll and I thought he'd take me, he hesitated.

He lay over me, both hands in my hair, his breath thundering on my cheek as he kissed me, and he just... froze.

I was gripping his neck, sliding my fingers into his hair as well, and I went still. My eyes flew open—to find him staring down at me, a startled expression on his face.

"What?" I whispered. "What's wrong?"

With a low, rumbling growl, he kissed me, his tongue demanding, insistent, his body pinning me to the bed, and his arousal pressed *so close*. He kissed his way from my mouth, down to my neck, then back to my ear, holding my head so that I couldn't turn from him.

"You are *mine*, Yilan!" he rasped.

"Yes! Yes, that's what I'm-"

"But if you ever betray me, you will succeed in destroying my people as well." His eyes were dark, his face tight and pained.

I blinked, staring at him as he rolled his hips and slid against me, so my jaw dropped.

"Melek, what—"

"I cannot be defeated by weapons, Yilan. But you? You would stop my heart. And so take down the greatest army of all time with a simple word."

Tears blurred my vision. "I would never—"

He plunged into me, snarling his need and his invasion was such a shock I gasped and clapped an arm to his back, clinging as he took me, his breath thundering in my ear, his body shaking, his *love* thrumming in the bond. And then he threw himself backwards, gripping me, pulling me with him so my stomach plummeted as if I'd fallen from a great height. And when I shrieked and clung, it was to find myself in his lap, his arms around me, his hands clamped on top of my shoulders, holding me down into his thrusts. His head thrown back, and his great, gorgeous throat bare, those tendons at the sides of his thick neck standing proud as he gritted his teeth against losing control.

I was helpless in his grip, capable of nothing except to ride the wave of pleasure of joining with him when he was so desperate.

"Melek... *Melek!*"

"Hold onto me. *Hold me, Yilan!*"

He was a storm of need. A hurricane of want. His body probing, pounding, his cries guttural. I was overwhelmed—the force of him within me sending waves of pleasure radiating from where we joined.

And then he tilted his hips and leaned me back, pulling me down so my body arched from where he took me, my breasts bare and bouncing as he dropped his chin, hands still clamped on my shoulders, pulling me into him, and watched himself take me.

"Oh, Yilan... *fuck!*"

I couldn't speak, couldn't do anything but grab his thick arms and hold on, my nails biting into his flesh. My body began to pulse, my breath catching as he held me into the peak of each thrust, pleasure sparking, growing, expanding with every new joining.

"Yes... *God, yes, Yilan,*" he grated. *"So fucking beautiful..."*

That need in my belly tightened harder.

"Mine... you're mine..."

I was sobbing, crying for him, wordless in pleasure, climbing towards that crest like clawing up a steep hill.

Then he growled my name at the same moment he lifted his hips and impaled me. "*YILAN!*"

I broke in his arms, lungs seizing, body shuddering, the entire *world* disappearing so that I was aware of nothing but what he inspired.

He roared again, then again, and somewhere in the back of my mind an alarm bell rang, but I couldn't even form the thought.

Then he snarled my name once more, falling backwards onto the bed, and pulling me with him so that I slumped over his body, quivering, shivering, panting, my face in his neck.

And then he wrapped his arms around me and held me so tightly I almost couldn't breath.

He stroked my hair back, pawing at me, trembling as well.

And when he turned his head a moment later, it was to pant in my ear.

"You hold the keys to my soul, Yilan. And the weapon to take down my people... please do not make me a fool for loving you."

Still barely able to breathe, I shook my head and turned my head to brush a kiss to his sweaty neck. "I will never choose *anything* to hurt you, Melek. You have my word."

48. Just Talking

~ MELEK ~

We were still on the bed, though I'd stopped sweating. I was on my back, my head towards the footboard, my feet at its head. Yilan lay over me, her arms folded on my chest, her chin resting on the back of her wrists.

She gave me the most beautiful, soft smile as I stroked her jet-black hair back from her face, tucking it behind her ears. The bond hummed, warming my chest, prickling my skin—and reminding me that I was going to be forced to leave her soon.

God, even with the lies and my anger at her for it, I believed her when she gave me her word. The conviction was there in the bond. And in fact, as I lay there with her, the bond humming like a tuning fork, I realized it was becoming clearer to me. Or rather, she was. The bond wasn't like reading her thoughts. It wasn't like her ability to place images in my head. But it did give me insight.

And right now, she was happy. Relieved. And... in love?

I hardly dared hope that she felt as intensely as I did. She'd been more circumspect from the beginning. Unwilling to set her biases aside. Yet now...

She sighed and closed her eyes as I stroked her hair again and let my hand trail down her spine.

"Your touch feels so amazing, Melek," she breathed, arching into my hand like a cat.

Seeing her, flushed from my love and smiling because of my touch, was the most gratifying experience I'd ever had. I would have given up everything else in my life to simply spend every day that way—with her, in the quiet, making love and seeing her smile.

"I love your touch too," I murmured. "Feeling your weight on me… Feeling your claws in my back," I rumbled, grinning and raising my eyebrows.

I smiled broader when her cheeks pinked.

"You big oaf," she muttered, hiding her face in her hands.

I chuckled, but pulled her hands away from her face when it was obvious that she was truly self-conscious.

"Yilan, don't be embarrassed with me. Ever. I *adore* it when you want me. God, loving you is the most thrilling thing I've ever done."

She lifted her chin enough that I could see her eyes over her fingers. "Truly?"

"Truly," I said. When she smiled and dropped her hands, I grinned again. "Definitely worth a few more scars."

She spluttered and slapped my chest as I laughed.

But suddenly there were footsteps, the tent flap snapped and a deep voice hushed, "Melek, I found Gall—*oh shit!*"

Yilan gasped as I rolled to my stomach, pushing her to my side, snapping my wings out to cover her, and snarling at Jann. But even though he'd turned his back to give her modesty, he didn't leave.

"Jann, get the fuck out of here, *now!*"

Yilan twitched under my wing, but didn't push it back because she was completely naked.

'I can't—Melek, he's coming. You have to—"

"Who's coming?"

"Ga—"

Jann tensed as the tent flap twitched back again and Gall entered, a spear gripped in his hand, and in full uniform.

I frowned and lifted my head. "Gall, what are you doing dressed? It's still the Days of Peace—"

"I asked him to show me where your tent was." That voice, so deep and bored—and just slightly slurred—chilled my blood, because it was immediately followed by the appearance of Gault, the King. He strode into the tent, ducking to get in through the door, then stopping two steps inside to straighten and survey my tent with a pompous frown, as if he were slightly repulsed. "Is this truly how you live? How… humble of you."

Under my wing, Yilan startled and twitched.

I froze, reaching out under my wing to grasp her hand but unable to find it and unwilling to look away from Gault.

The King. *In my tent.* And he'd followed Gall. His son.

My son. Who now stood a few feet inside the doorway, staring at me, his brows drawing tighter and tighter over his nose.

What the fuck was going on?

"Gault—I mean, Sire—"

"I'd heard you were busy, The *whole camp* heard," he said with a leering smile, but there was a glint in his eyes that raised the hair on the back of my neck.

I looked at Gall, but he was staring at me with the strangest expression. I couldn't tell if it was pleading, or hopeful, or... something else. I frowned, then turned back to Gault.

"To what do I owe this... unexpected honor?" I asked carefully, praying Gault wouldn't notice my wing twitching as Yilan moved under there, presumably to pull the fur around herself. Still on my stomach, I leaned slightly away to give her as much room to maneuver as possible, praying she'd manage it in time. There was no way Gault was going to allow me to—

"Lift your wing, Melek," he purred in a deep, guttural voice that filled my head with visions of slitting his throat.

"Sire," I said sharply, then looked at Gall—whose face was pale. "He isn't—"

"Lift. Your. Wing, *Melek,*" Gault said, no hint of a smile or suggestive purr this time, but every ounce of the entitlement of King who was absolutely within his rights to require me to reveal what I had hidden.

Praying she'd had time to cover herself, I ruffled my wings as if I was irritated, then drew them both back, never taking my eyes off of Gault.

"I only hid her from the boy. He's still quite inexperienced with women—"

I was trying to distract him from Yilan, but Gault laughed. Which confused me. But it was Gall whose eyes went wide as saucers, then his face turned from pale to beet red. He gripped his spear as if he'd use it, then his eyes cut to me, and he snarled as fiercely as any Nephilim in his prime.

I snapped my head to look at Yilan, horrified and expecting to see her naked, reaching for a fur to pull over herself... only to find her laying on her stomach, her back bowed and both hands drawn back to meet her ankles which she'd pulled up behind her.

I was *horrified* at the sight—my precious mate bound and hobbled like a common beast. Until I realized what she'd done.

Using that looped cotton at her ankle, she'd twisted it so it looked as if her wrists and ankles were bound together. A close inspection would reveal that she could free herself at any moment, but from across the tent, and distracted by her nakedness... She'd made it look like I had her bhoar-tied on my bed. Her face was red and her hair messy from my wing. Her eyes shifting and darting with fear. If I hadn't known better, *I* would have thought they'd caught me in the process of raping her.

Clever, clever girl.

But my breathless admiration was short-lived.

"How *could* you?!" Gall growled.

Shit. "Gall, this isn't—"

"Oh for fuck's sake, you idiot," Gault sneered at him. "Grow up!"

Gall flinched when Gault snapped at him, then turned back to me, his expression one of horrified dismay. I tried to push up, to reach for him, scrambling for *some* signal I could give that Gault wouldn't understand, that would let my son know I hadn't done what he thought I'd done. But I was drawing a blank.

Jann slowly turned, keeping his pained and desperate eyes off of Yilan, but just as helpless as me.

"You said... You *always said—"

"You are a man, not a fucking *child,"* the King snarled at him. "Where do you think *you* came from?"

I was stunned. Not once in Gall's twenty years of life had I heard Gault acknowledge his connection to the boy. Gall and I rarely talked about the King, but when we did, it was to delicately discuss how to keep Gall out of his way.

How the fuck had they ended up together? And why *now?*

Gall stared at me in horror and rage. I stared back, silently pleading with him not to believe it.

"I need to speak with you later," I said as quickly and casually as I could. "Much has happened over these Covenant Days. Why don't you go rest and I'll come get you when I'm done with the King?"

Gall didn't respond. He didn't react in any way, except to look at Yilan. I couldn't follow his gaze, couldn't see what expression she had, or whether she was even looking back at him. But I prayed he gave us both a chance to explain.

There was no choice now but to tell him the truth and hope he could find a way to keep it secret.

"You..." Gall said thickly. "You always taught me—"

"Oh, fuck off, you little toad," Gault said, bored and irritated, flicking a dismissive hand at Gall as he stepped past him towards me.

I gave Gall an apologetic look, but raised my chin quickly towards the door, telling him to go ahead and leave. "I'll find you when we're done," I said, praying he would wait and not run off again because he was stressed.

Because he was very definitely stressed.

Enraged.

His hands gripped the spear until his knuckles turned white. I was about to urge him sharply to go before Gault lost his patience, when Jann caught his elbow, leaned into his ear, and tugged him towards the door.

I sent Jann a grateful look, then pushed up to sit as Gault approached, completely ignoring his son as if Gall and Jann weren't even in the tent.

Then they were gone, and my heart was racing, because Gault had come to stand near the end of the bed, his arms folded, looking down on Yilan with an ugly smile on his face.

"You clever prick," he muttered, though he was still smiling. "You really did have us all convinced that you were too good for this." Then he looked at me, and his smile faded, leaving only a dark, blank expression in its wake. "I thought the green eyes said it all."

My blood ran cold.

"What... what are you doing here, Gault? It's not safe for you to roam around camp with no one but Gall as a guard," I said as casually as I could. "He's strong, but he doesn't have the skill in subterfuge. I know it's the Peace, but still—"

"I gave my guards the day. I was bored, and he was returning from... somewhere. He knew where your lair was," Gault said flatly. His eyes had returned to Yilan and the heat in them made my hackles rise.

No.

Absolutely not.

I cleared my throat to get his eyes back to me. "You needed me? You could have sent a messenger—"

"This isn't a game, Melek. I needed to see what you were up to. Now I know." he smiled again. "Interrogation, *indeed*," he said huskily.

Yilan paled, but bowed back as she was, she couldn't move away from his gaze.

My heart broke. She must have been in so much pain. Her hands were turning bright red because the loops on the cotton were cutting off her circulation. I needed to do *something*. So I pushed off the bed towards Gault to cover her at least a little, and picked up one of the furs as I moved. "We were just having a conversation," I said honestly.

Gault guffawed. "Is that what you call it? I call it rutting."

Disgust and rage burned through my veins and my instincts began to scream. My throat wanted to scream.

I am not a *predator*.

I'd always known this about my people—especially during war. Especially out of the city. The Nephilim were a culture literally born of the rape of women by fallen angels. Of course their offspring were casual about it.

But I had chosen differently. Had led differently. Had seen changes in those closest to me. I had hoped that, with time and generations, our people could become... redeemable.

Then I'd see something like this—from the King, no less—and it turned my stomach and washed me in despair.

Tossing one of the furs over Yilan's back and praying she could allow at least one of her hands some relief, I turned to face Gault and spoke through gritted teeth.

"I have only hours until I need to go. If you're just being social—"

"Oh no, I'm not just being social," he said, his eyes gleaming, licking his lower lip as he stared at *my mate*. "I need you to leave earlier. I have had some urgent news and it requires my immediate reply. Since you're going anyway, and you have one of the beasts, you can travel faster and take it with you."

I shuddered, hands clenched at my sides, twitching because I wanted to clamp them on his throat.

"That's... well, I'll be disappointed to miss the last Day of Peace, but I suppose I can pack now and then get moving. I'll deliver her to you in an hour. Two at mo—"

"No, Melek," Gault said, taking the last strides to the side of the bed and extending a hand.

There was a shining, crystalline moment where everything within me recoiled—and roared, my hands actually rose as I instinctively moved to catch him as he reached for my mate with his thick fingers.

But Yilan shot me a dark look past him and I froze.

Unaware of how closely I'd come to restraining him, Gault tipped up her chin and forced her to meet his eyes as he let that long tongue of his snake out to slowly lick his upper lip. He rattled an approving growl.

"The message must be delivered immediately. And I find I'm feeling like... celebrating. You go. I'll have a servant pack for you and follow. Your things will reach you by tomorrow. I'll take her now."

Her eyes were wary and locked on him from under her lashes. She shivered. But I reminded myself that she wasn't actually bound under that fur.

If only I'd given her a weapon. *Fuck!*

Then Gault hummed and pinched Yilan's chin between his thumb and forefinger. "I will make you scream," he said in a low, guttural rasp. "Even more than the General. I will make you wish you'd never been born."

Panic and revulsion lit a fire in my chest. I had no way to slip her a weapon as he watched. And no believable excuse to take her away. But there was *no fucking way* I was leaving her with him.

When I looked from her to him and realized his breath was getting shorter, rage hit me in the solar plexus like a charging bear, so hard that I grunted.

I was shaking. My mind shifting to battle plan.

Ten feet to my weapons. Twelve at most. I could have my spear in my hand in two or three seconds. Gault was armed, though only with blades—could he throw? I didn't remember. *Fuck!*

He was two inches taller than me, slightly broader, but not as fit. He had been well trained in his youth, but he hadn't had to meet a true challenge in probably five years and he'd slacked on training during the war. He was a thick, brute of a Nephilim, and our King for a reason. But he was staring at my mate like she was a pig on a spit, and he was starving. And her eyes were swimming in fear.

Did she really believe I'd let him take her?

I could have his throat slit in seconds—but before he could shout? Jann had taken Gall out, but had he stayed outside? Had Gault brought other guards he'd left out there who might hear?

If I let him think I would give up Yilan, he might be distracted enough not to notice before I got the blade into him, but letting him touch my mate—even his fingers on her chin—was making me murderous.

I was going to kill him.

I was actually going to fucking *kill him.*

He plunged one hand into the pocket of his leathers and cast around in there so much I thought he was beginning to pleasure himself.

"Gault," my voice was thick, my throat wanting to close as he stared at her with a sick light in his eyes.

He cursed, then looked down, dropping her chin and shoving both hands into his pockets, then others, then cursing again.

When his head snapped up, his eyes were glazed with lust—but also flashing with irritation. "Fuck. I've left the written message in my tent. We'll go now," he said, then turned for the door, snapping his fingers at me.

Relief rocked through me, a tidal wave ready to take me off my feet. But then he looked back once. "Bring her," he said hoarsely, then reached for the tent flap. "You can leave her with me there."

49. Judas

SOUNDTRACK: *Step Into Darkness*   by Dubkiller
and Archer

~ MELEK ~

We walked the back trails through the camp towards his tent, and I was shaking.

All around us, in every corner of the camp, the Nephilim were celebrating, cheering, playing music, dancing. They sounded *happy.*

I walked this trail as if it led me to the executioner's gallows.

The fact that I was the one carrying Yilan was the only thing keeping me sane. But with every step we drew closer to his tent and the moment when he would expect me to relinquish her to his hands.

Never. Fucking. Happening.

Breath short and shallow, I silently pleaded God's forgiveness for this treason, begging Him to understand that I could not allow her to be harmed.

In my arms, Yilan was wrapped in the fur that I'd tossed over her, and her hands and feet were released. I'd quickly returned that precious cotton to her ankle as I pretended to sort out the best way to carry her.

Now she lay in my arms, pale and silent, her head turned and looking at Gault who walked behind me so he could follow to his tent. He said he didn't know the way. I suspected it was a ruse.

He played the thug, often. Brutish. Piggish. Selfish and petulant. He made way for people to underestimate him—and in that way, identified those who were trying to manipulate, or outwit him.

They always regretted it.

Gault was lazy and selfish. He was also sly, and very, very strong. When he was unbridled, he didn't just cow a foe, he tore them to pieces. Literally.

He'd been born to the throne, yet he might have lost it to some of the others who were close cousins. Yet, he had ruled since his eighteenth year—when he killed his older brother—and he had faced every challenge since.

When it mattered, he unleashed. He became a roaring, ferocious beast of strength and cunning.

There was every chance this was all a ruse, all a ploy to get me alone and away from my weapons.

Or he could legitimately have forgotten the message and was now making me carry my claim to him, a public display of my submission because it bolstered his smug ego to have others see me do so.

I would put nothing past him. But since he'd told me to go first—claiming he didn't remember how to reach his tent from here—I was forced to walk with him at my back, leaving me no easy room to simply toss her aside, or flee with her.

He was leaving me no choice but to kill him.

I looked down at her, and her eyes cut up from behind me, to meet mine, wary and alert.

I wish I could speak into minds, or share images as she had. Reassure her that I would not fail her.

But to my surprise, she inserted herself into my mind, an image of herself holding and petting me. Soothing. Reassuring... and the dead King on the dirt behind me.

I swallowed hard, but nodded once. Her eyes flashed with surprise and she tucked her chin down, but turned back to watch Gault over my shoulder—the image now shifting to what she saw so I'd know if he came at me from behind.

I hated this. Hated knowing there was no other choice. But it was clear that my honor would no longer carry me safely through this war. I was being set up. Either the King truly wanted to touch my mate, or he wanted to use her as a pawn in his game to destroy me. Regardless, the end result would be the same.

I'd cut off any limb he so much as brushed her with. Starting with those fingers, and that tongue. And yet, even as that conviction settled in my chest, even as I accepted that there was no other course, grief made my steps heavy. Not for Gault—the man was a pig. But for Yilan. I would gladly lose my life to the executioner in defense of her… but I had to find a way to kill the King and get her away quickly enough that she wasn't simply taken by someone else as she fled.

And then I remembered the Fetch and my breath caught.

Yilan glanced up at me, then went back to watching Gault.

"Sing," I said quietly, remembering she'd said that's how she called them. "Sing the song that takes you away… you'll need it," I murmured.

She took a deep breath and I thought she'd sing. But she shook her head and the words rushed from her in a breath.

"There's no point." She placed an image in my mind then— empty forest. No Fetch close enough to hear.

I was looking for careful words to encourage her to sing anyway, just in case, when Gault spoke up from behind me.

"You will not be denying me *anything,* Fetch. Not even once. Your General may be lax in his discipline, but I am not. You will obey the very time I speak, or you will pay. Do you understand?"

Yilan shrank in my arms and I almost tossed her aside and just went for him then—but there was too much risk of someone else stepping into the trail and seeing before I could get her away—or catching her while I fought him.

I had to get him in the tent. I had to get a hand on one of his weapons.

And I had to kill him.

My pulse thrummed in my skin and my breath was short. The hair on the back of my neck stood up, my instincts expecting attack from behind at any second.

Yilan kept her head down and her expression miserable, but I felt her tensing, preparing.

"You need to be good," I muttered as if I was preparing her for the King to take her. "Do as you're told and nothing more. Stay out of the way unless you're instructed otherwise."

"Do not interfere. Leave this to me," she breathed.

Before I could tell her *fuck no,* we were at Gault's huge tent. I turned sideways, putting her back to the flaps that covered the doorway, letting her get a straight look at Gault, to remind her what we were dealing with, as I used her back to push the canvas aside.

I scanned the tent immediately, walking her towards his bed at the other end of the massive tent, looking for his weapons. They were always plentiful, and sharp. I needed to get one myself, without letting him get close enough to grab one for himself.

Several blades, swords, and spears leaned against the furniture at the back of the tent—behind his bed. Clocking their locations, I determined that I would lay her on the bed and make a fuss of settling with her to give myself time to grasp whichever was closest before Gault could get a hand on her—

Skin prickling with nerves, my steps got faster as I hurried her towards the bed. Behind me Gault entered and made straight for the writing desk at the side of the tent, rummaging through things there until he came up with what he'd been looking for.

He nodded, and rumbled, rolling it and tying it off with his royal knot as he approached, smiling that dark smile as I lay her down on his bed.

Her fingers dug into my forearm, but I ignored it, eyes on Gault, mentally preparing for the moment he'd look away, so I had half a second to whirl and grab one of the weapons—

"Take this to the generals. Then lead the advance." Gault stalked towards me holding out the rolled parchment. "In a few days, when we hear of your success, I will kill her. But in the meantime…" He leered at her and I stiffened. "I will keep her busy."

I closed my eyes and took a breath. He wasn't going to look away. I needed to just do this, as quickly as possible. I'd go for the spear because his arms were longer than mine and it would give me better reach—

Gault laughed. "I know you claimed her, Melek. If it helps, I will tell the men you gave her to me as a parting gift."

I was shaking, starting to turn as if I'd face him, but mentally aiming to whip around and grab that spear—just two steps away and—

Instinctively, I froze.

She was not property. She was *mate.*

She would not be defended in subterfuge. He would know that I stood for her, and that he paid the price.

I straightened from the bed, hands open and ready, body tensed, and Yilan gasped.

"Melek, don't—"

"She is mine," I growled. Gault's eyes flashed. "She is not for sharing."

His chin dropped, but he smiled. "I am King. What is yours is mine. I will share her with whoever the fuck I want."

"No, you won't," I said, taking one step forward, just one more to the left and this would begin.

Gault's eyes lit up. "Are you *challenging me?"*

"Only for her, but the result will be the same."

"I knew it," he breathed. "I knew you and your *fucking honor* were all an act. A ploy to win the men."

I darted aside for the spear and in the same blink Gault turned, drawing a two-handed sword from somewhere I hadn't known it was secreted and whirling smoothly to bring it up *En guard.*

There was a flash of fear in the bond as Yilan watched us stare at each other.

The area where we stood was only about fifteen feet wide, leaving both of us very little room to swing. And yet, we both knew the other was restricted as well.

We began to circle, weapons wide—I forced him towards the bed and away from the other weapons I could see, though it was clear he had them hidden in places I didn't know all over this tent.

"She belongs to me," I growled. "I've taken her. And kept her. She doesn't need your dirty prick."

"Oh, but she needs yours?"

"Yes." *Mate. Soulbond. Mine.*

Gault laughed and swung the sword, I blocked it once, his sword clanging against the butt of my spear—shaving a sliver from it—and shoved him back, then we began to circle again.

"This is perfect. I knew you were far more cunning than you let on, but I thought you were too cowardly to actually challenge me. The *great* General Melek," he purred. "Always full of surprises."

"No, just strength and certainty."

Gault sneered and the sword flashed—but when I stepped in to block again, he instead whipped to his left and clamped a hand on her ankle.

Yilan yelped and grabbed for the furs as he began dragging her off the bed, holding the sword up towards me. My heart screamed as she was dragged backwards, grasping, but unable to get a grip on anything substantial until he had her almost off the bed. And because she was halfway between us, it restricted my options for attack.

I growled and danced aside, trying to get access myself and keep him farther from her. But Gault kept turning, dragging her across the corner of the bed to keep her at least partly between us— but then she finally clamped her hands on the footboard and, for a second, she stopped his retreat.

I roared forward, darting, stabbing with the spear in a flurry of whirls and thrusts, forcing him to let her go and bring the sword up in both hands.

The impact of the weapons rang through my arms as surely as the blade of the sword sang in the clash. But at least he wasn't touching her anymore.

Yilan was scrambling back over the bed to get behind me as I pushed him back, deeper into the tent, teeth bared and snarling.

"She is mine."

"Everything that is yours is *mine,"* he spat back, twisting that sword and swinging it up unexpectedly. I only managed to jerk aside at the last minute and that razor's edge of a blade shaved the hair from my arm.

"Bullshit," I grunted. "She's no simple conquest."

Clang, stamp, whirl and clang again.

"Oh? Are you breeding her?"

"God willing. You will not take her, Gault."

He was beginning to sweat, but very little strain showed on his face, the smug fucker. "So you think she's strong enough to survive?"

He blocked my stab and sent her a lusty glance that made me roar and leap for him.

50. Truth and Lies

~ MELEK ~

"No, Melek!" Yilan shrieked as I rushed forward, throwing images into my head of him taunting me, intending to distract.

And she was right, I realized, as Gault met my flurry, calmly twisting to block my spear, then whirling aside. Now we made a triangle—Yilan behind the bed, me a few feet from its foot, and Gault on the opposite side, his back to the tent entrance.

"You were always just one step from betrayal," Gault snarled, panting harshly, though his limbs had not slowed, and his eyes were gleaming with bloodlust and smug satisfaction. "I knew they were wrong about you—even if I lose this, you will not win, Melek. They will see your true colors."

The rage in me blistered my skin. I wanted to rush him, but Yilan was shaking her head, her eyes on Gault as she stood, half crouched, appearing to try to hide her nakedness from him. She held one hand raised towards me in warning, the other hanging down near her knee as if to balance.

I would have bet my life that below the level of the bed she now held a dagger.

She glanced at me once, fear and admiration in her gaze, and my chest swelled with pride in her courage as she nodded.

We would advance together.

Yilan sent me an image—her leaping onto the bed like a cat, unconcerned with her nudity, a dagger flashing in the light of the lanterns as I rushed forward from his other side. Force him to fight us both at the same time.

But as we turned and she sucked in a breath, before either of us had advanced, Gault bellowed like a butchered beast, and his eyes went wide. He clutched at his stomach and his sword clattered to the dirt.

I was confused until a spearhead appeared, blooming from his stomach and through his hands like a deadly sapling reaching through the earth for sunlight, and a ragged voice screamed, *"You have no right!"*

Gault's face twisted between fear and rage, but his hands were pinned to his stomach by the spear now piercing him through.

Writhing and roaring, he fell forward to the dirt, revealing Gall behind him. Pale, shaking, tears running down his face, Gall yanked the spear out of the King, then turned it in his grip, holding it up then plunging it back down and into Gault's back again, screaming.

And Gault, who'd been twitching, roaring, shaking, went very, very still. His eyes still blinked, his mouth opening and closing... but then blood poured from his mouth and he coughed, spitting it, spraying the bed, my legs, and the ground in front of him.

His eyes rolled and his head was craned back, but his body didn't move.

We all froze, staring at him, gaping like a dying fish.

"Melek, get Gall!" Yilan cried as she clambered over the bed and yanked Gault's head up by the hair.

He stared her in the face, pain and rage burning in his eyes and she spat on him. "You deserve this, you fucking *pig,"* she hissed, then laid her blade to his throat as she leaned into his ear. "Die knowing that I am going to eat your testicles—fried. Your *royal seed* will die in the body of your enemy you sick *fuck."* Then as he gave a hoarse roar, she leaned back and drew that blade through his skin so that his lifeblood surged, soaking her legs, the dirt, and even parts of the bed beyond her.

She didn't flinch, but she made a strange growling noise as she continued the cut until he was half-decapitated. Then she cursed and threw his face into the dirt—muddy with his own blood—as she staggered back.

I was staring at her, admiration, fear, grief, and relief rushing through me. But then a shadow moved, and it was instinct. Reflex. Because we'd both almost died and now something was coming for her—I charged, leaping for her, tackling her, shoving her aside and rolling back to my feet with the spear up, and—*Holy shit!*

With a strangled cry, I threw the spear aside, and threw myself to the ground, just as Gall leaped at me, screaming.

"Stop touching her! Stop *hurting her!*"

"No, Gall!" I screamed and my soul almost left my chest when time slowed, and I saw Yilan, gasping, throwing herself between me and that spear.

I grunted with the effort to reach for her, to throw her aside, but I was too late.

There was a cry, and a clatter, a groan and a scuffle. I pushed to my feet, my vision blurred and head spinning in confusion.

Where was she? *Where was she?*

Then everything stopped.

"Melek... *Melek. I'm fine!"* she gasped, panting.

I blinked once, then again, trying to make sense of what I was seeing.

Gault on the floor, dead, his skin already gray.

Gall on his side, cheeks dirty and tracked with tears, eyes wide and hands clasped on the thin forearm that was wrapped around his throat.

And Yilan, grappling, clinging to his back like a monkey, only cutting off his air when he started to rise, whispering in his ear, her face pressed to his hair, and tears on her cheeks as well as she murmured over and over again, trying to get him to listen.

"It's okay, Gall. I'm okay. You did good. You did so good. Melek didn't hurt me. He never hurt me. It was only the King. Only the King, I promise... shhhhh..."

Gall struggled and gaped, his eyes rolling. He was overstimulated and afraid, and I was torn, yearning to hold my mate, to take her from all of this, to cover and protect her... and aching for my son. Knowing what he thought and why he was angry, flabbergasted by his courage, and so, so sad, because even when it was done in defense... the taking of a life never passed without leaving a stain on our hearts.

I was crouching on the ground, trying to reach for him, but he writhed every time my hand got close, then Yilan would be forced to cut off his air again until he stopped.

I sat down hard, watching both of them, on the edge of tears, as I realized I was only making things worse by trying to help. And so I was forced to watch my mate slowly, slowly murmur to my son, get him thinking again, get him listening.

And slowly, he started to breathe, though his breath hitched again and again. His tears rushing, rolling down his face and his chin trembling.

But he stopped fighting her.

"Why?" he coughed. "Why would you defend him? Why would you let him—"

"That's not what's happening, Gall. I give you my word. I told you... I will never lie to you, or hurt you. We are not enemies, remember?"

"But you said *he was!*"

Yilan's eyes closed and she laid her cheek against his hair. She still had him in a grip, her legs locked around him. Her arm in place at his throat... He couldn't get up without her releasing him. And yet...

She was hugging him.

"Gall, that was true when I said it. But things have changed. Melek and I... we're protecting each other."

His eyes flew open then and found mine—accusing. "*This* is protection?"

I sighed, shaking my head. "Gall... it's complicated—"

His entire body spasmed and his face went red as he screamed. "IT IS NOT TOO COMPLICATED! I CAN UNDERSTAND!"

Yilan sobbed, but swallowed it back, teary, holding him as he cried and struggled again.

But he was past hearing me. He trembled from head to toe.

I'd seen him overstimulated before. I'd seen him break down in fear or hurt. But this...

He was falling apart.

"Gall, please..." I begged.

"It's my fault, Gall. I didn't explain as things changed," she whispered. "I know that's confusing, but I need you to trust me. Melek is the father you always knew. He is a *good man.* There are things going on here that you don't understand, but they're good—

Gall roared and threw his arm wide. Using his elbow to leverage and throw them both over, Yilan shrieked and tried to cut off his air again—to still him—but because she'd been embracing him, her positioning was off.

"I UNDERSTAND MORE THAN YOU THINK! I AM NOT STUPID!"

With a roar, he flipped her over, his weight crushing her for a moment so she wheezed, and in that second her defenses were down, he ripped her arm from his neck.

I leaped to my feet towards them, ready to pull him away from her, but he already had his hand on the spear that had been thrown aside and he was rolling up, his training kicking in as he pushed to his feet with the weapon in place... and pointed at *Yilan.*

His mouth was open, his breath coming in harsh puffs. His eyes darted from her to me, but neither of us was close enough now to get a hand on that weapon before he could throw it or bring it to bear.

I stayed half-crouched, hands up in surrender, but started inching towards Yilan, so I could at least make myself his primary target instead of her.

"Gall... she isn't lying to you—"

"SHUT UP!"

I snapped my mouth closed, but took another half-step closer to her.

"Stop moving! Stop, or I'll hurt her!"

I did as he said, but shook my head, let him see my grief. "I'm sorry, Gall. I'm so sorry. I know this is frightening. I'm sorry I scared you. It was a ploy... to stop the others coming for her—"

"I DON'T GIVE A FUCK!" he screamed so hard he spit and his head shook.

Then, in a moment that would always break my heart, he took one hand from the spear and started hitting himself in the head. "SHUT UP SHUT UP SHUT UP!"

Yilan gave a little cry and covered her mouth with her hands. "Gall, please—"

"Leave me alone! Both of you," he rasped, shaking his head and backing away. "Leave me alone. You're liars and.... And monsters."

"No," I breathed. "Son, I—"

But his head whipped to me and his eyes, bloodshot and shining with tears, spoke every accusation his mind could conjure.

"My father is *dead,"* he hissed, and a tremor rocked through his body. "And I'll kill you too, if I have to. You're all just horrible, selfish, *rapists* who—"

"Gall... she's my *mate."*

His eyes widened and his jaw dropped. He gaped at me, then at Yilan—who nodded, her hands still pressed over her mouth.

"We didn't know, Gall. I'm so sorry. We didn't know at the beginning. But it was all—"

He threw the bloodstained spear aside like it was a serpent. I leaped between him and Yilan, hands up, but the spear clattered benignly to the packed dirt, and he turned, stumbling away, out of the tent.

"Gall… *Gall!*" I called after him, gathering Yilan into my arms.

But she shushed me, and held me as I watched my son reeling away.

And then he was gone, and we held each other. So tightly neither of us could easily breathe. And then tighter still. Trembling from head to foot.

51. Problems to Solve

~ YILAN ~

For a few breaths, we just held each other. But Melek shook with tension and I could *feel* his mind racing. The bond thrummed with alarm and grief and something I thought was his desperate need to protect.

He exhaled heavily, then leaned back, holding my arms and scanning me. "Are you hurt? Wounded? Even a little thing, Yilan. Sometimes we don't realize and we've been stabbed—"

I felt a flinch at the memory of those scars that peppered his beautiful hide, but I shook my head. "Just shaken. Bruised a little. There's nothing, Melek. No bleeding. I promise."

He turned me around once to check for himself, then exhaled again. "Do not move," he ordered me before whirling away and dropping to the dirt next to Gault, lifting his head to see the wound at his throat, before sagging.

"Definitely dead," he said.

I tried not to be irritated that he thought I might not have been sure. But either he didn't notice my bristling, or he didn't care, because he returned to me, taking my hand and dragging me towards the back of the tent.

"He always keeps clothing here for his bayan girls. Quickly. We need to get you dressed."

Then he trotted to a set of drawers near that armoire where I had watched Gault's disgusting habits, digging through three drawers, cursing at each. "…wisps of *nothing* because he was only ever trying to paint them, *fuck.*" But a moment later, he lifted a pair of leggings out of the bottom one. There were cutouts on the sides of the legs, but he tested the material and obviously found it substantial enough because he gave them to me, then started unbuttoning his own shirt, hurriedly whipping it off his shoulders and wrapping it around me while I was still getting the leggings on.

"Melek, just breathe. I'm fine."

"It's not you I'm worried about right now," he muttered, hurrying over to the entrance of the tent, picking up that bloodied spear on his way and using the handle to stand back from the door and push the flap just barely aside so he could peer out without sticking out his head.

"There's no one coming that I can see. We have to pray no one heard the ruckus over the celebrations."

I listened for a moment, nodding. The camp was full of music, shouting, and laughter.

Then he was back at my side. I'd finally buttoned that shirt and he just gathered me into his chest, breathing heavily. I knew there were things we needed to do, but I fell into his arms gratefully, realizing I was trembling too.

The moment we were still, gripping each other, that image of Gall smacking himself rolled through my head and my throat began to pinch again.

"Melek—"

"It's good that he ran. He needs to be alone for a few minutes when it gets bad like that," he breathed, but I could hear the hoarse doubt in his tone, and felt the flinch in the bond. "I'll find him before you leave."

I blinked. "Leave? I'm not leaving him—"

"You won't. I'll find him. I will." I felt his head turn and looked up. He was looking at Gault's body on the dirt. His face dragged down with tense lines appearing on his forehead and lining his cheeks. "I will find him, and then you'll go, and you'll take him with you," he muttered.

I looked at him sharply, a burst of hope and unease both tightening my chest.

"I'll take him, of course," I said, watching his face. "But… you're coming as well?"

Melek took a moment to turn and meet my eyes. "Yilan. I have to confess to killing the King. Neither of you can be here—"

"What?! *No*—you didn't—"

"Gall would be tortured and executed—or you. No one will believe it was in your defense—you're an enemy."

"Of course they will, because *you'll* be the one to tell them," I insisted. "Melek, I wasn't lying to you. These men are looking for you to—"

"Yilan, stop!" he gripped my arms and snarled in my face.

"No! I won't! You are *free* now, don't you see?! He's gone!" I hissed, throwing a hand towards Gault's body. "You can step into the crown with a *clear* conscience."

"No, Yilan—I can feed you and my son to the wolves, or I can own this and *possibly* be cleared in self defense."

I gaped at him. "No intelligent, powerful Nephilim is going to clear you of killing the King—and you didn't even do it!"

"I would have, though. It makes no difference. I intended to. I might as well have—"

"But you didn't!"

He glared at me. "And you *did,* so what do you want me to do, just let them kill you?!"

"NO! I want you to lay claim to his throne, inspire them, take control of this war, and *change the world!* This is obviously what God intended all along—"

"Get your fucking hands off of her," a voice growled.

We both whirled to find Turo standing in the back of the tent, stepping out of the shadows of the armoire, glaring at Melek, reaching back for his sword.

"Turo, don't you fucking *dare!"* I hissed. "We killed the king and we've already done this once, so just stay back and fucking listen!" I barked.

Turo's head jerked back and his brows rose. I felt a surge of amusement in the bond, but it was overshadowed by the alarm. I grabbed Melek's arm as he started to turn to face Turo.

"Don't you start, either," I snapped. "We're all on the same side here."

"I'm sorry, *what?!"* Turo spluttered, gaping at me. "I'm sorry I didn't get here sooner, but there were crowds and I wasn't expecting you at this side of camp... what the fuck did I miss?"

I glared at him. "You missed that we need you to dispose of a body," I said, opening my hand towards Gault. Because of his position on this side of the large bed, Turo was forced to creep closer—keeping eyes warily on Melek—until he could see Gault's body.

Then he visibly paled.

Despite the growing area of dark dirt under Gault's body, Turo advanced slowly, wary as a cat on a hot roof. He crept forward, poised for battle, his sword at the ready, until he was able to pick up Gault's head and, just like Melek had, checked both the wound, and his eyes.

"Holy shit," he whispered.

I folded my arms. "Honestly, your confidence in me is *heartwarming,*" I snapped. Melek gave a little huff until I glared at him too, "You didn't believe in me either."

Melek opened his mouth, looking like he'd try to soothe me, but

Turo dropped Gault's head and pushed to his feet, marching

towards me. "This is done. The mission is *done.* We need to get

you out of here. *NOW.*"

52. Never the Crown

~ *MELEK* ~

It was fucking annoying when the bossy Fetch agreed with me, because that meant I couldn't argue with him.

Yilan held no such compunctions. "I will go when Melek agrees to lead and take this opportunity he's been handed," she said stubbornly.

I wanted to throttle her. "We are *not* discussing this in company," I growled.

"Fine," she replied, then turned to Turo. "Take the body and dispose of it. Make certain no one's going to stumble on it. The longer we can make it uncertain what's happened to him, the better."

The Fetch hesitated, but then nodded.

"Gault is already more than twice his weight! He can't do that alone," I hissed.

"He's not alone," Yilan answered reluctantly.

And in unison, Turo muttered, "I'm not."

I blinked, but Yilan sighed as Turo gave a low whistle. A moment later, the shadows at the back of the tent began to move and first one, then a second, then a third Fetch appeared, all of them tense and watching me warily, but drawing closer as soon as they stopped being vapor, or whatever it was that they did to walk the shadows like that.

I grabbed Yilan's arm and pulled her behind me, but she just muttered something under her breath and put her hand to my back where they couldn't see as she spoke to them like they'd been there the whole time.

Had they?

"Take the body. Walk the shadows—I know it's risky, but we can't let anyone catch sight of him. Then wait for me at our meeting point. Keep one of the runners close to hear the song."

I looked at her sharply. She'd told me that they weren't close enough to hear her!

She returned my gaze, and I felt a thrust of reassurance through the bond, but she didn't answer the question, just continued softly but firmly giving orders.

And the men didn't question her.

Turo glared. The others looked at me nervously. All of them hesitated before passing close to me. But they didn't question her orders, and within a minute, they had Gault draped over their shoulders and they were walking him into the deepest of the shadows at the back of the tent.

I didn't miss that Turo shot a look at Yilan before they entered the dimness. But he said nothing. And a moment later they all disappeared into that shadow as if it were fog.

I took a deep breath and turned to Yilan, who was watching that same place with a frown on her face.

"Are they gone?"

She nodded, but didn't look away.

"Yilan," I said firmly. She blinked and turned to look at me. "Are they out of earshot?"

"Yes."

"You said they were earlier, also—yet here they are."

"We have... ways to reach. It's not as easy or as quick as just being close enough to hear, but I reached for them the moment Gault arrived in the tent. It just took time for them to arrive."

My jaw dropped. "You said you couldn't sing because they were too far away to hear!"

"They were—but I reached out in the ways I could. I just wasn't sure they'd hear me. Besides, I wasn't singing in front of that bastard. No way. That's... that's between us," she said, her eyes dropping and her body squirming uncomfortably.

I clawed a hand through my hair and just stared at her, overwhelmed with both admiration at her grit, and genuine unease.

"Yilan... are you lying to me?"

"No," she said emphatically, meeting my eyes without flinching.

"These men—you said Turo was the General of your people. Yet he's following your orders? And the others as well?"

She raised her eyebrows. "I know in your society women are nothing but chattels. But in ours it is... different," she said through her teeth.

I opened my mouth to reassure her, but she wasn't finished.

"I am the best shadow walker of our people. I had the best chance of infiltrating. The others worried for my safety because obviously I'm not as strong in a fight. But I wouldn't let someone else take a greater risk to *attempt* what I knew I could *achieve*. I am the best equipped, and so I am commander of this mission. You know how critical orders are in this kind of operation. When one Fetch is leader, all others follow, regardless of rank."

I stared at her. "Even the King?"

"A King, a Queen, a General—*anyone,*" she said pointedly.

My head was spinning. "How many Fetch are here?" I asked.

Her expression went uneasy. "A dozen," she said finally.

"What?!"

"They aren't all *here,*" she said waving her arms at the tent. "But in or around this camp. Watching and... studying. They take turns visiting the camp and listening. At any given moment there would be three or four within the tents, though not always close to yours. Your tent is well positioned, the rock behind keeps us from approaching on two sides—"

"I know," I growled. "That's why I chose the position. But Yilan... How long have you all been here?"

She squirmed. "Since you reached the swamplands," she said. "But those details are unimportant now. We need to—"

"Yilan, I don't wish to fight with you when we'll soon be separated... but if this is what you call honesty, if this is honor in your people—"

"Don't you *dare* judge me," she hissed. "I walked into this place ruled by men with *no* honor, and even less self-restraint. I did as I said I would and I helped you. But I would not give up my own people for Gault's trust. No. Never."

I stared at her. "Very few things worth dying for..." I muttered.

She nodded. "But not none."

We stared at each other and my heart was flinching. Every time I thought I'd found peace with her, every time I thought I truly could trust her, some other secret was revealed.

But I knew it was a question that couldn't be answered here and now. Gault's body was gone, but he would be missed within hours at the *least*. All it would take was the wrong servant or guard who'd been given instructions to come back and...

I cleared my throat and shook off the dark thoughts.

"I have to go—and so do you," I said just as emphatically as she'd given her little tirade.

"No," she said firmly.

"Yilan—"

"No. This is the time, Melek. This is an open door for you. You can take the crown and they will follow and—"

"And *I said no,*" I growled. "Dear God, Yilan, let it go. There are very few things in this world worth dying for—but you and Gall are it for me. I will *not* risk either of you to rumors and suspicion and the fucking chaos that's going to ensue here when they realize Gault is dead!"

Yilan's expression grew more worried than angry, but she folded her arms. "Your only options are to take the crown, or flee, Melek. But you have no reason to flee—you've done nothing wrong."

"I believe one thing we *can* agree on is that my brothers at arms are unlikely to see this that way," I growled.

Her eyes widened and she dropped her arms. "So... what? You just walk into that *cesspit* and get yourself blamed for my actions and killed for no gain? You are my mate, Melek," she hissed. "I will not let you do that. *I* will walk the shadows and tell them it was me if you try to confess to this!"

I took her arm and God help me, I shook her. "No, you *won't.* You will leave, and I will say you escaped in the chaos in the wake of the King's death."

"You can't put yourself on the line like this!"

"If you're so certain they want to follow me, why don't you believe they'll listen?" I snapped.

"Because we both know they won't *think* about this, they'll only act. Most of them are ill-disciplined, self-indulgent, *children!"*

"Children who will kill my son if they have even a *hint* that he was involved. No judges, no questions. They would tear him limb from limb before I'd even had a chance to shout. You expect me to leave him to that? I will not let him carry this!"

Yilan stared at me, those worry lines appearing on her forehead again, her eyes big and liquid and locked on mine.

"I wouldn't ask you to leave Gall to them," she whispered a moment later. "But—"

"I am a soldier, Yilan. I wasn't born to be King. I do not aspire to a crown, and I never have. If I were supposed to, God would have given me one."

Her jaw tightened. "He may not have placed a crown on your head at birth, but He has given you men you didn't ask for, land you didn't seek to possess for yourself—the entire fucking *continent* listens to you, Melek! You are already more than a General. You are a—"

"If I embrace what you say, I am nothing but an ambitious traitor and not anything that all these hearts and minds follow me for. No, Yilan. I will take my chances. I will protect Gall, and you, and I will pray that God finds a way through this for me. But I will not sit myself on a throne that was not mine to take."

"And if they forgive you... and crown you? You *did* win a challenge against the King."

"Then I would *consider* it only if no other strong male stepped forward," I said reluctantly, everything in me recoiling. "But hear me, Yilan, my goal is freedom to live in peace with you. *Not* to rule a nation." I was angry, bristling, ready for a fight—and frustrated. But to my shock and dismay, Yilan didn't push again.

Her chin trembled and she dropped her face into her hands.

And she sobbed.

53. Careful Now

~ MELEK ~

I sighed and pulled her close, holding her for a moment, closing my eyes and inhaling her scent, trying to fix the memory in my mind so I'd never lose it.

Then she relaxed against me, finally.

I was trying to figure out how to raise the specter of Gall—eventually I needed to find him and explain—when someone cleared their throat just outside the tent flap and I almost leaped through the roof.

Yilan drew her dagger, but I motioned to her to stay there as I started creeping across the floor towards it.

"Sire, may I enter? I have a message for the General."

Already halfway across the tent, I slumped. It was Jann.

Hurrying the rest of the way, I leaned out the tent-flap, scanning the area behind him as I grasped his shirt, pulled him inside, and hissed at him to draw no attention.

He came in, eyes down the way Gault would require, but then his gaze rose when he realized the tent was empty except for me and Yilan.

"Thank God you came," I whispered to him. "There's no time to explain, but I need your help."

He stared around the tent, but nodded. "Of course, but—"

"I need you to run messages. Tell the Council that the King is drunk and having one of his moments. That I'm trying to convince him to stick with the plan. And I need them to stay away so he'll relax and sleep it off."

Jann nodded, but he glanced at Yilan with a question in his eyes. I ignored it.

"Tell all his servants that he has ordered them to remain off duty until the end of the Covenant. We must not be interrupted before I leave tomorrow."

"Of course, but… Melek, where—"

Then his eyes fell on the stain in the dirt and the dark splatters on the bed and he froze.

His head snapped up to me and I saw the whites of his eyes. "Melek, what the fuck is going on?"

I put both my hands up. "It is truly not what you think, brother," I said quickly, praying he was too distracted to notice Yilan drawing her knife again, because the last thing I needed was those two coming to blows. "But I do need your help to delay any… attention in this direction."

Jann swallowed, looking at that dark stain again, then at me, then at Yilan, then back to me. Then he swallowed again.

"Don't be afraid, Jann," Yilan muttered bitterly behind him. "I assure you, he stubbornly clings to every last word he has ever given."

Jann turned quickly to look at her, frowning.

I nodded but clapped his shoulder to get his eyes back on me. "You have nothing to worry about," I said quietly.

Yilan scoffed, but Jann just stared at me. "And Gall?" he asked softly.

"I'm going to go find him when he's had time to calm down and then—"

"I'll do it," Jann said with another wary glance at Yilan.

I shook my head. "No, it really does need to be me. There are some things we need to discuss."

"But—"

"Jann, if you can help us keep everyone away from this tent, that would be the best help I could hope for."

He stared at me, and I knew he suspected. But he was also smart enough to know he didn't *want* to know.

Then he nodded and offered his arm for me to clasp. I took it and pulled him into a quick, thumping hug, praying that it wasn't the last time we'd have the chance to embrace. Then, nodding once to Yilan, he was gone. Yilan remained still, staring at the door where he'd exited.

"How long until you're—"

She hissed and snapped a hand up to stop me speaking, then stepped aside, into the shadow of a set of drawers, and then she was gone.

I gaped. Did she think we had people listening? Or was she just being cautious?

I paced the dirt, waiting. After a few moments, I was almost biting through my tongue to stop myself calling after her to make sure she was safe.

But then, finally, she stepped out of the shadow behind the armoire, frowning.

"We're alone," she whispered. "But Jann doesn't trust me anymore."

I was tempted to make a joke about how that might be smart given how easily she'd ended the King, but her skin was still pale and her eyes were haunted. It was too soon.

Death left a stain. Always. And not just in the dirt.

"Was he your first?" I asked her gently.

She gave a wide berth to that dark puddle on the floor, but shook her head. "No."

"So you truly are an assassin?"

"I am the best shadow walker of our kind," she said with a humble, one-shouldered shrug. "I was born for this."

"No. You were born for me," I said gruffly.

Her eyes lit up then and she made a beeline for me, coming to stand at my feet, staring up at me like she didn't quite believe I was real.

"Melek Handras—*General* Melek Handras, I love you," she said quietly. "I hate the decisions you're making, but I love you."

"I could say the same," I said, trying for humor. I even managed a half-smile. But she just plowed on.

"You need to let us find Gall," she said hurriedly, like she'd been thinking about it and anticipated that I wouldn't be happy.

"Absolutely not. If he sees you—or anyone else for that matter—materializing out of a shadow, he might actually lose his mind."

"And if my men return while you're gone, what then?" she asked tightly.

I sucked in a breath. "Then you go, and you stay safe."

"Melek—"

"No, Yilan. You gave me your word. I don't want to leave you, either. I don't want you gone. But if safety appears, you grasp it. You grasp it and cling until I make it through the ravine."

"How the fuck are you going to make it to battle if you are putting yourself before a Judge tomorrow?"

"I'm trusting that if we are intended to survive this, God is going to find a way. And if we aren't... well, then I wouldn't have anyway, no matter what course I took."

Her jaw flexed. "You say that so easily, as if walking away from me is—"

"Do *not* finish that sentence," I growled. "You know it isn't true... Don't you?"

She stared at me, but then she slowly nodded and her shoulders rolled forward. "I'm sorry, Melek, I'm just... there are so many other choices here and you're refusing to see them."

I sighed and stepped up to hold her arms, looking down at her so she'd see I was hiding nothing. "I have never denied that there are other ways to walk through this world," I said quietly. "But if you believe that others follow me, then you must know they do it because I walk with integrity and to serve. To run now—or to take the throne by force—would fly in the face of everything I have ever claimed to be. I meant what I said, Yilan. If there is any blessing on me, it is because God is pleased with me. I will not call down *His* wrath alongside the rest of this shit."

"But then that means we will have no choice but to say goodbye,' she said, her eyes welling again.

"I pray it isn't goodbye, but... *until we meet again.* I pray that fervently, Yilan. I promise you, there is nothing that I want more than to gather up Gall and run with you. Hold you. Be with you. Turn my back on everything and everyone else. But... I can't."

Her forehead pinched, but she reached up to cup my face. "I know," she whispered, blinking back her tears. "I do. I just..." She blew out a breath and looked down. "I'm sorry, Melek. I want to make love to you—it may be our last chance. But I can't... not here. Not in *his* bed—or even in this tent where he has violated so many." She glanced over her shoulder and shuddered.

"It's okay, Love," I whispered, pulling her in. "I feel the same. I have some time. Gall needs some space to calm down. So we'll use that to sit here and hold each other until your... friends return. Then we will say goodbye and I will find Gall."

I heard her swallow. She didn't nod, but she sighed and sat up, holding my face. "If you're traveling tomorrow you need to keep up your strength. I'm sure there must be snacks here, or something in this tent. You can't tell me that brute only ate at mealtimes."

I shook my head. "I couldn't eat," I said quickly.

"But—"

"I'm serious, Yilan. I think my stomach would revolt. If you're worried about it, let's get a drink from the casks," I said, nodding towards the back corner of the tent. "Something to fortify our nerves."

She bit her lip, obviously nervous about the idea of me suffering effects of alcohol. But I wouldn't drink enough to affect my mind. Just a little to loosen my tension.

Yilan sighed again and urged me to stay there in the chair while she found two mugs and filled them both from one of the casks, then brought them back to me, making a great show of presenting me one of them before holding her own up.

I raised mine and smiled when she offered the toast. "For the *great* General Melek Handras. My mate. Father to Gall. Defeater of the Pig King. And incredible, *soulful* man," she said, her voice trailing off to a whisper at the end.

We clunked the mugs and began to drink, but I was moved so deeply, I reached for her with my free hand before I'd even finished emptying the mug and tossed it aside. She made a little squeak as I pulled her back into my lap. But she was smiling.

And so, as she sipped at her mug, I stroked her hair back over her shoulder and buried my nose in her neck.

And as time dragged on and the adrenaline wore off, and we both started to feel drowsy, she urged me to lay my head on the back of the chair, then she lay against my chest, her temple resting on my shoulder.

I fought sleep, knowing her countrymen might show up at any moment, and I wanted to wallow in every moment until then.

"I'll take Gall," she whispered at one point, just as my eyelids began to close.

"Hmmm?"

"I'll take Gall with me," she whispered, then kissed my cheek. "No matter what, he'll be safer with us than he is here."

"I have to talk to him first."

She sighed and nodded against my shoulder, her hand stroking up and down my chest.

"I love you, Melek," she said in a tiny voice. "No matter what happens… I love you."

"I love you too…"

I knew I should say more. But I was *so tired.* And so I just held her to me and finally let my eyes drift closed and stay there. Before I sank fully into the dark, I lifted a plea to God to give us more time. Any more time. Don't let this be it…

Please…

54. Into the Shadows

SOUNDTRACK: *You'll Never Forget Me*   by
Future Royalty

~ YILAN ~

When Melek gave the long, low sigh of sleep overtaking him, I hugged him tighter.

Even in his sleep, he clung to me. His arms tightening in response.

I didn't move immediately, just lay there, smelling him, praying, until the powder Turo had passed me and I'd slipped into his drink truly took hold. His big hands slipped down, his arms went loose, and his head fell fully back, his mouth open and slack.

Even then I didn't move. I needed a moment.

Tears blurred my gaze, but I blinked them away and straightened in his lap, stroking his forehead as the lines of worry eased there, combing back his hair, twining his warrior's length around my fingers, wishing I could grip it and pull him to me and *force him to see the fucking light.* But I had tried. In every way I knew how.

He was more fucking stubborn than a Centaur stallion with the aroma of an in-heat female in his nostrils.

Before I called Turo back to help, I took a few more minutes to look at this from every angle, to make certain there was nothing I'd missed. No opportunity overlooked. But no matter how I parsed it all out, there was nothing.

Unless Melek was ready to declare—and yes, fight—for the crown, the Nephilim would only implode—and once they took the ravine, likely continue to advance, bringing their chaos with them. Even if we, the Shadekin, could stop them at the Shadows of Shade, defeating them would only leave a Continent in disarray, and all eight nations in upheaval.

Nephilim fighting for the crown would bring the fallen angels back—those fuckers could never just leave things alone down here. Even among their offspring, they meddled and manipulated, and incited violence. I couldn't imagine what would happen in this land if there was no immediate succession.

The possibilities made my blood run cold.

No… We needed Melek. All of us. The Nephilim. The Shadekin. And all the peoples he had conquered. If he couldn't see that, my only choice was to force all of us to brave the initial chaos—let him see the consequences of his choice—and pray he could be convinced in the wake of it.

Let him be the savior to solve the tribulation that was about to descend on the continent.

And that meant getting him and Gall the fuck out of here until the King's death was discovered and the Nephilim were scrambling.

Turo was *very* dubious. But I was in charge here.

I would take my mate and his son beyond the Shadows of Shade, into Theynor, my land, where he would be presented as the prize that he was.

They would try to use him for the sway he held over the Nephilim—and now the entire continent. I knew that. But there was no choice.

I would beg God to make Melek forgive me for forcing his hand. But I *couldn't* let him martyr himself!

Still stroking his face, I was overcome in a wave of grief and fear. What if he truly denied me because of this? What if he *rejected the bond?*

We were vowed and bonded, surrendered. But either of us could turn from that. Could choose to destroy what existed between us.

Severing a bond was painful and destructive to both mates, but it could be done. The question was, did he love me more than he hated the idea of being crowned?

God, I began to shake just thinking about it.

"Please, Melek," I whispered, praying the words would take root in his subconscious. "Please... this is *my* honor. This is *my* word. It is for *your* good, even if you can't see it. There is no one on this continent who deserves to live, deserves a *crown* more than you. No one better to lead *every* land. I wish you could see that."

I had to swallow the lump in my throat. I hugged him one more time, burying my face under his ear and letting only one tear slide down his neck before I closed my eyes and prepared to move.

Turo and the others had disposed of the King's body within an hour of leaving the tent. Then they'd found Gall.

At my orders, Turo had intentionally stayed, positioning himself at the edge of my reach, so I could call him when they were needed, but there was no chance they'd be discovered or drawn into... this.

Everything was going as planned, but now time was growing short.

Darkness had fallen. We needed to move while the camp was still busy with celebrations.

We had to be well out of the camp before things slowed—carrying two massive Nephilim—all while avoiding anything that would draw attention to the fact that the King was *gone*. It could take hours.

Forcing myself to focus on the task, and not on Melek's rage when he learned what I had done, I leaned my ear against his chest to check his heart and make sure I'd dosed him correctly. It was a relief to hear that massive thud, pounding away like a drum.

The sleep powder had slowed his pulse, but not alarmingly.

I turned my head to kiss the center of his chest, and then I reached for Turo in my mind.

'It is time.'

'Finally,' Turo responded immediately. *'What took so long?'*

'We had a visitor, and Melek took much longer to sleep than I anticipated.'

'These fucking Neph bulls,' Turo muttered. *'We'll be there in minutes. Half the camp is already passing out from drink. We need to move quickly.'*

'I know.'

True to his word, my helpers began to materialize within a couple of minutes. I motioned at them to keep their voices down just in case, and had to turn away while they bound Melek before bracing themselves to carry him.

'Where is Gall?' I asked Turo.

'Already on his way,' he replied gruffly.

I nodded. Turo had a soft spot for my sister, Istral, so understood why I wanted to take Gall from here. But he didn't like the added complication of hauling *two* Nephilim across an enemy nation.

"Thank you," I whispered, putting a hand to his arm. "You're a good man, Turo."

He sagged and quickly placed his other hand over mine before I could draw it off his forearm. Startled, I flinched and yanked my hand back before I caught myself.

The hurt in his eyes was... heartbreaking. He stepped right up to my toes, but thankfully, didn't touch me. "You do not need to fear me, Yilan," he breathed. "I won't push you. Not after all you've been through."

I shook my head. "You just startled me—"

But he hissed a curse and his eyes went fierce—in defense of me, I knew. Turo had never harmed me. He loved me. I knew that. I'd always assumed the admiration and gratitude I had for him would evolve into love over time. But now...

Raising his hand slowly so I would see it coming, he cupped the side of my neck, tracing the line of my jaw with his thumb. I had to brace not to shudder.

"They will pay, Yilan. We will *make* them pay."

I sagged, but he looked at me intently.

"Don't worry, we won't risk this mission," he muttered. "You've done well. But hear me, Yilan, when we're home and you're safe, when you see that you don't have to protect yourself anymore... then you'll tell me. You'll tell me, and we will grieve together."

I took a deep breath and nodded, though my heart sank because I knew he wanted to hear what had *truly* happened, even less than what he thought was coming.

Then I tensed, because his whisper grew fierce. "I vow to you, Yilan. I will kill anyone who so much as looked at you wrongly."

I wanted to tell him all of it, right then, so he didn't have to carry that rage anymore. But this wasn't the time, and I couldn't afford to distract him from the incredibly dangerous and risky path we were about to embark on. All I could do was meet his intense gaze and pat his hand to reassure him.

"I am well. The things that happened here will only make me stronger."

He opened his mouth to reply hotly, but then one of the others cleared their throats and we were forced to break apart—him reluctantly, me with relief.

It was time. Wrists and ankles chained, my unconscious mate lay on the canvas sling between two poles sturdy enough to be used to carry a horse. Four of my comrades were positioned, one for each corner, and two more, one on each side to give their partners rest when needed.

He looked so vulnerable—asleep and bound in the hands of those he'd name enemy, I wanted to weep. But I wouldn't leave his side until we made it to the Capitol. And then... when he was awake... then I'd explain.

And I'd pray that he could forgive me.

"Let's go," I said quietly.

"Yilan—" Turo started, but I shook my head.

"It's time," I said hoarsely. "We need to get well beyond the camp before the sun rises. Remember to keep walking the shadows until your power gives out. It will be impossible not to leave footsteps bearing that kind of weight. So spread the trail as much as possible."

The men—the biggest and strongest we'd brought on this mission, though each still less than half the weight of Melek—all nodded and leaned down, taking hold of the poles, but not lifting until their leader gave the command.

Turo remained at my side, one hand hovering near my back, though he didn't touch me, which was a relief.

We watched them together, carrying Melek to the deepest and widest of the shadows at the back of the tent, and when they'd managed to maneuver their large load so that all of him was covered by the dimness, the leader nodded.

"We're aiming for the twisted tree, thirty feet away. Concentrate."

The men all nodded, placing one hand each on Melek's bare arms or legs, and then they began to fade. The process was slower when they carried any burden, but one the size of Melek... I was stunned they were able to do it at all. But they did.

And then, just for a breath, Turo and I were alone.

My stomach dropped when he turned to me and offered his hand. "I will avenge you, Yilan," he said quietly. Fiercely. "These bastards will pay. You have served your people at cost to yourself and I will not stop fighting until every one of them knows it, and knows they pay the debt for what they did to you."

I slumped. "Turo, please…"

"You want me to just let them harm you? You expect me to stand by and just… forgive that?"

I opened my mouth, suddenly *needing* to tell him everything. Needing him to understand. But every instinct in my head *shrieked.*

He wouldn't be able to think straight for days. Possibly weeks. It would put all of us in danger. But especially him.

He watched, eyes angry, as I shook my head. "This isn't the time," I croaked. "Just promise me you'll take no action until we've spoken… about everything."

"Oh, I promise you, Yilan. I want every detail, to know *exactly* what I'm avenging."

I sighed, but nodded. Then he took my hand and led me to the shadows, and we both faded into them without another word.

55. Tied

~ *MELEK* ~

My first awareness was the freshness of the air.

Before I'd even opened my eyes, my senses perked. A breath of cool, clean air fluttered over my body and I *knew* I couldn't be in camp anymore. Where was the scent of shit-tainted mud? The heavy odor of unwashed male bodies, unwashed clothing, unwashed bedclothes—unwashed *everything?*

But my eyes wouldn't open. Despite my tension and questions, I sank back into sleep for a time.

When I woke again, my eyes were heavy, but fluttered.

I blinked.

And blinked.

And blinked many more times, trying to clear the crust and blur from my eyes, and also trying to find some frame of reference for what I was seeing.

But every time I opened my eyes, the sight was the same.

A huge, lavish room. Floor of stone slate. Walls built of huge bricks. I could see one shutter-framed window from this angle. The sill was deep enough for me to sit in it.

Still blinking, rubbing my eyes with half-numb hands, I slowly scanned the room, confused.

The furniture was large, but not nearly as big as ours. The fireplace was huge—large enough even for me to step into it if the hearth was cold. But there was a fire crackling merrily away, and a huge stack of wood next to it, as if whoever lived here thought they needed days of warmth.

It certainly wasn't needed for light. Bright but thin sunlight bathed the room, turning all the dark, carved furniture into gleaming luxury, velvet curtains into rich falls, and...

And none of this was Nephilim in style or size.

I sat bolt upright, hand clawing into the soft mattress on which I lay, head snapping left and right—but then I had to groan and let myself fall back again because my head spun and ached like a motherfucker.

I didn't know what had been done to me, or where I was, but it took minutes of laying there, eyes closed, to swallow back the wave of nausea that tried to punch out of my throat.

When it finally felt safe to open my eyes, I took it much more slowly.

The bed I lay on was massive—easily large enough for my frame—and had four posts, one on each corner, and a ceiling. Thick red curtains were pulled back to the foot and head, but they were held by a gold cord that could be released, and the curtains pulled closed along the rails between the posts.

Presumably, to block out that bright sunlight.

Where the fuck was I?

It took a great deal of time, and patience, rolling first to my side, then slowly pushing myself upright—and closing my eyes, breathing deeply for many minutes before the nausea passed.

Eventually, I was able to lower my bare feet to the floor. Then I had to spend time shifting my weight until I was steady enough to actually stand. And more minutes before I could walk. But I could feel my head clearing with every breath, and my body growing surer.

At some point, I stood in the center of that stone floor and turned a slow circle.

The room was six-sided. The most important side—the central block—housed a huge, arched doorway *with steel bars over it.*

Anger and unease twisted my chest, but I kept turning.

The fireplace took one side. Then the window. The bed. Another window—with drawers and a wash table underneath it— filled the fifth. The final side was covered in shelves, the lowest of which was thick and deep and held a row of large baskets. But the shelves above that were full of books, knick-knacks, and curiosities.

If it weren't for the bars on the door, I would have thought I'd been ensconced in a royal guest suite somewhere.

But why bar the door if the windows were open and accessible?

I shuffled to the nearest window—the one that let that breeze drift through the room—and found the answer.

Aware that I was still a little unsteady, I reached across the deep sill intending to grip the external ledge and lean over to see how the window was placed in the wall. It was big enough that I could crawl into it and launch from—

There was an electric *crack* and a jolt that started in my fingers. Nerve pain sang through my arms and into my chest. I gasped and pulled back, blinking.

At least I was more awake now.

Swallowing, curious, and a little fearful, I pointed one finger and reached into the open window slowly, uncertain if the—

The crack came again the moment my finger passed the edge of the windowsill, and my arm jangled with that pain.

Magik. Some kind of power shield.

Careful not to tip past the sill itself, I did lean into the space to look for the ground—and discovered it was easily a hundred feet below. I didn't know if that magik would follow me. If I threw myself through it, would I pass through?

Somehow I doubted it. And there was always the risk that the shock would freeze my wings.

No throwing myself out windows, then.

I made my way to check the other, but already knew what I would find, and sure enough, one more sizzle on my fingertip was enough.

No escape.

I began to sweat.

Then I discovered the tray resting on the top of the drawer set next to my bed.

Fruit. Bread. Cheese. And a small note in perfectly crafted handwriting: *Start slowly. Your stomach has rested for days.*

Rested?

Been starved, they meant. I huffed, shaking my head and tossed the note aside. But then my stomach gave a great clench and growled audibly.

I picked up the small loaf of bread, biting off a hunk and chewing on it as I walked another circuit of the room to see if there were any clues as to what nation I was in, or how I'd come to be here.

But there was nothing.

Yilan.

My heart raced.

Where was she?

Panic fluttered my heart and I froze, hand clasped to my chest, right at the center where the space that was *her* resided.

And only then could I breathe.

She was alive. She was nervous and unhappy, but she was alive.

I wanted to roar. But my head was still foggy and my thoughts came slowly.

We'd been taken, clearly. But by whom? Had her comrades betrayed us? Or had they inadvertently led our mutual enemies to us? Was she imprisoned too?

The Nephilim wouldn't have put us up this way. It had to be another—

Yilan.

I swallowed the mouthful of bread too early and it hurt going down, but I barely felt it as the memory rushed back to me.

"You hold the keys to my soul, Yilan. And the weapon to take down my people... please do not make me a fool for loving you."

Her eyes sang of sadness, but she shook her head then turned to kiss my neck. "I will never choose anything *to hurt you, Melek. You have my word."*

With a low growl, I turned that circle again and even though there were no direct clues, it made sense.

It made so much fucking sense.

Fucking Fetch.

Rage expanded my chest at the same moment something deep inside me screamed with pain. My mate was here. Somewhere near enough for me to sense her.

Lies.

Deception.

Betrayal.

Mate.

I was still reeling, still breathing against the fire of rage when there was a massive *clunk* and the twin doors that filled that doorway arch beyond the bars began to swing outward.

I whirled, throwing the bread aside, cursing my body for feeling so shaky and weak, but bracing so that it wouldn't show as the gap between the doors widened to reveal at least a dozen people.

The anteroom outside the door was dim, no windows or lanterns, but the light from the room was enough by which to see who stood there.

At the center, right at the front, a short, slim woman stood, dressed in finery the likes of which I had never seen. She wore a purple velvet cloak with a white fur trim that was clasped with a gold chain which draped across her collarbones.

Her dress under that was plainer—no embroidery or frill, but made from a fabric with such a lustrous sheen I instinctively didn't want to touch it in case I marred it with my soldier's hands.

Her chin was high so that she stared down her nose at me, though I was two feet taller than she was. There was a pretty circlet on her head, and a bright purple diadem hanging at the center of her forehead.

Unlike Yilan, her hair was curly and a warm brown, which was the first surprise. I'd thought all the Fetch were pale skinned with black hair and blue eyes, like Yilan and Turo.

But she was definitely Fetch. Of that I had no doubt.

I'd thought Yilan's mannerisms were her own, but now it was clear that my mate was deeply *Fetch.*

As the Queen was revealed, so was the entourage behind her. Several women, also in deep cloaks, though with hoods high, a handful of guards with stern faces and spears at the ready. Then another line of men behind them—one of them was Turo—standing with feet apart and hands on the hilts of the swords at their waists.

And every single one of them reminded me of birds—trim, powerful bodies poised on the edge of movement even when they only stood there. They didn't move, yet there was a *feeling* about them—as if they were only barely tethered to this world, and with one step, they could walk the wind.

Shadows, I reminded myself, grinding my teeth. *They walk the* shadows.

A memory rushed back to me, then. Yilan's words.

"...I walk the shadows, I do not serve them. There is a huge difference."

Was there?

The doors were drawn back, and the Queen drifted forward until she stood just outside arm's reach from the bars.

As if I would be able to attack her through them.

Smart woman.

"Bow to the Queen, General," a deep voice muttered from the back of the crowd. Turo, I thought.

I rolled my jaw, but reluctantly sketched a very shallow bow.

The Guards and other men shifted on their feet, clearly unhappy with my lack of respect, but they could all eat my shit.

The Queen, nose still high, let her eyes drag down my body—and for the first time, I considered my own clothing.

I was wearing a long, white shirt with loose sleeves, laced at the throat, hanging almost to my knees. But nothing else.

Her eyes scanned my shoulders, down my chest—did they hesitate at my crotch? I wasn't sure, but smiled as if they had because it would piss her off—then down to my half-bared thighs, my calves, and feet.

I opened my arms. "Do you like what you see, your Majesty?" I asked in a sarcastic growl.

Her eyes snapped back up to my face and her lip twitched as if she wanted to sneer, but was stopping herself.

"Are you truly the General of the Nephilim, Melek Handras?"

I huffed. "I would say *at your service,* but it would be a lie."

Her brows rose slightly, and I heard a muttered curse from behind her, but she raised one hand and no one spoke up.

"You are welcome here, Sir," she said calmly.

I pointedly looked at the bars between us, then back to her. "I can tell."

She arched one perfect brow and her lips pulled up on one side. "I am not certain you can be trusted. But... should you prove yourself honorable... you will be freed. Eventually. Now, ask your questions. I do not have much time."

"Where am I?" I was certain I knew, but I wanted confirmation.

"The Shadekin welcome you to our Capitol—and to the Palace. You are my guest here."

"Do you imprison all your guests?"

"When they have conquered a continent and killed a King? Yes," she said simply.

I huffed and rubbed my mouth to cover the smile that wanted to come at the pointed look in her eyes. But I wouldn't give in. And the most important question burned.

"Where is Yilan?"

"She is not far. And she will be allowed to visit you when it is safe. I asked to speak with you alone first."

My blood ran cold. "If you have harmed her—" I snarled, starting towards the bars, and in a blink there was a twist in the shadows just beyond the light cast from my windows, and suddenly four men appeared—including Turo—swords bared and marching to stand between me and the Queen.

Turo locked eyes with me coldly. "You speak one threat and it will be the last word that ever passes your tongue," he said calmly, but with great conviction.

I raised my hands to remind them that I was unarmed *and on the other side of fucking bars,* but the action raised the hem of my shirt and the Queen's eyes dropped… then widened.

I smiled.

Turo's gaze went flat. "Fucking *pig.* "

I tensed and so did he, but the Queen broke in. "Thank you, Turo. But let the General speak. Words cannot hurt me. While he is bested, imprisoned, and unarmed, it would be natural that his ego was… pricked," she said with a hint of amusement dancing in her tone.

The Queen stepped forward and the men parted, but stayed at the front, holding their weapons.

She folded her arms under her breasts and tipped her head.

"I have not brought you here to kill you—unless you try to kill me," she said.

"Then why?" Like I didn't already know.

"Because I have been told that you are, at heart, a good man. That perhaps you even possess a soul—remarkable among your kind, you'll agree."

I growled, but she ignored me.

"Your personal reign of terror on the Continent ends now, but that doesn't have to mean—"

"Thank you, Keely. I'll take it from here."

One of the women in the line behind her, face hidden in a deep hood, reached out for the Queen's shoulder, and the Queen immediately stopped, turning to face her.

I frowned, instincts alert—but then she flipped her hood back and my heart sang.

Black hair.

Slanted eyes.

Full lips that wanted to smile.

And eyes that lit up when she lifted them to meet mine.

Yilan.

56. Mate. Mine.

~ MELEK ~

Mate.
Soulbond.
Mine.

But then I inhaled sharply, because as she revealed herself, everyone in the anteroom—including the Queen—turned and bowed or curtseyed to her…

"Yilan—" Turo growled.

"Hush," she responded calmly, though I heard her tension. "You wanted to be sure he wouldn't jump to attack. He has not."

I blinked, confused for half a breath, until Yilan stepped forward, and the *Queen* took the circlet and diadem from her forehead and offered it on open, flat palms to Yilan, who took it and quickly settled it on her head, threw back the sides of her coat and walked right up to the bars.

The men twitched when they realized she moved closer to me, but she shot a look at Turo, then turned to face me… and they all remained behind her.

When our eyes locked, I was the only one who could see hers. And see the plea in them.

My breath stopped. She stood silently, her eyes big and deep, liquid. I wanted to fall into that gaze. My hands twitched to reach for her as her name tore from my throat and I stumbled forward—

but then drew up short when she only dropped her chin and gave me a fierce warning look.

"Turo... the General has been asleep for days and will be concerned about how his countrymen are faring," she said quietly. "Please give him the report you gave me an hour ago."

Turo spluttered. "But—"

"Now please, *General.*"

Turo gaped at her, then clearly gathered his thoughts. He raised his chin and cleared his throat preparing to obey, though his eyes flashed with anger when he turned to me.

"Our scouts have returned from their foray to the swamps. The Fallen King is dead. His people know that, but fight on. Rumors abound that the Shadekin have their famed General, Melek Handras, because he disappeared at the same time as the Fetch prisoner—whom they blame for the King's death. They've been unable to confirm that the General wasn't also killed."

He cut off then as if he was done. But Yilan shot him a look from the side. "And the rest," she snapped.

He glared back at her and there was a moment that it seemed their wills wrestled. But then he gritted his teeth and turned back to me. "The Nephilim are *stumbling* and *blind.* As concerned with fighting among themselves as they are about conquering the nations. They made it through the ravine under the leadership of Jannus the Halfling, but only just. They hold the land by their talons. There is infighting and challenges for ranks even among the soldiers." He glanced at Yilan, then smiled darkly at me. "The time to attack is now."

My heart sank to my toes, and the rage that I'd been holding at bay, all the thoughts of how I'd come to be here and what it meant, rushed to the surface as the pleading in Yilan's eyes suddenly made sense.

I stared at her, my heart twisting, flinching, *pained.*

The bond thrummed. And then it shrieked as it became clear that all my worst fears were realized.

For the span of a breath I was in freefall—my soul screaming for her, my body shaking with need, my mind pleading, praying, despairing.

And then I remembered.

"I will never choose anything *to hurt you, Melek. You have my word."*

It was like being stabbed right in the heart.

She was a lie. Every bit. A lie and a trap to defeat me.

She was everything I'd feared.

Everything I'd asked her to promise me, everything I had promised *her* was meaningless.

"Fucking *Fetch*," I spat.

The men roared and leaped forward, but Yilan raised her hand and they all stopped as if they'd been frozen in place.

Perhaps they had.

There had to be a heart of ice, pumping frigid water into those veins.

Perhaps she froze them in truth.

"I understand your concerns," she said formally, though her eyes were wide and dark, locked on mine. "I know it will take some time to... process. But I want to assure you—"

"There is no point speaking, Yilan. I will never believe another word that passes your lips."

Fear flashed in her gaze, then her eyes shuttered as Turo snapped forward again.

"You will *not* speak to our Queen that way!" But I ignored him, holding her gaze, letting her see every ounce of my disdain, every crumb of my disgust.

Liar. Liar. Liar.

Yilan hissed at the soldiers who were following Turo, crowding towards the bars, ready to come for me.

"Leave him!" she spat.

Turo turned on her. "He insults the crown and the Queen—"

"And I would remind you that I hold a life debt to him. Let him speak his words. They do not touch me."

I felt her heart's pang in the bond calling her a liar, and huffed a humorless laugh.

Turo, furious, whirled back towards me, his lips twisting in rage—but she caught his arm and ordered him back to his place. Ordered *all* of them back into the shadows of that anteroom.

The choice not to put windows there now suddenly made sense.

When everyone else had backed off and she stood closest to me again, her forehead was lined. Pinched.

Good. At least she retained enough humanity to have a conscience.

Then she raised her chin again and took a deep breath. "I understand your... anger," she said carefully, that pleading entering her gaze again, but it didn't touch her voice. "We will win this war with or without you," she said with conviction. "But my preference is to fight *alongside* the honorable General. Not against him."

And oh, the *layers* in that statement.

I shook my head, huffing in disbelief at the sheer audacity of her.

Unable to resist, I stormed up to the bars, ignoring her gesture to the men to stay back, though I didn't reach through. "I would not give an ounce of my strength to you... you deceptive *bitch.*"

Turo roared and Yilan whirled away from me, but I ignored the rest of them and kept my eyes on her with the kind of smile I reserved for enemies, knowing eventually she would see it.

"Out. All of you," she commanded. "Now."

Everyone except Turo immediately turned on their heels and started out of the anteroom, though some of the women cast worried glances back over their shoulders.

It wasn't until Yilan had taken a deep breath and was beginning to turn back to me that she realized Turo hadn't moved, but stood aside to let the others pass him.

"Go," she said firmly.

"But he's a fucking Neph!"

"And the fiercest—and most honorable of them! He is angry, but he would never hurt me!"

"You can't seriously believe—"

"Turo, do not make me discipline you," she said quietly. "Leave. He is weak and imprisoned. I am perfectly safe."

Turo grumbled and made a big show of re-sheathing his sword, glaring at me over her shoulder.

She sighed like a mother losing her patience, but only folded her arms and stared at him until he reluctantly turned and stalked after the others, his boots ringing on the slate floor. At the end of the anteroom, he grasped the doors, hesitating once to look at Yilan, a strange expression on his face, before walking through, closing the doors, and leaving us alone.

The hair on my arms stood up when her shoulders slumped.

Instinctively, I wanted to reach for her, gather her in, kiss her, plead with her, demand that she tell me if she was hurt, or—

But no.

No. There would be no kissing. No holding. No relief. No reassurance.

As she turned back to me and walked right up to the bars, as if *she* might embrace *me,* I took two, stumbling steps back, shaking my head, my lips peeled back from my teeth.

"Melek," she breathed, and her voice cracked. I heard the grief—felt the pang in the bond.

And I hated her in that moment. *Hated* her for her lies and deception. *Despised* her for how she had wrapped my heart and soul around hers. Because it hit me then, when she gripped the bars and pleaded with me to come closer and my body *ached* to give her what she asked, that I would never be free of her.

Never.

The fucking bitch had imprisoned me more perfectly than any cage ever could. Because it didn't matter if she opened these bars this moment and let me walk.

Because the deepest part of me was tied to her. And would remain so, no matter how much distance I put between us.

57. The King has Fallen

SOUNDTRACK: *Can't Help Falling in Love – DARK*, by
Tommee Profitt and Brooke.

~ MELEK ~

The despair was so overwhelming, the rage so white-hot, I did
nothing but stand there and tremble.

"Melek," she breathed. "Please."

"Please, *what?!*"

She stared at me like she was drinking me in—probably just as
frantically as I drank in the sight of her. But did she hate herself for
it as I did? Apparently not.

Then she swallowed. "I didn't lie about anything," she said
hoarsely. "I just… didn't tell you everything."

"Well you left out a *whole fucking lot!*" I roared.

There was a shout on the other side of the door.

I snarled. "Better go soothe your bond-vowed. He seems to be
losing his shit."

"I'm going to handle Turo. He will know the full story first,
before the others. He deserves that much. But for now…" she drew
herself up and I saw it then, that regal certainty—it flickered though.
Hints of the scared young woman peeking through. "For now, it's
important that you know that the only thing I didn't tell you was
that I was Queen. Everything else—my feelings, my convictions,
what I wanted for you… it was all true."

I took a step closer and her eyes widened as I leaned in and dropped my voice. "So… you still want me?"

"Of course I do! You're my mate!"

I tipped my head. "Better tell that to your bond-vowed *General*. Seems like you have a type, Yilan. Have you fucked him since you got back? The man clearly worships at your feet, so I'm guessing the reunion was *thrilling*."

"Melek," she choked. "Of course I haven't! Don't be cruel."

"Cruel? *I'm* cruel? Are you fucking kidding me?! You lied to me, drugged me, and stole me from my life! I *trusted* you!"

"And you should! Because you're mine. And I'm yours!" she hissed, glancing over her shoulder.

"Don't say it too loud. He might hear you."

She snapped her head back around, and some of her fire was back. "I know you're angry. And I get it—I would be too. But I *didn't lie to you*. And I would *never* betray our bond that way. The only reason they don't know is because I haven't had a chance to talk to *you,* so you wouldn't be used against your will—"

"Bullshit," I snarled bitterly, raking my hand through my hair. "Just stop. I don't believe a word anyway. A fucking Queen? I should have known," I said with a sneer. "The Royals always are the most conniving and vicious." I leaned even closer until my nose almost brushed the bars. "One of the reasons I *never wanted to be one*."

"Melek—"

"Suddenly all your ambition for me makes sense. Hard to get excited about a simple General, right? I mean, clearly. You already had one of those."

"That is *not* what is happening here!" she hushed, stamping her foot. There were tears in her eyes, but she stood with her hands balled at her sides and her chin high, meeting my snarling insults with a dignity I hadn't seen in her before.

One more thing she had hidden from me.

"I am going to forgive you," she whispered.

"So noble of you," I snarled.

She closed her eyes and swallowed, then met my eyes again. "I am going to forgive you for your harsh words because I know this is a shock, and… and I would feel betrayed at first, as well."

"At first?!"

"But I am not going to… to *spar* with you. Because I am not vicious, except in defense of those I love. And I love you, Melek. You're my mate."

"Another deception," I snarled. "How did you do it? How did you make me believe? Is this just a spell?" I hissed, pounding my chest once where the bond sang and screamed.

She shook her head, her eyes welling. "Trust me, this was far harder for me than it was for you."

"Such bullshit. You played a part, Yilan: Strong, beautiful, but vulnerable in a herd of Nephilim, right? Always the poor female that we needed to rush to save. Very, *very* well played. But make no mistake, I will not fall for it again. I will not play your games."

"I wasn't playing you! You were never a part of this plan. My mission was to kill you! And then I met you and…"

"Then you should have done it," I hissed, leveling a finger at her. "Because I will never serve a liar and a fiend!"

Her head jerked back and her eyes cleared. "You already did. Your entire life," she said incredulously. "That fucker deserved your loyalty, but I do not?

"That fucker was born with the birthright—"

"So was I!"

That stopped me cold, because as much as it grated to admit, she was right and I had to consider what that meant.

If she was truly their Queen, truly born to it, and leading… she'd done so at the front of the battle. She'd left her throne to examine and then solve the problem herself. Exactly as a good leader should.

No wonder they were all so twitchy about her safety.

In any other set of circumstances I would have *admired* that.

But this…

She must have felt me waver, because she gripped the bars again, leaning between two, pressing herself towards me. "I am your mate, Melek," she whispered. "And you are mine. God put us together for a reason. And that reason is to lead into truth."

And then it all became clear.

I was no longer snarling, or bellowing. I was even beginning to let my anger pass…

I was just cold.

"Yilan… you cannot lead into something you do not possess."

Her brows pinched and her forehead lined as she shook her head. "I understand your anger, but do not let it make you stupid, Melek."

I huffed. "I have been deceived. I *am* a fool. But I am not stupid. However, those people out there are if they believe you can lead them into *truth*. You don't understand the concept!"

"Then you show them," she challenged me.

I frowned. "What?"

"I said, if you don't think I can do it, *you* show them. I am Queen, Melek. The Queen of this people. In my land things work differently. The Shadekin birthright *always* passes to the female. The Queen. And then is balanced by the wisdom and strength of the man she chooses. Always," she said, swallowing hard.

I blinked. "What?"

"I am Queen, Melek. That makes my mate, my *pair,* our King."

For the second time in minutes, I was in freefall.

But Yilan didn't even hesitate. She set her jaw and pinned me with her eyes.

"Do you hear me, Melek? *You* said God chooses rulers. Well, He chose *you* as my mate. And in my culture, the King always outranks the Queen. It is the Queen's most important responsibility *to choose the right man for the crown.* And I did." She swallowed hard. "So if you're really my mate, that makes you King of the Shadekin. *Chosen by God.* If you really believe I can't lead them into truth, well… can you? Because you're about to get your chance. That is… if you are willing to claim me as mate and will allow me to do the same."

I was speechless, gaping. Utterly floored.

But Yilan's jaw just tightened. "I didn't wait to tell them about our bond because it was faked. I waited *because* it's real. And because the *moment* I acknowledge you, you become our King. And hear me, Melek: Mate or not… I *will not* hand my Kingdom to a coward."

Sneak Peek:
Slave to the Wolf King
1. Call the Reapers

Behold, I was brought forth in iniquity, and in sin did my mother conceive me.
Psalms 51:5

~ *CASIMIR (Pronounced "CAZZ-uh-MEER")* ~

I woke up needing to piss.

One of my toys slept face down with her arm thrown across my chest. The second was curled like a puppy on top of the furs at my feet.

Tossing the fur—and the unwanted arm—back, I turned to sit on the edge of the bed, elbows on my knees, running a hand through my hair while I blinked my way awake.

The toy who'd been embracing me rolled away with a tiny protest. I watched her over my shoulder for a moment, considering punishing her. But she only rolled to her back, her beautiful breasts bouncing slightly as she slumped back against the pillow. The strands of her dark hair that lay over her face fluttered when she began to snore quietly.

I shook my head and pushed to my feet, walking naked towards the bathroom.

Our underground chambers meant there was no morning light. No dawn at the window. No windows at all. Nothing to tell my body it was morning but sheer discipline.

Other wolves might have chosen to give in to the bestial urge to become nocturnal. We were creatures of the dark, after all. But I didn't will it. And while I didn't will it, the packs did not do it.

Our wealth was reliant on trade with the humans, who mostly kept what they called *office hours.* So I had determined that we wolves would, as well.

Of course, almost everyone slept late. Except me. A habit from my youth, at the urging of my father, the previous King.

The wolf of power plans while his enemies sleep.

My rage crackled at thoughts of my father, so I dismissed them.

The only other wolf more disciplined than me was my servant and advisor, Ghere.

Small and slight, Ghere was the runt of his litter. He should have been nose to the dirt—never hold the ear of the King. But in order to make up for his fine frame and delicate constitution, God had given the fucker a mind larger and sharper than any I knew.

And he never failed to step into my room the exact moment that I arose.

I suspected he stood at the door, his ear pressed to the frame, waiting. How he heard me pad across the stone floor every morning, I would never know, but he never failed me.

This morning, though, he scuttled towards me even faster than usual as I crossed the chamber, heading for the bathroom.

"Good morning, Sire."

"Is it?"

"Perhaps not," he said quickly, licking his lips in a nervous habit he had that always made my nose wrinkle.

I stepped into the bathroom, leaving the door open for him so he could follow. I was desperate to piss. The man had shadowed me into far darker spaces than this.

"What is making your balls retreat this morning, Ghere?" I asked, sighing with relief as I began to relieve myself into the bowl.

The humans had so many things wrong, but indoor plumbing and electricity were not numbered among them.

"Sire, the Queen is dead."

I went very still, only for a breath, guarding against the rush of rage and frustration. It wouldn't do to lash out at Ghere. He was necessary.

I cursed under my breath. "Did she leave a note?"

"Yes."

Fuck.

When I had finished and turned from the toilet to see him holding a piece of paper, I snatched it out of his outstretched hand. Walking slowly back into the bedchamber, I opened and read it, scanning it quickly. But there was nothing new.

Pitifully weak.

Crying for attention.

Miserable. Depressed. Unable to cope, blah, blah, blah.

Just like the last one.

Fuck.

I crumpled the paper and tossed it at Ghere, who snagged it deftly out of the air, but the tension in his features didn't ease.

"Sire—"

"She was too weak. Just like the others."

"Yes, obviously. But—"

"Call the Reapers."

"Of course, but I just wonder—"

"This time tell them to hunt the poor areas. The trailer parks and slums."

"Sire?"

I reached the bed and shook the toys awake. Miraculously, the blonde curled at the end of the bed was still wearing the wisp of lace and silk I'd given her yesterday. When she sat up, frowning and blinking, one side of it fell away where I'd bitten through the strap last night.

There were marks on her shoulder, scrapes in the shape of my teeth leading from her collarbone to the top of her full breast.

I smiled and reached for her, taking the weight of that pale globe and teasing her nipple with my thumb until it stood proud.

Flushed and messy from sleep, she still bit her lip, smiling, and leaned back on her hands, pressing her chest up for me.

Good girl.

I put one knee on the bed and her eyes brightened, so I crawled forward to kneel on it, nodding when she reached for me with a question in her eyes, burying a hand in her hair when she leaned down to take me in her mouth.

I let my head drop back and growled my approval of her talented tongue.

"Sire," Ghere said, averting his eyes from my toy. "I think—"

"Tell them to hunt the poorer areas, Ghere. The women there have suffered already. They'll be stronger."

"But... your offspring must be of the noble bloodlines. Taking a human I understand, but—"

I hissed and tightened my grip in the toy's hair, guiding her as pleasure coursed through me, lighting my veins. My second plaything was waking and crawling over to join us. I cut eyes to her to keep her from interrupting. The blonde was doing her work well. I would meet this dumpster fire of a day with my skin thrumming.

"There will be no noble bloodline if they keep dying before they bear young," I said through clenched teeth. "Find women who have lived in the darkness before. My blood is noble enough for both of us."

Ghere hesitated.

He was threatening to stifle my pleasure, so I let the power rise with the blood coursing in my veins and snapped a thread of compulsion at him—just a bare taste. But his breath rushed out of him and he bowed so low his hair brushed the tops of his feet.

"Yes... yes... of course."

"Do it now."

He scurried from the room as quickly as he'd arrived and I turned my full attention to the women.

Or tried to.

Something itched at the base of my skull.

Frustration.

Anger.

And something... shakier. But I shook it off. We'd already been through this twice before.

Women killed themselves every day in the modern human world. One more sad story wouldn't cause so much as a ripple in the thin veil that guarded our world from theirs.

I wouldn't let myself be disturbed. I'd find her, the woman capable of this. I would force her to submit, bear an heir with her and no longer be tormented by the clock ticking over my head. The clock that counted down to my defeat.

"What's wrong, Cazz?" the dark-haired toy whispered, coming to kneel next to me and leaning in to kiss my chest while her friend continued sucking me.

I hadn't compelled either of them this morning. Yet the blonde was remarkably dedicated to her task.

But despite her talent, my thoughts were too disturbed to let me focus. We'd played late into the night, so I was sleep-deprived. And now I was... tense.

And I had things to do.

"Fucking human women," I muttered. "You're always more trouble than you're worth."

Thrusting into the blonde's mouth, ordering her not to gag—her body would obey me, even to the point of stopping her heart if I instructed it—I took a handful of the brunette's hair and tugged her head back to bear her throat.

"Do you know why I bother?" I whispered to her.

She shook her head as best she could with the grip I had on her. She gasped as I leaned over her, pulling her head back until the tendons on her neck stood proud.

Her breath hissed in and out of her teeth and her chest rose and fell quickly. Unable to lift her head from my grip, she followed my progress with her eyes as I opened my mouth over that vein, pulsing thick, hot blood just under the surface of her flawless skin.

I latched on, sucking hard, needing to leave a mark. But I wouldn't let her relax into the pleasure of my touch thinking there was no danger. I let my teeth graze her skin and she shuddered.

Then I kissed the skin, laving it with my tongue to soothe the pain where the beads of blood rose.

"Every time a human submits to me, my power grows," I murmured breathlessly, the combination of the blonde's attentions and this toy's fear ensuring that my body was prickling with promised pleasure. I was beginning to sweat.

"I s-submit!" the brunette gasped. "I do!"

I tipped my head, staring down at her and her eyes widened further.

"You do," I murmured, pretending to soothe her.

"I'll always submit," she breathed. "Always. I'm here for you, Cazz. You can trust me."

A jolt of pleasure from the blonde's ministrations rocked through me and my eyes closed. I tipped my forehead against the brunette's, my breath rushing between my teeth and over her face.

"And you human bitches also... confuse lust... with love..." I growled. "Every. Fucking. Time." I dropped her hair, but whipped the hand around to close it on her throat, squeezing hard enough that her eyes bulged. "I don't need a lover," I hissed. "I need a fucking bitch in heat."

She opened her mouth but no sound came out.

"I didn't compel you, so why did you ask me what was wrong?" I snarled.

She was trying to shake her head, but I had her neck clamped in my hand, just one hair away from cutting off her air.

"Every fucking one of you decides that you have given your heart, and then you break, and then you die. I am *sick* of your failure."

I closed my eyes as the blonde redoubled her efforts and my body responded. For a moment I couldn't speak. But then I opened my eyes and caught the terrified gaze of the brunette.

"Good thing you're delicious," I rasped.

The brunette gave a little sob and my orgasm detonated at the base of my spine.

2. All Hail the King

"Beware those who come to you in sheep's clothing but inwardly are ravenous wolves."
- Gospel of Matthew 7:15

~ *JESSE* ~

The guards tipped us out into the room like puppies out of a bag.

I landed heavily on rough stone, scraping my knees and palms, hissing against the pain. But they'd freed my hands and ankles before they shoved me in here, so, with my heart thudding in my chest, I scrabbled to pull down the blindfold that was over my eyes and get my bearings quickly.

Dark room. Stone walls and ceiling. Warm lights. Cold air. Damp. Shadows my eyes couldn't penetrate—and more shadows behind us I wished they couldn't.

Left and right, women shrieked and sobbed, hitting the floor, some rolling, one planting face-first into the rock and laying there, unmoving.

Behind me, a cluster of guards filled the doorway, with more spreading out along the wall. They didn't carry weapons, but they didn't need to. They were all well over six foot and huge with it. Strong and rugged… feral. Brows and jaws heavy, and bodies that moved in that fiercely controlled way the wolves had that was riveting and terrifying at the same time.

So, when a low voice muttered, "Really? This is the best you could do?" and the guards shrank like they wanted to disappear through the wall, I whipped my head back around to see who was capable of scaring these monsters.

Then I couldn't breathe.

The back of the room was swathed in deep shadows so that at first it was difficult to make anything out. But as I blinked and tried to breathe, slowly he became clear, walking towards us out of the dark like an apparition manifesting out of hell itself.

He stood easily as tall as the guards, his shoulders just as broad and draped in thick fur from an open vest that fell almost to his knees. His chest was bare revealing warm-brown skin, the wide, flat planes of his pecs, and rippling abs so defined they cast their own shadows.

He stood staring down his nose imperiously at everyone in the room, one side of his upper lip pulled up in smug derision, and yet, somehow the ugly expression only emphasized the razor edge of his jaw, the full lips, and the dark hair that fell in loose waves around his face and to dust his collar at the back.

But that wasn't what made my lungs deflate.

His eyes glowed.

Incredible, stunning eyes, a blue so deep and shining it should have felt like staring into the waters of a tropical ocean. And yet those eyes were coldly cruel. Arctic waters, deep and flickering with shadows. Yet, glowing like moonlight through a sheet of ice.

Like all humans, I'd heard myths about the Wolf King and his packs—mostly the kind that were whispered at sleepovers or around a campfire. But as I watched him materialize out of the darkness, it was suddenly clear that those were not stories at all.

This man was very, very real.

Something deep and primal screamed that a predator was stalking me. Pushing to my feet, ready to run, I was forced to watch him because there was no room to move, stumbling back a step as he advanced on us, the dull, warm light that bathed half the room from lanterns on the walls finally falling on him, cutting hollows into cheeks shadowed by stubble and revealing him more clearly.

In the shadows he looked almost tribal—all leather and fur, with three necklaces at his throat.

But in the light, the perfect cut of his pants became clear, the sheen of soft, durable leather, the thick lushness of the fur around his shoulders, and intelligent disdain in those eyes that scanned each of us with such impatience...

This was no animalistic warrior.

Beast he might be, but he was a King. He exuded a fiercely masculine presence. A weight, as if the air around him was thicker. And a tingling, fascinating glimmer of power, light on the horizon that flickered in the corner of your vision, but disappeared when you turned to see it.

I couldn't take my eyes off of him.

And my guts trembled.

The creak of leather and rustle of heavy weights moving behind us told me the guards were all bowing, or offering some kind of acknowledgement to him. But he ignored them, instead scanning each of the women—there were eight of us—his expression growing more and more contemptuous with each passing moment.

"What the fuck is this mess?"

"They're from the poor neighborhoods, as you requested," one man, presumably the leader of the guards, offered tentatively.

Male. I had to remind myself, they called themselves males, not men.

Then the guy's words sank in and I bristled.

Indeed, they were not men. Taking women like commodities, herding them like sheep.

When I'd been thrown into their arms I'd been certain I was about to die.

Or worse.

It had taken hours of pretending to be asleep or catatonic with fear, to catch enough snippets of conversations between the guards to understand that they were wolves. And that I was one of what they called a Reaping.

That none of them would touch us, as long as we obeyed.

Not because they were honorable thieves, or had any scruples. But because we had to be untouched. Because we'd been chosen for the King.

I'd hoped I had that part wrong.

Clearly I didn't.

A snarl ripped through the room and the King bared his teeth.

The women around me cried out, or sobbed, all of them curling in on themselves, turning back and forth, shrinking from the King, but unwilling to get closer to the guards behind us, either. They turned impotent circles, shaking and crying. One even wailed like a child.

SILENCE.

I jolted as the word echoed inside my skull just as clearly as his voice had echoed in the tall chamber around us a moment earlier, an eerie thrust of power with it.

And the room obeyed.

All of it. All of us. Every one.

The noises from the terrified women stopped as if someone had muted the television.

I'd already been quiet, but I felt the conviction settle in my chest. I would not speak. My jaw clenched of its own accord, and any words on my tongue faded like smoke on the wind.

Then he looked around, those incredible eyes glittering with frustration and something I couldn't identify, and it was as if the air shifted.

Four of the women were still on hands and knees, bodies convulsing with tears, shaking with terror. Two had made it to their feet like me, but remained hunched. Cowering.

And one still lay unconscious where she'd fallen when the guards dumped her in the room.

The King shook his head slowly, then sighed, as if he carried a great weight.

"There's no need to cry. You have nothing to fear," he crooned. And then he smiled and the world tilted.

Power wafted off of him like a rich perfume, rippling as he moved and I felt myself changed.

My body thrilled.

He was King. He was male. He was everything I had ever wanted. The earth answered his voice and the sky stormed at his bidding.

Awed and breathless, everything within me ached to throw myself at his feet.

I wrestled it with the corner of my mind that understood that something was happening, something outside my control. That the thoughts suddenly clamoring in my head, admiring his beauty and strength, hadn't started in my mind.

And yet... I wanted him. Wanted to slide hands up his torso, curl fingers into his hair. I ached to hear that deep voice hushed in my ear, to feel those hands on my body.

My mind overflowed with images that stole my breath.

Images of him in the dark, our bodies entwined. Images of him in the light, standing over me and staring murder at any that would harm me. Images of him smiling, laughing, sultry and sweet, then dark and demanding, eyes glowing and breath hot—

I blinked, more terrified than I'd been even when the guards took me because while they might have forced my body, this man—this male—could control my mind?

I felt the desire to kneel before him like a hand planted between my shoulder-blades, yet no one was close enough to touch me. I shook with it, watched the woman to my right who'd made it to her feet, drop to her knees, then bow herself, face almost to the floor, as she crawled towards him, eyes shining and jaw slack.

He watched her come, tipping his head, though his expression remained blank. And then she reached a trembling hand toward the toe of his boot, her breath heaving in her chest like she was seeing the face of God.

My knees almost gave, my body wanted to give in. I wanted to tear her away from him and put myself in her place—

Please, I begged God. *Please... I can't...*

The King's sneer returned and he glided back a step, out of the woman's reach.

And just like that, the spell was broken. Nothing in the room had changed, and yet everything was different.

The women around me all froze, blinking, as if coming out of sleep.

I shook my head, more scared than I had ever been in my life.

That power he held... that compulsion... the intensity of it. Dear god, if he'd held that thrall a few more seconds I would have fallen to it as well.

We'd all heard the stories of his unquestioned authority, of his influence over others. But what I had just seen wasn't persuasive. It wasn't even intimidation. That was *control.*

He *possessed* others?

A cold chill prickled, like death breathing down my neck.

I looked at the women around me and saw it in their eyes... even as their minds cleared, even as they shuddered and breathed again... they'd stopped crying, stopped struggling. Even as their fear returned, something in them was drawn to him. Their eyes flicked to his face again and again, and they worried at their clothing as if they were suddenly self-conscious. A piece of that had stayed with them. A piece of them now belonged to him.

They had given in.

I began to tremble uncontrollably, my head screaming, my heart pounding so loudly it was all I could hear, drums beating in my ears.

I would not be a puppet to any man—any male—ever.

I could not lose myself to this!

When his eyes fell on me and he smiled so I could see the predator in him. I flinched.

Then he shifted his gaze to the others and I slumped.

"Now that we're all a little calmer… Welcome to the Sifting," he said, his voice low and gravelly as he scanned each of us in turn. One of the women sighed. "Before this day is done, one of you will be my mate."

He sounded like the idea made him want to vomit.

3. A B*tch in Heat

~ CASIMIR ~

I was horrified.

When I'd told Ghere to order the Reapers to find women from the human slums I had imagined the wicked types, like my toys. The women who embraced their fate and it made them bold. Instead I'd been sent a box of poorly bred puppies suitable only for drowning?

What the actual fuck?

"God help us," one of them murmured.

I snorted.

"I assure you, God abandoned this place long ago," I drawled.

The woman looked at me, shocked. It was the one at the center who'd stayed on her feet. She'd been staring around the chamber in horror, murmuring to herself, clearly forgetting that we wolves enjoyed heightened senses.

She remembered now.

The guards laughed, but the women's eyes snapped down to her feet. She dropped her chin. Her hair, a rich mahogany brown, the kind that would spark red in sunlight, fell around her face in long waves, though it was messy and matted now.

She was a thin little thing, though there was evidence of muscle under those terribly fitting clothes.

Then—noting the tear at the neckline of her shirt—I started paying attention. Which made me scan the others and grind my teeth. The Reapers clearly hadn't been gentle.

I cursed again. None of the women were even clean. I saw torn shirts, ripped jeans, even bruises. And one of them had hit the floor and remained there, as if she were already dead.

"Who is responsible for this shitshow?" I growled to Ghere below the hearing of the humans.

The male stepped up to my side, responding in kind so they wouldn't hear us. "Khush led this foray," he muttered.

"Order ten lashes. I asked for women who'd met darkness, not poorly freighted dolls."

"Consider the restrictions, Casimir: those who are virgins at this age are likely more timid in their approach to life."

"Timid? These women are helpless." Some of them, including the one who'd stared at me, looked malnourished. I was tempted to simply send them back and tell the Reapers to try again—with more stringent instructions on who and how to select targets. "Are they even fertile?"

"Impossible to know for certain with virgins, of course. But we know they all cycle regularly," Ghere provided.

I shook my head. "Look at the bruises on that one."

"I believe some of them fought—"

"I don't give a shit, Ghere. You want me to believe the guards couldn't control these frail birds without tearing their clothes?"

The male hesitated, obviously wanting to correct me, but unwilling to risk my ire.

I rolled my eyes and gestured at him to speak—I wouldn't punish him for raising truth, if he had it. But how the fuck was I supposed to name a mate from among these pitiful creatures without walking straight into yet another failure?

But Ghere must have read my wave to proceed as the signal to begin the rite, because he stepped forward and cleared his throat.

"Ladies, I know the day has been difficult, but I assure you, you are safe here. The King Himself, Casimir Augustus Klane, is here to greet and assess you. Despite our, er, unconventional beginning, I hope you understand that it is a great honor to stand here today. The King of Wolves seeks a mate. A human mate. You alone have been selected from among your kind for his consideration."

I was considering very little. If this was the best the human race had to offer, we were all in much deeper trouble than I had imagined.

"A mate?" the same woman asked quietly. "I thought… the stories said he was already mated?"

Ghere opened his mouth to reply, but I spoke first. No point avoiding the truth. "She died," I said baldly.

"May… may I ask how?" Her eyes were wary, but accusing. She was brave, this one. The others were all staring at the floor, though two of them seemed to still be at least partially in the thrall of the compulsion, because their eyes were glazed, and one was loosening a button at her throat.

I raised a brow, partly-amused, partly-impressed. "She suffered a mental breakdown and killed herself," I said with a warning smile. The woman blinked. "Being the Wolf King's mate comes with many privileges. But few humans are strong enough to live in my world. Hence, the Sifting."

Ghere leaped in then, as if he was afraid I'd give away too much. "Of course, we will provide everything you need to advance in this process. The King only wishes to identify which of you is most likely to thrive."

Thrive? These women didn't know the word existed. I stopped listening as Ghere continued to explain the process of the rite, the tests and challenges, and their role in them.

I was fast determining that this entire idea had been a poor one. These women didn't even have the *physical* strength to live here, let alone to keep up with me. Chances that they'd be capable of enduring the inevitable trials to come were miniscule.

The women's eyes grew wider as Ghere explained the wealth and opportunity that would be afforded to them, as well as the expectation of delivering an heir, and a second child to ensure the succession of the throne.

The two who hadn't shaken the compulsion began to shiver and stare at me with hopeful eyes.

I'd barely touched them with the power, but their minds were so weak, they were already more than half mine. It was pathetic.

"...our main concern is for your wellbeing," Ghere went on kindly. "The King's power relies on his utter domination of the packs. But especially those highest in the ranks of the hierarchy... which includes his mate. I am aware that your human society does not function similarly—but please, understand... the power you felt from Casimir when you entered was only a taste. He is the most potent ruler the wolves have enjoyed for centuries. You will not need to worry for your safety or provision. Our King is... formidable."

One of the women who'd given over to the compulsion shuddered and clutched a hand to her chest.

Holy fuck. Weak didn't cover it.

"Actually, Ghere, I think this has been a mistake," I said abruptly, interrupting him. "I don't believe my mate is here."

I began to turn away, muttering to him under their hearing. "These minds are far too weak. It's a waste of my time. We need a new pool."

"But, look, Casimir!" Ghere grabbed my sleeve, pulling me back to face them. "They're receptive, see? You've always said that a willing partner is worth more than someone who must be... urged."

It was true. I had. But only when their commitment rose from strength in themselves. Not wounded puppies who rolled over and showed their bellies to the Alpha with tails wagging.

I could see that the two women who'd never fully released from my power were beyond willing. They were already halfway in love. Which was our entire problem with these humans. This would not do.

"The position of Queen requires three things," I snapped impatiently. Let them hear the terms and reject them, then we could move on and find a new group of women. "Firstly, the ability to bear heirs. Secondly, submission to me as King and Mate. And third, acceptance that I will not offer love. Love is a sacrifice of self. My power relies on dominance. It weakens when I yield to another. I cannot offer it and remain King."

I was growing impassioned, so I stopped for a moment and took a breath, dropping my voice for the women who were all listening avidly. I met their eyes one by one until I landed on the warm-haired beauty who'd spoken up.

"My Queen will receive anything material she wishes. But she will submit to me, and I *will not bow*. She will share my bed, my power, and my wealth. She will not share my heart."

I'd been glaring down at them, impatient and determined. I lifted my chin and waited, but none of them spoke.

Good.

Too weak—or perhaps, strong enough only to see that they had frail hearts in desperate needs of the affirmation of a male's—

"What happens to the others?" the mahogany-haired one asked quickly. "You have eight women here. What happens to the other seven when you... when you choose?"

I smiled. "I assure you, mate or not, by the time the sifting is complete, all of you will *desire* to stay here with me. And if I find you appealing, I will not turn you away." Though, looking at this lot, most of them would be thrown back to their own world. I wasn't interested.

Ghere nudged me, but the two who'd already given themselves both looked ecstatic.

The one whose hair was so rich and warm frowned at the floor, her eyes flitting back and forth as if she searched her mind, her lips moving though she made no sound.

She was a strange little thing—courageous to speak to me without permission. She might be fun to break if she turned out to be strong-willed.

Ghere was dry-washing his hands, looking at each of the women in turn, clearly nervous about the direction this had taken. I wasn't sure why.

He cleared his throat. "As you've heard the King explain—"

"Are you violent?"

I turned back to the woman with a flat smile. "Show me a wolf who isn't. And I am the King of the others. What do you think?"

Her throat bobbed. The tear in the neckline of her cotton shirt offered a fleeting glimpse of plump cleavage. My cock twitched.

"I meant… I meant with women… um, Sire," she said uncertainly. "With your Queen. You said you have to dominate, that she has to submit. What is she submitting to?"

An image flashed in my head of that day just weeks ago when my second mate had killed herself. I'd had my toys, one of them by the neck.

I smirked. "I don't make a habit of leaving bruises," I said, letting a dark promise seep into my tone. "But they've been known to happen."

The woman flinched and I sighed, rolling my eyes. "I take no sexual pleasure from violence. I am a wolf, not a beast. A loyal, submitted female has no reason to fear me."

It was, perhaps, a *stretching* of the truth. But the woman looked relieved.

I was intrigued. Of them all, she'd shown the strongest spine when I compelled them. Not that that was any guarantee. The last two had been the strongest in their bunches as well, and look where that had gotten me.

Dark frustration washed through me again as I looked over this group of thin, dirty women and I shook my head. "Ghere, this is pointless—"

"I'll volunteer," the mahogany-haired one said quietly.

"You see," Ghere nudged my side nervously. "One offers to be sifted already. I'm sure the others will as well. There is no need to—"

"No," she said, then licked her lips and stepped forward. "I volunteer to be your mate."

4. Fascinating

~ JESSE ~

As I'd listened to the King's pompous tirade, it had become clearer and clearer to me that it was not just bad luck that I was here.

The question was, would I step out of the flames of one man's making, and straight into another? Or was this truly an opportunity for escape?

"I will be your mate... if you'll have me."

The King's eyes narrowed.

His servant's brows rose and he raised his hands. "Oh, I don't think you understood—"

"Why?" the King asked, his voice deep and skeptical. But I didn't miss the glimmer in his eyes. I'd surprised him.

I swallowed hard and prayed I'd understood all of this correctly. "I think... I know, I can give you what you want. And in exchange, you can give me what I need."

The King's brows rose then. "How very presumptuous of you. But I will take the bait: What is it that you want?"

"I propose... an exchange."

"Of what?"

"You take me as your mate and you keep me safe like you promised. Away from my world and... and anyone I knew. When I bear you an heir, you give me a house somewhere remote. Somewhere no one can find me. A couple of servants to run it and enough money to live modestly. You can have your family, and I can have solitude. And... and safety."

His eyes narrowed again. "Why would you offer yourself to this? To me, when I have not compelled you to do so?"

I hesitated, but couldn't find any reason to hide the truth. "Because you're the first man I've met with the power to free me from all the others."

The King stared at me as if I'd confused him. He tilted his head, his eyes pinning me to the floor. I was terrified he was about to unleash that power on me and steal me from myself.

I couldn't let it happen.

"I have terms, though," I blurted.

The King looked indignant—also a little amused. "You think you're in a position to set *terms?*"

I hurried on, praying he'd listen. "No violence. At all," I said, swallowing the pinch that was rising in my throat. "If I'm going to get pregnant, I can't be hurt. And... until I'm pregnant, you only have sex with me. No one else. You give me every chance to... to bear you the heir." The King snorted and fear jittered through me. "If you do, I'll submit. Truly. You won't have to use that... that power. I will do anything you say. I'll give myself to you. Willingly. Like... like a slave."

The room was silent except for our voices so at that word I could hear him suck in a breath. Flames flickered in his eyes—fire beneath the ice.

"Slave?" he rumbled.

I nodded, hands clenched at my sides, praying. Because it was better to humble myself than to be forced to it. I couldn't let him steal my mind. I had to keep myself. I knew if he used that awful power on me, I would lose myself completely with time.

"You said... you said your power was about dominance?"

"Yes."

"Well, surely, if someone gives themselves willingly... That must offer you more power? More than if you have to... make them?"

His face went open with shock, his brows rising as if they'd climb into his hair.

"You promise me a home after you have your heir, and that you'll never hurt me, or use that... that power on me. And I will give you everything you've asked. If I don't, well... it sounds like I'd be dead anyway."

He was still gaping, but as if he'd caught himself doing it, his eyes suddenly hooded and his mouth snapped shut. "That you would," he muttered.

I nodded. "So... what do you have to lose?"

~ *CASIMIR* ~

It was a fascinating proposal.

The moment she'd said she'd give herself to me willingly, my cock had twitched. Then, when she named herself a slave... my power *surged*. Even now, it raged in my veins as if it could reach through my skin to take her.

It was impossible, and yet, it couldn't be denied. Her choice to submit sent power coursing through me.

What would it do when she actually gave over?

Without compulsion?

I'd never thought... never even considered...

Fascinating.

I had to work not to swallow like a boy at his first mating. "And if you defy me?" I asked, indulging myself, because all I wanted was to know what she'd say—and see how it affected my power.

She raised her chin. Her expression was sad. "I won't defy you. I'm sacrificing myself to you. But in the end... in the end it's your choice. If I ever say no… well, it's not like I could fight you. Or your power. I'd be trusting you to… to keep your word."

"You can't actually be considering this?" Ghere hissed at me below the humans hearing, through unmoving lips. "What about the rite?"

"The rite hasn't worked for us so far," I snarled back.

Her eyes hadn't left me.

She was too small, too thin, too wiry—though I suspected all of that would change if she was properly fed. And yet…

When our eyes locked, a jolt of desire and a correlating wave of power washed through me.

A slave. She would *make herself* my slave? Willingly?

"Do we have an agreement?" she asked, her voice shaking as if she were losing her courage.

"We certainly do."

Every wolf in the room gasped, but I couldn't have cared less what they thought.

I didn't take my eyes from hers—hazel eyes, I realized. Brown at the center, bleeding to a soft, gray-green at the outside of the iris. I inhaled, picking out her scent from the crowd, drinking it down.

She would be my mate.

She would be my Queen.

She would *choose to* be my slave.

I physically shuddered. God, I was going to come.

Without breaking eye contact with her, I snapped my fingers. "Take the others away and bring the Cleric," I muttered.

Ghere bowed stiffly, then gestured to the guards, who immediately gathered up the other women—shrieking, crying, some pleading for me.

But I barely heard them.

As the room filled with the noise of moving bodies, of guards muttered orders, and women's cries, my new mate's eyes widened.

"Cleric?" she asked hesitantly. As if she were afraid of the answer.

I frowned. "Did you think we would conceive the royal heir out of wedlock?"

Want more? Find the complete *Slave to the Wolf King* series in paperback or on Kindle/Kindle Unlimited:

Grab it in Paperback

Or binge the whole series on Kindle!

Or turn the page to try my dark contemporary stalker romance, *Hunt for You!*

Sneak Peek: *Hunt for You*
1. Show Me in the Dark

~ BRIDGET ~

SYSTEM NOTE: CHAT ENCRYPTED END-TO-END. ENSURE ALL ACCOUNTS ARE LOGGED OFF BEFORE DISCONNECTING.

SleepingBeast: Why would you even consider this?

DeadGirlWalking: Long story short: Everyone in my family dies young. Cancer and heart attacks mostly. Somehow, I hit the genetic lottery, and got the genome markers for both.

DeadGirlWalking: I am almost thirty years old. My body is a literal ticking time-bomb. And my life is hell.

DeadGirlWalking: Let me rephrase that. My *non*-life is hell: No drinking. No drugs. No fatty foods. No elevated heart-rate (so, no sex, or any other form of extra-curricular fun. I can't even watch a scary movie). Apparently, if I do absolutely nothing, I will probably get to do it for a pretty long time. Except, maybe not. Maybe I'm sitting calmly in the café reading a very unexciting book when I twitch once and fall face-first into my frappucino.

DeadGirlWalking: I am *done* living in fear of what is inevitable. I need to feel alive again.

SleepingBeast: You think me murdering you is going to make you feel alive?

DeadGirlWalking: No, I think knowing that my day is coming soon will make life a lot more interesting until it does. And then when it finally does, I won't have to think about it anymore at all.

SleepingBeast: That's dark.

DeadGirlWalking: You're homicide-for-hire and you're calling *me* dark?

SleepingBeast: Touche.

SleepingBeast: Though, for the record, I'm not for hire. You won't pay me a cent. And I'm not homicidal. I classify my services as *assisted suicide adjacent.*

DeadGirlWalking: Did you hear that? It was my snort of skeptical derision. You get off on killing people. Pretty sure that makes you homicidal. Or is there another name for it if it's a kink?

DeadGirlWalking: Found it. Apparently you're a Erotophonophiliac (Erotophonophilian?) God, what a mouthful.

DeadGirlWalking: THAT'S WHAT SHE SAID.

SleepingBeast: Nope. I get off on the hunt.

DeadGirlWalking: Well then, let's be clear: I'm no sub. I just want to run for my life, and lose.

SleepingBeast: We're clear. I am a Dom. But I'm happy to provide additional services until it's my turn to die.

DeadGirlWalking: Such a giver. So, will you also be finding some dude on the dark web to knock you off when that time comes?

SleepingBeast: I expect to take my last breath gasping, laying in a pool of my own blood because the FBI finally caught up with me.

DeadGirlWalking: Suicide by cop?

SleepingBeast: More like government sanctioned murder.

DeadGirlWalking: Geez, and you call me dark.

SleepingBeast: No… I call you *prey.*

DeadGirlWalking: Holy shit. I just got goosebumps. So I guess that means we're doing this?

DeadGirlWalking: Beast?

SleepingBeast: Go back to your non-life, D. Sweet dreams.

DeadGirlWalking: Wait, are you coming for me or not? Because if you aren't, I need to find another whacko.

SleepingBeast: Goodnight D.

DeadGirlWalking: Just answer the question. Are you, or are you not, going to hunt me down to primal-fuck me, then kill me?

DeadGirlWalking: TELL ME.

DeadGirlWalking: Beast?

DeadGirlWalking: For fuck's sake.

DeadGirlWalking: This better be part of the game, otherwise I'm reporting you to the Manager. Call me a dark-web Karen.

DeadGirlWalking: Seriously, I need confirmation here. You said this could take weeks—months? I can't go through another Christmas alone because you got bashful. If you aren't coming I need to find someone else.

DeadGirlWalking: I'm doing this with you or without you. You get that, right?

DeadGirlWalking: Would you just answer the fucking question?

DeadGirlWalking: This brings a whole new meaning to "the strong, silent type."

DeadGirlWalking: Fucker. Or should it be *non*-fucker?

DeadGirlWalking: Just tell me.

DeadGirlWalking: Is this one of those moments when a guy thinks what he's doing is foreplay, but it's not? Because it's not, just in case you were wondering. I'm being fucked right now. And not in the fun way.

DeadGirlWalking: Beast?

DeadGirlWalking: Fine. I guess I'll just wait and see. But I'm keeping my options open. If another dude shoots his shot (literally) and beats you to it, that's going to be your fault for not making your intentions clear.

DeadGirlWalking: Should have put a ring on it. Just sayin'.

SleepingBeast: Stop whining. We'll meet.

DeadGirlWalking: Thank God. How soon?

DeadGirlWalking: Growl once for "this week" and twice for "this calendar month."

SleepingBeast: Goodnight, D.

SleepingBeast: Sleep while you can.

DeadGirlWalking: Wait! Don't you need my address or number or something?

[SleepingBeast has left the chat.]

I pushed away from my desk, heart racing so fast I wondered if I was going to pass out. My vision was tunneling.

Holy shit, this was really happening.

Finally.

It was strange blinking back to my real life and my real body. Every time I was online I kind of got lost in the virtual world.

My psychiatrist called it *escapism.*

I called it relief from *existential crisis and the utter fucking tedium of this world.*

Tedium? Not for much longer. Not if Beast was really who I thought he was.

Unable to resist, I clicked through to the screenshots I'd kept of his response to my post in the definitely *not* government sanctioned forum called Weirdos Whackos and Freaks Playground.

I'd been ranting that night, drunk and despairing. The responses had mostly fallen into two categories: Those who were frantic to help me feel better, and those who hoped I would kill myself and were willing to incentivize me.

Not him, though.

He had been a man of few words, right from the start.

I know how to make you feel alive. Then a link.

That was it. I'd assumed he was some pervert hoping to find a desperate woman who'd fall into bed with anything that pretended to care. Or maybe he just wanted to find a woman period and it didn't matter what she thought about it.

I was open to either scenario.

His profile picture was a muscular guy, standing with his feet shoulder width apart and his hands at his sides, kinda clawed, like he was ready to fight, silhouetted by glowing flames.

I would have bet real money he was ex-military. Or he'd dedicated himself to some kind of organized training.

He was clearly aggressive. Strong. Probably abusive.

Hyper-intelligent. Extremely self-reliant. Definitely a loner. But decent social skills. All the better to lure in vulnerable women.

The only reason I'd clicked the link was because I didn't give two shits if he hacked me. I wanted to see if there were any clues to whether I was right.

I'd expected to find his amateur pornography—why did men always believe that all it took was a visual of them strangling their own purple-headed wonder worms to make a woman shiver?

I'd figured there was an outside chance he ran a sex club, or some other IRL experience he was selling to the kind of people who looked for things on the fringes. As in, me.

But the link only led to a profile page. That was my first surprise.

Cain.
Experienced primal dom.
Seeking real life prey.

I'd been immediately intrigued. And then I talked to him and got consumed. And then obsessed.

And then… eventually we got here.

Sighing as the adrenaline in my veins slowly faded, I closed all the windows on the screen and began to shut the computer down, but my hands were shaking so badly from the rush that I kept accidentally using the wrong key commands. I had to make myself slow down and focus. But when the laptop finally whirred to silence and I was left sitting in the silent blackness, I still didn't move away from the desk.

I could see the light-glare of the words from my screen across my retinas in the dark.

Seeking real life prey.

And he wasn't bluffing. I'd done my homework.

I had to take a deep breath to calm the new wave of flutters in my stomach. It took a moment to put a name to what I was feeling because it had been so long…

I was *giddy*.

Cain, AKA: SleepingBeast, a primal Dom, probable serial killer, and bona-fide *whacko* had taken my case. I was now officially *prey*. The game of cat and mouse was about to begin. I wouldn't know when, or how. But at some point soon, our paths would cross. He would make certain they did. And if he liked what he saw when he found me, that moment would spark a hunt that might last weeks, or even months.

He'd warned me that he would toy with me. That thought brought a whole new rush of adrenaline, and a hum between my thighs. I was counting on it.

I gave a weird, cackling laugh that sounded way too loud in my dark little closet of an office.

Cain was coming for me.

Life just got very, very interesting.

Thank God.

2. The Scent of You

~ BRIDGET ~

The next morning I woke up to the usual hollow emptiness in my chest—until I remembered what had happened the night before and adrenaline began to thread through my system, making me shiver.

I knew it was unlikely, but I couldn't resist logging on to the dark web forum *just in case* he'd messaged again, or was giving me some clue of when or how he might show up.

But of course, there was nothing.

Then I decided to check my email because I hadn't done that for a couple days, and it was time for my monthly payment.

I immediately regretted it.

FROM: Asshole (Jeremy Haines)
TO: Bridget
SUBJECT: You agreed to the rules

Ugh. I hovered the mouse over the email for a moment, considering opening it. But the truth was, I knew what it was about, and I didn't want to think about that yet.

Muttering a curse under my breath, I marked the email as "read" knowing he'd get a notification of that. It would hold him off for a time.

Jeremy was an asshole, but a fairly patient one. He believed in letting people think about stuff. If he thought I'd read it, he'd give me a couple days before he'd decide he needed to up the stakes. And by then I might feel differently.

Or I might be dead.

I giggled as my skin goosebumped and sparkled and my heart raced. But then I put Jeremy out of my mind, closed out my email, made sure my computer was logged out of everything before disconnecting the VPN and turning it all off.

Looking at that blank screen made my skin itch, so I slapped the lid of the laptop down and pushed out of the chair.

I'd go to the gym. Then at least I'd feel shaky from tiredness instead of anxiety.

I also smiled at the idea that Cain might already be coming after me. And when he found me at the gym he'd be pissed. *I thought you weren't supposed to raise your heartrate?*

Shouldn't and *wouldn't* were two different things.

Some things were worth the risk. Namely, my sanity.

I liked living on the edge.

So I dressed quickly, shoved my black hair up into a ponytail that, because it was cut in a blunt bob, was really just a sticky-uppy top-tie that made me look about six years old, but kept most of my hair off my neck, then jumped in the car, watching the rearview eagerly for any sign of a car following me as I drove the fifteen mile route to the only decent gym in the area.

A heavenly scent assaulted me the minute I walked into the actual gym, but there were already dozens of people there, and lots more than half of them were men. I considered taking a quick circuit of the room and seeing who'd picked the gorgeous cologne, maybe asking him what it was. But he'd think I was hitting on him, so I walked over to the weights praying that whoever he was, he'd walk past at some point and maybe he wouldn't be a dickhead. He smelled good enough to lick.

In today's world there wasn't enough licking outside of preschool in anyone's life, in my opinion.

Then I was at my first machine, and I had to pretend I was totally casual about messing with the hardware on my body. At least I could just slip my arms inside the big hoodie I wore and do it out of sight. Let them think I was messing with my bra straps or whatever.

As a concession to the doctors, and because they really wouldn't let me do *anything* if I didn't have some kind of observation, I wore a heart monitor while I worked out, or any time I thought I'd be walking more than a mile. Because my resting heartrate was sixty-five, I wasn't allowed to let my working heart rate exceed one hundred or the fucking monitor would start screaming louder than a church lady at an R-rated movie, and everyone at the gym would look at me.

It was a royal pain in my ass, because it meant that between sets on the weights I had to sit there like an idiot while it lowered—which inevitably invited *comments* from the gym monkeys who thought I was a princess who didn't want to break a sweat.

"You need a towel over there, sweetheart? I'd be happy to come wipe you down."

Fuck around and find out, douchebag.

"I'm good." I didn't even make eye-contact. There was no point. I might actually topple him off his too-high center of gravity with the force of my disdain.

When I'd done all my sets, I went to the bank of cardio machines and *almost* jumped on the stair-stepper. But that really would get my heart rate up too fast. And besides, those machines had their back to the room and the pitbull was still glancing my way once in a while. I didn't want him leering at my ass.

So I stepped up to my usual treadmill. But just as I was turning the machine on, I took a quick glance out the big window to the street three levels below in case there was any sign of a dark, probably homicidal maniac following me.

My heart rate jumped high enough for the monitor to give a faint beep when I saw a guy leaning in a doorway across the road, smoking a vape. He had hair as black as mine, shaved on the sides and long enough to fall into his eyes on top. He was pierced through every visible orifice and protrusion, and he was *strong*. Athletic and muscular without the ridiculous bulk of the body builders in here. *That* was a body that had been honed for moving and dominating, not just to impress the eye.

He was frowning at the doors into the gym and for a moment I stopped breathing and my heart rate jumped up another notch. But then another guy trotted up to him and they kissed briefly, then disappeared into the apartment building.

Oh well, maybe not.

My heart monitor gave one more warning beep before I snapped out of the thrill-trance, took two or three deep, controlled breaths, then turned on the machine and started a slow jog that I could sustain for an hour at a heart rate of ninety-five. I wouldn't though. Just five miles today. I needed to preserve *some* energy, just in case Cain really did show up.

My heart monitor peeped at me again, but I was smiling that time.

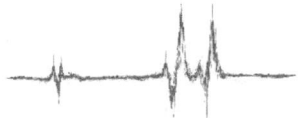

~ *CAIN* ~

She was more aware of her surroundings than I would have anticipated, but pretty soon it became clear why.

Every time she turned her back in this room, the fuckers that were supposed to be here working out, but had really come here to see and be seen, were following her with their eyes, murmuring to each other—slapping chests and snorting as they said things that I would cut their tongues out for actually speaking if I got the chance.

And yet, a part of me understood the allure. One particular part of my anatomy, understood a great deal. And that was *not* good.

I had learned years ago that any kind of emotional, or sexual attachment beyond the hunt itself not only complicated the game, but threatened *my* safety. It influenced my objectivity.

For that reason, I'd almost left the moment she walked in, turned my back and never contacted her again. Because the first time I clapped eyes on her it was like the air in the room shifted.

I'd positioned myself strategically behind a few weight machines so I could see her, but wouldn't be easily seen myself. I knew roughly what she looked like, but it still punched me in the solar plexus when she actually showed up.

I almost laughed at her raven-black hair sticking straight up on top of her head, like a five-year-old's. Especially since she'd hidden the rest of her trim body in a thick, black hoodie that would have been big enough for me—was it her boyfriend's? Did he know what she was doing? Who she was talking to at night while he slept?

Or maybe he was behind this?

The hair on the back of my neck stood up. Maybe it was something they did together? It wouldn't be the first couple I'd met that were into dark shit together. And she wouldn't be the first woman who pretended to be single and was actually looking for someone to help her make it a reality.

But as she strode into the gym with a little bag over her shoulder, swimming in that massive hoodie, her skin-tight shorts hugging only the top half of her tight thighs, my entire body went still and my heart began to thud against my ribs.

Despite the fact that she'd done everything she could to hide it—she was *stunning.* When she turned her head to look through the glass doors behind her, her eyes were so big and penetratingly bright, for a second I stopped breathing.

The handful of photos I'd seen online didn't do her justice *at all.* They were all from college, before she was really a woman.

Her hair was shorter and a lot more severe now. And her skin, while unblemished except for what appeared to be a scar on her forehead, looked *too* pale. Like she didn't get enough sun. Which was probably true, considering what she'd told me about her health issues. Yet, not only was she a member here at the gym, I'd found an old archive clipping from her childhood hometown in which the local newspaper showed her and a dozen other high school students who'd received belt promotions at their local Karate dojo over a decade ago.

She definitely moved like someone who knew her own body. But then, a lot of women did—especially when they knew men were going to be looking at them. It didn't necessarily mean she'd kept up with her training.

I was both fascinated, and frustrated.

Records of her had been easy to find after she was ten years old, which was about the age most people started leaving a trail online. But while I could dig up school records and sports teams and even what appeared to be a college degree earned online, it was like she had only existed in the most shallow ways.

No social media at all, not even old ones. Not even an old *Facebook* account that uneducated parents might have suggested and then monitored while she was in high school. Which was shocking in this day and age.

And no work history, which made zero sense.

It was like she'd dropped onto the planet at the age of ten, then disappeared again as soon as she got her degree, six or seven years ago. No birth certificate that I could find, definitely no marriages. She had to have a legal name and identity I was, as yet, unaware of.

That was okay. I liked a challenge. A lot.

And, of course, I was still working on the darker side of her online life. I knew there'd be a real harvest there. It was a helluva lot harder to pin down, though. I'd been stalking her profile in the dark web forum we shared since the day we *met*, but it didn't save history. Public chats only stayed visible for twenty-four hours, then were wiped. So except for our direct messages, and the homework I'd done following her in real time both online and in person, she was an enigma.

Fucking fascinating.

And that was a problem.

I felt the clench of arousal low in my belly when she sat down on the bench to do some curls and opened her knees, and my brain immediately conjured *everything* under those shorts.

Or tried to, at least. There were too many questions still unanswered.

My heart was beating faster, which it always did when I was stalking prey. But she shouldn't have affected me so deeply yet, because I hadn't actually decided whether to take her or not.

This was what I affectionately called the *interview* stage: Seeing whether she was realistic about what she wanted—and just how much she was lying to me. Because everyone lied some. The question was whether they did it to protect themselves from *everyone*, or just to misdirect me.

Was she a desperate woman looking for that heady rush that only danger could bring?

Or was she a manipulative bitch getting her kicks out of toying with a man online?

I didn't know yet. That wouldn't have been a problem— I was a patient man. But the way my soul sucked towards her the moment she showed up, and the resistance I now felt in my skin the second I started thinking about leaving, definitely was.

She was my *type*.

I couldn't decide if that would make this whole fucking game easier, or harder. And *that* was a problem. Because she wanted me to kill her.

I needed my head clear. I needed to be decisive. I needed to be in control of every step of this journey.

I didn't need to keep wondering what she looked like under that hoodie.

Nope.

Nope, nope, *nope*.

Shaking my head and taking hold of my balls—metaphorically—I let the weights I'd been using clank back to earth and pushed off the machine.

It was time to go. She wasn't right. Or rather, she was *too* right. I wasn't going to be able to disconnect from this one and that made the whole endeavor way too dangerous for *me*.

I'd already packed my stuff up and slung my backpack over my shoulder and was wiping my forehead with the little towel, looking for the route through the machines that would take me to the door without crossing her path, or being obvious about avoiding her, intending to go home, block her profile, and never speak with her again—even if that thought did give me a little pang. But as I was weaving between machines and drinking from my waterbottle, keeping my eyes off of her and my head slightly turned away, one of the gym bums who was here to build useless muscle for the sake of it, made a sly comment to her and her head jerked up.

It was reflex, when someone moved that quickly, to check and see where the danger came from.

"I'm good," was all she said. She didn't even look the guy in the eye. But that meant that her face was turned a little towards me and even though she didn't look at me either, I could see her clearly.

See the empty, hollow darkness behind those startling eyes.

I sucked in a breath and my step faltered. And right then I knew I was fucked. Because that was the moment I started planning how to intercept her in broad daylight without her seeing my face.

It was my favorite tease. And the way I introduced myself to prey whenever possible.

And I shouldn't have been planning that for her.

But damn... I *wanted* to see light behind those eyes. Even if it was only the spark of survival fear.

So I kept moving, and I left without looking back. But I didn't leave the property—just that room.

I had a plan in place for her before she finished her workout and trotted out to her car, looking over her shoulder and in every direction.

Looking for *me*.

I smiled.

Good girl.

3. See You Soon

~ BRIDGET ~

I dropped into the driver's seat in my car considering whether or not to stop for coffee on the way home when that heavenly smell washed over me and my entire body thrilled.

I gasped, tensing, beginning to turn just as a thick, man-hand whipped out from behind my seat and clapped over my mouth and pulled my head back against the headrest. I struggled for a second, kicking against the floor of the car, fingers clawing into that hand as I screamed behind it, but then that scent got stronger and warm, and a smooth cheek brushed my jaw at the same time a very deep, gravely male voice whispered.

"I told you I'd see you soon."

I froze, eyes wide, my breath tearing audibly in and out of my nose.

"Just breathe," he said, and I could *hear* the smile in his tone. But my pulse was so loud in my ears it made it hard to hear him.

I tried to take in every detail I could—the scent, the size of his hand over my mouth, the callouses on his palms, the unique timbre of his voice. My senses were heightened, but focus was impossible, my heart racing so fast I was glad I'd already taken the monitor off because the doctors would have *flipped.* Lights sparkled at the edge of my vision.

"Relax, Bridget. I'm not going to hurt you—I just wanted to introduce myself."

He knew my real name already?

I stopped trying to claw his hand off my face and after a few heaving breaths through my nose, made myself drop my hands to my lap, gripping the hem of the hoodie instead, but my heart was still going a mile a minute, and my panting was loud in the car.

I felt something brush the side of my head and realized he'd buried his nose in my hair and was inhaling deeply. I didn't know whether to blush or fistpump.

"Are you calm enough to remember what I'm about to tell you?" he rasped a minute later.

I nodded. My breath was still coming in deep pants and my hands had started to shake, but I was gripping the hoodie and praying he wouldn't notice that.

"Very good." He was still whispering, still keeping his voice in a gravel barely above the volume of my pulse so that his actual voice was masked. "We're going to have a few rules. Blink once to tell me you understand what I'm saying."

I blinked hard, squeezing my eyes shut for a second then opening them again to stare through the windshield at the blank, cinderblock wall of the gym, feeling both idiotic and *ecstatic* that I'd parked back here. But as he continued to speak, I couldn't help smiling behind his hand. The initial panic was quickly being replaced by a *rush* that was going to leave me shaking for hours, I was sure.

"First rule: No one knows the game we're playing. *No one.* Do you understand? The moment I learn that you've spoken to *anyone* about me—and I will find out, trust me— I'll disappear and you'll never hear from me again. Blink once if you understand."

I squeezed my eyes shut and opened them again, bolt upright in the chair, my feet planted hard on the floor.

"Second rule: Until the final hunt, either of us can stop this game at any time. I'll send you a message before the first hunt with a safeword that I'm assigning you. That word crosses your lips in my hearing—or on any communication we might have—just once, and you'll never see me again. Blink once if you understand."

I blinked again.

"See how easy this is? Third rule: Tomorrow I'm going to send you a list. Within 48 hours of receiving that, you'll visit a pharmacy or drugstore and pick up every item. Every single one—and in the quantities that I assign to each. Even if you have to visit more than one store. When you have all of it, you'll take a picture of all of it on your kitchen counter and post it as a unique post in the forum where we met. If you have skipped anything or don't have enough of something, you'll never seen me again. So don't post it until you have everything. Blink once if you understand."

I squeezed my eyes closed, my mind whirring with curiosity. When I opened them again it was just as he moved, turning his head to look out the passenger window to see if there was anyone who could see us. I realized then that I could make out a very faint reflection of him in the windshield. I locked eyes on it and tried desperately to memorize the details, but couldn't see much more than a strong, square jaw that was cleanshaven, full lips, and the tip of his nose because he was wearing a hoodie that shadowed most of his face.

When he turned back, he kept his chin low so I didn't see anything more. Disappointment fluttered in my stomach.

"Final rule," he growled. "You give *no* indication to anyone in your life that you know you're going to die. If you have legal or financial details to put in place, you do so casually—you're just being responsible. But you don't say goodbye. You don't give things away. And you don't breathe a word to anyone in your life that you wish to die, or that you plan to. Leave notes or instructions with a lawyer if you need to. If I hear even a *hint* that someone suspects what we're doing, I will disappear and you'll never see me again. Blink once if you understand."

I blinked again, my breath still coming in short, sharp puffs through my nose.

"Now… I told you that I knew how to make you feel alive. I wasn't lying. I'm not a liar. Remember that. It'll be important later. But for now, just know that I won't warn you when a new hunt begins. Between hunts you may go days, or even weeks without seeing or hearing anything from me. But just because *you* don't see *me* doesn't mean *I* don't see *you*. At times I might choose to leave you signs that I'm near, or I might not. But I *will always be near.* Whether you're aware of it or not. So don't get complacent and break the rules, or you won't see me again. Blink *twice* if you understand."

I did as he asked, my heart trilling in my chest.

"Good girl," he purred and a zing of need like I hadn't felt for years jolted behind my navel. He leaned closer again and I swallowed hard, inhaling that scent deeply, crystalizing it in my senses, knowing for as long as I lived I'd associate that smell with him.

There was a pause, and the clunk of the car door handle. My stomach dipped, but he didn't let me go even when he swung the door open and the cool morning air rushed in, taking some of his scent away and replacing it with the smell of warming cement.

He paused again, and I braced, expecting him to run and getting ready to turn and look as quickly as possible, see if I could catch a glimpse of his face. But he gave a low, disapproving growl like he knew what I was thinking.

"You won't see my face, Bridget. Ever. When we meet it will be darkness, and I'll wear a mask. And if it's the latter and you try to remove it, it will be the last thing you ever do... do you understand?"

I nodded quickly and he paused again, sinking down a hair behind me as if he might be about to leave, but then he froze.

"I almost forgot," he whispered. "As the hunt progresses it will get... aggressive. I don't expect you to submit. You can fight, you can resist, you can run—you can try to escape me any way you want. In fact, I encourage it. But our agreement involves no weapons. Everything that happens between us, happens organically. We use our bodies, and anything we find in the vicinity of wherever we meet. If I find you carrying a weapon, you'll never see me again. And if you bring a weapon against me, it will be the end. Do you agree?"

I swallowed hard and nodded under his hand.

For a moment, he was still and quiet, then his thumb moved to stroke my cheekbone.

"You're a very beautiful woman, Bridget. What a waste to take you from this world." Then his other hand snaked around the seat, his fingertips stroking down my throat, then along my collarbone as he audibly inhaled. His hand over my mouth loosened just a hair.

"This is your one and only chance to prove you'll play by the rules, Bridget. If you don't, you'll never see me again. I'm going to remove my hand from your mouth, and you're *not* going to scream. You're not going to move at all. You'll keep your eyes on that wall in front of you and answer my questions. Then, when I leave, you will give a slow count of thirty during which time you won't turn around to watch me go."

I waited for the instruction on whether to blink or nod, but then he gave a little rumble in his chest and suddenly the deathgrip he had on my face loosened, then his hand was gone. But he was still there, breathing in my ear.

I froze, my heart hammering.

"Very good girl," he whispered hoarsely.

My stomach thrummed. I swallowed and breathed through my mouth, gulping at the air, my heart pounding like it might actually break through my ribs.

"Now, answer my questions quietly, but quickly. Do you know the man who was leering at you in the gym today?"

I blinked. I wasn't sure what I'd expected, but that wasn't it. "No," I said quickly.

"Have you seen him there before, or spoken to him at all?"

"I've seen him, but we haven't spoken before. Except... like that."

He was silent for a second. He cleared his throat and I thought I heard a hint of his actual voice, but when he spoke again it was still in a whisper.

"Why do you want to die?"

I blinked. "I told you, I have—"

"There are plenty of people in this world who would happily take every day of health that was available to them. There's something else in your life that makes you want to die. What is it?"

My heart rammed at my ribs. I gripped the hem of the hoodie tighter. "Life is… empty," I said. "Boring. Hollow. Whatever you want to call it. There's *nothing* here. What's the point?"

"A nihilist?" he asked, sounding a little amused, which pissed me off.

"My psychiatrist calls it fatalism, and says I confuse thrill with purpose."

He hesitated. "Do you want to die? Or do you want the thrill of being hunted?"

"It isn't a thrill if I can't actually die," I said without hesitation.

"That's not the question—"

"Yes, it is," I interrupted him, then blinked, wondering if that was breaking any rules. But he paused, so I swallowed and plowed on. "The only time I feel *alive* is when I feel like life might be taken from me. For real. You said that the first day. You said you knew that."

He grunted again. "So you'd give your life up in search of the ultimate thrill?"

"No," I said. "Giving my life up *is* the ultimate thrill."

He huffed. I couldn't tell if he was laughing or disapproving and I caught myself about to turn to measure his reaction. My heartrate hit the ceiling.

"Do you have any questions for me?" he finally asked, still whispering.

"Why do you do this?"

I waited. The car jiggled as if he'd shifted his weight like he was squirming in his seat. But still he didn't answer.

I licked my lips. "I'm not judging," I said. "I'm just curious. Is it just the… the Erotopho-whatever it was?"

"I am not *turned on* by death. Or by killing," he hissed.

I frowned. "Then why do you do this?"

He hesitated again, and every hair on the back of my neck stood up. It felt like my *skin* was listening for his answer.

And when it came, it was a low grunt—almost his natural voice, which was still rough and deep, but warmer than I'd expected.

"For exactly the same reason you do," he said finally. Then the car jiggled and eased up like a weight had been lifted.

Shit! He was leaving?

I sucked in a breath at the patter of quick footsteps on the cement outside, grabbed the arm of the car door, but remembered his rules and didn't turn around. I made myself keep my eyes forward and started counting slowly, breathlessly to myself, my pulse threatening to lift the top off my skull.

30... 29... 28...

The second I got to the count of one, I whipped my head around, but of course he was gone. My heart was pounding mercilessly and my head was beginning to ache with it. But I deflated immediately.

He was gone. And that delicious scent was fading because the back door was wide open, allowing the morning air and sun to pour in.

Cursing to myself, I clambered out of the car on shaky knees, slammed the back door closed, then looked over the car to search the parking lot.

But it was empty, the morning sun cutting an angled shadow from the building, slanting across the cement.

Just as empty as my chest suddenly felt as the adrenaline from his visit began to ease from my veins and all the strength went out of my legs so that I had to sit in the seat for a few minutes more before I could turn the car on and drive.

But at least when I did, I was smiling.

Because he was real. And he was here.

I could smell him on my hair.

Read *Hunt for You* now in paperback or on
Kindle/Kindle Unlimited!

Acknowledgements

Jesus, thank you for saving me from myself. Thank you for bringing so much love into my life, and showing me that you aren't afraid of the ugly in this life, and I don't have to be either. Thank you for these gifts you gave me. I hope they delight you.

Alan, a lot of people think we're #couplegoals, and you and both know, that's a hard-won place to be. Thank you for inspiring romance in me. Thank you for being better than romance, but offering real intimacy and connection. And for being my cover model since the very first book. Thank you for helping and supporting, and not being threatened by made-up men. I couldn't do all of this without you. And I wouldn't have gotten this far without your support. Thank you for trusting my judgment, and putting our money where my mouth is. I'm praying God blesses *you* for being an amazing, loving, and strong husband and father.

Harry, I can't believe you're almost old enough to read this stuff. If you got this far, well… let's talk. Thank you for getting my jokes, and for giving hugs when I'm sad. You're already an amazing young man, and you're going to make some lucky woman very, very happy some day. I pray when God shows you the right woman for you, you'll grab her hard and never let go. And that she'll love you just as fiercely in return. Now… I guess I can't tell you not to read this stuff anymore. But insert a "Mum look" here. But feel free to tell your friends to read my books. They might learn something. *Wink*

Tessa, I have to give you the ultimate thanks for bringing me the spark for this story. I know it isn't quite what you envisioned, but I hope when you read it, it brings you joy anyway. (If not, you can just stfu and sit down, because children should be seen and not heard.)[1]

I have a HUGE thank you to my Beta Development Reader crew who showed up and have put up with my sporadic writing, my stress, and all the debates on character motives:

Anna, Bobbi, Cindi, Despina, Doina, Jasmyn, Jeannie, Jennifer, JK, Linda, Mariela, Melody, Nikki, Rini, Rose, Sally, Sarah K, Sarah M, Sherri, Sravanthi, and Susan.

---

[1] I *almost* kept a straight face for that.

You have helped me throughout the writing process, both with feedback, and cheering along. Your theories are food to my soul, your arguments are #AuthorJoy, and your hearts and minds are a huge asset to me. Thank you for taking this journey with me!

No Acknowledgement is complete without a *massive* thank you to every single member of *Author Aimee's Reader Tribe* on Facebook! You continue to be my happy place. All the laughs, all the support—for me and for each other—and all the Jasom Momoa memes a girl could ever want. Thank you. I tell you in every book that you made my dreams come true because it's true. You literally make every day a joy, every book a triumph, and every #AuthorFail a funny-rather-than-embarrassing moment. I'll never stop thanking God for you.

And finally, thank you to you, dear reader, for taking the time and investment to be here. Without you I couldn't do what I do. I hope you'll seek me out on social media and say hello (you can find all my links on www.authoraimee.com) I've been wishing to have you in my life since I was seven years old. So, thank you.

You all changed my life. I will never not be grateful.

Aimee

Made in United States
Cleveland, OH
22 May 2025

17110574R20256